THE
LAST
OLYMPICS

THE LAST OLYMPICS

Author Revealed August 4, 1996

Wessex House Publishing
Franklin, Tennessee
ISBN: 0-9646872-2-4

This book is dedicated:

To my wife and mistress (the same person),
who though she could never quite understand my devotion to
either the Centennial Olympic Games or this story,
nevertheless tolerated my zeal for both;

To my daughters, who give so much meaning to my life;

To the many friends I have made in the Olympic
movement—may they not take offense at this work of fiction.

But understand this: If the owner of the house had known at what hour the thief was coming, he would not have let his house be broken into.

—Luke 12:39

AUTHOR'S NOTE

This is a work of fiction. Though parts of it are based in fact, the main events of this narrative never occurred. It is nonetheless my opinion, confirmed by experts on the subject, that the story's depiction of a terrorist attack is a realistic scenario for what could have happened in Atlanta during the Centennial Olympic Games. Therefore I have waited until the conclusion of the Games to publish this book, in order not to endanger the safety of anyone attending.

Likewise I have no desire to cast aspersions on the Olympic governing body, the International Olympic Committee. For the purposes of the story, it was necessary to include the IOC, but my portrayal of it is intended to be read as fiction, not fact. Those IOC members with whom I have become acquainted over the past eight years know that I maintain the highest regard for their organization and its president.

The same goes for the Atlanta Committee for the Olympic Games. Just as it would be impossible to write about the 1996 Olympics without including ACOG, a story without conflict is no story at all; therefore it was inevitable that ACOG should be a part of the conflicts that (I hope) make the plot entertaining. But I would never want any member of that fine organization to confuse my portrayal of it with my true feelings.

ACOG, and the Games that it brought to fruition, are a monument to the vision, boldness, and tenacity of one inspirational leader. Ignoring the naysayers, he persisted in his belief that his city and his people could do something truly great. Along the way toward the realization of his dream, he brought on board thousands of committed staff and volunteers, of whom I am one. It has been my great honor, over the past eight years, to labor alongside some of the finest professionals I have ever known, on a project that will forever change the city of Atlanta and its position within the world community.

PART ONE

THE OLYMPIC GAME

PROLOGUE

At 4:00 a.m. on Tuesday, September 5, 1972, six men wearing track suits and carrying gym bags climbed over the fence of the Olympic Village in Munich. A telephone lineman and a mailman saw them, but because they wore the uniforms of Libya, Lebanon, and Saudi Arabia, the workers assumed they were athletes returning from a night on the town.

Once inside, the men moved quickly down a street called Connolystrasse to No. 31, a squat three-story building that housed the teams from Uruguay, Hong Kong, and Israel. There they split up, three of them going to the front of the building and three to the back. The steward and concierge were both asleep, and the outer lobby doors stayed unlocked. The intruders had no trouble getting in, where they joined two others who worked in the Village.

Now eight strong, they had a key, but the door of Apartment 1 was stuck. They pushed on it. This woke up an Israeli wrestling judge, who tried to block them, but they burst in just as he shouted to his friends: *"Terroristen!"* One of the athletes managed to break through the French doors in back and run to the nearby South Korean quarters for help. Meanwhile the terrorists overpowered, bound, and gagged the four men they found in Apartment 1.

Moshe Weinberg, a wrestling coach and veteran of Israel's wars, had been out all night with friends. He walked up on the terrorists just as they were about to enter the next apartment, quickly sized up the situation, and knocked down one of the intruders. They shot him in the face, but he refused to die; he still had enough of his wits to tell the intruders that Apartment 2 housed Uruguayans, not Israelis.

The terrorists believed his lie, and went on to Apartment 3. There they took six men, one of whom escaped as they led them out the back door toward Apartment 1. Weinberg took advantage of the confusion to overpower another terrorist and pick up his rifle. They shot him again and left him for dead.

As the captors herded the Israelis into Apartment 1, two more prisoners tried to escape. The terrorists shot both, but one of them managed to stab his killer between the eyes with a kitchen knife. And Moshe Weinberg still would not die: stumbling in from outside, he grabbed another knife and stabbed a terrorist before the invaders finally shot him to death.

Later on, many of the Israelis' neighbors would claim that they slept right through the noise. Just two days before, everyone in the Village had awakened to the sound of gunshots from a triumphant Olympic shooting team, so if anyone did hear anything, they probably thought it was another false alarm. But what about security? How had the intruders gotten this far without detection? The answer to that question lay thirty-six years in the past.

Wanting to overcome the stigma of the last Olympics in Germany, Hitler's Berlin Games of 1936, the Munich organizers called the 1972 event "The Games of Peace and Joy." The Munich Olympic Village— blocks of pastel-colored towers with wide bands of glass, bright fountains, and exposed water pipes everywhere—looked more like a space station than an armed encampment, and everything was designed for easy access. The perimeter fence stood only six feet high, without barbed wire, and its chain links made easy footholds for an athlete sneaking back in after a night of partying. Once inside the Village, visitors found plenty of helpful charts and diagrams giving the locations of each national team.

Yet the Germans had detailed more than 24,000 police and troops to the Games, and they had night patrols on duty in the Village. But no one saw or heard anything; it took the two athletes who had escaped to alert the authorities. Only then did the security forces start to gather, and as the morning wore on, Connolystrasse filled with armored vehicles and jeeps, ambulances and fire trucks.

The media followed, and suddenly the eight *fedayeen*, or "defenders of the faith," had a worldwide audience of one billion. They called themselves Black September after an incident in September 1970 when Jordan's King Hussein had turned against his friends in the PLO. The PLO's leader, Yassir Arafat, had organized the group, and Muammar Qaddafi may have provided their funding.

From the window of Apartment 1, the fedayeen dropped an ultimatum typed in English. It demanded the release of 234 political prisoners mostly held in Israel, and three planes to fly the prisoners, terrorists, and hostages to an undetermined location where they would exchange the hostages for the prisoners.

The statement had a 9:00 a.m. expiration, then only two hours away. Over the next hours, in a series of tense negotiations, the authorities would get this pushed back: first to noon, then to 1:00 p.m. and still further in two-hour increments until all the deadlines ran out at 9:00 that night.

In the meantime, the police considered using gas, chemical weapons, or an armed assault on the building, but ruled all of them out as too dangerous. At lunch they tried to send in heavily armed "cooks" with the food, but the eight fedayeen were smart enough to meet them on the street and take delivery there.

Black September wasn't the only problem security faced. Even though they'd sealed off the Village, they still had crowds of onlookers, and that night a riot nearly erupted when the mobs learned that the scheduled soccer matches had been canceled. But the worst interference came from the media. Journalists sneaked in using passes borrowed, bought, or stolen from authorized personnel, despite the fact that the ID picture often didn't look at all like the bearer. ABC had a great view of No. 31 from a nearby hillside, but they were ordered to take down their cameras when the police realized that the fedayeen were getting too much information from the TV reports.

Just a few blocks from Connolystrasse, life in the Village went on with eerie determination. People still shopped at the stores, athletes trained, and that night many of them would come out to dance and party at the discotheques. The Games went on too, that is until the organizing committee canceled them at 6:00 p.m.

The basketball semifinal between Egypt and the Philippines was set to occur before the cut-off, but it never took place. Both countries had withdrawn to show solidarity with the people in No. 31—and in Egypt's case, that meant the terrorists. The rest of the Arab world either praised the attack or remained silent, and the only Middle Eastern leader who condemned it was King Hussein of Jordan. Late in the day, when the organizing committee ordered all national flags flown at half-mast, ten Arab nations demanded that theirs be raised again.

The authorities lacked such a unified strategy. The Germans and Olympics officials wanted to negotiate, but the Israelis refused: Israel had never given in to terrorists, Golda Meir's government proclaimed, and it wasn't going to now. The leadership of the International Olympic Committee (IOC) split over who should take charge. Should it be their outgoing president, who had already given his retirement speech, or the new one, who was out on the Baltic Sea with the yachting teams? The retiring president wanted to run the show alone, but against his wishes his subordinate—a gifted young Spaniard named Juan Antonio Samaranch—managed to convene the executive board for a meeting.

By the time the board met at 7:00 that night, time had nearly run out at Connolystrasse 31. Willy Brandt, the German Chancellor, tried to get President Anwar Sadat of Egypt on the phone to work out a solution, but this was not the mature Sadat of later years. After several tries, Brandt could reach only a subordinate to the Egyptian President. "May I know to what I owe the pleasure of your call?" the official asked coolly.

At 10:00 p.m., the terrorists came out of Building 31 leading the hostages in groups of three, tied ankle-to-ankle. A bus transported the terrorists and hostages to two Bell-Iroquois UH-1D helicopters in which they rode to the airport, where a Lufthansa 727 sat waiting to fly them to Cairo. But the Germans had planned a few surprises. Five snipers had taken up positions on the control tower, two more just north of it, and two more underneath a fire truck. Three Munich policemen, dressed as pilots, sat in the cockpit of the plane, and five others hid in baggage compartments or behind seats. Another 100 border guards protected the tower and kept the airstrip sealed off.

The five snipers on the tower—a tiny group by the standards of later hostage rescue teams—had the primary responsibility for taking out the terrorists. The police had lit the area well, actually too well since the bright lights made confusing shadows. Nor had anyone thought to equip the shooters with infrared rifle sights or even walkie-talkies. Beyond all that, a contingent of armored vehicles couldn't make it to the airport on time because the road was clogged with media and spectators. So the fake flight crew, realizing their impossible situation, abandoned the plane against their squad leader's orders.

The two helicopters touched down thirty meters apart at 10:34 p.m. Inside sat the nine Israeli hostages, tied with rope and belted into their seats, guarded by six of the terrorists. The other two members of Black September quickly jumped out to inspect the plane.

As the two were coming back, the snipers on the tower began shooting. One of the terrorists was killed, but the fedayeen killed a policeman and shot out the glaring lights. Then, just as the six armored vehicles arrived, the Black Septembrists tossed a grenade into the first chopper. It exploded with five hostages inside, and the terrorist guarding the other four Israelis opened fire on them.

All the fedayeen ended up dead or captured, and a few days later, their alleged "last will and testament" aired over Libyan radio. "We are neither killers nor bandits," it stated. "We are persecuted people who have no land and no homeland. . . . It would do no harm to the youth of the world to learn of our plight only in a few hours. . . . Why should the whole world be having fun and entertainment while we suffer with all ears deaf to us?"

By executing their attack at the Olympic Games, Black September had taken center-stage. They got their wish of "educating" the planet, at least for a few hours. But the authorities took away a different lesson. After Munich, counterterrorism became a growth industry, not only in Germany but in France, Britain, and America.

By the time Israeli agents had hunted down and killed the last members of Black September in 1979, the world had become a very different place—a little less optimistic, a lot more cautious. Olympic organizers wouldn't think of hosting the Games without providing their athletes' village with the kind of security normally reserved for presidential mansions and nuclear missile silos. They would keep intruders out at all costs, and nothing like Munich would ever happen again.

Or would it?

1

Two silent figures waited in the shadows of an apartment building just outside the Vila Olímpica. Clad in black with ski masks, they watched as two armed guards leading a German shepherd passed by not thirty yards away before rounding a corner and moving out of sight. It was Sunday, July 26, 1992, the first day of the XXVth Olympiad.

"Alright," whispered the shorter of the two men, "that means we should have twenty minutes till the next patrol."

"But where's the signal?" asked the other.

"Don't you know that nothing in Spain is on time?" the first man said with a low chuckle. "Wait—there—it's starting!" They watched the light on the horizon, rising to the sky. "Okay, it's nearly five minutes late. Let's go."

"I gotta grab our silent partner," the tall man said, hoisting a heavy object onto his shoulder.

Suddenly, fireworks began going off in the sky over the bay more than a kilometer away. The two men could see flashes and brightly colored flowers of light that hung suspended in the air before floating lazily earthward. From this distance, the visual effects came into view first, followed a fraction of a second later by the loud noise of the explosion.

Within sixty seconds, the two men and their hefty piece of baggage had passed through the double security fence, unseen but not undetected. Sensors had picked up the movement, and soon these electronic guards would signal the breach to Village Security Headquarters.

They'd known this would happen, and had timed their break-in to coincide with the nightly fireworks. The confusion gave them the extra few seconds they needed to dash to the nearest doorway and step out of their black coveralls wearing blue and white warmup suits. Now they blended right in with the other 13,000 athletes and officials in the Residential Zone of the Village.

Four minutes later, a Village Security team arrived at the scene of the breach and discovered a body between the fences. He wasn't dead, only passed out and reeking of alcohol. They turned the drunk over to local police, who questioned him, but he could barely remember his own name, let alone the fact that he'd been abducted from a nearby alleyway and hoisted over the outer fence to be left as a decoy.

The Village duty officer had no reason to investigate further. How could he know that this was only the beginning? Meanwhile the two intruders moved confidently but cautiously deeper into the Residential Zone. Entering one of the two cinemas, they watched the second half of *Ruthless People* and the first half of *Jean de Florette* in French before leaving at 1:45 a.m.

"You'd think they could have gotten some more current movies," observed the tall man. By now activity in the Village had died down, and as they made their way, they found it easy to avoid the few people still moving about at this late hour.

After a couple of turns, they arrived at their destination: the U.S. Olympic Team quarters. The two exchanged glances for a split second before pushing open the door like two athletes returning from an evening out.

They strolled up to the front desk, where the night-duty steward looked up at them with mild interest. "What can I do for you fellas?" he asked.

"First," said the shorter man, who stood to the right of the desk, while the second man locked the door behind them, "give us the room number of Elroy Hubrick."

"He's asleep now," the night-duty man said, sitting up straight in alarm. "What do you need him for?" As he spoke, the taller man stepped around behind him.

"Because we have something to show him," said the first man as he pulled back the jacket of his warmup suit to reveal what looked like the butt plate of an automatic pistol shoved into his pants.

The steward put up his hands, his mouth struggling to form the words, "*Nooooo*—don't shoot!"

The tall man grabbed his shoulders and held him effortlessly in his chair. "Sit still and be quiet!" he hissed. "Now where's your room roster and key safe?"

Trembling, the steward answered that the roster was in his top right drawer. But the key safe was in the office of Chef de Mission Hubrick, head of the U.S. delegation.

"And the key to the safe?" The grip didn't relax for an instant.

"In my center drawer."

"Good," said the voice, now close to his ear. "Now, get in that closet"—the steward felt the hands behind him turning his head toward a door in the corner—"and don't say another word. Don't try anything stupid, because I'll be right here at your desk."

The smaller man headed through the back door and down the hall to the apartment occupied by Elroy Hubrick. The intruder had a penlight, and he quickly located the living room telephone and disconnected it before moving on. Because the rooms weren't air-conditioned, every door was open. He stopped and listened at the first before moving on. The chef de mission would have a private room, and since he could hear two men snoring, he knew this one couldn't be the chef's.

In the second room he heard just one man's breathing, so he crept in and shined the tiny penlight onto the suitcase under the bed. The nametag read *Rusty Griffin, Assistant Chef de Mission, United States Olympic Committee (USOC)*.

Entering the last bedroom, he checked the accreditation badge on the nightstand, then brushed the sleeping man's face with the tiny beam of his light. Yes, this was the one. He switched on the overhead light.

Chef de Mission Elroy Hubrick bolted awake, his face alive with shock. "Don't!" he shouted.

"It's okay, Dr. Hubrick," the intruder said softly, switching off the overhead light and turning on a bedside lamp. "Sorry to have startled you. If you will assemble your assistants in your office in five minutes, I will explain."

"Who the hell are you? And what are you doing in my room?"

"Sorry, sir—I'm Thomas Mason, Special Agent, United States Department of Defense Intelligence Agency."

Hubrick sat up in bed. "You got some credentials to prove that?"

Mason smiled coyly. "I'm sorry, I don't." He held up his hands. "But don't you think if I'd wanted to do you any harm, I would have by now?"

Hubrick grunted and grabbed a shirt hanging on a hook from the wall. He shot an angry glance at Mason. "You wanta watch me dress?"

Mason apologized and started to leave the room, then turned around. "I'd suggest you don't call Village Security—I don't want to embarrass them."

Hubrick shook his head, got out of bed, and pulled on a pair of pants. A former Olympian himself, Dr. Elroy Hubrick had already been appointed Director of Operations for the 1996 Games in Atlanta, and everyone expected him to later become the first African-American President of the U.S. Olympic Committee.

Five minutes later, Hubrick and his four assistants, including the night steward, sat in the delegation's office. The other three who'd been asleep sat around in bathrobes or tee shirts and sweats, rubbing their eyes and wondering aloud what was going on. None of them seemed nearly as awake as their leader, who was boiling with rage. "Now," he said, "would you mind telling us why you interrupted our precious few hours of sleep, Mr.—what was your name again?"

"It's Thomas Mason, and this is Greg Robbins." The two were sitting at the far end of the table. Mason was in his early forties, with wavy sandy-blond hair and mustache, both going gray around the edges. His face had a hard look to it even when he smiled, thanks to the scar on his left cheekbone, which was accentuated by the bright fluorescent light. He had a stocky build, and at nearly six feet tall he didn't look short except when placed next to Greg Robbins, whose 6'4" frame towered over him even sitting down. Robbins had a much milder face, with a mop of straight brown hair and a gentle smile that contrasted with his earlier behavior at the front desk.

"Within the next few minutes," Mason continued, "we will be joined by several of my colleagues, and each of them will tell you how they got in. Then I'll be able to explain to you the full purpose of this exercise. If you don't like the explanation, *then* you can call security, and we'll allow ourselves to be arrested. But give us ten minutes."

Hubrick sighed. "Alright. I don't suppose a real terrorist would say that. But look here, how'd you get into the Residential Zone of the Village? This is the highest security area in all of Barcelona."

"That's what we're here to talk about," said Mason with a smile. He began telling the officials how he and Robbins had gotten in, but at that moment two men walked in through the front door, which Robbins had already unlocked. The chef de mission and his assistants started at the sight of the two, one dressed in ordinary street clothes and the other in the uniform of a Village employee.

"Guys, how about explaining to Dr. Hubrick here how you got in?" Mason pointed to the first one, a lanky young man with a shock of blond hair across his forehead. "You first, Adam."

"Well, sir," said Adam, standing at modified parade rest along with the other new arrival, Julio. "I was hanging around the front entrance at about 1500 hours—3:00 p.m., that is—when two of the access-control guys went around the corner to smoke a cigarette. I went up to the one guy on duty and started speaking Russian. I pointed to the entrance like I wanted to go in, and he tells me 'no' in Spanish, but then I opened my briefcase to show him about fifty pins."

The lapel pins, displaying flags, coats of arms, or company logos, had become a second form of currency in Barcelona. Adam's fifty pins would fetch about $200 in the open-air market at the Parc Ciutadella just outside the Village, where he'd bought them.

"So the fella's eyes got real big," he continued, "and he looked around to make sure no one was watching. Then he took the pins and sent me on my way through the magnetometer and into the Village. No questions asked."

"But there are armed guards out there!" shouted Hubrick with outrage.

Adam shrugged. "They don't do anything unless access control alerts them. So now I'm inside, and I know that to get from the International Zone to the Residential Zone, I need a meal ticket."

Of course, he said with a grin, only official team members can buy meal tickets, but 2,000 pesetas plus ten more lapel pins with the logos of various NOCs (national Olympic committees) did the trick.

"So then I go downstairs to the cafeteria and eat," he went on. "I have to say that the food here is good, and the service is quick."

"Get on with it," Hubrick growled.

"Okay, after dinner, I just walk into the kitchen, acting like I know what I'm doing, and wander around till I find an exit into the Residential Zone. I walked out past a couple of kitchen personnel who were outside cooling off and shooting the breeze. Once in the Residential Zone I sort of disappeared—took in the activities, you know—until now. Piece of cake."

"Excellent report," said Mason. "Julio?"

A Cuban-American who could easily pass for Spanish, Julio gestured toward his Village uniform. "I bought this from a guy in town for seventy-five bucks, then I walked through the gate while Adam was talking to the access-control guy. I had my employee accreditation badge, which I'd 'borrowed' off someone on the Metro, so I just walked around and played video games for awhile, caught a movie. . . ."

"Let me see that badge," Hubrick demanded, then looked back and forth from the badge to Julio's face. "This doesn't look at all like you."

"No, sir, but how about your own photo?"

Out of habit, Hubrick had clipped his badge onto the shirt he'd put on a few minutes before. He looked down at it.

"With all due respect, sir," Julio said, "that's a bad likeness—anybody's ID picture is gonna look like a mug shot. And when you've got unmotivated conscripts working the gate, by the end of their shift they're hardly gonna glance at a badge. So anyway, I'm hanging out, and all of a sudden, who do I see but John Major? There he was, the British Prime Minister, near the U.K. team area with press all around him. I got no more than ten feet away, and I could hear every word he said. If I'd been some nut with a pistol, there would have been nothing to—"

The door opened and two more strangers entered the office—one of them a woman. Mason's eyes followed Hubrick's. Maybe the chef de mission was thinking *Even a girl managed to get through*, in which case Mason could have straightened him out, because this particular woman could do almost anything a man could, and then some. Or maybe he was thinking something else entirely.

Mason could certainly tell what the other men were thinking. The one who'd been on duty jumped up and offered her a chair while the others, half-dressed, nervously tried to cover themselves up and ran their hands through their tousled hair.

"Dr. Hubrick," Mason said, "meet Michelle and Lamont."

Nobody even glanced at Lamont; Michelle was striking, cover-girl gorgeous. Nearly 5'11" and lean, with short black hair and vivid blue eyes, she had long, athletic legs displayed to advantage by a ridiculously short miniskirt and high heels, and her low-cut halter top revealed the contours of two exquisitely proportioned breasts. Mason couldn't help but smile when he saw the men (with the exception of Hubrick) sitting up straighter and squaring their shoulders to make their chests look bigger.

"I told you to be inconspicuous," Mason chided her in a fatherly tone. "You're about as inconspicuous as a fire engine."

"You told us to use any means necessary without hurting anybody," Michelle said pertly.

"Fair enough," he replied. "Now tell us about your victim."

It wasn't hard to imagine how she'd managed to entrap an unaccompanied Italian gentleman as she stood around the day-pass control center fifty yards outside the main entry gate. She'd had to tell several other prospects to get lost when she saw that they didn't have the right credentials, but one wore a high-status badge that allowed access to the

Residential Zone. "Just to make it interesting," she said, switching into accent, "I passed myself off as an Australian."

Returning to her normal voice, Michelle explained that when the official asked her where she was staying, she had blushed and said she'd rather he gave her a number where she could reach him. "So while he was writing it down, I lifted his pass." She pointed to it proudly. "And of course, the nice thing about visitor passes is that they don't have photographs, so no one would know that it belonged to a man."

"Those Italians," Hubrick chuckled in spite of himself. "They can't resist a pretty face, can they?" Mason could read the unspoken thought at the end of this: *Who could?* In a more stern voice, the chef de mission added, "Y'all are nothing but a bunch of pickpockets."

"Do you think pickpocketing would be beneath any terrorist?" Mason shot back.

"Humph." Hubrick couldn't think of anything to say for the moment. He turned to Lamont, a young black man with a beard and mustache, and demanded, "How did *you* get in here? And don't tell me you came in disguised as John Major."

"No, sir," said Lamont with a grin. "Aaron and I—he should be along any time now—just pulled onto the shoulder of the motorway that runs under the Village. While he pretended to change a flat tire, I climbed through an opening in the retaining wall that we'd noticed before. I could have come through the sewer system just as easily, but I figured why put up with that smell when I can just walk right in? And the fence between the Residential Zone and the International Zone wasn't any problem either. There aren't any alarms or barbed wire, and in most places the posts aren't even in the ground—just up on concrete cinder blocks. Beside the money exchange, there's an eighteen-inch gap where folks have pushed back the chain link so they'll have a shorter walk to go cash their checks. It was easy enough to slip through while the access-control guard was hitting on a girl."

Mason looked at his watch, then turned to Hubrick. "While we're waiting for Aaron, I'll bet you'd like me to explain why we've done all this."

"Yeah, that crossed my mind," mumbled Hubrick, obviously displeased with the events of the past few hours.

Mason nodded to Robbins. "Greg here is going to head up security in the Olympic Village when the Games come to Atlanta in '96, and the rest of us will be there in an advisory capacity. We'll be keeping a low profile, trying to make sure there's no serious security violation, and going into action if one happens. So we're here to test out the situation and make recommendations for Atlanta—and to let you know of the dangers here so you won't feel overly secure."

"You don't have to worry about that now," Hubrick said ruefully.

The phone rang, and one of the USOC men answered it. "Yeah? Uh-huh. Okay." He turned to Mason. "It's for you."

Surprised, Mason took the phone, then suddenly brightened. "Why, Eli, you old dog," he said. "Haven't talked to you for awhile. What's your company doing here?" He nodded his head knowingly. "Oh, I see, just dropped by. Yeah, sure, he's mine—nice Jewish boy. Have your folks bring him over, would you? Ha, ha. I'm sure he was creeping around someplace he shouldn't have been. Listen, you and I need to talk later on. I want to get your feedback on security in the Village. Alright."

Hanging up, Mason turned to Hubrick. "That's a friend of mine from Israel." He didn't say it, but Eli worked with the Mossad, one of the world's most sophisticated intelligence and counterterrorism units. "Now those guys never take security for granted—no doubt they've got around-the-clock armed guards."

"Great," said Hubrick. "But what about us?"

"Okay, I can assign one man"—Mason glanced at Michelle—"or rather, person, each shift. They'll be unarmed, of course."

"Unarmed?" asked the man who'd been on duty at the front desk when Mason and Robbins came in.

"We can't carry weapons here in the Village," Mason said flatly.

"Then what about that pistol of yours?"

"You mean this?" Mason pulled the object from his pants and tossed it across the table. It was a wallet with its back side painted to look like the butt plate of an automatic. "It can work in some situations," he explained, "though I don't think it would fool anyone with any training in these things. But anyway, we can provide this watch for you if you can give us some kind of ID so we won't have to sneak back and forth into the Village every time."

"Please don't," said Hubrick. "We can get you day-passes."

"And some warm-up suits would be nice," Mason added. "Just so we'll blend in."

There was a knock at the door, and two men in Israeli team warmups came in, leading a third. After exchanging a few words with Mason and Hubrick, the men, who weren't athletes but Mossad agents, released Aaron Stein and left.

"Aaron, Aaron, Aaron," Mason chided. "What happened?"

Stein shook his head and looked at the floor in embarrassment. "Sorry, Chief. I was running late, and I walked right smack into the middle of the Israeli quarters." In spite of himself, he laughed. "Wouldn't you know it? There I was, surrounded by the toughest security in the whole Village, and it didn't take them two seconds to figure out I wasn't one of theirs."

Mason nodded intently, then turned to Hubrick. "If Aaron couldn't bluff his way through with those folks, I sure couldn't." He smiled at Stein. "Your little wrong turn may have been the most useful aspect of this whole exercise, Aaron, because it illustrates why you can't ever let time constraints push you into a position where you don't want to be."

"Speaking of time. . . ." Hubrick pointed to his watch.

"Sure, sure." Mason stood up. "We'll let you get some sleep."

"If we can," said Hubrick. "Y'all folks sure as hell have got me scared now."

At nearly the same moment, two men were standing on the twenty-fifth floor of the unfinished Ritz-Carlton Vila Olímpica Hotel overlooking the Village. The hotel had been scheduled to open before the Games started, but a series of strikes and fires later attributed to arson had delayed completion. So it stood an empty shell, a monument to frustrated plans and lost millions.

But these two didn't care about that. Holding out his hand toward the Village, one of them said, "Look at this golden city, Hafiz. See how it glows."

"It is beautiful," said Hafiz with admiration.

"And just think," said the first man, "of how we could make it glow even more with the fire we bring!"

"Yes, but Ahmad—"

Ahmad, caught in his own revery, was not listening. "And think of the humiliations our people have endured. Think of our enemies. . . and right down there in that Village, their athletes are sleeping in the belief that they are secure. If anyone wanted to make a statement, this would be the place and time to do it."

"Aren't you getting ahead of the plan a bit?" asked Hafiz.

Ahmad shook his head. "I am thinking of the future, that is all. For now, our mission is only to go into this Village and find out how easy it is to penetrate its barriers. And when these Games are over, we begin to prepare. Four years." He snapped his fingers. "It will go by like a flash, but it's enough time."

"Yes," said Hafiz. "A flash. They will think they are safe in the United States, and we will have a surprise for them."

"*Alto!*" The two turned around to see an unarmed security guard standing behind them, his flashlight shining in their eyes. The poor fool hadn't thought to call a backup before he went to investigate the noise on the twenty-fifth floor.

On Tuesday morning, a small column appeared buried on the fifth page of Barcelona's largest paper, *La Vanguardia*:

Security Guard Dies From Fall
At Ritz-Carlton Construction Site

BARCELONA—Security guard Jordi Diaz, 33, fell to his death from the twenty-fifth floor of the Ritz-Carlton Vila Olímpica early yesterday morning. The building, which had been scheduled to open earlier this month in conjunction with the Olympic Games, remains unfinished due to a series of construction and labor problems, according to a spokesman for the Bectell Corporation here to oversee the troubled project. Because of its proximity to the Olympic Village, there is the fear of foul play, but local police believe the fall was an accident.

2

On Sunday, August 9, two weeks after their first strange encounter, Hubrick and Mason sat together near mid-field at the Estadi Olímpic. This Olympic Stadium had been built in 1929 with the hope that the 1936 Olympics would be played here. When the Games went to Hitler's Berlin instead, Barcelona had attempted to put on a "Popular Olympiad" as a protest, but the Spanish Civil War interrupted those plans. More than half a century later, the city had finally gotten its chance to host the world.

As Hubrick and Mason watched, the Closing Ceremonies of the XXVth Olympics began upon the completion of the marathon. King Juan Carlos entered the stadium to the anthems of Catalonia and Spain. After he was seated, a local theatre group staged a parody of an Olympic race to enormous cheers and laughter from the crowd.

"Well, that's another set of Games put to bed," said Hubrick, "and safely, thanks to you."

Mason nodded. "Glad we could be here—not that anything necessarily would have happened if we hadn't been."

"So y'all just got a free vacation, huh?" asked Hubrick with a smile.

"Some vacation."

Just then a youthful-looking man with dishwater blond hair sat down beside them. Hubrick greeted him like an old friend, then introduced Mason to Steve Kirk, who would direct Olympic Village Management in Atlanta.

Mason chatted with Kirk. Just about all the chefs de mission he'd talked to, Kirk said, had told him they liked the Barcelona Village much better than the ones in Seoul or L.A. Only a few problems had come up, mainly the lack of air-conditioning, which forced them to keep the windows open and let in noise that kept athletes awake on nights before competition.

And then there was the problem with the buses: drivers who didn't know their routes and couldn't read the maps because they were in

Catalan, not Spanish. "It was like *Gilligan's Island*," said Kirk with a sigh, "but they solved the problem like Americans—by throwing money at it. They hired taxi drivers to ride on each bus, and they got the job done, but in general I'd call their management style here. . . *interesting*. I mean, from what I could tell, the whole Village Management team took siestas every day. Can you imagine if we did that in '96?"

Kirk seemed pretty high-strung, and Mason certainly couldn't imagine him taking a siesta. "Yeah, I'd call their access-control setup pretty interesting too."

"Tell me about it!" chuckled Kirk. "I was there the day Magic Johnson and the rest of the Dream Team showed up. It was star-struck city. The whole Village swarmed over the accreditation area trying to get a look at them, and you could have walked right through without any problem. No wonder he and Michael Jordan decided not to stay in the Village." He shrugged. "But what do you expect? These security guys are just military recruits who had the option of working here instead of going to boot camp. I guess they figured anyone smart enough to make that choice is smart enough to check access."

"I sure as hell didn't feel safe," Hubrick volunteered, gesturing to Mason. "Not after all that this guy told me."

"The venues are too big, too open, too complex, and there are just too many people moving in and out to have any guarantees," said Mason. "It was a nice touch putting all those tanks all over town—if I were some thug, I'd think twice if I saw an M-1 Abrams taking up a couple parking spaces—but we won't have that option in Atlanta."

Kirk laughed. "I can imagine the kind of grief the civil liberties types would give us if we did."

"At least we'll have some state-of-the-art biometric equipment to make sure the person coming in through the gate is who he says he is, but machines aren't really the key anyway—people are—and even then, there's no way to absolutely ensure safety." Mason looked at Kirk, who frowned. "So Steve, sleep peacefully for the next four years, but once the Games start, pray every night."

The men stood for the national anthems of Greece, the original home of the Olympics; Spain, the outgoing Olympic host; and the United States, the future host.

"I just couldn't imagine a terrorist attack on U.S. soil," said Hubrick as *The Star-Spangled Banner* came to a close.

"To be honest, I can't either," Mason replied, "and maybe that's our whole problem. Someday we'll wake up and find that somebody's blown up the Empire State Building, or some federal installation out in Utah or some place like that. But I know if I hated America and I wanted to hurt her in a big way, there wouldn't be any better opportunity than in Atlanta."

"But the number-one sponsor of terrorism doesn't even exist anymore," said Kirk as the future hosts began to put on their show, first with a film introducing the city of Atlanta to the world.

"You mean the Soviet Union? Sure, but that only means the situation is harder to predict than ever. Back in the good old days of the Cold War, you at least knew where the crap was coming from, and there was even a chance to make a deal, like the Spaniards apparently did with the ETA." The ETA Basque separatists of northern Spain had conducted an IRA-style war against Madrid for the past thirty-three years, but they'd kept amazingly quiet during the Games, and Mason figured the government had paid them off. "I'd put the Palestinians in the same category—my friend Eli, who's about to be posted as bodyguard for the new prime minister, Rabin, says he thinks they're about a year away from striking some kind of sweet deal.

"That old-fashioned kind of terrorist seems positively warm and fuzzy compared to the ones I think you're gonna see in the next few years," Mason went on. "There are groups out there like the Shining Path in Peru who never depended on the Soviets—hated them as much as they do us, in fact. They believe in their cause like a religion, and they know there's not a chance in hell for the majority in their countries to accept them unless it's by terror tactics."

"You're really concerned about the Shining Path coming to Atlanta?" asked Hubrick with a smile.

Mason shook his head. "I'm not nearly so worried about groups who want their countries to go Communist as the ones in countries that have just dismantled Communism, or are about to. Look at what's happening in Yugoslavia. The hatred between ethnic groups there has been around for hundreds of years or longer. The Communists kept it under wraps for awhile, but now it's back worse than it ever was."

On the field below, performers had begun putting on a literal song-and-dance number highlighting Atlanta. The men fell silent to watch.

"Elroy here introduced me to the folks you're gonna be working with in the Village," said Kirk a few minutes later. "Looks like a great team you've got."

Mason nodded his head. "The best."

"So, uh, what's the word on Michelle Hinton?"

"She's tough as nails, I'll tell you that."

"Damn right, she's tough," said Kirk with admiration.

"No, I mean tough like she'll kick your balls off."

"No way."

Mason nodded his head and smiled. "Trust me." He had spoken the truth, but he'd also gotten used to protecting his talented agent from the attentions of overly amorous males. Still, Kirk seemed like a nice enough fellow, so he obliged him with a little more information. "She was Miss Kentucky 1981, and she probably could have gone on to the Miss America title if she'd wanted, but she's too much of a tomboy for that. So she got her criminology degree at the University of Kentucky instead, then came on board with me." He couldn't help but add one protective warning: "She's very professional."

"Oh, I'm sure," said Kirk. "I understand what you're saying: look but don't touch."

Mason laughed. "No, she can handle herself, and I'm not her father. I'm just saying I know she wouldn't screw around unless that was part of the job, and then"—he looked away—"I'm sure she'd be world-class."

They watched the Atlanta extravaganza on the field, but at least two of the three men were thinking of Michelle. Mason remembered how his wife had reacted when he'd told her he was adding a woman to the team, especially when she saw Michelle's picture. So on the day he'd introduced them, he'd made sure to put Sandy at maximum advantage and Michelle at maximum disadvantage. He and Sandy were dressed to go to the theatre, and Michelle had just finished a workout. The two women got along just fine.

Mason glanced at Kirk—it was easy to see from his far-off gaze what he had on his mind—then looked across the stadium at the hillside beyond it. Two helicopters hovered with their lights shining on the ground.

Hubrick saw it too. "What the hell—?"

"I guess their sensors must have picked up some movement," Mason explained. He pointed out the royal box several rows below them, where King Juan Carlos sat with his family and IOC President Juan Antonio Samaranch. "That hillside's one of the few places outside the stadium where a sniper might be able to get one of them in his rifle sight."

"That must be eleven or twelve hundred yards!" Kirk said incredulously.

"You'd be surprised, with modern weaponry," Mason said. "Look—see how the Spanish are moving their troops onto the slope?" The hillside now swarmed with soldiers, probably responding to a false alarm. But if there had been any trouble there, it was over now.

Soon the ceremonies reached their finale. Plácido Domingo sang the Olympic Anthem, the Olympic flag was lowered, and the Olympic Flame extinguished. A dance company appeared on the field to perform a climactic closing number, the "Ritual Fire Dance." Then the ensemble raised a silver boat aloft to launch it—with Cobi, Barcelona's canine mascot, who poked his head out mischievously to wild applause—on an endless voyage into the stars.

The final dance of fire began with vast and colorful explosions in the skies above the Estadi Olímpic. This wasn't the ordinary nightly fireworks show that had provided Mason with cover for his break-in two weeks before; this was the grand finale, and within seconds the air was thick with fire and smoke and deafening noise. Neither Kirk nor Hubrick, Olympic veterans though they were, had ever seen anything like it—only Mason had, more than twenty years before as an infantry officer in Vietnam.

The shock waves echoed around the stadium, and the crowd roared. Another Olympics had ended in success.

Across the field, Ahmad and Hafiz watched the fireworks display. "Isn't this amazing?" asked Ahmad. "What does it make you think of?"

Hafiz shivered. "You *know* what it makes me think of—*INCOMING!* I almost climbed under my seat at the first salvo."

Both of them silently imagined the scene four years from now, when real explosives would take the place of fireworks, and the crowd would scream in terror instead of delight. The drama would be beamed live via satellite to the entire planet, and the whole world would tremble.

3

Thomas Mason flew out of Barcelona the next day on his way back to Washington, carrying with him Olympic souvenirs for his kids, Jennifer and Mike, and a handmade Spanish tablecloth for Sandy. They had lived in a comfortable split-level home in Maryland for the past four years—their longest stay in one place ever, as Sandy liked to point out—and he'd hated telling them they would have to move to Atlanta. Jennifer would be in eleventh grade and Mike in ninth, hard ages to switch schools and towns, but it was either that or have their father gone for the next four years.

Four years: by then he'd be forty-seven, and he'd promised Sandy that after Atlanta his days of chasing all over the world on Defense Department business would be over. He'd take an assignment as an intelligence analyst in some cozy corner of the Pentagon, and they wouldn't ever have to move again. He was tired of moving too, but he wouldn't let himself think about it till then.

At the age of twenty-one, he'd finished college and gone straight to Vietnam. That was in 1969, at the height of the war, when the Army conferred the gold second lieutenant's bar on countless ROTC graduates who believed that duty and honor were necessary requirements for citizenship. As an infantry officer he'd found himself in the position of forward observer, where one constantly put oneself out on a limb, then proceeded to saw the limb off.

He'd learned more than he ever could have back at Ohio State, in a classroom that extended from the grimy, leech-infested jungles to the seedy bars of Saigon. But somehow, the place must have met some unknown need in him, because he'd signed up for another hitch when his year ended. And then one day he had walked straight onto the path of a Viet Cong sniper.

If Mason hadn't taken that bullet, his unit might have stumbled into an ambush. The shot had sliced into his cheekbone, a fact that still made him queasy with the knowledge of how close he'd come to losing an eye. But compared to some of the men he saw coming back from 'Nam in wheelchairs, it hadn't really been a serious wound, though the Army thought enough of it to give him a Purple Heart. Still, lying in his bed in the hospital at Subic Bay in the Philippines where they'd taken him by medevac for his surgery, he'd already decided that he'd had enough of the adventurous life. At least he thought so then.

During the early '70s, he'd finished college and married a high-spirited young woman from North Carolina. He still joked with pride that it was her fault he hadn't ended up in some safe, dull corporate job forever.

He'd gotten his degree in risk management and gone to work for an insurance company. He had liked studying the theoretical side of assessing risks, but he quickly found he didn't care for the insurance business itself. After watching him leave for the office every day for three years, looking like a man on his way to pay off a loan shark, Sandy had said, "Do something that interests you. I don't know—go back in the Army or something." And that was exactly what he'd done.

Only this time he'd taken a behind-the-scenes role in military intelligence. After more than a year for his training, they had gone to Germany, where he worked with a unit monitoring Soviet troop movements on the other side of the Berlin Wall. From there, it was Korea, where he analyzed enemy activity along the DMZ. Then, as he moved up, the assignments became shorter and more exotic: Egypt, where he got his first and best exposure to the underworld of Islamic fanaticism, and the Dominican Republic, where Jennifer was born.

In the early '80s, he landed an assignment that Sandy and the kids liked, a stint with NATO Headquarters in Belgium. He'd made rank quickly, but he knew he might sit at major for the next five years or so, and the analysis work which had seemed so fascinating a decade earlier had grown tedious. Once more he wanted a change, something less in the background—something close to the edge.

The time was right for a move from counterintelligence to counterterrorism. After the failure of the Desert One rescue mission to Iran in April 1980, the Defense Department had realized the need for more elite special operations units, and Mason knew a colonel named Norbert Helms who'd been promoted to brigadier general and picked to head up a group within the Defense Intelligence Agency called the Response Support Team (RST). Helms had invited Mason to come on board with him, and after a good long talk with Sandy, Mason had accepted.

The Response Support Team assisted American military and civilian installations in sensitive locations with the identification and reduction or elimination of threats. "Elimination" usually didn't mean what it did with other covert operations, because the RST operated on the principle of preventing violence *before* it ever occurred. Its clearly defined mission, and General Helms's strict adherence to it, kept it out of the kind of hanky-panky that brought down Oliver North and a number of classified operations such as Yellow Fruit in the late 1980s. Thus when the Pentagon began to scale back on some of its more adventurous undercover programs with the end of the Cold War, the RST had survived and even prospered.

For that reason—not to mention his record of judicious intelligence work that put him ahead of men with more experience—Mason had been assigned to Atlanta. He would work with Greg Robbins in the Olympic Village until the summer of 1994, when they would be joined by the team who had helped them successfully carry out the "raid" in Barcelona.

Mason called them "the kids" because they were all much younger than he, but he had never worked with a finer group of professionals. Between them they spoke fourteen languages. Adam's command of Russian could have fooled a Muscovite into believing that he came from some outlying former Soviet republic, and Aaron Stein spoke Yiddish, Hebrew, and—most important of all—Arabic like a native of the Middle East. They could go anywhere and mix so well that not a soul would notice anything out of place. Lamont, though he'd gone to Georgetown, could talk and act like a homeboy from the 'hood, then turn around and pose as an exchange student from Kenya, and Julio had already proven he could pass for almost any Latin nationality.

And then there was Michelle. It didn't matter that she was the toughest woman Mason had known other than his wife: when she played the damsel in distress or the coquette, she could manipulate almost any man who came to her with the wrong intentions, like the guy in Barcelona from whom she'd stolen the pass. Of the whole team, she had the coolest head, which was why Mason had placed her second-in-command. She was a pilot too, and that impressed him greatly since his only flight time had been as a passenger.

Now on the plane home to Washington, he thought about this as he gazed out of his window. *It must be a major head-rush to fly one of these things*, he mused. *I'd hate to have the responsibility*. He smiled at the irony of it: more than anybody, Greg Robbins included, Mason had to ensure that nearly 14,000 athletes and officials from all over the world got safely through their thirty-three days in the Olympic Village. Flying a jet seemed easy compared to that. *At least I've got four years to prepare*, he reminded himself. *Four years to plan ahead for every possible snafu.* That was the only way, to plan. If you waited till things actually went wrong, it was usually too late.

In a suite at the Princess Sofia Hotel in downtown Barcelona sat a high official in the Democratic People's Republic of Korea, known to the West as North Korea, with the head of that nation's Olympic committee.

"So, Comrade Lee," he said, tapping a pencil on the desk while admiring the new Rolex he'd purchased for himself a few days before, "once again your athletes have disgraced our Great Leader: only three gold medals, and a total of thirteen."

"Comrade Chun," said the subordinate, sitting up straight in his seat, "we would no doubt have done better, except for the bias of the judges against our nation and our people. As our Great Leader has said—"

Chun cut him off. "The Great Leader wants medals, not words."

"I see." Lee drew in a breath. "It is true, Comrade Chun: our enemies to the south continue to outdo us."

"That is right, Comrade Lee," said Chun dryly. "This year alone the fascists won thirteen gold medals, and a total of thirty! I did not think that after the debacle of 1988, we could ever again be so humiliated, but now I'm having my doubts."

The North Koreans had tried to get a share of their southern cousins' limelight in the 1988 Olympics, even building a stadium in Pyongyang larger than Seoul's. But the IOC had rejected their invitation to host festivities in the nightmarish capital of the world's strictest police state, and North Korea—doubly disappointed when China and the U.S.S.R. refused to join it in a boycott—kept its athletes home.

"Until 1972," Chun continued, "we earned not a single medal, while the South took home one after another, and ever since then, our athletes have failed to perform on the same level."

"Yet there is no reason this should be," said Lee optimistically. "Look at our comrades across the Yalu River. This year the People's Republic of China won seven gold medals in swimming and diving, yet where were they in the last Olympics?"

"What is this to us?" said Chun. "They are a much bigger country than we are."

"But Comrade Chun," Lee countered firmly, "there is also the example of the German Democratic Republic: in 1988 that country, with fewer than sixteen million people, had nearly as many medals as the U.S., a nation whose population is twenty times as large."

"It has been nearly three years since the reactionaries of Germany overthrew the democratic government there," Chun pointed out with a scowl. "You seem to be avoiding the subject at hand."

"Begging your pardon, Comrade Chun, my point is that in China, it is not the quantity of people, it is the training and techniques they have learned from the former coaches of the German socialist teams." With a sly smile, he added, "And something the Germans bring with them, a guarantee of victory through sophisticated science. I'm not talking about diet supplements either."

"I know what you mean," Chun snapped.

"There's more," said Lee. "Several East German coaches have spoken to me, and they wish to offer their services."

"Why?" asked Chun, narrowing his eyes.

"Because they would rather help a socialist government than a capitalist one," Lee replied. "And because they are not looked upon favorably by the new regime in Berlin."

"Any other reason?"

"Yes. . . their services do cost money."

"Of course," said Chun. He thought for a moment. "But it may be worth it, depending on the price. Everyone knows that our race is the strongest and most intelligent. Why should those dog-faced whites or the American Negroes outdo us?" He stood up abruptly. "I don't care how you do it, Comrade Lee—deliver me Olympic gold-medal winners, and you will become a national hero."

"Yes, Comrade Chun," said Lee, taking the other's lead and standing. "I will meet with the Germans and report to you what they say."

A week later in Paris, a man sat at a small bistro reading a foreign newspaper and sipping Perrier. Anyone who noticed him would have had a hard time placing his nationality. From his ruddy complexion and dark eyes that flashed back and forth, searching the passersby, he looked like a southern or eastern European, but his dark suit was of a better cut than the clothing typically worn by emigrés from the former

Communist countries. His lack of a tie might identify him as a Muslim, or it might only indicate the stifling late-summer heat that hung over the Boulevard St. Germaine.

The man waved to another man approaching him, dressed in a sport coat. He stood up to shake the visitor's hand. "Thank you for coming, Herr Zoeller," he said in German, motioning for him to take a seat.

"How could I refuse, Herr Drabeznic?" Zoeller replied. "You sent the ticket."

After he'd ordered for his guest, the man named Drabeznic went straight to business. "I called you because I believe my country can help you—and of course, because I believe you can help my country."

"Your country?" asked the German, confused. "You mean—?"

Drabeznic shook his head. "Forget about Yugoslavia. I mean *my* country, Bosnia."

Herr Zoeller chuckled, then said philosophically, "A nation dies, another nation is born—a familiar theme where I come from." Formerly a team handball coach for the German Democratic Republic, he had recently found himself out of a job and, because his Communist past made him an object of suspicion, virtually a man without a country.

"We intend to build a team," said Drabeznic. "The best money can buy!"

"I don't get your meaning."

"Herr Zoeller, there is far too much turmoil in my country to put together a team of natives. Therefore one of your primary responsibilities will be to buy players from elsewhere and ensure that the team qualifies to attend the Games."

Zoeller thought about this. "Well, if you have the money, we can certainly find the players," he said. "After all, handballers don't earn what basketball stars do—not five percent as much! But how will we be able to prove that they're Bosnians?"

"Don't worry about any of that," said Drabeznic. "I'll see to it that the entire operation is completely legitimate in appearance. Citizenships will be granted, and of course you'll have to recruit players of reasonably similar ethnic background—Italian, Romanian, Greek. . . . But let me attend to the bureaucratic end of things. You don't need to deal with anyone but me."

"Interesting," Zoeller replied. "Very interesting. . . . Yes, it just might work."

Two weeks after the Games ended, the President of the Premiere Bank d' Nationale in Lausanne, Switzerland, met with his senior investment officer.

"No doubt you know who has just become our largest single account," the investment officer said.

"That's not too difficult to guess," said the president.

The officer nodded his head. "It's interesting. Just think, eight years ago they were virtually bankrupt, and now they have a balance of 965 million francs."

Even the bank president, who was used to dealing with enormous amounts of money, gave a low whistle at this sum, which equated to $650 million. "How about outflow?"

The officer shook his head. "It's incredible. I've never seen anybody make as much money with such low overhead except maybe—you know." The president nodded his head, recognizing the reference to the bank's Colombian depositors. "For every franc they put out, they make fifty, a hundred, two hundred. . . . I believe it would be safe to say that by 1996, the International Olympic Committee's account will well exceed $1 billion U.S." He sat up straighter in his chair. "It could even be as high as $1.5 billion."

4

Somewhere around 776 B.C., the peoples living near the village of Olympia on the Peloponnesian peninsula began holding a quadrennial religious, artistic, and athletic celebration. Originally the athletes competed in only one event, a foot race of approximately 200 yards first won by a cook named Coroebus of Elis. Other events were added and the Games stretched from one day to five as their fame spread throughout the known world. After the Battle of Thermopylae, a Persian officer who had questioned his Greek prisoners about their Olympic Games remarked in amazement, "What manner of men are these we are fighting? It is not for money they contend, but the glory of achievement."

But kings and other men of means saw the political ends to be gained by winning. Dionysius the Elder, tyrant of Syracuse, created the first free agent in history when he persuaded Dicon of Caulonia to run for his city. Sparta initiated the first sports boycott in 420 B.C. rather than pay a fine for breaking the Olympic truce, which prevented member cities from attacking one another during the Games. Emperor Nero competed in 66 A.D., managing to win the chariot race even though he'd been thrown from his chariot and hadn't even finished, and left with more than 1,800 first prizes. In return for these unearned honors, he cut the Greeks' taxes.

The takeover by politicians and wealthy men, the bribing of athletes, and the exploitation of the festivals for political purposes brought on the end of the Games in 394 A.D. Olympia fell silent, the stadium and hippodrome were destroyed, and the statue of Zeus was carted away. An earthquake in the 600s sent nearby rivers flowing over the site, covering all traces of the ancient Games' former splendor.

But the memory remained alive in historical writings, which inspired a young French baron named Pierre de Coubertin, who conceived the idea of reviving the Olympic Games. For a long time his vision remained his alone; then in 1894—exactly 1500 years after the ancient Games ended—he formed the International Olympic Committee, which put on the first modern Games in Athens in 1896.

Coubertin wanted the new Olympics to be free from the twin curses of political and economic manipulation. All athletes would be amateurs, even at the cost of such ugly scenes as Jim Thorpe returning the gold medals he had earned at Stockholm in 1912 when it was revealed that he had once played professional baseball. But because of their very success, the Games were changing. They added on sports unknown to the Greeks, not to mention the entirely novel concept of Winter Olympics, which began in 1924.

Coubertin died, penniless and forgotten, a year after the Berlin Games. War cancelled the next two Olympiads, and the Games didn't hit their stride again until Helsinki in 1952, when the Soviet Union took part for the first time. From then on, the Olympics would be a proxy Cold War between the West and the Communist Bloc.

Melbourne in 1956 was the last of the pre-commercial Olympics, thanks to the new medium of television. The city received only £80 for the rights to televise the Games; just twelve years later, ABC paid what then seemed a staggering $4.5 million for the TV rights at Mexico City. (In 1992, NBC would shell out nearly ninety times that much.)

Then in the mid-1970s, Horst Dassler, son of the Adidas shoe empire founder and nephew of the rival Puma magnate, had an obvious—and revolutionary—idea: what if major corporations were to "sponsor" sporting events as a form of advertising? The first big Olympic sponsorship program in 1983 brought in $10 million *each* from such corporate giants as Time-Life, Visa, Kodak, and Coca-Cola.

And in 1984, Peter Ueberroth disproved the conventional wisdom that cities always lost money by hosting the Games. Los Angeles came in $215 million in the black, and the IOC, which had never offered to pay a cent for any losses, demanded a cut. The committee ended up getting a mere $7 million, but future host cities wouldn't get off so cheaply.

Juan Antonio Samaranch, who became IOC President in 1980, oversaw an expanding organization that included representatives of Communist, African, Asian, and Latin American countries, as well as the traditional Euro-American power blocs. This made the IOC seem more democratic, but members from such impoverished nations could easily be influenced by the benefits that came with membership.

And benefits there were. Paid staff at Olympic Headquarters in Lausanne, Switzerland did all the actual work, while the IOC President and his nine-member executive board made most of the decisions. The remainder of the IOC had only two jobs: to travel around the world and be treated as royalty at major athletic events, and to meet once a year. At every fourth meeting, they selected the cities which would host the Summer and Winter Games six years later; then in 1986 they decided that the Winter Games would take the even-numbered years between Summer Games starting with 1994, a move which doubled the commercial potential of the Games—and the committee's exposure on the world stage.

A nod from the IOC meant so much money and prestige that cities bidding for the right to host the Games invested enormous sums to win members' votes. The thirteen municipalities vying for the Winter and Summer 1992 Games spent $61 million collectively, or $700,000 per IOC member. Athens alone would shell out $40 million of the total $85 million that would be spent in the bidding for 1996.

Few city organizing committees ever offered a brazen cash bribe, but they performed little favors such as reimbursing airfare (even though tickets had already been provided), or lavishly entertaining delegates. In 1993 China donated a statue valued at $100 million to the IOC's pet project, the Olympic Museum, which seemed suspect in light of the support given by the IOC President to Beijing's ultimately unsuccessful bid for the 2000 Games. At the Tokyo bidding in 1990 for the '96 Games, the Greeks flew in a dozen of Athens's most attractive call girls, officially designated as hostesses, to entertain IOC delegates. The Atlantans dubbed the women "The Wet Dream Team."

The power of economics and politics eventually affected the athletes, those healthy youths who performed all the spectacular physical feats on which the Olympic empire was built.

Doping, the use of steroids, drugs, or other novel means to enhance performance, became widespread in 1970s and '80s. Steroids helped athletes put on muscle, but caused breast development and shrinking testes in males; deep voices, facial hair, nymphomania, and an enlarged clitoris in females; and psychological disorders in both. There would be scandals for the West, such as the stripping of Canadian sprinter Ben Johnson's gold medal at the Seoul Olympics; and after the fall of Communism, state archives in East Germany and the Soviet Union would reveal doping programs on an enormous scale.

Thanks to a 1984 rule change repealing Coubertin's requirement that all competitors be amateurs, the players themselves were given a much greater financial stake in the Games. For the IOC, this meant that they could bring in more top-billing acts, such as the NBA superteam that dominated the Olympic basketball courts in 1992.

Nor were athletes immune to politics, including boycotts imposed by their governments. Twenty-two African nations stayed home from the Montreal Games of 1976 to protest the fact that New Zealand's rugby team had played in South Africa. Then the U.S. and its allies boycotted Moscow in 1980 because of the Soviet invasion of Afghanistan, and the Soviet Bloc returned the favor during the 1984 L.A. Games. All this meant that some of the world's greatest athletes went a full twelve years without meeting one another in international competition, and many promising careers stalled along the way.

The Olympics were getting out of hand, and with all the money the IOC controlled, it wasn't surprising when more Third World countries began clamoring for a bigger share. The organization had a private-club structure, a relic of the aristocratic past, which created some unusual circumstances. Luxembourg, smaller than Rhode Island, had a seat; so did Liechtenstein, whose princess represented all 29,000 of her citizens; and so did Monaco, which would fit many times inside of New York's Central Park—with fewer people than the latter at lunch hour. Yet some of the world's most populous countries such as Indonesia, Iran, and Vietnam had no seats on the IOC, and China, Pakistan, and Nigeria held only one each.

The Norwegian gold medalist who opened the '94 Games in Lillehammer publicly criticized the IOC President, and said that the IOC "should be given a different, democratic structure." It began to look as though the Olympic machine was out of control.

Like the modern Olympics themselves, the Atlanta Games began as the dream of one man. A Georgia lawyer named Bobby Joe Watkins got the idea one Sunday on his way home from church, and like the leader of a religious sect, he gradually assembled a small band of followers. Together they laid out the plans for the '96 Games at his kitchen table one weekend.

These founders of what ultimately became ACOG, the Atlanta Committee For the Olympic Games, had to be true believers, because anyone else would have laughed at the idea that Atlanta could host the Centennial Olympics. Everyone knew *that* honor would go to Athens. It had history on its side, and grandeur; Atlanta had freeways and malls, racial tension and crime. Besides, the Games had just been to the U.S.

in 1984, and wouldn't likely return for several more Olympiads. But if Watkins wanted to waste his time and other people's money, the USOC would let him, and they gave their approval (perhaps tongue-in-cheek) for Atlanta as the designated U.S. bid city.

Yet Watkins and his town had more on their side than the rest of the world could fathom. Mayor Andrew Young, former lieutenant to Martin Luther King and Ambassador to the U.N. under President Carter, joined Watkins's team and began bringing international guests to see the city for themselves. And a surprising thing happened.

By the late 1980s, everyone had begun talking about "infrastructure," meaning roads and other necessary facilities, because Barcelona's lack of it had them worried. Ancient buildings and narrow streets made old European cities quaint and attractive, but they gave planners a headache. With the 1992 Games still a few years away, every hotel room in Barcelona had been booked, and the idea of holding the 1996 Olympics in a place that had built its economy on the transportation and convention industries was looking better all the time.

Just before the IOC met to make its decision, Atlanta's morning newspaper, the *Constitution*, gleefully reported the sign seen by an Atlanta couple in an Athens hotel:

> The hotel will suffer from periodic power cuts. Should you need candles, ask housekeeping. National and private banks in Athens are not in operation. You will be experiencing difficulties when you dial due to the Greek Telephone Co. not operating. Any mail will be delayed reaching its destination until the Greek Post Office strike is over. We have no way of knowing in advance which flights will actually materialize, international or domestic.

On September 18, 1990, the same hometown paper proclaimed the IOC's decision in three-inch headlines: *IT'S ATLANTA!*

All that day and night Atlantans celebrated their victory and toasted their new hero, the hard-driving Bobby Joe Watkins, who had made his million-to-one dream a reality. Dignitaries gave speeches predicting greater success for Atlanta than L.A. had enjoyed; no one mentioned Montreal, whose citizens were still paying off the debt incurred when they hosted the Games in 1976.

Winning the bid was not (to paraphrase Winston Churchill) the beginning of the end, only the end of the beginning. Watkins's powerful, persuasive ego—which had made him just the right kind of

salesman to win over the IOC—wouldn't allow him to admit that his
Games would do any worse than L.A.'s, and he refused to consider outside help for funding. If L.A. could produce more than $200 million
profit on a budget of $600 million, surely Atlanta could generate at
least that much with $1.5 billion to play with, and that money could pay
for the enormous promises he'd made in order to get the bid.

But Watkins didn't follow the pattern of frugality which had made
Peter Ueberroth's Los Angeles Olympic Organizing Committee such a
success. Whereas Ueberroth had maintained the impression up to the
last minute that his Games would barely break even, ACOG started out
portraying itself as a successful corporation, as though it already had
the $200 million in hand. Therefore a modest operating environment
like the one in L.A., an airport hangar with used military furniture,
would not do: ACOG opened its headquarters in the posh Inforum
Building on Williams Street.

When the local media published the salaries of the top ten ACOG
executives, Atlantans were aghast to learn that these people (some of
whom had no experience beyond organizing local benefit functions)
commanded salaries in excess of $200,000. Watkins himself, at over
$650,000 a year, had the highest income of any non-profit executive in
the world.

Nor did Watkins take into account the fact that he wasn't the only
one who'd learned that the Olympics could make money for a city. This
time around, the IOC stood poised to siphon off a huge portion of the
revenues, sponsorships, and television rights in return for the privilege
of using the name "Olympics" and the magic five-rings symbol. And
just behind them waited plenty of others, each expecting their own cut.

Considering all the money ACOG threw around, who could blame
Atlanta politicians for demanding their own oversight committees,
complete with "fact-finding" trips to Barcelona, the Bahamas, and
Monte Carlo? Or the Georgia state government, which would receive
$450 million in new infrastructure absolutely free, for charging rent to
use its facilities? Or the sports federations, who wanted a separate
Village in Athens, Georgia to accommodate the rhythmic gymnasts;
extra quarantine facilities for equine diseases; VIP suites in the
Olympic Stadium; and extra dockage for the yachts in Savannah?

The list of those making demands went on and on. Local Civil
Rights leaders expected Atlanta's private African-American colleges to
receive the same levels of investment as the state-owned universities
across town. And the USOC took a twenty-percent cut of everything its

"partner" ACOG received, which meant that if someone donated an item, ACOG had to fork over twenty percent of its value in cash.

Each of these expenditures ate away at that mythical $200 million profit, but more than anything else, Watkins had himself to blame. Everyone knew that success or failure rested on marketing, so at the behest of experts he had hired one of the top sports marketers in the country to run ACOP, a joint venture between ACOG and the USOC. But the two men's egos failed to mesh, and after less than six weeks, Watkins replaced the expert with a less ambitious group of early retirees from IBM who lacked the experience to successfully market the Games. ACOP ultimately fell short of its goal by over $100 million, a number that would have been larger if a half-dozen Atlanta-based firms hadn't taken the initiative of sponsoring the Games.

Then there was the Olympic Stadium, a monumental error of timing. A temporary facility could be built for only $75 million, but Watkins wanted a permanent edifice, which cost $220 million and which the Atlanta Braves would receive at no cost to them after the Games. He planned to make up for the difference from the $600 million he expected to make from the sale of U.S. television rights, but if they were going to build the permanent stadium, they needed to make that decision in the summer of 1993. Thus, even though the IOC urged him to wait it out because the current advertising market was weak, Watkins went ahead and bid the rights—and NBC paid him only $456 million. The full magnitude of his poor timing would become apparent two years later, when the network gave Sydney, Australia $250 million more for the 2000 Games.

With all this taken into account, the stadium actually cost Atlanta an extra $300 million, and the projected profit of $200 million soon became a memory.

IOC President Samaranch had been scheduled to step down in 1995, but he left early when King Juan Carlos requested his help in forming a new government. The IOC needed a new president, and a power struggle raged for a few months until someone put forth the name of Jason Blanchot.

Nominally an African because he came from the Seychelles, 700 miles east of Madagascar, Blanchot had lived in Paris ever since being exiled from his homeland after a 1977 coup. He had the fine features of his mother, a Creole woman, and the elegant speaking voice of his father, half-French and half-Asian, thus combining all three of the world's major races in his lineage. He also had the advantage of being old: in two years he would turn seventy-two and his membership would expire, at which time the postponed conflict over control of the IOC would resume.

And so it fell on Jason Blanchot to oversee the century-old organization at the time of its greatest power and its greatest vulnerability. He knew that he could either be the man who saved the IOC and the Olympics for the world, or the one who lost them; at his age, he must have wondered if he was up to the task.

5

Planners selected the Georgia Institute of Technology as the site for the Olympic Village because of its location just north of downtown Atlanta, and because it already had extensive infrastructure in place. Though nearly $160 million in new housing would have to be built, the expenditure seemed justified because the buildings could become dormitories for Tech and its downtown neighbor, Georgia State University, after the Games. By early 1994, much of this construction had begun, but in general, Tech looked like any other large urban university.

On one unseasonably warm afternoon in January, McMillan Street on the northwest end of campus teemed with students coming and going between classrooms, dining halls, and dorms. Others sprawled on the grass in front of the Couch Building across from Fitten Residence Hall, enjoying the weather.

The sun-bathers left a wide arc around a worker in a Georgia Tech Plant Operations Department uniform repairing a window on the Couch Building. He was tall, with blond hair and a handsome, ruddy face. His coworkers called him "Tex" because of his deep Southern drawl, though he insisted that he'd lived in Springfield, Missouri, all his life until moving to Atlanta in 1991.

From time to time, Tex looked up from his work in the direction of Fitten dorm across the street, watching students enter and leave. To exit, they simply opened the door, but to enter they had to punch in a code. Tex observed several groups of two and three going in by this method.

After half an hour, Tex had sealed in the new windowpane with caulk. Then he gathered up his tools and, taking one last look at Fitten Hall, returned to the plant operations department for his next work order.

Visitors to the ACOG offices in the Inforum Building went through a series of security checks before getting off the elevator at the sixth floor, where they walked past a long streamlined receptionist's desk and a "Countdown Clock" showing the number of days till Opening Ceremonies on July 19, 1996. Today, the clock showed 892 days to go. Down the hall to the left, behind a door with a sign that read *Steve Kirk, Olympic Village Managing Director*, Kirk had just chased everyone out of his office except for Thomas Mason and Greg Robbins.

They had come to discuss one of the most crucial aspects of Olympic Village planning: keeping out unwanted visitors. The Georgia Tech campus would be divided into three zones: a "research zone" outside the Village, where the work of Tech scientific researchers would go on more or less as usual; a large Residential Zone, where the athletes would live; and a tiny International Zone that would welcome media and guests. A chain-link fence ten feet high, with nineteen entry control points and almost 250 cameras, would meander for more than seven miles around the Residential and International zones of the Village.

Only a very few people would know the exact outline of the fence prior to its installation, and some of the world's most sophisticated access-control technology would ensure that no one got through it except those with authorization. Visitors with day-passes would sign in at the Atlanta Civic Center more than a mile away, have their names checked off a list, then board a bus for the International Zone entrance. There they would first pass through a sensor which would read their accreditation badges, then they would proceed through a magnetometer or metal detector, and finally an X-ray machine. It would be even more difficult to access the Residential Zone, where a hand-geometry scanner would read each person's hand measurements and fingerprints, comparing them with data already logged into the system.

Kirk listened thoughtfully to Robbins's report on these security steps. "So this stuff is all pretty reliable, huh?" he asked finally.

Robbins hesitated. "No problem in sunny weather, but when it rains, a few bugs may come out in the works."

"Oh shit," said Kirk, folding his arms and saying with a straight face, "but of course, it never rains in Atlanta, does it?" All three men laughed.

Robbins explained that every scanner would have a dehumidifier installed in its housing, and the equipment supplier would have a repair staff on call in the Village twenty-four hours a day. But until they repaired a malfunctioning scanner, Village Security would have to maintain manual observation. "That's the thing about electronics," he observed. "It works great when it works, but when it doesn't. . . ."

"People are always going to be the key," Mason pointed out, observing Kirk's frown as he said it.

Having brought his family south—Sandy and the kids liked Atlanta, he was glad to discover—Mason had been working with Robbins for months now. He had made plenty of recommendations about the access-control systems, but he was afraid that all their thinking revolved around a faulty premise. They operated under the assumption that the worst threat would come from outside the Village.

But what about inside?

On the corner of North Avenue and Techwood, just across from the Georgia Tech campus, wrecking crews had knocked down a dilapidated hotel, an unappetizing-looking Wendy's, a dowdy old Tech dormitory built by the WPA in the 1930s, and a portion of the Techwood Homes public housing project. What they had left was a magnificent 8.5-acre site on the edge of the major motorway through Atlanta, where I-75 and I-85 joined to make the Downtown Connector, and on this spot would go one of the most prominent Olympic construction projects of them all.

These were the University Apartments, so named because after the Games they would go to Georgia State University for student housing. The brick Gothic structures—some of them six stories tall and some as high as twelve—would cut a striking figure through the skyline along the Downtown Connector. Architect Niles Bolton had designed them to create a pleasing visual link between the low-rises, also Gothic in style, of the Georgia Tech campus to the north and the post-modern skyscrapers of the city center further south. Thus at street level, the apartments would appear to scale with buildings nearby, yet from the expressway they seemed fitting structures to face the NationsBank Tower, Atlanta's tallest building at 1,050 feet.

After fierce bidding, ACOG awarded the job to the Ellis-Don Construction Company in early 1994, and work soon began on the $62 million project. The enormous crew included two quiet men known collectively as "the Hungarians" to their coworkers. Both stocky and round-faced, they had perpetually placid faces that made them particularly unnoticeable, and since their English wasn't good, no one made an effort to talk to them very often.

If the foreman noticed anything unusual about the two men, it was their relish for hard work, which set them apart from their American cohorts. He'd even found them working late one night—off the clock—sweeping up and preparing their area for the next day's labors.

The night watchman soon grew accustomed to the Hungarians, too, and after the first frustrated attempts at conversation, he usually waved them through the gate without question. One night he thought he saw flashes of light coming from Building D, but he knew little about the construction work, so he didn't ask any questions.

Another time, six months after that, the two Hungarians drove up to the gate in a truck with several thirty-gallon drums in the bed and two other men in the cab.

"What you got there?" the guard asked. From his shack behind him shone the glow of a TV set. It was Tuesday, another episode of *In the Heat of the Night*: Sheriff Gillespie was closing in on tonight's batch of criminals, and the guard resented the interruption.

"Delivery," answered the driver, the taller of the two Hungarians and the one who spoke something close to intelligible English.

"What is it?" The night watchman got out his clipboard to make note of the delivery.

"Mud," said the driver, "for sheetrock."

"Mm-hm." The guard wrote this down on his clipboard. "And who's that with you?"

"They help."

"I know, but what are their names?" The man held his pencil at the ready.

"First man, István Szakasits."

"How do you spell—?" The night watchman made a face. From the TV came sounds of gunfire and a high-speed chase. "Aw, hell," he said with a shrug. "Go on through."

The driver nodded his head and drove on in the direction of Building D.

Of the seven players on the first string of Helmut Zoeller's Bosnian handball team, only the three on his back court had actually been born in Bosnia. His three forward court men—an Italian, a German, and an Albanian—and his goalie, a Turk, had a more tenuous connection to the nation. Their Bosnian lineage could neither be verified or disclaimed because the government in Sarajevo, or what passed for a government in its beleaguered situation, had more pressing matters to attend to.

Despite broadcasts from Radio Television Belgrade that accused the

Bosnian Muslims of being radicals like the ones in Iran, the Bosnian leadership was anything but fundamentalist. The government included, and encouraged cooperation between, Orthodox Serbs, Catholic Croats, and Muslims. Therefore they were enthusiastic when an unknown named Hakija Drabeznic had approached them with the concept of a Bosnian handball team, which he would fund, and which would be composed of players from many nationalities. It brought to mind the glory days of a decade before, when the Yugoslav handball team had dominated the sport and Sarajevo had hosted the 1984 Winter Olympics. Perhaps this team would help to show the world that the many national groups in Bosnia could live in harmony.

Not only did Drabeznic pay the players' expenses, he had set up the first team and the second team (players no one on the first team had ever heard of) in a compound outside of Sarajevo. There, just a few miles from the scenes of fighting between Serbs, Croats, and Muslims, they lived in relative comfort, protected by nearly a dozen armed men. The latter got along well with the team members, and when they weren't on duty, played matches with them. Of course the real players always won—at least, the first team always did—but it was good fun for everybody.

Soon the training would begin to bear fruit. Drabeznic wanted the team to prove its ability in matches with other countries leading up to the world championships, so they would be spending a lot of time on the road throughout 1995 and 1996.

With the cuts that seemed to come every six months, the staff at ACOG had to be skilled and dedicated to keep operating. But by the final budget cycle in October 1995, when paid personnel and even volunteers had been reduced by twenty-five percent, most of them felt they could stretch no further. For all the whittling away at departments, certain sacred cows remained—anything that had to do with Olympic pomp and ceremony, corporate services, or special treatment for VIPs whose good favor the IOC wanted to curry—and ACOG wasn't about to touch those.

And there were continuing frustrations in the marketing area. The Centennial Brick Program, designed to finance Watkins's dream of converting twenty-one acres of urban blight in the middle of downtown into a park where the citizens of the world would gather, was a massive failure. Instead of the $10 million profit projected, it resulted in a $10 million loss for ACOG. And in 1994, Watkins had been out-negotiated by the Winter Games hosts in Lillehammer when it came to dividing up rights to sponsorships sold by the IOC. This constituted only a $2 million loss, but by that point, every dollar counted.

The decisive blow came in October 1995. The bureaucrats Watkins hired to run the transportation department had to be fired due to lack of expertise, and when the new transportation director presented his budget, it indicated that his predecessors had underestimated their needs by $80 million. Now ACOG executives, reeling from this news, went back to their operating departments and ordered them to slash their remaining budgets by another forty percent.

But the budgets had already been cut to the bone, and reductions of that magnitude were out of the question. Nor were there any more sponsorships left to sell. As for ticket revenues, sales for the most popular events had already exceeded expectations, and even though several million tickets remained unsold, few spectators were interested in watching field hockey, archery preliminaries, or baseball games between such "powerhouses" as South Korea and the Philippines.

So that was it. ACOG had gone bust. It had three options: it could cancel the Games, produce them on a much smaller scale, or look for a white knight—some entity with enormous finances—to assure that everything would evolve as originally envisioned. The first of these choices was unthinkable, the second almost as bad, leaving only the hope of a savior.

But who could save the Games? The City of Atlanta couldn't, and the State of Georgia wouldn't. The federal government was out of the question, particularly with the White House consumed by one or another of its endless ethics investigations. Nor was there time for a bailout by corporate America, particularly when ACOG was still publicly proclaiming that it would make a profit.

On the first of November 1995, the money spigot dried up at its primary source, the banks. ACOG had exhausted its available credit lines, and the lenders' projections forecast no possible recovery of the $60 million worth of credits already outstanding, not to mention any future cash advances. This left 2,000 employees on a tightrope. Since July there had already been a hiring freeze, and those who still had jobs held their breath whenever they went to cash their paychecks.

Bobby Joe Watkins had prepared a voice-mail message announcing the termination of all positions and asking anyone who could continue without pay to remain until he found another source of funds. But he had one more trump card, and on the Thursday prior to the scheduled broadcast of the November 30 doomsday message, he faxed its text to the organization that had the most to lose if ACOG went under: the International Olympic Committee.

Upon receipt of Watkins's fax, the IOC executive committee convened for an emergency session. Jason Blanchot established an operating committee which immediately flew to Atlanta to begin negotiations, and they issued interim guarantees to the banks for payroll purposes. So ACOG's employees went back to work as Watkins had hoped, but Watkins himself did not. Salvation had its price: effective December 1, executives chosen by the IOC would replace the top layer of ACOG management.

Thus the monumental project of putting on the Games resumed, though with a marked shift in attitude. One of the hallmarks of the Atlanta committee had been its tremendous sense of community spirit, making it easy to mobilize large numbers of volunteers who routinely worked long hours out of sheer pride and dedication to getting the job done. But now morale dropped, and the formerly united staff began to divide into two camps, the Atlanta partisans and the Olympic occupation force.

Symbolic of the new leadership was the dictatorial style of Bobby Joe Watkins's replacement, Hans Bliecher, an Austrian management consultant with one aim: to cut the cost of the '96 Games without hurting the image or long-term plans of the IOC. That meant that there would be no lasting benefit to the community if he had anything to do with it. He immediately began eliminating ACOG departments that he dismissed as unnecessary—community relations, governmental affairs, Olympic legacy.

Bliecher sent an edict to the construction department stating that any remaining plans for permanent structures should be replaced with temporary facilities as much as possible. "With this project so much in the red, the hell with the permanent legacy!" he thundered. "If we screw this up, these Games will not come back to America, let alone Atlanta, in ten lifetimes!" Likewise, entertainment budgets for local companies virtually disappeared, as he curtly informed the head of Sponsor Relations, "Because they won't be around next time." But he made no such cuts for perennial sponsors such as Coca-Cola and IBM, who the IOC counted on to purchase sponsorships in the next Olympiad.

Under Hans's guidance, the Games would be functional and efficient, but warm and fuzzy they would not be. This was the icy business environment of Germanic efficiency, hardly a corporate culture in which Southerners were likely to take comfort. Quickly Hans earned the nicknames "The Butcher" and "The Big Cheap," and out of his earshot the younger associates took to mimicking him in an Arnold Schwartzenegger voice saying, "You will do it my way."

But not everything Bliecher did was unpopular. He cut legal expenses and eliminated the risk management department, whose function had been to analyze and mitigate any possible claims against ACOG. "This organization doesn't plan on existing in 1997," he said, "so let them sue the hell out of us then!" He also cancelled the Games insurance, required primarily by the TV networks to protect them against loss if the events did not take place. The renewal premium of $10 million had come due, and there would be another one in '96. But on the basis of the IOC's strong balance sheet, Bliecher got the networks to back down from the requirement. And by bringing about numerous resignations with his authoritarian style, he further downsized the organization, such that within four months of his takeover, ACOG's monthly costs had dropped by about thirty percent.

The IOC President, Jason Blanchot, wondered in private if canceling the insurance had been a reckless move. But he'd based Hans's compensation almost entirely on any savings he could realize (with a $2 million bonus if he cut losses to below $50 million), so this type of cost-cutting was exactly what the IOC had expected. Still, the insurance issue haunted Blanchot.

The black Porsche 928 eased onto the southbound lane of the longest bridge in the world, Lake Pontchartrain Causeway just north of New Orleans, and rapidly accelerated to 120 miles per hour. It was after 10:30 p.m. and the driver, tipsy from a bottle of fine French Bordeaux consumed during dinner, kept his eyes focused on the road and the lights flying by as he passed car after car after car.

The man was trying to sober himself up, thinking how he would explain to his wife that the U.S. equestrian team board meeting had run late. Therefore, between the wine and his imagined conversation with his wife, he barely noticed what the young blonde in the seat beside him was doing.

She had firm, smallish breasts. He'd noticed that at dinner, when he'd put on a pretense of asking her about her riding career and tried hard to fight away the image of her legs wrapped around a saddle. But even then he'd noticed that she had on a strapless gown—no bra. And when she'd excused herself to go to the ladies' room, she'd returned minus her black panty hose. So now, as she slid out of her black chiffon evening gown, she had nothing to cover her toned, tanned body but the single long-stemmed rose he'd bought her at the restaurant. She ran it gently over her rock-hard thighs, then down across her silky blonde mound, then up to her firm stomach and erect nipples. Finally she leaned back against the seat and slid the rose across his lips.

She moaned. He smiled back weakly as he took his foot off the accelerator. "Jo—uh, Ms. Cunningham—"

But she had slipped into a distinctly non-verbal mode.

She didn't say a word as she reached over and ran her hand over his lap, where his erection pressed upwards against the steering wheel. As he slowed the car down, she unzipped his pants and started working them down his hips with one hand while using the other to massage him.

The same cars he'd passed were now whizzing by, a fact he noticed just as he realized that with one motion the graceful young woman had straddled his body and lowered herself onto him with a deep sigh. She laid her head on his shoulder, and he could feel her breath in his ear.

There was no place to pull over, and he strained to watch the road as she put her open mouth over his, and her taut buttocks began to work up and down on top of him.

She was calling out his name, and he had started to call out hers when he saw the lights of the toll booth less than two miles away. He had to finish now, which wasn't difficult to do. He let go inside her as she screamed, "Yes! Yes! Yes!" just like the *whish! whish! whish!* of the cars passing by.

She dismounted as quickly as she'd mounted, and slipped on her dress as he struggled to zip up his pants.

They rolled into the toll plaza so slowly that the attendant must have thought the Porsche was running out of gas. But he didn't ask any questions.

After the driver had paid his toll and resumed normal speed, he looked across at his companion and smiled. "I've seen some great try-outs," he said, "but that has to be the best ever."

JoEllen Cunningham smiled, too. This gentleman, one of three male judges on the five-member U.S. equestrian team executive board, had a family and a reputation, both of which he could forget about if she ever released the contents of a microcassette tape still recording in her purse. But if all went well, she'd never have to.

She was an excellent rider, but selection to the U.S. team had more to do with the whims of the highly political committee than it did with the more objective criteria that governed swimming or track. She had only two more trysts like this one to go through, with the other two judges, before she would surely win a majority vote with the board.

"Listen very carefully," a voice hissed into the receiver.

"What?" Michelle Hinton sat up abruptly.

"I said listen very carefully. You have exactly three hours to comply with our directives, or eight American athletes will die."

Michelle was on her feet and looking out the window, but she saw only darkness. Grabbing a pad, she made a note: *Male, age unknown, possibly foreign.* "Who is this?" she demanded.

"All you need to know now is this. For crimes committed by the government of the United States, we, the Defenders of America, will act as judge and jury on these representatives of the Zionist Occupation Government unless our demands are met before midnight tonight."

"And what are your demands?" she asked frantically.

The voice ignored her question. "Make no attempt to contact your commander, Mr. Mason. He has already been informed of our intentions, and his telephone has been implanted with an explosive device. Any attempt to breach the perimeter of his quarters will result in death. I will call you again in exactly fifteen minutes."

Michelle acted quickly. Fearing that her colleagues' phones had been tampered with as her commander's had supposedly been, she contacted the other Response Support Team members by radio. Within three minutes, the other four had joined her.

Lamont rounded up their eight-man tactical force from the Georgia Bureau of Investigation (GBI), while Aaron and Julio went to check the area around Mason's quarters. They returned to report that it was all dark, and there were no signs of anyone inside, but they had found wires running across his door and windows. They didn't dare touch them until they had a better picture of what they faced: Mason had trained them too well for that. Michelle designated Adam as the negotiator, and he waited beside the phone while she and Lamont rushed about setting up a command center.

When the phone rang, Adam began taking notes. Lamont tried to trace the calls—there were four as the night dragged on—but they never lasted long enough for him to put the trace on them. Finally Adam had compiled the list of demands from the terrorists: the release of thirty-one political prisoners, a jet to take them to an unnamed location, a CNN camera crew to report the story, and $50 million in unmarked bills.

"All of that by midnight?" Michelle asked, glancing at her watch. "That's only ninety minutes away."

Adam shook his head. "No, I talked him into pushing it back to 3:00 a.m."

"That's still no time," said Michelle without having to voice the thought on everyone's mind: *We don't have the Chief to tell us what to do.* "Do you know where they are, and how many there are?"

Adam didn't have any idea of the size of the force, but he'd gotten their location.

"So they're right here," Michelle said in wonder. "Do you think—"

"Oh," Adam said, "and they want supper for themselves and their hostages, ASAP."

Over the next few hours, a frantic scene unfolded in the makeshift command center. Having delegated authority to Adam, Michelle went along with his suggestions, if somewhat hesitantly. She especially questioned her negotiator's advice that, as a wedge for bargaining, they should withhold food.

"I just don't see your logic," she said.

"Look, there's no way we're gonna meet their demands, right?" Adam reasoned. "So if we stall on the food issue, and keep them thinking about that, they're gonna get desperate and give in."

It turned out Adam was wrong. At sunrise, a very angry terrorist leader called to say that they would begin killing a hostage for every fifteen minutes that the authorities withheld food. At that point, Michelle had no choice but to send in the tactical forces, which had been waiting anxiously for the order to begin the attack. The ensuing firefight took out three terrorists, but it also ended in the deaths of all the hostages.

Everyone knew that they were in the midst of a *simulated* terrorist incident, sprung on them by Mason at a weekend retreat outside Atlanta. He'd told them they'd have a chance to rest up before all the long days and nights ahead, and then. . . .

The bullets fired were blanks, and if the bomb squad had gotten a chance to dismantle the device outside Mason's cabin, it would only have set off a tape recording of an explosion. Afterward the security team, the "terrorists" and "hostages," and those who had played the part of media personnel gathered in the conference hall of the retreat center to review the exercise.

The media personnel were real, journalists recruited for the job by the simulation specialist Mason had contracted to put on this show. But many of the hostages and terrorists were acting students who improvised their roles, and a political science major from Emory University had composed the group's manifesto of political intentions. She had chosen to go for a white supremacist scenario, but her paradigm had one inconsistency: the leader of the terrorists (though security would not know this until near the end of the exercise) was black.

His name was Allan Boyd, and he introduced himself simply as a lieutenant in the U.S. Navy. What the rest didn't know, and what Mason would explain to his security group later, was that Boyd came from the elite of the elite, the Sea-Air-Land operations unit better known by its acronym, SEALS. He and his team had seen duty in Grenada, Desert Storm, and countless other unpublicized actions, often going into the most hostile of all situations long before the infantry landed. When the Games began, the SEALs would be in Atlanta on a special mission; but that would only be revealed much later.

For now, Mason talked to his people about the obvious lessons to be learned. This one was just a drill. But the next time they got a call like the one Michelle had received, it might be the real thing.

PART TWO

THE COUNTDOWN

6

Slightly over 10,000 medals had been awarded to Summer Olympic competitors over the century leading up to 1996, but of the 197 countries coming to Atlanta, over half had never won anything. More than a quarter had fewer than ten on their balance sheet, and another one-eighth had winnings in the 10-to-100 range. Only twenty-three nations had won more than 100 Olympic medals, and aside from Japan and China (which hadn't even begun to compete until 1984) this inner circle consisted of Western or former Soviet Bloc powers. Even there, the "distribution of wealth" ran on a sharply sliding scale: Great Britain, at number four—the only country to win medals in every Summer Olympics since 1896—had just over half as many as the number three country.

The top three nations had taken home a staggering forty percent of all the Olympic medals ever awarded. Germany, in its various incarnations, had garnered over a thousand. In second place was the former U.S.S.R., which had placed first in all but three of the Summer and three of the Winter Games in which it had competed. But the end of the Cold War had splintered that country into fifteen teams. Therefore, center stage belonged to the all-time Olympic champion, the United States, which boasted almost 2,000 medals.

The coaches at the U.S. gymnastics training center in Indianapolis predicted great things for their 1996 team, whose acknowledged star was Melody Johnson of Concordia, Kansas. A curvaceous eighteen-year-old, Melody made an unlikely heroine: not only did she lack the streamlined, almost boyish, figure of a Cathy Rigby or a Mary Lou Retton, but her age made her over the hill by gymnastic standards. Yet Melody had swept the U.S. preliminaries, and with her good looks and sunny personality, she had sponsors vying for her endorsement on their products. One cereal company had already done a mock-up of her face on their box, with production schedules only waiting for the results of her performance in Atlanta.

That caution was most likely linked to memories of the Dan-and-Dave fiasco of 1992, when Reebok signed decathletes Dan O'Brien and Dave Johnson even though neither had yet won the gold. As it happened, Johnson only got a bronze medal, and O'Brien didn't even qualify in the U.S. team tryouts. Conserving his energy, O'Brien had elected not to pole-vault at lower levels, starting instead at an intermediate mark that he'd previously carried with ease. But he failed to clear the bar, receiving no points and missing the chance to participate.

Thus people in the industry doubted the wisdom of Hypertonic, a South Korean athletic shoe company, when it introduced its new Hypershoe line with a $2 million endorsement by two untried decathlon hopefuls. Joe Bob Sweeney from Texas A & M and Curly Rogers, a handsome blond southern Californian, both had good prospects, but neither had ever competed in the Olympics. It appeared to be a replay of Dan-and-Dave, but Hypershoe wanted to make a strong initial impact, and its executives believed that the Sweeney and Rogers ad campaign would pay for itself in name recognition.

Among the Americans going to Atlanta, there were "sweethearts" like Melody and heartthrobs like Joe Bob and Curly; then there were the others that fans loved to hate. Journalists called it the Tonya Harding Effect, after the skater accused of ordering a hit team to remove her competitor from the 1994 Winter Games, and this year's Tonya Harding was JoEllen Cunningham. Surely the most well-known competitor in a sport that normally didn't attract much attention in the U.S., she had gained considerable notoriety because, as one sportswriter said with a wink, "She has ridden her way to the top." Nobody doubted her skill as an equestrian, but there were ugly rumors about how she'd gotten on the team. "People want me to be prim and proper and traditional," she told a reporter. "They just can't handle the fact that I'm a strong woman, so they make up stories."

In contrast, the newest star of the exceptionally strong U.S. swim team was the picture of an all-American heroine. Barely seventeen, Elizabeth Taggart had smashed the U.S. backstroke record in both the 100 and 200 meters. She would be one of just three native Atlantans representing their city in the '96 Games—and certainly the only one whose father worked with ACOG. Ben Taggart, who had volunteered with the Atlanta Committee almost since its inception, would serve as Director of Protocol at the Village where his daughter would reside. It was a good human-interest story, and the media had interviewed the two of them together several times. "Do you or Elizabeth's mother have any misgivings about her being in the Olympic Village?" one TV reporter had asked Ben Taggart. Taggart, visibly annoyed at this question, said, "Why should we? This is the safest Olympic Village ever."

The athletes of the former Communist Bloc had trained as hard as the Americans, but with far less hoopla. The governments that had once funded their sports programs had collapsed, and the short period of free-market economics had not yet spawned companies capable of providing lucrative endorsements, leaving many of the athletes to fend for themselves.

There was Olga Shcharansky, a fifteen-year-old St. Petersburg gymnast who had participated neither in the school program nor the national training camps. Instead she had trained with her mother, a retired national champion, in a public gym. Like Melody Johnson, she had earned the love and respect of her country as she rose from nowhere to find a place on the national team. But though she was as pretty and petite as her American counterpart, hers would be a much more lonely and much less lucrative journey: Olga's biggest hope was that if she won in Atlanta, her family of six would find a way out of the two-bedroom apartment where they struggled to survive.

Katarina Heindrich of Dresden, in the former East Germany, had feared she might not make the track team. But she was a strong athlete, and even if no one expected her to win any medals in the 200 meters (U.S. sprinters now dominated that event), she had gained respect throughout Germany for her speedy recuperation from an automobile accident only a year before. Now she would go to Atlanta along with her new friend and fellow sprinter, Heidi Hirsch, who came from the west side of Berlin.

The most spectacular track-and-field competitor from the former Warsaw Pact was unquestionably the decathlete Sándor Lukács of Hungary. In the Hungarian and European championships, Lukács had broken the previous world record by exceeding 9,000 points, becoming the favorite for the gold. Ironically, this win came just as Hypershoe launched its commercials featuring Curly and Joe Bob bantering back and forth as to which of them would win the decathlon in Atlanta. The way things looked, neither could hope for anything better than the silver, second-place to the Hungarian.

Of the few remaining Communist teams, only two—China and North Korea—attracted any real notice.

Before the 1992 Olympics, the Chinese had promised big things for their female swimmers. Their team, the "Five Golden Flowers," named after a popular film from the 1950s, came away with four gold medals and five silvers, placing them second only to the powerful U.S. women. At their National Games in Beijing the following year, no Chinese women set records, but they established a staggering depth of talent: for instance, in the 50-meter, their swimmers took first through sixth places in the world.

Likewise their breadth of talent had expanded. None of the Golden Flowers competed at the World Aquatics Championships in Rome in 1994, their place being taken by the "Ten Little Flowers," which actually consisted of twelve women. In Rome the People's Republic of China won two-fifths of all medals, and five of the ten records set were theirs. They even managed to break the time set by a U.S. *male* swimmer for the 100-meter in 1992. But for the U.S. women, Rome was a disaster: their four gold medals marked the lowest total ever for a U.S. championship team.

The rise of Chinese female swimmers in the late 1980s and early 1990s had been breathtaking. The number who ranked in the world's top ten for thirteen different events had gone from zero in 1980 to nine in 1989 to fifty-two in 1993, meaning that the Chinese held forty percent of the top slots. One swimmer, who ranked thirty-fourth for one event in 1992 and did not even make the top 150 in her other two events, was number one in all three competitions a year later.

Many found all this just a little *too* remarkable, and wondered whether these flowers of China had a little extra fertilizer in their soil. Spectators in Rome held up syringes with "China" written on them, and disgusted American competitors began to see a case of déjà vu. At Montreal in 1976, American swimmer Shirley Babashoff had been accused of sour grapes when she remarked on the East German women's deep voices. One German coach had quipped, "We have come here to swim, not to sing," but time had vindicated Babashoff. After the Berlin Wall fell, investigations confirmed that the secret police or "Stasi" had been doping East German athletes for years.

Once Communism fell in eastern Europe, widespread doping had gone into hiatus, but now observers of swimming began to notice ominous parallels in China. Just as the East German women had done much better in a comparative sense than the men, the Chinese women outperformed their male counterparts for gold medals and records. The East Germans had skipped some competitions, most likely for fear of testing, as did the Chinese. In each case, the strongest showing was in sprint versus distance competition, where steroids were less effective. But most damning of all were the strange physical changes in the Chinese competitors: exceedingly well-developed muscles on the girls' legs and excessive acne on their faces.

Beijing's response to accusations of doping ranged from professions of openness to outright hostility. The Chinese admitted that they'd hired an East German coach and taken training from the Soviets and Hungarians prior to the fall of European Communism, but they gave other reasons for their success: the international pool of competition for women was of lesser quality than that for men, and Asian women were more equal in size to their non-Asian counterparts than were Asian men. And when all this reasoning failed, the Chinese accused their critics of racism.

Soon the drug busts started to come in fast and furiously. In 1993-94, eleven Chinese swimmers tested positive for steroids, compared to ten other swimmers in the rest of the world during the preceding twenty-two years. Other countries became so concerned that in an unprecedented move, they banned the Chinese team from the August 1995 Pan-Pacific Championships in Atlanta, the "dress rehearsal for the Olympics." This startled the Chinese, who then admitted that forty-eight of their athletes had failed drug tests since 1987. But an inquiry team from the swimming federation found nothing; therefore the new Chinese women's team, "the Twenty Little, Little Flowers," would swim in Atlanta.

With all this attention directed toward China, it was easy to miss what was happening in its Communist neighbor to the east, the Democratic People's Republic of Korea. But Olympic Village planners couldn't help but notice: allocations for residential space were based on previous team sizes, and whereas North Korea had sent only sixty-four players to Barcelona, in Atlanta they would have 302.

Among those on the North Korean table tennis team was Lee Chin. Before leaving her village, she had promised her family she would return with a gold medal for them and the "Dear Leader" who controlled the nation. Like many of her teammates, she felt she'd embarrassed her country in Barcelona, and over the four years since then had worked incessantly to improve her skills. This time she knew she would prove herself.

But when she happened to see some of the swimmers and runners at the Olympic Training Facility on Kwangbok Street in Pyongyang, Lee Chin was amazed at how they had grown—not only in the size of their teams, but the size of their bodies. She wondered where, in all the glorious reaches of the Democratic People's Republic, the "Dear Leader" had found such women.

Only twenty African countries had ever won an Olympic medal. Their combined continental total was 172, the lowest in the world, and nearly a third of their medals had come from a nation that didn't even compete in the seven Olympiads from 1964 to 1988. And though South Africa had changed, its biggest star seemed like a throwback to the past.

He was the white super-heavyweight boxer Christiann Vervoerden, who at 296 pounds and nearly seven feet tall was surprisingly agile. A relative unknown two years before, he had burst quickly onto the fight scene, and remained undefeated after twelve matches. There was talk that this Afrikaner giant from the hinterland had killed two men with his bare hands. Whether or not that was true, Christiann definitely had a habit of focusing on his opponents with the "evil eye" of a witch doctor. As he entered the ring, he would let out a shrill, blood-curdling yell that made even his most loving fans tremble.

Twenty-eight years old, red-haired and bearded, with a ruddy complexion, he compared in build and size to American basketball star Shaquille O'Neal; in fact the press in Pretoria had nicknamed him "The White Shaq," a name which reportedly enraged him. Vervoerden had a reputation as an unreconstructed racist, and some said he even belonged to the Afrikaner Resistance Movement, a neo-Nazi paramilitary force that invaded the constitutional talks in Johannesburg in 1993.

Whatever his politics, Vervoerden was an outstanding fighter. Qualifying at the Pan-African Games, he easily won four fights in the heavyweight division: three of these were first-round knockouts, and in the fourth his terrified opponent refused to leave his corner.

The Olympic Village in Atlanta would host nearly 14,000 athletes and officials, making it a city larger than most towns in America, but it still couldn't hold all the men and women who hoped to compete in the Games.

Every nation had the right to send four competitors regardless of their qualifications, and only athletes from high-profile Olympic nations faced stiff competition for a slot; in other countries, particularly of the Third World, athletic ability had little to do with it. Often the national leaders would simply sit down and make up the list of those they wanted to send, and if the team had little chance at medals anyway, the lucky few would most likely be children of wealthy or powerful countrymen to whom the Olympics simply represented a world-class vacation. There were also athletes willing to change their citizenships to smaller, less notable countries to increase their chances of making the team. Marginal players from the United States, daunted by the selection process, would switch to the Virgin Islands or Puerto Rico (which had their own teams despite being U.S. possessions), or any other nation that would sponsor them.

Clearly the term "Olympic athlete" did not necessarily mean world-class athlete. At Calgary's Winter Games in 1988, an incompetent and thoroughly unqualified ski jumper nicknamed "Eddie the Eagle" had competed for Britain, and though he provided comic relief to the world as well as terrific embarrassment for his homeland, British Olympic officials had been terrified he'd break his neck.

By the early '90s the international federations that governed each Olympic sport had become wise to the Eddies of this world and began tightening their standards, forcing competitors to undergo preselection trials. Qualifications put everyone on an equal footing, and sometimes they resulted in surprises. A great athlete might have a bad day, as had happened in 1992, when world record-holder Carl Lewis missed out on the 100-meter dash qualifications and Dan O'Brien had his fiasco. Or an athlete who'd only hoped to compete might, by doing his best at just the right moment, find himself among the Olympic chosen few.

Such was the Bosnian handball team. In spite of the continuing war in their country, they had swept through the qualification rounds for their region and played exceedingly well in test matches against several of the stronger European teams. A Serbian news agency had investigated the players' backgrounds and discovered that a number of them were professionals from other countries, Bosnians only in the sense that they had been rapidly conferred citizenship from Sarajevo; but given the biased nature of the source—and even more so the fact that no one really cared about the Bosnian handball team anyway—most of the world press ignored the issue.

Soon all the contrasting teams and individual athletes would come to Atlanta. Some would succeed while some would fail to meet the goals they'd set for themselves. Christiann Vervoerden and the swimmers from Communist Asia would become the focal point of bizarre sideshows. Others would take part in the central drama that would characterize the 1996 Games, a drama that had nothing to do with sports.

7

The Games would begin on July 20, 1996, exactly 132 years after General Sherman's attack on the city of Atlanta. Sherman had begun marching his troops in May 1864, and in May 1996, a new breed of attackers marshaled their forces. But instead of cannons and rifles, this army came with computers, fax machines, cameras, and microphones.

Bobby Joe Watkins had sold his hometown to the world by emphasizing its facilities and its warm spirit of cooperation between the races; now the media would dissect and un-sell it by portraying Atlanta's lack of history and culture, its crime, its decaying urban center and sprawling suburbs, and the racial tension that was alive and well behind the smiling patina of Southern charm.

The first cannon-shot came from overseas. A German TV network ran a "documentary" which portrayed Atlanta's blacks living in slave cabins while the whites luxuriated in mansions. The British press had plenty to say about a racial brawl involving some of their black sprinters training in the south Georgia town of Americus. The average Briton, the London papers reported, would be safer strolling down Falls Road in the heart of Belfast's combat zone than on Peachtree Street. One tabloid went so far as to display Atlanta's weekly murder count on its sports page, as if it were the box score of a ball game.

Then the American media set themselves against what some called "The Bubba Games." *The New York Times* observed that in Atlanta, "ancient history means before shopping malls." Even Southern papers got in their licks. Referring to an Atlanta restaurant with special Olympic menus in nineteen different languages, the *Houston Chronicle* pointed out, "All it means is now there are nineteen different ways of telling the waitress whether you want your barbecue chopped or sliced."

Looking for negatives, the media found plenty to exploit. There was the cold shoulder Atlanta had consistently given Freaknik, a spring break festival which brought in thousands of African-American college students from all over the country to cruise the streets of Midtown and wealthy suburban Buckhead. Though the city's ill will had to do with the massive traffic congestion, not the color of the visitors' skin, the shutting down of local malls and restaurants on Freaknik weekend looked like a throwback to the old days of "whites only" lunch counters.

Then there were the problems between homosexual advocates and suburban Cobb County following a 1993 county commission resolution condemning the gay lifestyle. When activists learned that ACOG planned to use Cobb as the site for Olympic volleyball competitions, they threatened massive marches by "hundreds of thousands" of gays around the world. Rather than undergo that battle, ACOG pulled out of Cobb in July 1994, but even that wasn't enough: militant gays prevented the Olympic Torch from passing through that hated piece of ground.

The media assault culminated when one of the major television networks began an exposé entitled *Atlanta: A City Divided*. The mayor, the governor, and ACOG's Director of Public Relations had received advance notice of the special, and each called the network president and pleaded with him to stop the broadcast. The only impact of the pleas was to strengthen the network president's resolve that the show would run. The network, hoping to boost ratings it had lost by not winning the contract for the Olympics themselves, wasn't about to hold back on such a juicy story, especially when it would be reported by two award-winning anchors, Tim Barakoff and Margaret Winters.

Atlanta: A City Divided began with Tim Barakoff walking along a crowded city street. He was at Peachtree Center in the middle of downtown on a workday, he announced. "This is the Atlanta that's been advertised to us, the Atlanta promoted by its Committee for the Olympic Games, a city—in the words of a former white mayor—too busy to hate."

The camera panned up the glass-enclosed elevator of the Peachtree Plaza Hotel, then tracked across the skyline. It cut to the same view at night, with thousands of lights shining in the towers that stretched up Peachtree from Five Points into Buckhead. When Tim reappeared, standing on the same spot as before, the bustle of midday had died down with the coming of night. A few partygoers passed by on their way toward Planet Hollywood behind him; a few cars went by on the street, one of them pouring out rap music from its speakers; and a policeman stood talking to two homeless men who had wandered in front of the camera. "Looks a little different, doesn't it?" asked Barakoff. "That's because very few Atlantans would be caught dead downtown after dark—and being caught dead is exactly what they fear."

Margaret Winters made her first appearance standing in front of the Hightower Homes housing project in southwest Atlanta. Behind her had gathered a collection of black children and adults, the youngsters giggling and making faces but most of the grownups staring ahead with sullen expressions. She had come with three armed security guards, she explained, "because this is one of those areas that neither the Olympic Committee nor the leadership of this city wants outsiders to see."

The camera made another pan, this time to show the ruined buildings and people of Hightower Homes: windows broken or boarded up, paint peeling, scruffy children playing in a bare-dirt yard, crack addicts passed out in doorways. A variety of sounds came with the picture: shouted epithets, screams of sirens, and the ever-present thunder of rap from a boom-box. "There are many who would say that *this* is the true City of Atlanta," Margaret announced, "and indeed I'm standing inside the city proper, a shell with some 411,000 inhabitants surrounded by a sprawling metropolitan area of 2.7 million. The disparity grows daily, as more and more residents flee downtown for the safety of the suburbs, and who can blame them?"

Another segment found Barakoff in the emergency room of St. Joseph's Hospital, in an area near Dunwoody called "Pill Hill" because of its high concentration of health-care facilities. It didn't appear that they had many emergencies in this clean environment of stainless steel and white enamel, so quiet one could hear the Muzak emanating from the P.A. system. The head physician looked fit and rested, and when Barakoff asked him how many gunshot victims they received a day, he chuckled. "Better make that *a month*, Tim, and I'd say maybe one or two. Most of those are hunting accidents, or the proverbial guy who was cleaning his rifle and it 'just went off'."

"No murders?"

"Sometimes, but most of what we see is considerably less exciting. Our cases are generally accidents: a man falls off a ladder in his backyard or a child gets too close to the barbecue pit. And of course there are the heart attacks, too. We have a famous heart center here, you know."

The scene cut to Margaret Winters in the emergency room at Grady Memorial Hospital in downtown Atlanta. Dozens of patients, almost all of them black, crowded on benches or leaned against walls, some of them holding their heads or stomachs and groaning, some of them visibly ill and in dire need of attention. Suddenly a medical team burst through the ambulance entrance with a patient on a gurney while a voice on the P.A. system shouted "Code Blue Emergency Room!" There was no Muzak at Grady.

The view switched to the operating room. The patient had defibrillators on his chest, and as his body jerked with the electrical shocks, a voice-over of Winters announced, "Another shooting statistic for the city of Atlanta, but hopefully this one won't become the tenth fatality of this young month. Grady Hospital is a place where many Atlantans begin their lives. Yet for many more, it's the end of the line."

Even the most obtuse viewer could not fail to observe the contrast with St. Joseph's and its rich white patients who, if they weren't tinkering with their houses and gardens, were barbecuing in their backyards or getting heart attacks from enjoying too much of the good life. But no one mentioned the fact that Grady was the designated trauma center for the city, and that all emergency medical teams had specific instructions to bring trauma cases there.

In the final segment of the show, a camera followed Moores Mill Road, crossing Marietta Boulevard to leave behind the mansions of Buckhead and enter the poor neighborhoods of south Atlanta. The last shot was a dissolve from the Olympic Torch to a scene from the 1992 Rodney King riots at Five Points.

Back in the studio, Margaret gave a few statistics on "the murder capital of America," with its 16,000 violent crimes a year and one murder every forty-four hours. Tim shook his head. "Margaret, it's hard to believe that you and I were in the same city." Then he looked at the camera for the wrap-up. "So there you have it," he said. "Two Atlantas: the picture offered by the Olympic salespeople, a city of peace and prosperity and shady trees, with gorgeous skyscrapers and a world-class airport—"

"And the other Atlanta," said Margaret, "a place of abject poverty, rampant crime and murder, racial discrimination, and hatred. When the world comes here for the Olympics in July, what will it see? One Atlanta or two? I'm Margaret Winters."

"And I'm Tim Barakoff—hoping that, during the Olympic Games, Atlanta will truly be the city too busy to hate."

Many viewers around the country accepted the series at face value, and soon other networks ran their own, very similar, pieces—all networks, that is, except for NBC and CNN, both of which were accused of bias because the former had an Olympic contract and the latter an Atlanta address. The spark set off by Barakoff and Winters caught fire across the world: people who'd planned to attend the Atlanta Games now had second thoughts, and several tour operators had to declare bankruptcy because they couldn't turn back the airline tickets for which they'd prepaid. Soon IOC members found themselves openly challenged as to how they could possibly have selected Atlanta as the site for the Centennial Olympic Games.

In the remaining weeks of May 1996, two other Olympic stories made the headlines; fortunately for ACOG, neither had anything to do with Atlanta.

The first and much more prominent item involved Sándor Lukács, the Hungarian decathlete who would have given Joe Bob Sweeney and Curly Rogers tough competition for the gold medal. Lukács had been driving near his hometown of Buda when a rental car overtook him, running him off the road and into a ditch. He came away with only a broken hand, but this rendered him unable to compete in four of the ten events of the decathlon. The mysterious driver vanished, and the car, which turned out to have been stolen from a rental agency in Buda, was found two days later parked near a railroad station on the Austrian border.

With the case closed for lack of evidence, the Hungarian press began making insinuations that Hypershoe's $2 million endorsement deal with Lukács's two prime competitors gave the company plenty to gain by eliminating him from Olympic competition. This spin didn't get much play in the English-speaking world until the British tabloids picked it up, comparing it to the Tonya Harding-Nancy Kerrigan scandal.

Hypershoe responded by hiring a team of attorneys who began filing libel suits in Budapest, London, New York, and anywhere else in the world where journalists impugned its name. This did little to improve their damaged image, but their sales soared, giving credence to the old public relations adage: "It doesn't matter what they say about you, as long as they're saying something."

At least Lukács could hope to compete in the 2000 Games. But the so-called Bosnian handball team (or at least, its first string) would never play again. They'd been traveling in three buses from their last competition before Atlanta, a match in Milan which they'd won 24 to 17, when the first bus had skidded on a high mountain pass and gone off the side, killing the driver and all eight passengers. The other two buses carrying the remaining team members had managed to stop before careening down the mountain.

Without Coach Zoeller and his seven best players, Hakija Drabeznic's Bosnian team would have a tough time living up to the expectations they had created in the preceding three years. "But we're still going to Atlanta," a somber Drabeznic said in an interview with *Radio-Televizija Sarajevo*. "Our team qualified, and they're still going to play. These weren't the men we had planned to put on the court, yet they have the example of their fallen comrades. And I believe they're going to give a performance the world will never forget."

His prediction would turn out to be correct.

8

In just six weeks, what the Atlanta newspapers called "the largest peacetime event on earth" would begin. Never before had Olympic venues been so widely spread—1,200 miles from Miami's Orange Bowl to RFK Stadium in Washington, both sites of soccer matches—or so concentrated in a city center. Of the thirteen competition sites inside Atlanta, eight lay within easy walking distance of one another.

Walking itself would be an entirely different matter, because during the seventeen days of the Olympics, downtown Atlanta would be wall-to-wall with spectators, delegations, and locals out to join in the experience of a lifetime. Every imaginable type of sales would take place on and above the streets: airships, planes, helicopters, and giant wall murals displaying corporate logos; people handing out coupons and free samples; pin hawkers, food vendors, and makeshift newsstands selling papers from Tokyo and Berlin; street evangelists and political activists for every cause from the Nation of Islam to the North American Man-Boy Love Association. Less visible forms of sales would take place too, as visitors from a hundred different countries employed the services of gorgeous local escorts and packed the numerous strip bars, consistently rated as Atlanta's number-one attraction by visiting conventioneers.

As many as two million extra pairs of feet would walk the concrete expanses of Peachtree and Marietta streets on any given day, and ACOG's transportation coordinator, a former Army logistics expert, might have wished that everyone would walk. The freeways, rapid-rail lines, and buses would be taxed to capacity, and unless one happened to be a member of the IOC, parking inside the city (or even the use of a private vehicle) would be out of the question. Instead, spectators would leave their automobiles in gigantic park-and-ride lots, some as far away as Chattanooga 120 miles to the north, and board buses to take them to the venues. Even when they got to the nearest approach, they might walk as much as a mile from the curb to their seats. In addition to the

700 buses belonging to MARTA, Atlanta's public transportation system, ACOG had 2,000 more on loan from other cities. Along with all 240 cars of MARTA's rail line, they would operate around the clock.

In the midst of this, ordinary life inside the city would virtually cease. Though only three streets had been closed, many more had been converted to one-way, and even the garbage collection crews had to implement special plans to get their job done during the Games. Businesses were encouraged to let employees work at home, or to have them take their vacations, and Georgia State University would shut down classes.

Another campus just a few miles to the north would be more completely transformed than any other part of Atlanta: the 320 acres of Georgia Tech, which for thirty-three days between July 6 and August 7 would be the temporary home of 13,900 athletes and officials. Its daytime population, with 9,600 ACOG staff members and volunteers, 5,500 visitors (including media), and 2,600 Georgia Tech employees, would make the Olympic Village the sixteenth largest town in Georgia.

Because it occupied a much smaller space than any municipality its size, everyone would either walk or take one of seventy-five electronic "trams" around the Village. Like any other town, this one would have a bank, a post office, a library, a clinic, its own newspaper and radio station, and service and entertainment facilities ranging from an optometrist's office to a video arcade. There would be churches as well, though few Georgia towns could boast their own Buddhist and Muslim centers.

The athletes would come to Atlanta to sweat, and when they cleaned up they would use enough towels to cover 139 football fields. Village occupants would eat more than a million meals, drink more than half a million gallons of bottled water, and consume nearly two million individual soft drinks.

As head of Village Management, Steve Kirk had to allocate space for the 14,000 temporary residents of the Village, which required endless computer simulations. Projections based on figures from Barcelona were virtually useless because of the addition of twenty-two new teams created from the breakup of the Soviet Union, Yugoslavia, and Czechoslovakia. No machine could process all the variables involved, and Kirk's people ended up running the figures manually. But when the final team rosters came in, they presented still more surprises: some athletes, including Sándor Lukács, had dropped out; others such as the Bosnian handball team had changed personnel; and still others had just qualified. Therefore Kirk could only hope that when the teams arrived, their numbers would approximate the ones he'd received in the "final" roster.

Once they had some idea of who would come, Kirk's people then had to decide where to put them, an equally difficult task because all space was not created equal. Naturally, every delegation believed that it deserved the best facilities available, and Kirk had to balance that desire with an often conflicting one: to make sure that no one rubbed elbows with anyone they didn't like. Official Olympic literature seldom mentioned the fact, but common sense dictated that they couldn't put the Iraqis next to the Iranians, the Chadians next to the Libyans, or anyone at all (except possibly the Americans) next to the Israelis.

With these delegations together in such close quarters—some from countries at war with one another, some sharing ancient rivalries, some supporters of terrorism and some its victims—Village Management had made security its top priority. Aside from the fence and the biometric access-control equipment, a large portion of the 23,000 security officers detailed to the Games would be present in the Village. There was just one catch: in the words of one memo, "security should be perceived as invisible."

Outside the window of Village Management Headquarters, a constant parade of groundskeepers, maintenance men, and construction crews worked around the clock. Not long before, the room in which the four people were sitting had been an office in the Georgia Tech Student Services Building, but now the building had a new temporary function, and Steve Kirk had commandeered this office for a security briefing with Tom Mason, Greg Robbins, and Michelle Hinton.

"Well, folks," Kirk began, "the countdown is progressing. Are we ready?"

Michelle crossed her legs, folded both hands on her knee, and smiled at Kirk in an inscrutable way that he found slightly unnerving. He had sat in meetings with her for well over a year, plenty of time to become accustomed to the sight of her deep blue eyes peering across a table at him when she said something funny and then waited for his reaction, straining the fine contours of her mouth to keep a straight face. But the fact that he considered her the most gorgeous woman he'd ever seen hardly distinguished him from hundreds of other men. Yet Michelle exerted a magnetism over him that wasn't only physical. He found himself trying to avoid catching her eye. Once he'd recoiled when she had reached out and touched his hand to make a point. Many times he'd felt a thrill just talking to her, and would later laugh at his own foolishness. He had two divorces under his belt already, he told himself, so he ought to know better.

But there she would be, smiling back at him in a way that she didn't look at Mason or Robbins or the others, and he wondered if she felt what he was feeling or if she was only playing with him because she could read his thoughts. Whatever the case, they both had a job to do, and neither of them would do anything unprofessional. But in a little more than two months, the Games would be over, and then. . . .

Mason chuckled. "Good question, Steve," he said. "But if you have to ask that, maybe we're in trouble."

"What's that? Oh yeah, well, you know me—I'll keep asking right up to the last moment." Kirk took his eyes off Michelle and sat up straighter in his chair. "In the meantime, you folks have to brief me, while I in turn have the enviable task of getting to brief the Butcher."

"How is Hans anyway?" asked Robbins with a grin.

"Still looking to cut expenses, Greg," Kirk replied, imitating ACOG chief Hans Bliecher's Austrian accent.

"You can tell him from me that I'm glad he bought into all the Atlanta exposés on TV," said Robbins. "They scared him into doing something we never could, which is put more money into security."

"Yeah," said Kirk, "he still thinks the federal government will bail him out, and that the IOC won't have to pay for it."

Robbins snorted. "With all the shit going down in Washington, I doubt the Games are very high on their agenda. I've been trying to get them to allocate more people down here for two years now. But," he added with a sigh, "at least we know we'll have enough security here for a couple hours, anyway—when the President drops by."

Kirk groaned. Just two weeks before, a Secret Service agent had called Robbins to apprise him that they would have a very special visitor on the day of Opening Ceremonies. "I just hope it's not like when Reagan came to the Village in Los Angeles," he said. "You security types shut down an entire training site for thirty days just so he could show up once, and we can't put up with that here. And then there was Barcelona—King Juan Carlos decided to stop in, so all of a sudden the entire Village had to be closed to everyone except athletes."

"Don't worry, Steve," said Robbins. "Nothing like that will happen here. And if you keep the number of day-passes down—"

"Well, let's talk about that," said Kirk. He explained that even during the President's visit, there would be 1,100 sponsor support personnel in the Village, but some of the other numbers were more flexible— for better or worse. The media had become so adept at sneaking into the Residential Zone in Barcelona that this year, the chefs de mission for the national delegations were as eager as Village Management to keep them out. Only 400 members of the press would be allowed in the International Zone at any one time, and their presence would have the effect, as Kirk put it, "of a guy with B.O. on a crowded bus" because star athletes who tended to draw big crowds would steer clear of the International Zone for fear of being mobbed by reporters.

But demands from politicians counterbalanced the unexpected break because of the media. Kirk had fought long and hard to keep the number of day-passes down to 4,000 a day, twice as many as security would have liked, and if the numbers went anywhere, it would be up. Every official remotely connected with the Games wanted to bring guests as a way of showing off their importance, and they would all be pressuring ACOG to issue more passes.

When Robbins heard this, he reminded Kirk that their access-control system wasn't set up for numbers much higher than 4,000 a day. "Surely Hans is going to realize that this'll increase costs, and we all know that's his hot button. Maybe you can get him to back us up and say no additional day-passes—he must be good for something!"

"Yeah, but Blanchot's more of a politician," Kirk replied, referring to the IOC President, "so he's liable to bend to the pressure. Now, talk to me about that fence of yours—how soon is it going to be finished?"

"A couple of days more," said Robbins. "Now that school is out at Tech, we can seal it up. And it's one mean mother, too—a major improvement over that joke they had in Barcelona." But, he explained, Village Security lacked the manpower to adequately patrol the five-mile perimeter, and though motorcycle-mounted officers would cover as much area as possible (Robbins had asked the governor to deploy the Georgia National Guard to help), it would still be difficult. Someone could break through in a secluded area, and though the SWAT team— Allan Boyd and his SEALS—would come out once the breach was detected, nobody wanted to bring it to that point.

"In a lot of ways this is harder than putting up a fence around a military installation," Robbins continued. "There, the only people who are gonna want to break in or look in are spies, whereas here you'll have all kinds of rubberneckers hoping to get a glimpse of the athletes—especially around the swimming venues, because they're close to the fence."

After discussing the fence, Kirk turned to Mason. "But enough about equipment; let's talk about personnel. I'm eagerly—but not too eagerly—waiting for you to tell me which teams pose any particular security risk, besides Israel."

"Oh, I wouldn't worry about Israel," replied Mason. "Just like El-Al is the safest airline in the world, terrorism-wise, there's no other team better equipped to handle an incident than those guys. My old buddy Eli and his team will be on hand to protect them."

"Eli. . . Eli. . . ." said Kirk, trying to remember the name.

"Yeah, he was in Barcelona, and then. . . ." Mason stopped.

"And then?"

"And then they detailed him to guard Prime Minister Rabin."

"Wow," Kirk said. "I guess that didn't work out, did it?"

"He wasn't on duty the day of the assassination." Mason sounded a little touchy about the subject. "You can bet he's on guard for any kind of security breach."

"Their security guys—are they armed?"

Mason gave a coy smile. "We don't talk about that a whole hell of a lot, but let's just say that they're prepared. It's a fact of life, even if it's a little-known one."

"What if other teams find out?"

Mason shrugged. "They won't, unless there's an incident. Now, we've done some checking up on various organizations—Tamil Tigers from Sri Lanka, IRA sympathizers, etc.—and I've got a few concerns."

He went on to talk about several potentially volatile teams from Muslim countries: Iran, Iraq, Syria, Libya, Lebanon, Sudan, and even Palestine, granted participating NOC status in 1993. "But even if we did find some dirt on one of these teams," he concluded, "we don't have any choice but to let them in anyway." By the Olympic Charter and an agreement with the U.S. government, all members of a national delegation had the right to enter the country, and this included "athletes" who otherwise wouldn't have received a visa. "Bottom line is, we've got quite a few folks here who support some version of jihad."

Kirk completed the thought: "So they don't mind dying, because martyrdom means a direct pass to heaven."

"You got it."

"And they're in my Village." Kirk frowned. "Are we gonna watch 'em?"

"I wish!" said Mason. "To provide total surveillance, we'd need four operatives just for one player. For the six Palestinians, you'd need twenty-four." He threw up his hands. "Besides Michelle, I've only got four other people on my task force, and I know Greg's not eager to commit a bunch of folks to this."

Even though the city, state, and federal governments had committed large numbers of personnel to the Games, surveillance was a touchy matter in a country that prided itself on civil liberties. For months now, Mason and his team had run into problems checking out the teams coming to Atlanta. The U.S. government was reluctant to play its Cold War role of spying on enemies, and of course foreign delegations were hostile to unpleasant questions or security checks. In the end, Mason realized that for all his hopes of identifying every possible threat, his job had come down almost to pure guesswork and instinct.

"But maybe," he went on, "we could pool the different agencies and put a few people posing as hospitality clerks in each of the potentially volatile teams' quarters. They would file daily reports, and they'd need some kind of communication system to get in touch with me in case of an emergency. We'd have to have three people to work eight-hour shifts on each team, so you're talking about several dozen folks."

"Okay," said Kirk, jotting this down. "I'm gonna tell Hans that this is a must."

"I tell you what," said Mason, "I'd be willing to give up one of my precious few to watch this Bosnian handball team. I don't have any specific data on them, but I've got a gut feeling after that bus crash."

"The only thing I know about them is not to put 'em anywhere near the Serbs," Kirk observed. "That and the fact that their delegation size has grown. In Barcelona, there were only nine Bosnians total, but now they're gonna have seven players, nine alternates, and four coaches for team handball alone. Besides that, they've got their chef de mission, three other athletes, and two coaches—twenty-six in all."

"What about these new players?" asked Michelle. "Are they any good?"

Kirk shook his head. "No one knows, because they don't have any previous record as players. The guys who died were good enough to qualify, but they weren't likely medalists. I doubt if this new team can even win a match."

"Then why are they here?" she asked. "I mean, this isn't the team that qualified."

"Well, that's the thing, the *team* did qualify. It doesn't make any difference who the players are, it's a team sport, and they have the right to make whatever personnel changes they want to."

"Like I said," Mason repeated, "I'd just like to keep an eye on them. Let me detail one of my people—Adam, say—to watch their delegation."

"Okay." Kirk looked around at the others. "Well, folks, the one thing we can for sure expect in the next six weeks—"

Mason completed the thought. "—Is the unexpected."

9

Two men sat at the kitchen table, one of them working on something and the other one watching. Four years before, Ahmad and Hafiz had dreamed of this time as they watched the fireworks exploding at the Closing Ceremonies in Barcelona.

In October 1995, they had rented a farmhouse just off Georgia Highway 34 outside Newnan, twenty-five miles south of Atlanta's Hartsfield International Airport. Besides Ahmad and Hafiz, three others lived in the house, but the neighbors seldom saw the others. If anyone approached during the day, which rarely happened since the farm lay at the end of a dead-end dirt road, they would find a burly man riding a John Deere tractor out front, presumably plowing up the pasture land for future planting. Nobody ever got close enough to see that the gate to the fence around the farm was padlocked, or that the tractor operator had a walkie-talkie and an automatic weapon. The noise of the tractor covered up any sounds coming from the barn, 100 yards to the rear of the farmhouse, and because it lay on the other side of a hill from the gate, no one could have seen the occasional blue flashes coming from within at night.

Inside the barn, a single fluorescent bulb cast a dim, sickly glow, hardly enough light for the delicate work taking place, but the two mechanics there kept at their task long after sunset. From time to time their welding torches lit the room. The air was thick and smelled strongly of acetylene, and though the heat made it almost unbearable, the doors stayed closed and locked.

The mechanics had worked on two projects for the past few weeks. The first of these was a 1993 LTD Crown Victoria, a non-descript model with few luxury items that had served the Alabama State Patrol for two years as an unmarked car before being purchased for cash at auction. Like all "unmarked" vehicles, its color, model, and lack of detail identified it from a mile away, and they had selected it for that very reason; in fact, they'd gone to great pains to make it a very marked car. They had installed Wheelen blue lights on the top, a police radio with an antenna, and a security screen between the front and back seats. Then they had painted the vehicle white and stencilled on the familiar red and black insignia of the Atlanta Police.

The other vehicle required much more extensive alterations—hence the welding equipment. A 1988 Mack DM 690-S eight-speed concrete truck with a 10.5 cubic yard drum, it could carry more than 45,000 pounds of concrete or any other, similarly dense, material. It had been purchased with cash at a bankruptcy sale outside Jackson, Mississippi, and then brought here for the make-over.

On each side of the engine, quarter-inch steel plates and large louvers in front of the radiator had been welded to allow air to enter but prevent normal small arms fire from penetrating. The bumper had been replaced with a large I-beam which slanted from the sides and came to a point so that it could be used as a battering ram. It had been covered in vinyl and painted black, so that from a distance it looked like a normal bumper.

In the cab, the passenger's side was sealed shut. Half-inch steel plates were attached to both doors up to the windows, and the side windows were replaced with sliding enclosures of quarter-inch steel which latched at the top. A similar panel which would cover the windshield had slits two inches high and six inches wide to allow the driver to see. This cover would not be attached until the truck reached its intended destination.

Finally the workers had filled the tires with polyurethane foam, a technique often used on heavy construction equipment such as earthmovers and quarry machinery. It prevented blowouts—or in this case, any attempt to shoot the tires. This made for rough highway driving, and would eventually cripple the vehicle if it were driven at high speeds over any distance. But they didn't intend to drive it far.

On the wall of the barn hung enlarged photos of equipment from Atlanta's biggest supplier of ready-mix: Williams Brothers Concrete, whose vehicles Atlantans had seen in the hundreds, going to and from Olympic building projects over the past few years. No one would give the armored vehicle a second glance once it was repainted to look like a Williams Brothers truck.

This truck would not carry concrete, but something with the consistency of mayonnaise and the odor of dog excrement. It went by the generic name of emulsion slurry, specifically ANFO, or ammonium nitrate fertilizer and diesel fuel oil. All it needed was a container of nitroglycerin to break the weak bond holding the nitrogen to the other molecules, and it could blow up a large public building.

Ahmad and Hafiz had obtained the materials for the bomb through a series of carefully orchestrated robberies that began before they rented the farmhouse. Raids—scattered by time and distance—at an agricultural products plant, soap factory, and fabrics manufacturer had yielded the nitric acid, glycerol, and sulfuric acid to make the nitroglycerin. Then, starting in May 1995 with the theft of 1,500 pounds of ammonium nitrate from a lawn and garden store in neighboring Fayette County, they had begun accumulating quantities of fertilizer and fuel oil. These robberies had culminated in early October 1995, when they stole eleven fifty-pound bags of ANFO and more than a thousand blasting caps from a company in the Gwinnett County suburb of Norcross. Hafiz called in an anonymous tip that white supremacists had taken the explosives to use against the Million Man March set to occur in Washington later that month.

Though a fertilizer bomb is among the least sophisticated types of explosives, the relative ease with which its materials could be obtained had made it the method of choice on two other notable occasions. The terrorists who detonated a bomb in the World Trade Center garage in February 1993 had used nitroglycerin to set off their own slurry, a mixture of urea fertilizer with sulfuric and nitric acids, and the Oklahoma City bombers in April 1995 had followed the ANFO recipe. But this bomb would improve on its predecessors by sheer size: the two other bombs had been delivered in rental vans that could only haul a ton of slurry or less, whereas the cement truck would hold thirty times as much.

When the two men in the barn had finished their work, they moved quickly to the house and then went upstairs to shower. Because of their known affiliations with terrorist organizations, they had entered the United States illegally, and had to stay inside at all times. Upstairs they encountered the man who drove the tractor all day long, a soft-spoken, dimwitted giant with the nickname of "the Turk" because he had the same first name, Suleiman, as a famous Ottoman sultan. "Are you finished with my truck?" he asked as he did every night, and the other two told him they would be soon.

Downstairs the farmhouse had little furniture except for a few cushions strewn about the living room floor, a TV on CNN with the volume turned down, a police scanner, a tape deck from which emanated a speech by an angry Islamic priest, and the kitchen table where Ahmad and Hafiz were seated.

Both men spoke fluent English, Ahmad having attended NYU and Hafiz MIT. They had entered the U.S. through official channels, though they used false identities to do so.

Earlier that day, Hafiz had visited several Radio Shack stores in the metro Atlanta area to obtain materials Ahmad had sent him to buy, and now Ahmad busied himself with putting them to use in constructing a detonator. He'd learned the skill at a training camp in the high plains above Jalalabad in Afghanistan, where the victorious mujahideen had begun using weapons left over from their war with the Soviet Union to turn the country into a vast "University of Jihad," training Islamic terrorists to wage holy war all over the world.

One detonator would be plenty, but being a perfectionist, Ahmad was making two. The first had a timer that the driver could switch on before jumping from the truck, allowing the vehicle to move toward its target and explode 180 seconds later. The backup had a remote control device that could be activated by the mere push of a button, or by a radio, from two miles away.

Hafiz, who up to now had watched in silence as his comrade worked, suddenly spoke up. "The Turk can't wait to make his delivery to the stadium."

Startled, Ahmad fumbled with his detonators and growled at his companion. "This is delicate work."

"Don't be so jumpy—we're weeks ahead of schedule."

"I want to be prepared," said Ahmad, finally setting his work aside.

"You worry all the time," Hafiz chided. "But the Turk, he worries about nothing. If anything, he feels honored to be the one chosen to drive the truck."

"I'm sure he's had good practice driving the tractor here for the past few weeks."

"He didn't ask me, but I'm still wondering how we'll get the vehicle under the stadium."

"It doesn't have to be exactly underneath," Ahmad answered. "Just close, and in any case that is why we have this police car as an escort."

Hafiz thought for a moment. "You know, I wish we could have obtained real explosives instead of this fertilizer."

"If we had purchased 'real explosives,'" said Ahmad, who was partial to the fertilizer bomb, "we would both be sitting in prison at this moment. The amount of TNT we need can't be bought without a permit; otherwise you have to go to an arms dealer, and I suspect all of those are watched very closely."

Hafiz still didn't look convinced.

"There will be 85,000 people in those seats," Ahmad continued, "of which we expect to kill most. And think of the panic! The survivors will be trampling one another trying to escape, and many more will die or be injured that way. And all of it will be broadcast on live television to the entire world!"

"It is fitting that it should occur in that $200 million monument they have built to their own egos," Hafiz agreed, taking heart.

"Yes," said Ahmad, gingerly lifting the detonator and holding it to the light as though it were a jewel. "Three weeks from tonight, at precisely 9:00 p.m., the American viewing audiences will be settling down in front of their TVs to watch the Opening Ceremonies at the Olympic Stadium. But what they will see instead will be an explosion that will blow that stadium to bits and send tens of thousands of infidels to hell!"

On July 1, 1996, five days before the Village opened, security did a final "lockdown" exercise, bringing dogs into all the buildings to check for hidden explosives or firearms. Everything went fine until one of the dog teams got to University Apartments.

Lamont, from Tom Mason's Response Support Team, had come along to observe the inspection. Later he reported to his boss that the dogs behaved as though someone had put out a plateful of raw meat. They went wild, sniffing everywhere but finding nothing.

Yet these were dogs trained to sniff out explosives, and it had to be something else. Mystified, their handlers took them from one apartment to the next, and the dogs had the same reaction almost everywhere they went in four of the five buildings. Security called in a crew from Plant Operations to tear into several of the walls, but finding nothing, they patched the walls back up again.

One of the Plant Operations men, a tall Texan with blond hair, sang so loudly that Lamont had to ask him to be quiet while he talked on his cellular phone to the lab analyzing paint samples from the inside of the apartments.

"Mm hm," said Lamont into the phone, troubled by what he heard. In the background, the worker, with *Jon* stencilled on his shirt, was singing the song "Knock Three Times" in a subdued voice. "So that's it?" Lamont asked.

"Well," said the lab technician, "I suppose you could condemn the whole complex and let us do a thorough check, but I don't think that's what you want to do."

"No, of course not. Thanks."

The Texan kept singing the old Tony Orlando song, which urged the girl in the downstairs apartment to announce her intentions by knocking either on the ceiling or the pipe.

Lamont sighed. How could he tell Mason that some element had gotten into the paint which caused the dogs to react, making it impossible to search effectively for explosives in the new buildings?

Two weeks before the beginning of the Games, on Saturday, July 6, 1996, the Olympic Village officially opened. It looked spectacular: "Better than Main Street in Disney World," said one commentator. Its staff appeared well-prepared, and it had all somehow come together on time.

On the first day, only about 300 Olympic occupants showed up, mostly chefs de mission and their assistants, there to set up offices before the athletes arrived. Each team had an assigned Atlanta envoy, many of whom were immigrants from that particular country, and Kirk began holding daily meetings with the chefs and envoys to resolve any difficulties that surfaced as teams settled in.

At the first chef's meeting, the Japanese delegation complained about the softness of the mattresses and the few choices of sushi on the dining room menu. Kirk listened to these complaints, nodding and smiling and speaking soothing words. The North Koreans claimed that their rooms were not as good as those of the South Korean team, even though the facilities were exactly the same, and Kirk explained this as politely as he could.

Other than that, there were other minor issues such as washing machines not functioning, or a towel shortage—all of them easily resolved, and none of them nearly as serious as problems at the Barcelona Village four years before.

At 7:00 p.m., Kirk called his staff together to review the spectacularly uneventful day, and they spent most of the hour talking about an incident concerning some Australian soccer coaches.

Even the Director of Olympic Family Relations, who'd had to bail the two Aussies out of jail at 2:00 in the morning, had a laugh over it. It seemed that the two ardent footballers, who would be leaving town in a few days to go to one of the distant soccer venues, had stuck around Atlanta long enough to learn about the Cheetah III strip bar, conveniently located just a block from the east entrance of the Village. Having each imbibed enough tequila to incapacitate three ordinary men, they had found a dancer they particularly liked, and jumped up on the stage beside her. While one held her, the other began putting ten-dollar bills into her garter with his teeth. This amused the dancer, but the bouncers—who could have passed for Olympic weightlifters—wrestled the offenders off the stage and had them arrested. The visit to the local jail quickly sobered the two, who placed a call to their delegation. They were released on $1,000 bond each, and they would no doubt have a quick hearing.

"Well, let's just hope the press doesn't get ahold of it," Kirk said. "Anything else?"

Someone mentioned a concerted effort by Cuban expatriates from Miami to buy out all the baseball tickets and load the stands, a possible setup for mass defections by athletes from Havana, but Kirk shrugged this off. "Let the State Department handle that—that's why we've got one of their reps on hand. Anyone comes to you with a question about defection, you play dumb and turn him over to State." He glanced at his watch. "Alright, it's 8:00, time for you folks to go home. But remember, people, when the Games get started we won't be able to take off in the middle of the afternoon like this. Me, I've still got a security meeting to go to."

They gathered in Greg Robbins's office at Village Security HQ, deep inside the Naval Reserve Building on Plum Street: Robbins, Steve Kirk, Tom Mason, and the Director of Protocol for the Village, Ben Taggart.

At first they chatted about the number-one Olympic athlete from Taggart's point of view, his daughter Elizabeth. For the past year, she'd been swimming twenty hours a week, which sounded like a lot to the others, but Taggart assured them the Chinese made their girls work twice as hard. "I've seen some of those Chinese swimmers," he said. "They're nearly as big as Greg here, and fast too. So we'll just see how she does, but however it turns out, Susan and I are proud of her."

After that they got down to business, reviewing the minor access-control problems they'd had with fans trying to sneak a peek at their favorite stars. Mason had checked out a few suspicious characters hanging around the venues: "Nothing serious," he concluded, "and my folks are keeping a close watch. Still, to repeat what I said to you four years ago when we first met, Steve—and I know you're doing this—pray every night."

"Thank you, Tom, you are the great soother of all pain." Kirk sighed. "And now to the big item on the agenda: I guess what's-his-name is still coming to my Village?"

Robbins wagged a finger at Kirk. "Now, Steve, you know that our U.S. team can't win without your President coming to encourage them."

"Yeah, right—*they* need *him*," said Kirk sarcastically. "Meanwhile, he's gonna disrupt everything around here."

"Maybe it's a good thing Washington wouldn't bail ACOG out," Taggart observed. "Can you imagine? He'd expect to move in!" The others groaned at the thought.

"But with the way he's slipping in the polls, he'll grab at anything he can to prop up his image," Mason observed.

"Yeah, well, if the public only knew the strain it puts on security for him to be here, I'm sure his PR coup would backfire." Kirk let his voice trail off. "So when's he going to be here?"

"Looks like 5:30 in the afternoon on Friday the nineteenth," Robbins answered, "so he and the First Lady can go to the Opening Ceremonies that night. The White House wanted us to let him jog around the Village and shake hands, but of course we nixed that. All there's gonna be is a pep rally and photo op with the U.S. team before they load up for Opening Ceremonies, then he's outta here."

"Five-thirty?" Kirk asked sharply. "On the day of Opening Ceremonies? You must be shitting me! That's our busiest time!"

"I know, Steve, I know."

"Didn't you tell the Secret Service that?"

"Of course I did," said Robbins, "but they do what the President wants, and he wants to be seen with a bunch of young, virile athletes. It's politics."

With a sigh of disgust, Kirk said, "Don't they see how much this is gonna mess up our schedule for getting the athletes to the stadium?"

Robbins and Mason answered almost in unison: "You think they care?"

"I guess you're right," said Kirk with a defeated tone in his voice. "Alright, Greg, how do you plan to run this dog-and-pony show?"

"The way I see it, we can get him in and out pretty quick. They wanted to use the practice field to land his chopper, but I suggested another plan: Air Force One lands at Dobbins, then the Presidential limo comes down I-75 with Secret Service and police escorts. Once they enter the gates, the motorcade goes to the International Zone and lets the President off just twenty yards from the amphitheater for the ceremony. Then the photo op, and thirty minutes later—*voila!*—we load him back up and out of here. So the only place in the Village he'll be is in the International Zone."

"Yeah, but that's your least secure spot," Kirk pointed out.

"Normally, but that afternoon there won't be any guest passes issued, except for dignitaries. We'll have athletes and staff, of course, but they will have already passed security checks anyway. And then media—unfortunately, we'll have to double the number of press passes to 800—but again they'll have cleared."

"And the place will be crawling with Secret Service," Mason said. "You won't be able to fart in there without four gorillas wrestling you to the ground. Besides that, if we keep him near the amphitheater, that's not a spot that allows a lot of opportunities for an attack anyway, and Michelle and I will be in a chopper overhead to watch for anything squirrelly."

"Alright," said Kirk finally. "It's getting late, so—"

"You know, it's funny," Taggart interrupted. "We sit here and we talk about dangers in the Village and how someone might take a shot at the President. . . and all of that goes with the territory." He gazed at the others. "But I can't look at this quite as objectively as y'all do, not when my own daughter is going to be right there, too."

10

"As Director of Protocol," Ben Taggart began, repeating words already very familiar to him, "I am pleased to welcome the athletes, officials, staff, and chef de mission of the Bosnia and Herzegovina National Olympic Committee, along with their special guests, to the Atlanta Olympic Village."

It was Friday, July 12, and they had gathered near the center of the International Zone in the amphitheater, a building constructed for the sole purpose of holding the team welcoming ceremonies. The steps and seats were of stone, but a brightly colored cloth, which rippled in the faint summer breeze, served as the walls of the building. Behind it stood the Theatre for the Arts, and in front of it what had once been an open expanse of grass and walkways between buildings, transformed by the Olympics into a festival area. Banners hung from guy wires attached to two 100-foot towers that bisected the plaza at an angle. To the southeast stood the Kessler Campanile (affectionately nicknamed "the Shaft" by Georgia Tech students), an eight-story structure made entirely of slender stainless steel slabs stacked one upon another and rising to a point.

When the President arrived next week on the day of Opening Ceremonies, the place would be brimming with press, athletes, and officials; but today there was only Taggart, a few people from his Protocol staff, the twenty-six men of the Bosnian delegation, plus a few members of the media who'd come out for the obligatory "Scarred By War, Bosnia Hopes For the Gold" story. Taggart knew his words by heart, and as he spoke, he thought of the many more hours of handshaking, smiling, and chatting ahead of him.

The welcoming ceremonies, in which the Director of Protocol and the Village Mayor officially recognized the entry of each NOC to the Village, were saturated with the pomp and circumstance for which the Olympics are known and loved. After Taggart concluded his pro-forma speech with a wish that the friendships between countries made here would extend far beyond the seventeen days of the Olympic Games, he would introduce the envoy, who would then introduce the chef, and each in turn would speak a few kind words. Then a small band would play the country's national anthem, and an honor guard would raise the flag—in Bosnia's case a navy blue shield with a diagonal white stripe and six fleur-de-lis on a field of white. After that, the Village Mayor would present the chef with one of 396 quilts individually hand-sewn by women around the state of Georgia. Then everyone would pose for group photographs, before the national flag was placed alongside those of the other countries already welcomed to the Village.

An identical ceremony would occur for each of the 196 other nations coming to Atlanta. These events had to be fairly simple, because the mere staging of them required endless attention to seemingly artificial but in fact crucial details. Even the name of a country could evoke reactions, as in 1960, when the Taiwanese at the Rome Games had been humiliated by the IOC's refusal to let them present themselves as representatives of China. This year, Taggart expected a similar controversy over the name of Macedonia, which like Bosnia was a former Yugoslav republic. Greece, which had its own region named Macedonia, didn't like the implication that another country wanted to lay claim to it.

Then there was the matter of the national flag, of which there were many new ones and many others altered by the removal of the Communist star. Quebec separatists objected to the Canadian Maple Leaf, but it would have to fly—though Taggart had jokingly warned his people not to make the same mistake as some hapless Fulton County Stadium employee had during the 1992 World Series, when he flew the banner of Toronto's home country—upside-down. And then there was the South African flag.

Gone were the old orange, white, and blue stripes with the symbols of the three black "homelands" in the middle, replaced by a distinctly African-looking banner that reflected the country's black majority. But the new South Africa still contained many whites, some of whom rejected the changes brought about by the Mandela government, and when the flag was raised at the welcoming ceremony, one white member of the team had turned his back.

This gesture had brought gasps of shock and anger from many of those present. Photographers snapped the unforgettable picture, reminiscent of the Black Power salute given by American sprinters Tommie Smith and John Carlos in Mexico City twenty-eight years before. But even without these theatrics, the South African athlete would have been noticed anyway: he was Christiann Vervoerden, the boxer favored to win the gold.

Afterward, Vervoerden told a CNN reporter, "I box for South Africa, but for the real South Africa—not those monkeys who are running the place now." The correspondent asked him what he meant by *monkeys*, at which time Vervoerden's trainer tugged on the boxer's mammoth biceps and pulled him away from the throng that had gathered around him.

Such big challenges, plus a thousand little ones, had plagued Ben Taggart and his team as they worked at breakneck speed to welcome the 197 teams to the XXVIth Olympiad. In the case of the Bosnians, he had prepared for a disagreement over symbolism, with ethnic Serbs or Croats refusing to recognize the flag or the national anthem. But he'd learned from the envoy that most of them were Muslims, and since all but six were handballers, they had a considerable sense of team spirit.

"Just about everyone I talked to here at the Olympic Village," said a local news correspondent, standing in front of the International Zone entrance, "has been enthusiastic about their accommodations. In fact, one coach from Bosnia, who told me he was glad to get away from the war in that country, described it as 'just like a dream.' And speaking of dreams, Dream Team II, the U.S. basketball team, arrived here today for check-in, but without much fanfare. Steve, why was that?"

"Where's the mute button?" Steve Kirk asked, fumbling with the remote control as his televised image appeared on the screen. He had stopped by to see Thomas Mason at the Renaissance Hotel across the Downtown Connector from the Village, where Mason had moved in mid-June after bidding farewell to his family for the next six weeks. The absence of Sandy's influence in his life, combined with his nonstop schedule, would have made his room a pigsty had it not been for the hotel's housekeeping. As it was tonight, when the two men shared a quick meal before going over a few details, there were dirty socks on the bed, clothes on the floor, and a pile of papers and photographs at the desk where Kirk sat.

"I don't think it has one," said Mason, sitting on the bed and reaching for another slice of pizza from the box beside yesterday's socks. He laughed. "Besides, the novelty of making the eleven o'clock news shouldn't have worn off so quickly for you."

"It wore off ages ago." By now the Steve Kirk on the screen—dressed in the same shirt that now had a blotch of tomato sauce on the collar and the same tie which he'd long since loosened—was saying, "Well, Angela, as you may recall, there was a lot of excitement surrounding the arrival of the first Dream Team in Barcelona four years ago. That of course had something to do with the fact that 1992 was the first year NBA players were allowed to participate in the Olympics, and there was the star factor too: you had Magic Johnson, Michael Jordan, Larry Bird, Charles Barkley. . . . We learned our lesson from Barcelona, and security around Dream Team II was so tight that most of the other athletes and Village employees didn't know they'd gotten here until it was over."

"You should be glad you've got such an articulate Village Management Director," said Kirk, smiling. He muted the TV, set down a half-eaten slice of pizza, wiped his hands, crumpled the napkin, and tossed it into the wastebasket on the other side of the room.

"Two points," said Mason. "Now—let's talk about business."

Kirk smiled tiredly. For weeks now, both men had concentrated on nothing but business. They couldn't even leave the Village for an hour to eat a meal without turning on the TV and seeing an update on it—and the Games themselves still lay a week away. "Alright," he said, pulling out a notepad. "Ben and I have done a pretty good job of keeping your potentially volatile teams isolated. I don't think the Libyans were too happy with their location, but it'll work out. So far no Cubans have defected, and no Serbs have done any ethnic cleansing that I've heard about. Now, you say you've got some photographs to show me?"

"Yeah, Aaron tailed this guy for a couple days and took these," Mason said, reaching across Kirk into the desk drawer and pulling out a manila envelope from which he retrieved a dozen grainy black-and-white photos. They followed the progress of a single man, his face circled in red on pictures where he appeared in a crowd, as he loitered around the Village perimeter and visited several downtown sites, including the Olympic Stadium.

"So?" asked Kirk, handing the photos back. "You could track a thousand other people going to the same places."

"Something about the guy seemed suspicious," Mason said, "so we ran his photograph through the FBI, Interpol, etc. He's gone by tons of pseudonyms, but his real name is Ahmad Mahfouz, and it looks like he could be linked to Sheikh Omar Abdel Rahman."

"You mean the guy behind the World Trade Center bombing?"

"The same one."

"What do you know about him?"

"Not much *to* know. He hasn't got any history of personal involvement in terrorist activities, but he's been photographed at the mosque in New Jersey where the Sheikh used to go before he was arrested, and he seems to spend a lot of time wandering around near the Village and the venues."

"Doing what?"

"Just looking around. And he's also been seen with some other Middle Eastern-looking character in town, but we weren't able to photograph him. Obviously, it's a situation we need to be cautious about."

"Cautious, hell!" Kirk raised his voice. "Why don't you arrest him?"

"On what charges, Steve? Walking around? He hasn't done anything. This may be your Village, but we're still operating under the Constitution."

"Come on, Tom!" snapped Kirk, standing up and walking to the window to look out over the city. "If U.S. intelligence wanted to, they could find some reason to hold him for the next three weeks—and they would, too."

"Hardly," Mason said in a patient voice. "Can you imagine the field day the U.S. media, let alone the world press, would have if they found out about this? I'd say you're looking at a considerable downside here."

"The downside is that this nut could blow up a building," Kirk countered, turning from the window.

"Like I said," Mason replied calmly, opening a Coke and taking a drink, "all we can do right now is watch him. He's probably harmless."

PART THREE

LET THE MAYHEM BEGIN

11

Thirty-six hours. The Games were that close. It was the morning of July 18, and Steve Kirk had sat down with his Food Service, Transportation, and Protocol directors to review their plans for the Opening Ceremonies of the XXVIth Olympiad. They had to transport the entire Village to the Olympic Stadium, a mammoth logistical task not unlike marching an army, and the last thing Kirk wanted was a repeat of Barcelona.

No one four years before had thought to feed the athletes and coaches before they went to the Estadi Olímpic; so by the time they'd paraded around the stadium and lined up along the end field to watch the flame being lit, it had been nearly six hours since these 13,000 men and women—with some of the highest metabolisms in the world—had received anything to eat or drink. Once they got back to the Village, they stormed the dining facility and overwhelmed its capacity of 4,000. It was a miracle no one got hurt, because a riot nearly broke out as athletes pushed themselves against the glass entry doors.

The Atlanta dining facility had as many as twenty food-service lines operating at once, although it couldn't seat many more than its Barcelona counterpart. But once the athletes returned on opening night, they would have the option of either going to the dining hall or picking up a box lunch without ever going inside. There would be no repeat of the Barcelona debacle: Kirk had seen to that.

Besides getting the athletes fed, the second major headache for Kirk would be taking them safely to and from the stadium. Fortunately, he didn't have to rely on Village Security—at this moment up to their elbows in plans for the President's visit—but would instead use the services of the Fulton County Sheriff's Department, whose experience with transporting prisoners made them ideal for the job.

Intensive inspections would ensure that each of the 330 buses was "clean" (no weapons, bombs, or unauthorized personnel on board), and therefore they would drive directly up to the athletes' housing units. Every single athlete would have to show an accreditation badge with an A_A on it before boarding.

At precisely 6:30 p.m. the buses, each with an armed guard, would begin departing for the Olympic Stadium, driving the three miles on a dedicated lane with a solid line of green lights so no would-be terrorist could take advantage of a sudden stop to attach a bomb or climb onto the roof of a bus. (Just in case, every vehicle would be searched again upon its return.) After letting the athletes off, the buses would park in a secured area, and when the show ended, the athletes would re-board to be escorted back up the same dedicated lane from which they'd come. By midnight they should all be back, safe and sound.

Having reviewed all these details, Kirk turned to Taggart. "Everything on schedule with the welcoming ceremonies?" he asked.

"We've got twenty-five teams today," answered Taggart, "and the last twenty-three tomorrow."

"Any snafus?"

"Nothing major—not since Vervoerden and all that business with the South African flag. We almost had a little trouble with the Poles and the Indonesians because their flags look exactly the same, only reversed; and there was some disagreement over the Byelorussian national anthem, and of course the Greeks gave us a little grief over Macedonia, which they insisted should be called 'The Former Yugoslav Republic of Macedonia.' But we sorted all that out. We had State Department folks there to check out all the details and verify, then we double-checked with the ambassadors."

"Mm-hm," said Kirk, only half-listening because he was jotting down notes about transportation and food service. Then he closed his notebook and looked up at Taggart and the others. "Alright then, we all know what we need to do. Buckle on your seat belts, 'cause here's where it gets bumpy. If we can get through today and tomorrow, we've got it licked."

Being a news junkie, Ahmad had learned of the President's visit to the Olympic Village and the Opening Ceremonies before anyone else at the farm. As soon as CNN reported it, he'd told Hafiz, but he didn't seem excited.

"Is this not wonderful news?" asked his partner. "He will be in the stadium at the very moment when—"

"Yes, but don't you see?" Ahmad replied irritably. "If he's there, that means there will be more Secret Service there too, and more security for us to contend with."

"True," said Hafiz. "But the Turk is fearless, and he'll go anywhere we tell him to."

"The Turk is a fool," Ahmad shot back, "and it's our job to make sure he can get through with the truck."

With the Opening Ceremonies drawing ever closer by the hour, Ahmad had walked about the farm nervously, checking every detail. The men in the barn had completed their work on the vehicles some days before, and now with the paint fully dried, no casual observer could have detected any difference between these and a real Atlanta Police car and Williams Brothers concrete truck. Last night, they'd tuned up the engines and done a test-drive around the farm, less cautious now because their mission would shortly be complete.

Early that morning, as soon as the Turk had turned on his tractor to generate some background noise, Ahmad had test-fired one of his detonators in a large hole on the back side of the farm. He had then instructed Hafiz to drive two miles down the road in their "civilian" vehicle, a brown VW minivan, and activate the transmitter. Both the detonator and transmitter had worked just as flawlessly as the vehicles did. Ahmad only hoped the human element of their mission would do as well.

When he returned to the farmhouse that morning, Ahmad found Hafiz posing in front of a mirror in his Atlanta Police uniform, purchased by mail order from an out-of-state security supply firm. In his blue-black garb with his belt, nightstick, sidearm, and realistic insignia, he looked very convincing, all the way down to his posture and his walk.

"I'm impressed," said Ahmad. "You look just like the real thing."

They sat down on the bed in Ahmad's spartan bedroom, and he began drawing out a schematic of the attack for one last review. "Remember," he explained, "there are two levels of security we must penetrate to get to our objective. The first is here, about half a mile from the stadium, beyond which point all the streets are closed off with police vehicles and barricades. But they open the barricades for service vehicles, and they will let our police car and cement truck through because of our 'written orders'."

Hafiz had forged the orders based on a set found in a trash can near the stadium months before; only the date had to be filled in. Though it might have seemed a bit suspect to be bringing in a cement truck just before the Opening Ceremonies, the orders explained that the inner security ring of concrete barriers needed repairs, and as Ahmad reminded Hafiz, police officers would not question such an official-looking document.

"Alright," he continued, quizzing Hafiz, "what if they do give us a problem?"

"Then we drive away quickly, and while they're busy chasing us down, the truck will crash through the wooden barricade." Hafiz paused. "But won't they leave guards at the barricade, Ahmad? They're not *that* stupid."

"Certainly they will—but how can they stop our bulletproof concrete truck?" asked Ahmad. "If they alert the inner ring of security, where they have the concrete barriers and a double fence all around the stadium, the Turk will just have to pull the truck as close to the stadium as possible, smashing through police cars and even the concrete barriers if he can." Ahmad held the end of his pen to his lips, pensively. "Despite his willingness to be a martyr, it's important that the Turk believes he has plenty of opportunity to escape in the event his courage should fail him."

"I've explained that so many times he understands," said Hafiz. "Once he comes to a stop, he'll cut off the engine and remove the key. He'll have his radio to communicate with us, and as far as he knows, there will be a five-minute period before the bomb explodes." He paused. "Though of course we will detonate immediately."

"Excellent," said Ahmad.

"But. . . ."

"What now?"

"I just don't know how well the concrete truck will ride on those foam tires, especially with the heavy load it's carrying."

"There's nothing we can do about it," said Ahmad dismissively. "Now let's go check on the others."

The one-story Naval Reserve Building on Plum Street had such an anonymous appearance that few passersby would have given it a second look, and that was just the way the Village planners had wanted their Village Security office to look. But inside, of course, there was a constant buzz of activity. Phones were always ringing, faxes pouring in around the clock, people scurrying up and down the hallways, and at any hour of the day or night, a fresh pot of coffee was brewing somewhere in the building. This morning found Greg Robbins and Tom Mason in the briefing room along with more than a dozen representatives from various agencies providing security to the Olympics in general, and the impending Presidential visit in particular.

Robbins turned the agenda over to the Secret Service advance agent, who started giving the President's itinerary, beginning with his 5:00 p.m. landing at Dobbins Air Base.

"Don't forget what county Dobbins is in," said the deputy sheriff for Cobb County. "There's liable to be protests by the gay activists."

"We considered a last-minute switch to Hartsfield for that very reason," said the Secret Service agent, "but that would have been an absolute security nightmare."

"Besides that, we can't give in to every dissident group that wants to use the Games for its own agenda," Mason pointed out.

"Well, it's easy to forget that when you're looking at the possibility of 200,000 screaming assholes and twenty miles of traffic jams," drawled the Cobb County deputy.

"The official line is that Dobbins is federal property and not legally belonging to Cobb," the Secret Service agent went on. "Now, for his motorcade we'll have I-75 cleared"—he glanced at the Georgia Highway Patrol rep, who nodded his head—"then he'll get off at Tenth Street and come into the main Village entrance, which is the area that poses the most risk because that's the only time he'll be out in the open."

"And that has been the obsession of Mason and me, night and day," said Robbins. "We're not allowing any visitors in on Friday—"

"I'm more worried about what's gonna happen when he leaves the Village and goes to his suite at the downtown Ritz-Carlton," an FBI agent interrupted.

"That's our job," the Secret Service man countered. "We have the entire top floor plus the floor below it, with our men on the roof. The building's secure."

"I'm not talking about that, I'm talking about Fidel staying in the same hotel. We've got a rumor that the two of them are going to have a private meeting."

"Well, you know about rumors."

"That they're usually true?" the FBI agent shot back. "We're already gonna have a major population from Miami in town for the Games, and this is liable to create an incident of some kind."

"Precisely," the Secret Service operative replied. "That's why there's no comment being made on this matter, and no one knows anything. But I'd suggest you gear up for some picketing by the Cuban-Americans."

"When were you gonna tell us about that?" asked Red Anderson, Atlanta assistant police chief. "Don't look to me for backup—we're already taxed to the limit downtown with all the other shit."

"Everybody is, Red," said Mason.

"Shit." Anderson wrinkled his brow. "That means I've got to pull some blues off the street somewhere. All we need is for some damn tourist to get popped off around here."

"What we need to do," Mason suggested, "is see if the mayor will get in touch with the White House. Maybe he can talk the President out of having the meeting."

"I doubt it," Anderson replied.

"Maybe we can get the National Guard to cover you on the other end." The Secret Service agent glanced at the Georgia commander, who looked away.

"We've got to do something," said Anderson firmly. "We've got local thugs who've been planning their moves for months, and they could end up proving everything those TV people said about crime in Atlanta." He looked around at the others. "And listen, while I've got the floor here, let me tell you about our body count: the good news is that it's not as bad as it could be, and the bad news is that in the two weeks since the teams started arriving, we've had thirteen murders. Now we all know that the rate goes up in the hot months, but this is a fifty percent jump over the normal rate for that same time frame. Not only that, but petty crime is up significantly too."

"At least we haven't lost any tourists yet," the FBI man pointed out.

Robbins turned to the Secret Service agent. "And then, after the Ritz—?"

"The stadium," the agent replied. "Just before the ceremonies start, he'll ride in with an armed motorcade, and drive right up into an entirely secured area."

"Any bomb threats?" Robbins asked.

"Ha, are you kidding me?" said an ATF agent, and several of the others nodded in agreement. "We're like a Domino's Pizza, taking orders, which could mean we've got a bunch of kooks out there, or it could mean we've got someone who knows what he's doing, and is throwing out so many red herrings we won't know when the real one comes. You can imagine the manpower it takes to check all these out."

The agent from the President's advance team sighed. "And of course we've gotten the usual assassination calls. It's the same situation as with the bombs: leads that go nowhere, which may mean nothing, or. . . ." He let his voice trail off. "Not to mention ones who might want to knock off some other head of state or government minister."

"You've got Secret Service detailed to all of those?" Mason asked.

"Mostly, yeah, though a lot of them have bodyguards, too. Any of those leaders, whether it be Russia, Great Britain, or Japan, could be a target. Not to mention Fidel—there's plenty of Cubans who wouldn't mind being a hero, or what they would think is a hero."

"The tough thing about all this," said the FBI agent, "is that we know there are plenty of 'actives' wandering about, guys known to have been associated with terrorist organizations, but we can't get 'em for anything because they haven't done anything."

The State Department representative spoke up for the first time. "The upside is that most of them can guess that their organizations have been penetrated even if they don't know who the moles are, so if they're gonna do anything, they have to keep it on a very small scale and not let anyone know about it."

"I'm just worried about the ones who don't know they're being watched," Mason observed ruefully.

"Well, one thing we can do," Robbins pointed out, "is make the stadium totally secure: check all entrants for metal objects, and sweep the surrounding area."

"Damn," said Anderson. "I thought these Olympics were supposed to be entertainment, but they're turning out to be the biggest pain in the ass I've ever seen."

"You got that right," said Robbins. "Compared to your usual low-level pain in the ass, this one's a hand-grenade enema. They say three billion people will be tuned in by electronic media, plus we'll have every major newspaper on the planet represented." He laughed. "Not that that should make anybody nervous or anything."

12

The President of the United States had a tendency to arrive late wherever he went, and Air Force One did not make its scheduled 5:00 p.m. arrival at Dobbins until 5:15 on Friday. His limo, flown down the day before in a C-47, was waiting for him as he stepped off the plane to begin the twenty-mile journey to the Olympic Village, and since the gay demonstrations had been headed off, the motorcade emerged from Dobbins onto Delk Road without impediment.

All entrance ramps along Interstate 75 had been shut in sequence minutes before, and a few stalled or stranded cars along the shoulder had been removed by wreckers earlier that morning. Except for one or two state troopers posted at every entry or exit, the mile-long cordon with the limo, its Secret Service cars in front and back, and its police escort were the only vehicles on the road.

The President's party cruised at a steady seventy miles per hour, with three helicopters flying overhead, and at 5:41 the limo approached the Tenth Street exit. High above in a Jet Ranger chopper, Thomas Mason observed the movement below. For the past hour he'd listened through his headset to the radio transmissions of the various law enforcement personnel involved in moving the President from Dobbins to the Village, a task that had required the allocation of 150 officers. It seemed an awful waste of manpower to him. "All this for a photo op?" he said to Michelle, his pilot. "We've got some screwed-up priorities here."

To ensure a large turnout, the White House advance people had arranged for the entire U.S. team to gather in the amphitheater before boarding buses to go to the stadium. Besides this group of almost 800, there would be another 150 dignitaries including the U.N. Ambassador, the Secretary of State, various Olympic officials, the mayor, and the governor, plus the 800-strong media pool. When the crowd saw the President's party coming toward them—their view of him shielded at first by his Secret Service escort—the team sent up a hearty cheer, and a moment later the President and First Lady emerged from their limo, waving and smiling as the cameras rolled.

Up above, Mason gazed down through his binoculars at the Secret Service operatives surrounding the couple. Even from that distance (and in spite of their trademark dark glasses) he could see the concern on their faces. The Olympic Village might be one of the most secure spots in the entire universe, but their agency never took anything for granted; they had looked foolish enough when John Hinckley managed to shoot President Reagan fifteen years before. Just now the Commander-in-Chief motioned to the Secret Service team leader to indicate that he wanted to move about in the crowd of athletes and shake hands, and the team leader spoke into his lapel before nodding to his boss. Mason watched the President walking through, stopping from time to time to exchange a few words with the athletes.

By 6:00 p.m., the President and his human shield of agents had wound their way to the platform of the amphitheater. *This is the time,* Mason thought to himself grimly. *This is the place if someone wants to take a shot.*

The President made his speech, he gained the political points he wanted, and a few minutes later he was on his way to his hotel with the First Lady to get ready for the Opening Ceremonies that night.

"You're right, it was a damned waste," said Michelle after she'd landed their chopper. "I just hate to think what might have been happening while we had our hands full with this nonsense."

"Bite your tongue," Mason said, but he had the same thought.

As Ahmad noted with approval, the three vehicles departed the farm fifteen minutes ahead of schedule: first the Turk in the concrete truck, then the police car with Hafiz at the wheel and Ahmad a passenger. In their uniforms, both men looked very official. The other two men in the brown Volkswagen van brought up the rear. It was just before 7:00 p.m., and Ahmad had carefully ascertained over the preceding week that there wouldn't be much traffic on Georgia Highway 34 at this hour, a good thing because the truck's tires (not to mention the load) made for slow going. By the time they pulled out onto I-85 to begin the main leg of the forty-mile trek, forty-five minutes had passed.

On the interstate, the Turk managed to increase the speed to fifty-five miles an hour. The police car followed by a quarter-mile in the right lane, always staying close enough to remain in sight but far enough away that they didn't look like they were together, and the van kept pace from another quarter-mile to the rear.

Cars coming up behind them rapidly decelerated when they saw their police markings. Observing this in his rearview mirror, Hafiz laughed. "Look at these fools slowing down!"

"Keep your eyes on the road," growled Ahmad. If everyone stayed behind them all the way to Atlanta, they would have a line of cars five miles long—hardly an inconspicuous way to enter the city. "I wish these damned Americans weren't so afraid of a badge," he said. "Go on, idiots—pass us! We've got better things to do than to stop you."

"Wait, look!" said Hafiz, pointing toward the concrete truck ahead. Something had dropped down and was dragging the highway, making bright sparks. Hazard lights flashing, the truck pulled off to the side with a horrid screech of metal.

"Pull up behind him and put your blue lights on so no one else will stop," ordered Ahmad.

Once they had eased onto the shoulder behind the Turk, Ahmad got out and walked up to the door of the truck. Cars passed by at the speed limit, their drivers probably glad they hadn't gotten stopped themselves.

"What's wrong?" demanded Ahmad.

The Turk scratched his giant head with a forefinger the size of a carrot. "I don't know. It began making this terrible sound like something broke."

By now Hafiz had gotten out, and after squatting down on the other side of the truck, he discovered that the universal joint had sheared off, leaving the drive shaft dragging the ground. The Turk, walking around toward Hafiz with Ahmad behind him, said helplessly, "Hafiz, there was nothing I could do."

"Of course not," said Hafiz reassuringly, standing back up. "It's not your fault. Ahmad, we have a problem—it's that damned foam in the tires that caused it. I don't believe going sixty miles an hour works with this load."

The van behind them pulled up and the two mechanics jumped out. "Universal joint sheared!" Ahmad yelled to them. "Can you fix it?"

One of the men said he'd check, then crawled under the cement truck. Not thirty seconds later, he had climbed back out and told the other mechanic to get the welding equipment and jacks from the back of the van.

"Well?" demanded Ahmad.

"We can fix it," said the mechanic, "but only temporarily."

"What are you saying?"

"The shaft will be out of balance, and it's going to be a rough ride. It could come apart again in one mile, or it could last all the way."

"What if we go slow?" asked Hafiz.

"The slower the better, but there still aren't guarantees."

"Just make it work!" Ahmad ordered.

Ahmad hovered over the mechanics, as though watching them work would speed up the job. Hafiz, meanwhile, watched the highway. It occurred to him to go turn off the flashing blue lights of the police car so as to attract less attention, but just as he was leaning over into the rider's side, he saw something in the rearview mirror that froze him: a Georgia State Patrol car pulling in behind the three vehicles.

He took a deep breath, then turned around and walked back toward the patrol car. To calm his nerves, he took out a stick of gum and popped it into his mouth, and he tried to seem as casual as possible when he leaned over into the trooper's window and, chewing loudly, said in unaccented English, "How's it going?"

"Fine," said the patrolman, a middle-aged white man. "What's happenin' with you fellas?"

"Well," drawled Hafiz, "that there cement truck broke down, and those boys are trying to repair it enough to get it off the road. We thought we'd just offer a little safety light here until they got this thing moving."

"I hear you," said the state trooper, studying Hafiz's face. Hafiz could guess what he was thinking: *Mexican? Puerto Rican? Or an A-rab?* And it was clear that he had taken note of the Atlanta uniform and car. "So what are y'all doin' all the way down here? We're a long ways from Atlanta."

Hafiz shrugged. "They just told us we needed to escort this truck up to Centennial Park—they're makin' some kind of emergency run so they can put in a walkway or something before tomorrow."

"Hell, I'd a thought they'd have all y'all busy around the stadium or someplace," the state trooper observed, "what with all them extra people in town, and the Olympics starting tonight and all."

Hafiz hoped he didn't seem nervous as he smiled and said, "Don't ask me. All I do's take orders." He'd noticed some movement from the corner of his eye, but he didn't look up.

The patrolman didn't realize that someone had walked up on the other side of his car until Ahmad flung open the passenger door, aimed a pistol at the trooper, and fired twice into his chest.

"Great, you idiot!" shouted Hafiz as the blood-spattered body of the officer slumped limply in the seat. "Now you've really managed to get us noticed!"

"Shut up," said Ahmad, holstering the pistol. "Prop his body up so he'll look like he's just sitting in the car."

"How much longer?" asked Hafiz as he reached in to pull the dead weight up and lean its head back.

"Ten, fifteen minutes."

"We've got to hurry. The dispatcher's going to call him on the radio for something before too long."

What the two men didn't know was that a northbound motorist had already dialed 911 on his car phone. When he reported to the local dispatcher that he thought he'd just seen an Atlanta police officer shooting a highway patrolman, he had to repeat the message three times to the disbelieving clerk.

She still didn't take any action until another call came in from someone in the southbound lane who'd seen what looked like a sleeping state trooper in his car on the other side of the road. The dispatcher had trouble finding anyone to go check the situation out, because local law enforcement had been stretched incredibly thin to make up for the concentration of Atlanta police and other forces around the Olympic Stadium. The closest patrol car, eight miles to the north, was finally dispatched to the scene.

Hafiz was kneeling beside the truck, watching the two mechanics put the finishing touches on the jerry-rigged universal joint, when he looked up and saw the flashing blue lights in the southbound lane less than a mile away. Suddenly the car slowed to cross the median. Hafiz jumped up to look for Ahmad. He found him sitting in the fake police car with the engine running, and he raced over to the side of the car, but as he put his hand on the passenger door, Ahmad turned to him. He could see in his eyes what he was about to do.

Before Hafiz's fingers had wrapped around the handle, Ahmad punched the gas and shot out onto the northbound lane without even looking to see if anyone was coming. Hafiz shouted curses over the sound of the squalling tires.

The state trooper had pulled onto the pavement of the northbound lane, fishtailing as he began to accelerate in pursuit of Ahmad. In seconds, the Atlanta Police car had reached nearly seventy miles per hour, and Hafiz knew what was about to happen.

Without shouting to the Turk or the other two men underneath the cement truck, he began racing up the embankment along the highway as fast as his legs could carry him.

Ninety seconds later, Ahmad had reached a speed of 105 m.p.h., his blue lights flashing. The few cars on the highway in front of him had pulled into the right lane, so he didn't have to dodge any vehicles. He took his eyes off the road long enough to reach down and depress the detonator button.

For half a second, nothing happened. Then he felt his car shudder violently, its rear end lifting two feet off the ground as his back window shattered into thousands of pieces. Just as a searing heat hit the back of his neck, he heard the blast behind him, a sound like ten thousand thunderclaps all at once. He glanced into his rearview mirror to see an orange flame rolling toward him, engulfing the trooper's car barely half a mile behind him. Vehicles around it were tossed into the air, end over end like toys.

Ahmad slammed his hand against the steering wheel. "Damn, damn, damn!" he shouted. He could only imagine what would have happened if they had delivered their goods to the Olympic Stadium as they had planned.

13

The blast destroyed everyone and everything in the immediate area, including an overpass. All six northbound and southbound lanes were blown to rubble for a mile in both directions, leaving a crater forty feet deep and 200 feet across. The devastation spread out for miles, and it would take days to ascertain that some forty-five cars and trucks had vaporized, some of them on the highway and some crossing the overpass, a few more at a BP station on the exit. The secondary explosion of the gas pumps destroyed a Waffle House across the road, and the final body count would reveal that more than a hundred people had died along I-85.

Within minutes, every television network except for NBC stopped its regular programming to cover the aftermath of the blast. It was obvious that this bomb had not been intended for the isolated spot on the highway, but for the Opening Ceremonies at the Olympic Stadium. Panic spread, and soon tickets to the ceremonies, which scalpers a day before had sold for three or four thousand dollars apiece, were going for less than face value, if at all.

The President called up the National Guard, and the troops soon swelled the security force around the stadium to three times its original size. Cement barricades were brought in to block all streets, and armed guardsmen protected every checkpoint. From now on, no vehicle—not even a police car or one belonging to an IOC member—would get anywhere within a half-mile of any venue.

The athletes of the world cannot simply meet and begin competing; the festival of Olympic competition, once considered sacred and still treated with reverence, must include great pomp and circumstance. Los Angeles introduced itself to the world twelve years before with a long countdown on the stadium's giant screens, and a fanfare, followed by the stirring sight of a man with a jet-pack on his back rocketing high above the field below. Barcelona's opening had featured the powerful voice of Plácido Domingo, an Olympic ring dance by 600 performers, and a spectacle commemorating Hercules's voyage on the Mediterranean.

Following suit, Atlanta had planned a gorgeous spectacle, with hundreds of dancers and musical performances by Ray Charles and Whitney Houston. As in Los Angeles, giant screens had been placed along the tops of the stadium walls, and on these the countdown of minutes to the beginning of the ceremonies progressed. Up above, the Goodyear blimp looked down while searchlights from the ground skipped across the darkening sky. Yet the events of the early evening had put a palpable damper on tonight's celebration, and the crowd seemed nervous and subdued. When the clock on the screens ticked down to "0," the opening fanfare began with the release of thousands of balloons, and a cheer went up. But neither this nor the response to the stellar performances by Whitney and Ray and 400 local dancers would have broken any applause meters.

The lack of enthusiasm was due, in part, to the fact that not everyone had arrived yet, and those who had were fighting to get to their seats. The presence of thousands of extra troops in and around the stadium had caused congestion beyond anyone's worst dreams. Long, irate queues of spectators bottlenecked around the entry points, where each ticket holder had to pass through double magnetometers while purses and other belongings underwent inspection.

In fact 20,000 seats, including the two set aside for the President and First Lady, would remain empty for the rest of the night, and some of the brave souls who did come weren't seated until forty-five minutes into the ceremonies. It was a good thing that the planners had not attempted a display like the one in Los Angeles and Barcelona, when spectators had held up colored cards to make a ring of world flags around the stadium. That would have looked ridiculous with so many empty seats.

After the musical numbers, hundreds of marchers, each bearing a tall white flag, began to promenade in a tight platoon formation down the track. At the center of this group, by itself and held higher than the others, was the Antwerp flag with the five Olympic rings, so named because it had first been presented in that city at the 1920 Games. By now the crowd had begun to settle in, and they cheered more spiritedly as excitement built toward the central event of the night, the March of the Athletes.

One by one, all 197 teams would enter the stadium, each to be greeted by tumultuous rounds of applause from the spectators. If everything had gone as planned, there would have been forty-five heads of state and other national leaders in the VIP stands. They would have been cheered along with their nation's team, as had happened when Nelson Mandela appeared at the Barcelona Olympics. The VIP seats would also have been filled with 150 members of Congress, all 106 IOC members and their spouses, and other influential persons. But the VIP section was practically empty: only the IOC members had shown up, and even then it had been under orders from their president, Jason Blanchot. If *they* didn't come, how could they get anyone to believe them when they said the Games were still safe?

The athletes and officials of Greece, who by custom go first in the march, paraded out onto the track, followed by the tiny Afghanistan delegation, clad in billowy native pants and colored tunics. Many of the smaller teams appeared in native garb, like the three athletes, one chef de mission, and two trainers from the sultanate of Brunei, who looked magnificent in their brightly colored silks with broad shoulders, balloon pants, and decorative scimitars.

One by one, the announcer called the names of individual countries, and the newest nations got the loudest cheers. As the Bosnian delegation came forward, their handball coach, Hakija Drabeznic, waved and smiled to the crowd, which gave his embattled country some of its strongest applause. Namibia, former colony of white South Africa, got a special ovation, as did South Africa itself, along with Russia, the former Soviet republics, and the other independent states of the former Communist world. Even the Serbs, marching near the end under the Yugoslav name and flag (minus the Communist star) got applause in spite of American revulsion at their behavior in Bosnia.

American patriotism ran high despite, or perhaps because of, the premature terrorist attack just a few hours earlier. The stadium gave a standing ovation when the athletes of the host country, by far the largest delegation here, marched out last. This atmosphere of joy turned the appearance of the U.S. team into a happy, haphazard affair, with members stopping to pose for photographs and others breaking ranks to take pictures of their own teammates. It was a nightmare for security, but everyone else loved it.

By the time the U.S. team took its place with the others, each grouped by country under their individual flags at the center of the field, nearly ninety minutes had elapsed since the beginning of the march, and now the spectators were in high spirits in spite of every-thing. It took several minutes for them to settle down so that Hans Bliecher, as President of ACOG, could speak.

As lacking in diplomatic skills as he was, Bliecher understood that many in the stands that night wished Bobby Joe Watkins could have been in his place, and he filled his ghostwritten speech with glowing references to the people of Atlanta and the United States. This received polite applause, but unlike in the case of the enormously popular Peter Ueberroth twelve years before, no journalist would write that Bliecher deserved a gold medal.

Next came Jason Blanchot, inaugurating his first Olympic Games—and last, because of his upcoming retirement—and he too was generous with kind words. But people were hardly listening, because everyone had their eyes on the next item in their programs: *Welcoming Proclamation By the President of the United States*. But he was not here tonight, and though no one could blame him, it would no doubt hurt his standing in the polls. Instead, the Mayor of Atlanta said the magic words: "Celebrating the XXVIth Olympiad of the modern era, I declare open the Games of Atlanta."

The remainder of the Opening Ceremonies was a high-spirited event, with the singing of the Olympic Hymn and the presentation of a gigantic Olympic flag carried by great American stars of previous Games. At the raising of the flag came a slight sour note, when 2,000 white pigeons were released to boos and catcalls by animal rights sup-porters in the crowd. But the boos were drowned out by the cheering, and the pigeons—in spite of fears about their poor night vision—sailed out of the stadium to safety.

Finally, the most celebrated moment of the Opening Ceremonies had come. The lights went down. All over the stadium, spectators switched on the tiny flashlights they'd been furnished upon entering, a gift from a sponsor who manufactured batteries, and the pinpoints of light gleamed like diamonds. Then down the entry ramp came a small flicker, moving onto the track. The Olympic Torch had arrived.

It had begun its journey on Mt. Olympus and traveled more than 15,000 miles, crossing forty-two of the United States on a zigzagging path, sometimes in the midst of controversy and danger to the runners. But now it was about to reach its destination. As it came into view, the crowd assumed the closest thing to silence possible for such a large gathering, and the people in the seats nearest to the field heard (or imag-ined they could hear) the jarring footsteps of the flame's bearer as he bounced along the track. Those closest began to clap in rhythm, and the cheer caught on throughout the entire crowd.

There had been much speculation as to who would have the honor of completing the last leg of this epic torch relay to light the flame that would burn throughout the sixteen days and seventeen nights of the Centennial Olympic Games. The face of the runner remained indistinguishable in the dim lighting and even on the screen up above, but the crowd roared with approval as his name was announced.

The cheer rose as he rounded the track, and the decibels increased as he passed each section, climbed the stairs, crossed the steel bridge, and then ascended the final seventy-five feet to the edge of the Olympic cauldron. He looked back over at the audience and lifted the torch skyward to light the flame as the cheers rose to a deafening pitch.

The Olympic Flame sputtered, flickered, and then began to burn brightly. In the seconds that followed, its glow would spread across the world. In the six time zones of the United States, it would shine through TV sets in bars, restaurants, hotel and motel rooms—and most of all in the 93 million households with televisions.

Four thousand of these had sets wired to monitoring technology called "people meters," and at 3:00 on Saturday morning, the readings from these meters would feed into the home computer of the A.C. Nielsen Company. The overnight reports from these would reveal both good news and bad news for NBC. The good news was that for a ten-minute span of time around the torch lighting, the network had enjoyed a 51% rating. The bad news was that after the network went to a commercial, the figure dropped back to where it had been for most of the night: less than 10%. The Olympic Games were a big show, with lots of color and drama, but they couldn't compete with the great audience-grabbers of the '90s: the Gulf War, the O.J. Simpson Trial—or the explosion on I-85.

As soon as the story broke, every other network in the United States (and many throughout the rest of the world) had preempted their regular shows for live nonstop coverage. Media graphics departments hastily concocted logos using any relevant image except the Olympic Rings, available only to official sponsors, with typefaces reading *Tragedy In Atlanta*, *Attack On the Highway*, or *Olympic Disaster*. Anchors and reporters canceled their weekend plans, and news teams enthusiastically prepared to reap the unexpected windfall. But the anchors wore grim expressions as they announced, "For those of you who have just joined us. . ." to the millions of viewers who'd switched from the Opening Ceremonies.

In the months and years leading up to the Games, NBC had prepared ratings projections supposedly correct to the nearest one-tenth of one percent, then sold airtime to sponsors on a cost-per-thousand viewers basis, negotiated down to the penny. Now all this painstaking work had gone out the window, victim of unforeseen circumstances, but network executives could not merely go back to their advertisers and apologize. When they found out how few people had actually watched their commercials, the sponsors would demand "make-goods"—more airtime to compensate for the lost viewership—which translated into net losses for NBC. As remote controls around the country clicked on Friday night, those losses quickly rose into the millions of dollars.

The ironic thing was that the other networks had nothing new to report. It was all rehash, with clips of the explosion site played over and over, "experts" giving their impressions of what had happened, and repackaged summations by commentators.

Print journalists followed the lead of their television colleagues. As the Saturday morning editions began to hit the stands in the wee hours, every paper in the country featured screaming bold headlines about the bombing, with a photograph of the Olympic Flame lighting in the lower right-hand corner. The *Atlanta Constitution* filled its first six pages with reports on the incident, and the sports section had little commentary on the Games except for pre-written descriptions of the U.S. team, the events, and the schedule for the upcoming week.

The bomb might have missed the Olympic Stadium, but it had hit NBC dead-center, right in its pocket.

14

As though Atlanta didn't have enough traffic woes with the Olympics in town, a five-mile stretch of I-85 south of the airport was shut down because of the blast, and wouldn't be usable for months. Hundreds of FBI and ATF agents had descended on the epicenter of the explosion, searching the rubble as rescue teams collected bodies and body parts.

As the death toll rose, the agents looked feverishly for clues. Their best hope was to find a vehicle identification number that might lead them to the people responsible for the bombing, but the prospects for finding a VIN on any of the twisted and charred pieces of metal appeared slim.

The media were more confident of the bombers' identities. Two years earlier, they might have suspected Muslim fundamentalists, but that was before Oklahoma City. After initially blaming Islamic militants, many reporters had to back-pedal when that bombing turned out to be the work of home-grown fanatics, and no one wanted to go on record as a racist this time. So commentators peppered their reports with references to the fact that these events had occurred "in Newt Gingrich's backyard," the buckle of the Bible Belt, where there were plenty of right-wing fanatics itching to use the Olympics as a chance to make a statement.

Reporters in the Village managed to corner a haggard Steve Kirk, who gave them assurances from Jason Blanchot and Hans Bliecher that no further incident would happen during the Games. The Village itself was not a happy place over the weekend—certainly nothing like its planners had envisioned—and compared to the heightened security at entry points now, the original setup seemed casual. Every visitor had to undergo careful scrutiny of his accreditation card, then a comparison of his face with a computer-enhanced photograph on a screen, while dozens of Village Security officers and armed National Guards looked on.

The lines of people waiting in the hot sun became so long that a person had to truly be determined to enter the Village, and visitors who had misplaced or changed their badges found no sympathy. It didn't matter if they'd waited forty-five minutes or two hours; they weren't getting in.

Nerves became raw, particularly among the National Guard troops. Unlike Village Security, they hadn't been expecting to perform their jobs, and since there was no place to put them, they had to live in tents near the Atlanta Water Works. For the first twenty-four hours, they seemed a little starstruck by the opportunity to work "at the Olympics," but as the grinding reality of their long days in the July heat set in, many of them only wanted to go home. Therefore they weren't inclined to be as polite to an irate visitor, and Kirk had to field complaints from dozens of international guests.

To Tom Mason, the intensified security measures were reassuring, but he wondered how much the President's visit had caused them to let down their guard—and what would happen if they let down their guard again. His own Response Support Team's role did not substantially change because of the bombing, except that federal agents had become particularly interested in any information they could glean on delegations from politically sensitive nations. It was clear that contrary to media speculation on domestic terrorists, the federal investigators suspected foreigners, and they went through Mason's dossiers on the various Middle Eastern teams extensively.

Mason knew they wouldn't find anything, because he'd been so hampered by Olympic rules that his investigations could only be very superficial. There was the suspicious individual photographed by Aaron, for instance: the feds took copies of those pictures, but Mason didn't have much information on the man because he hadn't done anything illegal, and therefore nothing had been done to investigate him further.

Agents also questioned Adam from Mason's team, now working the 8:00 p.m. to 4:00 a.m. shift as "hospitality clerk" with the Bosnians. All that Adam could tell them was that the handball team members seemed to be taking advantage of their stay in America to buy up radios and TVs from various electronics stores. There was nothing threatening or illegal in that.

Mason and his people maintained a behind-the-scenes role, and hardly anyone outside of the federal agents and Village Security knew they were there. But his was not the most secretive organization in the Village. That distinction belonged to a group of twenty-eight men who lived in Burge Apartments on the other side of North Avenue from the main campus, a transitional facility that did not house any single team for an extended period.

Therefore no one spent enough time around the clean-cut, well-mannered young men at Burge to ask many questions. Because they walked about the Village in U.S. team uniforms with the credentials of American athletes, anyone would have assumed that they were exactly that. They certainly looked young and athletic.

But in reality, they were a highly trained SWAT team, the best in the world. Since the time they'd helped Mason put on his terrorist simulation exercise more than a year before, these Navy SEALs and their commander, Lt. Allan Boyd, had been very busy in other parts of the world. But where they had been was a secret, and if everything went well for the remainder of the Games, no one would know they'd been in Atlanta either.

Meanwhile, the Games began.

Saturday's schedule included competition in fourteen different sports, with medal events in several of them, but American viewers didn't care much about judo and shooting, and as for basketball or gymnastics, it would be several days before they got to see Dream Team II or Melody Johnson compete for the gold. Weightlifting began with the flyweight class, and boxing wouldn't really take off until Tuesday afternoon, when the most controversial pugilist since Mohammed Ali, South Africa's Christiann Vervoerden, entered the ring. So for the first few days of the Games, virtually all the attention focused on the Georgia Tech Aquatic Center and the swimming competitions.

Through Monday, swimmers would compete in preliminary rounds during the morning, and the top eight qualifiers would swim in the finals that evening. Eight others would swim in the consolation heats, a practice unique to this sport, which gave competitors out of the running for a medal at least a chance to perform. No more than two swimmers per country could enter any event, but if both swimmers qualified, they could go on to the finals and increase the odds of a medal for their nation.

Saturday featured the men's 100-meter breaststroke and 200-meter freestyle, and qualifying went much as anticipated, with two Americans in each event going on to the finals. That night they came away with one gold and one bronze—not their best performance ever, but still a respectable showing.

Yet a big surprise awaited viewers of the women's competitions—or at least, it surprised anyone who hadn't closely followed the world of women's swimming over the past four years. The women competed in the 100-meter freestyle and 400-meter individual medley or IM, and America's team swam like champions. But when the top eight qualifiers were posted for the two events, only one American had made it in either, along with a scattering of competitors from traditionally strong countries such as Germany, Australia, and Russia.

Only two countries managed to qualify both their swimmers in each event: China and North Korea. NBC's commentators knew plenty about the "Twenty Little, Little Flowers," China's third-generation team, and everyone had expected them to do well; but no one had ever heard of the North Koreans, who hadn't competed in pre-Olympic meets. By the end of the night, the two Oriental teams had virtually swept both races and broken several world records; only a German who won the 100-meter freestyle bronze by 0.02 seconds over a Chinese swimmer got to share the medal stand with them.

The former Olympians on the NBC staff had a hard time suppressing their disbelief at the North Koreans' emergence from nowhere. April Saunders, who swam in Barcelona, observed dryly, "These women have awfully broad shoulders, don't they? Looks like they've been hitting the weight benches pretty hard."

Late Saturday night, Steve Kirk finally made it back to his quarters and stretched out on the couch, too tired to undress and get into bed.

In the wake of the bombing, he'd been forced to add another duty to his already full plate, sitting in on the 5:30 a.m. security briefings since he knew more about the Village than anyone, even Greg Robbins. That gave him a little extra time to catch up on work between the briefings and the 8:00 a.m. chef's meetings, but it left him more exhausted than ever. There was only one mitigating factor to the security briefings: he got to see Michelle Hinton.

Tomorrow being Sunday, though, they wouldn't have the briefing until late in the morning, and there wouldn't be any chef's meeting at all. But he knew the phone would start ringing at 6:00 a.m., and wouldn't stop until late Sunday night, so Kirk had to follow the advice he always gave his people—"sleep fast."

Just as he'd drifted off, he heard a knock at his door. Grumbling, he got up and answered it.

"Not sleeping, are you?" asked Tom Mason, himself a little punch-drunk from the exhausting weekend that was only a little more than halfway over.

"Who, me?" said Kirk, rubbing his eyes. "No, I was just inspecting the back of my eyelids. Come on in."

"Look, I won't stay." Mason stepped into the entryway and shut the door behind him. "I just wanted to tip you off about the bomber."

"Yeah?"

"I have a hunch it might have been *him*—the guy in the pictures I showed you. Or at least, let's just say the feds are real interested in those photos, and I suspect—"

"He was gonna blow up the Village?"

Mason shook his head. "No reason to believe that, considering the timing. Everyone was gonna be at the stadium. The only good that's come out of this is the beefing up of security, but I just wish they'd been this serious about letting us check out the teams 'way back when."

"It's incredible," said Kirk. "Years of work putting these Games together, and some SOB could have ruined it all in a second. For five years now, I couldn't wait for this thing to start, and now I can't wait till it's over."

"And on that cheery thought, I'll leave you to your dreams." Mason opened the door and turned back to Kirk. "You look like you need a rest even worse than me, Steve."

"I'm so tired, I'll probably need you to remind me tomorrow what we even talked about. Goodnight, Tom."

He had just fallen asleep again when another knock came at the door. "Damn it!" he said aloud. He jumped up and, without even looking out through the peephole, threw the door open.

It was Michelle.

"Oh, I'm sorry," he said. "I thought you. . . is something wrong?"

He was still dressed, except for his tie and shoes, but she wore distinctly off-duty clothing: Reeboks, running shorts, and a tee shirt. She held her hands behind her back, which made her breasts stand out more, and he noticed that she didn't have on a bra.

"No," she said. "Everything's fine. I was just so keyed-up from everything that I needed to wind down. I thought maybe you were in the same state, and you'd help me with this." She brought out what she'd been hiding, a bottle of wine in a brown paper bag. "But of course, if you're sleeping, I could. . . ."

Trying to seem nonchalant, he took the bottle from her and pulled it out of its package. "Let me see this: '63 Lafite Rothschild—how'd you swing that?"

"One of the French coaches was in a generous mood," she said casually as she stepped in. She started to walk around, looking at his apartment. He had clothes slung everywhere, along with newspapers and memos and empty coffee cups.

"Sorry for the mess." He reached to pick up a shirt that hung over the back of a chair, but he let it go. No need to seem more nervous than he was.

"You must not bring a whole lot of young ladies back here," she teased.

"Oh, sure I do—in all that spare time I have between midnight and 6:00 a.m. You just missed one going out."

"Funny, she looked a lot like Tom to me."

"What did he say about you bothering the Village Management Director?" Kirk called over his shoulder from the suite's tiny kitchen, where he'd retrieved a corkscrew and two wine glasses. As he started to open the bottle, he saw that his hands were shaking. He drew a deep breath.

"I didn't tell him I was here," Michelle said.

They sat down on the couch, toasted the Frenchman who obviously had admired Michelle tremendously to part with such an expensive bottle, and fell to talking about work. Kirk's nervousness disappeared as they chatted, and in the middle of saying something he absentmindedly reached up and rubbed his neck.

"Let me," she said, setting down her glass. "God, you're tense." She stood up and put her hands on her hips. "Okay, you lie down and let me rub your back."

He readily complied, and as her slim yet muscular fingers began to massage his shoulders and lower back, he might have fallen asleep if he hadn't had the picture of her in his mind. Or maybe he was dreaming. Was she really here, and was this really happening? He opened his eyes. It was really happening, and he knew that he had to seize the moment.

He rolled over, pulling her on top of him. He knew she could feel how excited he was. He started to pull her down to him, but she put her index finger over his lips and stood up.

She walked toward the door. *Great!* he thought. *I've blown it now.*

She was just trying to be nice, and I— But she wasn't leaving; she was only turning off the foyer light so that the only illumination in the small living room came from a lamp in the bedroom down the hall.

She walked back over and knelt beside the couch. As their lips met, her dark hair fell over his face, and she reached to push it back, but he grabbed her wrist and pulled her closer. Everything about her—the way she smelled, the way she tasted, the way she felt—was even better than he'd imagined for the past months.

After several minutes, she stood up and kicked off her Reeboks, then started pulling off her shirt. A man would have grasped the neck and lifted it over his head, but she did it much more sensuously, crossing her arms and pulling it up from the bottom hem. Her breasts were superb: certainly not too small, and not a centimeter too large—firm but soft, and perfectly shaped to fit in his cupped hands. Then in a single motion, down came her shorts and panties, and she stepped out of them to reveal the finest body he'd ever seen.

Again, she knelt over him, and as they kissed, she undid his belt and unzipped his pants, caressing him and running her hands over his body. In his mind, Kirk had gone back to the possibility that maybe he was dreaming all this, but he didn't care if he was.

She pulled away from him, and he opened his eyes to see her spreading her knees to either side of his now naked thighs, then bending down over his prostrate body and guiding him into her. In the dim light, both of them could clearly see their bodies joining—then pulling apart as she leaned back, supporting herself with her hands on his knees as she rose—then, as she came back down, joining again. And again and again. . . .

The morning light woke Steve Kirk out of the most relaxing sleep he'd had in two months. He looked at his watch. It was 8:15. "Damn!" he said aloud as he sat up on the couch. Why hadn't the phone woken him up by now? Then he looked down and saw that the jack was pulled out from the wall.

What a fantastic dream! But it suddenly felt real. "Shit, am I cracking up?" he asked the empty room. He'd been working too hard, he knew: maybe these Olympics had finally snapped his mind. . . .

He plugged in the phone and trudged off toward his bedroom to get ready for another long day. But as he passed the tiny kitchen, something caught his eye: an empty bottle of '63 Lafite Rothschild.

He smiled—a deep, warm smile. This weekend had started out looking like the worst one of his life, and now he felt like the luckiest man alive.

NBC's programmers had expected strong ratings over the weekend. The Olympics in general draw in viewers who don't normally watch TV, let alone sports, and Americans love to see the competitions in which their teams do best. With the work week over, everyone would be home, gathered around their televisions, and it wouldn't be just men either: unlike boxing, for instance, swimming appealed to the female audience as much as males.

To counter this, the network's competition had lined up baseball games with title-contending teams or box-office hits that hadn't yet made it to video, but they had ended up preempting these for non-stop reports on the bombing. Even without this huge news story against it, NBC would have done poorly anyway, because Americans simply weren't winning the gold the way people had expected them to. On Sunday, the Chinese and North Korean dominance dipped a bit, but no U.S. swimmers of either sex made it to the medal stands. By the next morning, the network showed a Nielsen score about sixty percent below projections.

And as the Monday morning papers rolled out, the only Olympic news that made the front page of *The New York Times* appeared in the bottom right corner. It showed the lone American male gold-medal swimmer, who had won the 200-meter freestyle in a new Olympic record time, with the headline "Sun Sets on American Swimming Hopes—Is A New Sun Rising in the East?" Out of four weekend events, the U.S. men had produced only two bronze medals to go with the one gold, and their female counterparts were shut out completely. By contrast, China's women had won three gold, one silver, and one bronze; and the North Koreans had already earned a gold, two silver, and a bronze to take back to Pyongyang.

The top spot on the front page, of course, belonged to a headline about the bombing and the ongoing investigation south of Atlanta, where throngs of reporters had decamped for the next installment of the hit show now known as *Olympic Tragedy*. The remainder of the page indicated the relative importance of news stories from the weekend, with reports of starvation in Africa and the continued fighting in Bosnia taking precedence over the Olympics.

NBC's executives felt the noose tightening. Athletics, or track and field—always a top draw—would not begin until Friday, and the intervening days promised more lackluster U.S. performances against the Asian swimmers, as well as plenty of sports considered marginal by the American audience. Gymnastics or boxing might save the ratings, but in the meantime other networks had mined a whole new vein of ratings gold.

None of this had been lost on the sponsors of NBC's Olympic programming, and the network's top brass had already begun receiving angry phone calls over the weekend. Advertising fortunes would have to be committed to compensating for airtime that didn't come close to meeting viewership projections, and the network was fast running out of make-good slots.

Throughout Saturday and Sunday, as Jason Blanchot appeared in the stands at various competitions and greeted Italian cyclists and African weightlifters, the IOC President had dreaded the call he knew would come. And it did, at 5:45 on Monday morning.

"Blanchot!" a voice growled on the other end of the line. "Ira Greenberg here." The man didn't apologize for calling so early: as President of NBC, he wasn't used to making apologies of any kind, particularly to someone in whom he'd invested half a billion dollars.

"Ira, hello," said Blanchot, sitting up in the bed of his suite on the top floor of the Marriott Marquis. "How did you like our Opening Ceremonies Friday night?"

"I didn't call to talk about the floor show," said Greenberg irritably, "but since you asked, I think the whole event was a little sophomoric compared to Barcelona."

"Yes, I suppose you're right," said Blanchot good-naturedly. "It costs money to put on these kinds of. . . ." He stopped; he wasn't going to talk about money if he could help it.

Greenberg knew what he meant. "Yeah, and these are the Cheap Games, right?"

Blanchot checked his tongue. "The torch lighting was good, though."

"Yeah, it was alright, but I liked the thing in Barcelona better, with the guy shooting an arrow into the air to light the flame—that really came across well on TV." Greenberg paused. "But that's not why I called, Jason."

"Yes?"

"Look," said Greenberg, "I'm knee-deep in shit up here with sponsors demanding make-goods. They haven't said so, but I can tell they're starting to get gun-shy about Sydney now—you know, the one we paid you 705 million damn dollars for?" He caught a breath. "They're blaming me, of course, but you know who I blame for this? Not those assholes who set off that bomb, but you, Jason. It was your job to see that nothing like this happened."

"Look, Ira," said Blanchot irritably, "just how far do you think my jurisdiction extends? That bombing was thirty miles away from here. I can't be responsible for policing your entire country."

"Don't try that with me," said Greenberg. "If it's 'my' country, then it's also 'my' dollars—from U.S. TV—that make the Olympics possible. Your security people were supposed to stay on top of any threat."

"We have to balance the need for safety with the limits of our ability to investigate possible dangers, particularly in this litigious country of yours."

"Speaking of which, I expect you to make good on your promises to us."

"That's not in the contract."

"Maybe it is, maybe it isn't," said Greenberg. "I know you don't want me to sic my lawyers on you, and I can tell you that if you screw me, the other networks are gonna get the message loud and clear. We may fight between ourselves, but when we see one of our own getting the shaft from an outsider, we take the lesson to heart. Right now I'm figuring this bombing story is going to last at least until the Games are over, and if our market share doesn't get back up above projections, the cost will be $200 to $300 million."

"You know I can't do anything about that right now, Ira."

"No, but you can tighten down on your security so nothing more happens."

"I'm telling you, we've spent as much as we can. If we hire any more men, they'll be stepping on each other out there."

"That's not my problem—but let's just say it's in everyone's best interests for you to clean up your act."

With that Greenberg hung up, leaving Jason Blanchot still sitting up in bed and listening to a dial tone. He could tell it was not going to be a good week.

Monday morning's Olympic program began with various games of baseball, basketball, field hockey, softball, and water polo. Most of these would continue into the afternoon and evening, when they would be joined by soccer matches in Miami, Orlando, Birmingham, and Washington. NBC's cameras kept busy switching back and forth between venues and teams, along the way stopping to pick up the equestrian competition in Conyers, where America's notoriously seductive JoEllen Cunningham had just won the silver medal.

There she stood on the medal stand, shedding what looked like real tears as *The Star-Spangled Banner* played. "I'm just a small-town girl underneath it all," she gushed to a reporter afterward. Off-camera, three men who attached a special meaning to the phrase "underneath it all" each heaved a private sigh of relief that she had done well.

They were the male portion of the U.S. selection board, the sixty percent vote JoEllen had obtained through private exhibitions of her riding talent. Each of these encounters had been daring, involving maximum risk of exposure for the men, which only heightened their excitement: the one on the Lake Pontchartrain Causeway, another in a stable, the third on an elevator. None of the three knew about the "magic" she'd worked on the other two, and vanity wouldn't allow them to speculate. But all three had endured the skepticism of the two women on the board, each of whom had voted against JoEllen for the simple and unsporting reason that they didn't like her. Now the men felt vindicated, and even the women managed a smile of pride for "their" rider.

When the reporter asked JoEllen if she had her eye on the gold in Sydney, she sounded surprisingly off-handed. "Oh, sure," she said. "But I've got bigger plans than that."

Up next were the Chinese at the Wolf Creek Shooting Complex. Their nation's first gold medal ever had come from a free pistol shooter in Los Angeles who'd never competed until a year before, so the sport had a special place in their hearts. Today a Chinese athlete won the gold in the 10-meter air rifle, a victory marred only by claims from opponents that he'd taken beta blockers to steady his hands. About the same time, his compatriots in the women's rowing team took to the waters of Lake Lanier, where they placed well in the heats for coxed eights and quadruple sculls. Events there mirrored the world of swimming: again, the Chinese looked like the odds-on favorites, followed by the North Koreans—and again, both sets of women appeared remarkably husky.

In the afternoon, a North Korean weightlifter won the featherweight gold, and a female compatriot took the silver in the middleweight judo competition. Somalia's Ali Halaaf fought the first of two preliminary super-heavyweight boxing matches at Alexander Memorial Coliseum, his victory over a Colombian contender making the front page of the sports section only because this meant that tomorrow he would face the formidable Christiann Vervoerden.

That night there would be more team competitions in sports such as baseball and basketball, each of which had lengthy elimination periods. But the most important venue on Monday evening would be at the Georgia Tech Aquatic Center, and not because of water polo preliminaries either. Tonight the American swimmers had a chance to pull themselves out of the hole they'd dug over the weekend, and they did so in the men's competition, winning a gold in the 200-meter butterfly and a bronze in the 100 freestyle—just one bronze short of their tally for the previous two days.

In the women's competition, sportscasters predicted that the Chinese and perhaps the shadowy North Korean team would rack up the medals in the 100-meter backstroke and the 4x100 freestyle relay, but not make it to the medal stand on the 400 free. The commentators gave no reason for this, which amounted to a veiled charge of doping, because steroids and other drugs tended not to yield great benefits over longer distances.

In fact the American women did take their first medal in the 400 free, a silver, for which they shared the stand with the Germans and the Australians. American women also took the bronze in the 4x100—after the "Twenty Little, Little Flowers" (or at least, one-fifth of them) and a foursome from Pyongyang.

These were small victories—but welcome, and long overdue—for the U.S. swimmers. Unfortunately, not many Americans were watching.

If visitors had come late to the Olympic Games, they wouldn't have found a vacant hotel or motel room anywhere inside the I-285 perimeter around Atlanta, yet they might have hoped for lodgings far outside the city on I-85 south. But not anymore. Every single motel in the towns around the site of the bombing—Fairburn, Palmetto, Peachtree City, Tyrone, and Newnan—had *NO VACANCY* signs hung out, and restaurant staffs worked double shifts to keep up with the increased business from the thousands of reporters who'd come on the heels of the federal investigators.

The press interviewed plenty of locals, those who had lost loved ones in the blast and others who gave their recollections of hearing or seeing it. Correspondents asked people what they thought had caused the incident, and many blamed the Olympics, which seemed to confirm the media's theory that militant white supremacy was rampant in rural Georgia.

The authorities, meanwhile, had a lead they weren't sharing with reporters. About ten minutes after the blast that Friday evening, a man had been getting into his car after eating at a truck stop a few exits north of the site when an Atlanta policeman commandeered his vehicle, a gold Pontiac Grand Am. The man wasn't very happy to give up his car, but he assumed the policeman needed it because of the emergency, and he didn't argue.

He did take down the officer's badge number, and when he called the APD to ask what had happened to his car, he was told that the Atlanta Police did not have that badge number in its system. In other circumstances, the man might never have gotten his car back, but federal investigators wanted to talk to him, and they listened with interest to his description of the policeman: dark-skinned, perhaps an Arab (though he spoke flawless English), of medium build, with a mustache.

By Monday night, the authorities had located the vehicle in the parking lot of a Wal-Mart in Birmingham, Alabama—where another man had reported his own car missing, a '92 Ford Taurus. They tracked this one to the Mexican border near Laredo, Texas, and though they didn't find the thief, they did compile a sketch taken from descriptions by several people who'd seen him—all of which confirmed the information they'd received from the first car-theft victim at the truck stop. The sketch also matched the photos of the mysterious visitor to the Village and the stadium that Tom Mason had given the investigators, as well as the description given by a real-estate agent in Newnan who said he'd rented a farmhouse for six months, prepaid cash, to a Middle Eastern gentleman.

It would take the media another day to hear about this, and by Monday night, the film clips from the scene of the bombing, the speculations as to conservative leaders' roles in the plot, and the interviews with eyewitnesses had begun to run a little dry. Until they learned more, the networks would have to simply repackage what they already had.

15

It was clear that Americans loved three things: scandal, celebrity, and a hint of the macabre, which when combined with a fourth great love, of sports, made for marvelous television ratings. The formula had worked with Tonya and Nancy at the Lillehammer Games, and better still with O.J.; now a new legend was about to be born, and NBC would have a chance to win back many of the viewers it had lost to the weekend's melodrama.

Christiann Vervoerden had already inspired plenty of interest long before his preliminary bout with Ali Halaaf at Alexander Memorial Coliseum on Tuesday afternoon. Though many other boxing matches had plenty of empty seats, this one was a sell-out.

Vervoerden entered the ring with his trademark scream, a sound like a demon leaping out of hell. As this ghastly noise rattled off the rafters of the coliseum, Ali Halaaf stepped reluctantly into center ring for the customary touching of gloves before the actual fight. The Somali, with 287 muscular pounds stretched over a 6'6" frame, was no small man himself; but Vervoerden's presence—not to mention his extra five inches of height—made him look small. Halaaf made a point of avoiding the South African's legendary gaze, keeping his eyes on the other man's gloves as though wondering if their ten ounces of padding could soften the lethal force of his fists.

The boxers returned to their corners to wait for the opening bell, and Vervoerden glowered across the ring in magnificent silence while Halaaf exchanged a few hurried words with his trainer, who looked almost as concerned as he did.

The bell clanged. Vervoerden didn't walk into center ring as boxers usually do, to get a feeling for their opponent's strengths and weaknesses. Instead, he leapt at Halaaf, meeting him ten feet from the other man's corner with a flurry of blows and a yell that frightened even the spectators. Halaaf went instantly into a defensive posture, his hands protecting his face while the Afrikaner beat on them without mercy.

After just twenty seconds, Vervoerden knocked Halaaf to the canvas. The referee ordered the white giant to his corner while he counted down the fallen Somali, who lay prone until the count of five, then rose falteringly to his knees and looked up at his opponent's enormous back, still turned toward him. The sight of it seemed to make his decision for him; instead of rising, he stayed on his knees until the referee counted him out and raised Vervoerden's arm to signify that he had won.

Seldom in the history of the Games had anyone seen such a devastating attack in the ring, and the crowd went wild, screaming "CHRIS-TIANN! CHRIS-TIANN!" The noise filled the great hall, and NBC's Mike Ameche at ringside struggled to talk over the roar. "Well, I must admit that we're all a little taken aback," he shouted. "We knew he was big, we knew he was fierce—but this fast and this mobile? I for one am shocked and impressed."

Within hours, the *Atlanta Journal* would hit the stands with a front-page picture of Vervoerden standing over his fallen opponent, two clinched fists in the air, under the headline "Future Heavyweight Champion of the World?" The sports section featured reports of another fight that had begun as soon as the Vervoerden-Halaaf match ended—between promoters vying to sign Christiann for as much as $100,000. The Centennial Olympic Games had their first new star, yet Christiann remained reclusive, and his refusal to grant an interview after the Halaaf match only added to his image as a wild man who would rather fight than talk.

Actually, his trainer had forbidden the interviews, and denied the boxer something else that he liked almost as much as fighting; otherwise he would have stayed busy all night with women eager to subdue the world's most powerful man. Vervoerden needed his strength, because his other preliminary bout on Wednesday night would not be so easy.

On Tuesday morning, South Korea had defeated Uruguay in Game 9 of the baseball eliminations at Atlanta-Fulton County Stadium, and beach volleyball got started at the Atlanta Beach in Clayton County. Table tennis began too, and a nervous Lee Chin of North Korea (who would compete in the women's singles the next day) watched the doubles preliminaries on the TV of her Olympic Village quarters.

Most of the morning's programming went to gymnastics, for which Melody Johnson and the other U.S. women appeared at the Georgia

Dome. But by the afternoon the Russian gymnasts, especially Olga Shcharansky, would show that they could still give the girls from America a run for their money.

Because the Vervoerden-Halaaf fight lasted such a short time, NBC was able to cut away to a few of the Games' more underexposed sports. At Morris Brown College, Egypt trounced Sri Lanka in field hockey eliminations, and the Spanish judoist who won the half-middleweight gold showed that talent in that sport was not confined to East Asians. The Spaniards, never an Olympic power until Barcelona, also won the fencing gold medal in men's team epée; and later in the afternoon the scene switched to Wassaw Sound in Savannah and the yachting competition.

That night the U.S. male swimmers earned a gold and a bronze in three competitions, considerably better than the women, who were almost entirely shut out except for Elizabeth Taggart, who won a bronze in the 200-meter backstroke. The medal stand for the 100 breast—occupied by a Chinese, a North Korean, and a Japanese—looked like a scene from the Asian Games instead of the Olympics.

On Wednesday morning, NBC brought its cameras to the Georgia State University Gymnasium for the opening of badminton, and team handball began at the Georgia World Congress Center with a match between Romania and Côte d'Ivoire. Afterward, the network commentator interviewed a few coaches who had watched the game from the Village. "Do you feel intimidated at the prospect of facing a strong team on Saturday," he asked the Bosnian Hakija Drabeznic, "given the fact that you've had to deal with last-minute changes of team members due to the tragic bus crash?" Drabeznic smiled philosophically and answered, "Yes, of course, but I think a lot of people will be surprised when they find out what we can do."

In the afternoon, the cameras switched to Alexander Memorial Coliseum, but Mike Ameche had little to say about the bantamweight fight between a Filipino and a Costa Rican going on in the background. Everyone had their minds on that evening's match. "It's unusual to have so much attention focused on a preliminary bout," he said, "but then seldom do we get to see two such exceptional fighters pair off this early in the Games." As he spoke, the two men's pictures flashed on the screen: Christiann Vervoerden of South Africa, a blond Aryan, and Philemón Stevenson of Cuba, a black Hispanic.

The Cuban was the nephew of none other than Teófilo Stevenson, who had fought as a heavyweight and won the gold in three Olympiads.

Instead of going on to a promising career as a professional, the elder Stevenson had returned to Cuba, where he had such godlike status that people referred to him by his first name alone—an honor reserved for only two other men, Fidel and Che. "Like his uncle," Ameche said, "Philemón has suffered only one loss in his career, but unlike his father's brother, the younger Stevenson has aspirations of competing as a professional. Perhaps tonight's bout with Christiann Vervoerden will determine whether that will happen."

The match would begin at about the same moment the female swimmers lined up on the blocks at the Georgia Tech Aquatic Center to begin the 4x100 medley relay finals. NBC's programmers had no trouble deciding which competition to broadcast.

"Because tickets to Olympic boxing finals usually sell out quickly," Mike Ameche was saying from ringside, "fans often purchase package deals. These include plenty of preliminaries like the Pakistan-Indonesia bout going on right now, events ticketholders usually don't even bother to attend. But tonight"—the camera panned to show a capacity crowd in Alexander Memorial Coliseum, shouting and whooping as two unknowns battled it out on the canvas—"you can see that's not the case."

"You know, Mike," said his color man, Alf Stallings, "it's only the luck of the draw that places Vervoerden and Stevenson in the ring together so early in the trials." Because of the difficulty in assigning accurate rankings to unknowns from around the world, he explained, Olympic boxing matches aren't seeded. Therefore, they sometimes have a random quality. "Under other conditions, these two wouldn't have been expected to meet until much later, when the tension might be even higher."

"Of course it's pretty high as it is," laughed Ameche as the middleweight bout in the ring ended on a decision, to roars of approval from the seething crowd. "Just three more fights to go until the big match-up, and I don't know if you can feel it where you're sitting, but these boxers in the preliminary bouts are both the beneficiaries and the victims of a very excited audience. It's a little like being the opening band for the Rolling Stones—you get bigger exposure than you'd ever dreamed of, but the fans are just biding their time until the big stars come on stage."

Half an hour later, the referee introduced Philemón Stevenson, and the last syllable of the Cuban fighter's name died in a torrent of applause. It took nearly a minute to get the crowd quiet enough so that the ref could call out, "And in this corner, wearing the red trunks and weighing 296 pounds, for the Republic of South Africa: Chris-TIANN Ver-voer-DEN!"

This time the sound of thousands of voices rocking the coliseum buried the words entirely. When the pandemonium finally faded, Mike Ameche was saying, "We see the referee shouting something in Vervoerden's ear, and it doesn't look like Christiann is very pleased by what he's hearing."

"Mike, I'd imagine it's a warning against unsportsmanlike conduct," Stallings said. "The refs don't take kindly to antics like the trademark Vervoerden shout."

Warning or not, Vervoerden let loose with his hellish scream as soon as the bell sounded, and he charged at Stevenson just as he had Halaaf. But the earlier opponent didn't have Stevenson's experience and speed, and the Cuban easily side-stepped Vervoerden's initial thrust before landing several powerful blows into the midsection of the startled giant.

"Look at Vervoerden's face!" Ameche yelled. "I don't think any of those jabs did much damage, but there's an unmistakable expression of shock."

"These may well be some of the only direct hits Christiann Vervoerden has ever suffered," Stallings pointed out.

"—And tonight may have more surprises in store for him," added Ameche.

After a momentary retreat, the South African charged at Stevenson again, trying to force a left jab between the other man's upraised fists. But Stevenson parried the thrusts before going back on the offensive— moving in, jabbing, punching, then moving back out, only to begin another assault. "Again, it'll take more than that to do any serious damage to a man like Christiann Vervoerden," said Ameche, "but Stevenson is racking up points with the judges."

By the end of the first round, Stevenson had scored fifteen hits for a total of five points, and Vervoerden hadn't landed one significant punch. "Given the fact that this is only a three-round match," Ameche noted as the two men took to their corners, "all Stevenson has to do is win the second and avoid a knock-out in the third."

The roar from the crowd rose to deafening levels. It seemed like they couldn't stand to wait through the sixty seconds between rounds. "Of course, two rounds is a long time," Stallings managed to shout back at his partner.

"It certainly is, Alf, and we may be about to learn what Christiann Vervoerden is made of. There are many who say he's benefited from a stacked deck in the past, and may simply be too big to face a truly fast opponent."

"We see the two fighters taking encouragement in their respective corners," Stallings said as the cameras went in for close-ups. "No doubt Stevenson's lead trainer is telling him to keep his focus on scoring points while avoiding a direct hit from Vervoerden."

"Like I said, Alf, all he has to do is dance through two more rounds, and if there's anything Philemón Stevenson can do, it's dance."

"Mike, you mentioned that we'd find out what Vervoerden is made of—well, look at his corner. The only calm face there is his. He's saying something to his lead trainer, Pieter van Kleek. . . . I can't lip-read, and I don't know Afrikaans, but I'd be willing to bet he's telling him that he was just testing the waters in round one."

"Whatever it is, van Kleek doesn't look convinced," Ameche countered. "Here's the bell."

The boxers again jumped to their feet as the trainers removed the stools from their corners, and what followed left the audience—and Mike Ameche—speechless.

The South African seemed to come out completely transformed, like a witch doctor who shape-shifts to overcome danger. He jumped about, bobbing to the left and moving to the right. He jabbed with his left, and began a flurry of punches as fast and furious as those Stevenson had delivered in round one. *Boom-boom-boom*—three hits to the arms and shoulders of the smaller man. Stevenson tried to move back to the left, but Christiann moved faster, and the punches continued more quickly than the Cuban could fend them off.

"This is beginning to turn into a rout!" shouted Alf Stallings. "Stevenson's holding his hands up in a protective posture like Floyd Patterson once tried to do against Mohammed Ali, the peek-a-boo pattern, and Vervoerden is pounding away. Just look—he's knocking Stevenson's own fists back into his face!"

"Things are not looking good for Stevenson," Ameche had to admit. "At this point, all of his energy is going into fending off the blows. Look at that! A quick upper-body cut into Stevenson's chest, followed by another right into the side of the head."

"Watch how Stevenson moves to the left," Stallings said excitedly. "He's clearly running from Vervoerden."

"And Vervoerden's not letting up—he's matching Stevenson step for step." Ameche was beginning to get excited too. "Now he's got him on the ropes! Three, four, five, six punches to the stomach and the face, and now he's stepping back. . . ."

Vervoerden did step back—to let Philemón Stevenson, the up-and-coming boxer who had entered the ring with high hopes, tilt forward and fall face-down on the mat.

The referee rushed in, pushing the South African back into his corner and dropping to his knees beside the fallen Cuban. But there was no need to bother with the count: Stevenson was out cold. The Cuban trainers at their side, three medics jumped onto the mat and rolled the boxer over, attempting to revive him while the ref walked over to Christiann and lifted his right hand to signal the victory. The Afrikaner giant raised his other hand into the air and roared with triumph.

The second round had lasted twenty-three seconds.

The fans were on their feet, cheering and screaming with the enthusiasm of people who have gotten their money's worth. What they had witnessed was brutal, deadly, frightening—and they'd loved every minute of it.

"Vervoerden might well agree with Mark Twain's famous comment that reports of his death were highly exaggerated," mused Alf Stallings, now alone in front of the camera while Ameche tried to chase down the boxer for an interview. "It's clear in hindsight that he spent the first round just toying with his opponent, setting up Stevenson—and many others—to think that he couldn't get the job done. Well, he's gotten it done like no fighter I've ever seen, and he's proven he has every bit as much velocity as he does mass."

Stevenson still lay unconscious, and would for two more minutes. Even Christiann's own lead trainer, stunned by what he'd just witnessed, remained in the ring, but Vervoerden himself stepped out through the ropes and waded into the cheering crowd. He did not shout his own praises; in fact he said nothing at all as he walked toward the tunnel that led to the dressing rooms, his face blank like an animal satisfied with the blood of its prey.

Suddenly Mike Ameche jabbed his microphone into Vervoerden's face and asked, "Christiann, what was going through your mind as you delivered those final blows?"

Vervoerden looked down with contempt at the reporter, a midget at his side. Then in a deep and heavily accented voice he said, *"I vaz t'ink-ing how I vould kill dat black bastahd."*

Ameche, who had heard plenty of bizarre statements from boxers just out of the ring, looked stunned. "I'm sorry," he said, "I didn't hear you right—what did you say?"

"Perhaps my English is not so clear," Vervoerden replied. "I should say, 'I wanted to kill that nigger'."

Ameche's face went ashen. "You just mean that figuratively?"

Vervoerden began walking again. "I don't know what this means, 'figuratively'," he answered as Ameche struggled to stay at his side with the microphone. "All I know is that niggers such as this one have stolen my country from its rightful owners. You ask what I think about? I think about smashing that black head the way one would kick a head of cabbage."

His words went out live, and via satellite they would reach the rest of the world as soon as the two-second delay passed. A production assistant in the NBC mobile unit tried to shut off the feed before it was too late, but his producer held up a hand to stop him. This was pure controversy, and controversy could only be good for ratings.

By now Christiann's trainer had finally come to his senses, leapt out of the ring, and rushed forward to the boxer's side. "That will be all!" he shouted to the reporters, grabbing Vervoerden and tugging him toward the dressing room.

Mike Ameche watched Pieter van Kleek and his young charge disappear into the crowd, then turned toward the camera and struggled to come up with words. On his earpiece, he could hear the producer warning him that they'd already had seven seconds of dead air, an eternity on network TV, so he began simply recapping the fight.

"As for Christiann Vervoerden," he concluded hesitantly, "he seems to be a little. . . stunned after his bout with Philemón Stevenson. Boxers often come out of the ring saying things they don't even remember an hour later. . . ."

Vervoerden's words would be replayed on every news show in the United States by the next morning. The Thursday morning editions had already gone out in Europe, but American journalists shelved their Thursday columns and began writing furiously. By Friday morning, Vervoerden would dominate the editorial pages of the world.

Of course the shock waves spread fastest in Atlanta, where various black ministers appeared on the 11:00 p.m. news (and again on ABC's *Nightline*) to denounce Vervoerden and call for his expulsion from the Games. That night the neighborhoods of West End and Vine City erupted, and the mayor nearly declared a state of emergency before the police hauled in scores of rioters as the city fell into a troubled sleep.

The unrest bled over into the Village, even though the heightened security measures in the wake of the bombing had made it a quiet place. On Wednesday night, the South African team held a meeting and voted to send Vervoerden back to Pretoria, even though he would probably win a gold medal for their team if he stayed. Christiann's trainer went to Steve Kirk and asked him to find lodgings for Vervoerden, and Kirk went back to his old friend Elroy Hubrick, now Director of Sports for the USOC. As an African-American, Hubrick took offense at the racist comments, but he was a sportsman first, so he agreed that the South African could take an empty apartment in the U.S. quarters.

On Thursday morning, there was a showdown in Jason Blanchot's suite at the Marriott Marquis between Blanchot and Vervoerden's representative, a prominent sports lawyer named John Shapiro who'd volunteered his services. Blanchot's attorneys had counseled him that he'd be taking a risk if he tried to expel Vervoerden without the boxer's consent—particularly when he had the advantage of fighting his legal battle in the world's most litigious country. Several indignant African chefs de mission pointed out the example of Tommie Smith and John Carlos, who the USOC had expelled from the Mexico City Olympic Village in 1968 for their Black Power salute. That didn't matter to Blanchot, because the IOC itself had no precedent for taking action against an athlete for politically offensive behavior.

But there was a precedent for Vervoerden to continue competing even if his own country didn't want him. Just as athletes from the rapidly disintegrating Yugoslavia had done in 1992, he would box in the quarterfinals on Friday as an "Independent Olympic Participant." If he won, he would go on to the Sunday semifinals.

16

The Wednesday overnights showed NBC with a 16% rating during the Vervoerden fight, the highest since the Opening Ceremonies. But the numbers dipped during the hour following the fight, as the program moved to the Georgia Tech Aquatic Center just in time for U.S. viewers to see four extremely muscular lasses from north of the thirty-eighth parallel accepting the gold in the 4x100 medley relay. To the right, on the silver platform, stood the Chinese women, whose sinewy arms rippled as they waved to the crowd and smiled; and to the left, shivering in their swimsuits and looking very small, were the Americans. After the cameras moved to the Ukraine-Brazil volleyball game at the Omni, the ratings took a nosedive as viewers again switched to other networks for more news on the bombing.

By now everyone knew about the farmhouse outside Newnan, where the bombers had apparently constructed their machines of death in a barn that still had traces of ammonium nitrate. The media set up tents nearby, and in a few days, the little dirt road had experienced more traffic than it had in the preceding ten years. But the feds could not locate the bombers, except for a few body parts which seemed to indicate that anywhere from two to four perpetrators had died in the blast. They had alerted Mexican authorities to be on the lookout for one escapee, now identified as Ahmad Mahfouz, but he seemed to have vanished.

Friday the twenty-sixth marked the opening of the most prominent Olympic sport of all, track and field. America's attention focused on its two great hopes, Joe Bob Sweeney and Curly Rogers, who would compete Saturday in the first of two days of decathlon events. But something particularly ironic happened during an interview with the two American contenders on Friday afternoon, twenty-four hours before they entered the most important competition of their lives.

"I'm here at the chief police station in Munich," said a reporter on

CNN, standing in front of an official-looking building in the Bavarian city, where it was 9:00 at night. "Authorities inside are questioning a young man arrested last night in connection with the May hit-and-run accident that removed Sándor Lukács, the Hungarian decathlete, from this year's competition." The reporter could not say much about the youth, except that he belonged to a skinhead faction called the Beerhall Brownshirts, and had admitted that he'd received 10,000 deutsche marks, about $6,000, to injure an unknown victim whose identity he'd only learned from TV reports of the attack. After receiving 1,000 marks from a mysterious stranger to do some "ethnic cleansing"—harassing Jewish students at a local university—he was given another 1,000 marks and told to wait for a phone call explaining how he could earn more.

"By then he had received the equivalent of $1,200, a lot of money for an unemployed electrician's assistant, so when the man called him three weeks later, he was more than willing to do as instructed. Apparently he was given a train ticket to Budapest, another 3,000 marks, and a key to a locker at the Munich train station. Inside the locker he found another 5,000 marks, along with a photograph of Lukács, identified to him as a Jew attempting to relocate more Jews from Poland and Hungary into Germany. He also received instructions as to the time, place, and means by which he would injure the man in the photograph. Upon successful completion, he received another 10,000 marks by post, for a total of 20,000, and has never heard from the man again.

"As for the identity of the person who ordered this attack," the reporter concluded, "police have only a sketchy description, and they refuse to speculate on the cause for this vicious crime."

But the Saturday morning papers would not refuse to speculate. "This grievous action recalls the attack committed on Nancy Kerrigan more than two years ago," one U.S. paper editorialized. "In both cases, someone stood to gain by removing a particular athlete from the field of play." They could not say who that someone was, but in countries such as Japan where people were less afraid of lawsuits, journalists spelled it out in plain words: Hypershoe, the South Korean company that had invested $2 million in the success of Joe Bob Sweeney and Curly Rogers, certainly had the most to gain by eliminating their primary competition.

Gregory Bramble of NBC covered the last five swimming competitions on Friday night with former Olympian April Saunders. Together they watched the U.S. men earn only a silver medal in the 4x100 medley relay, while the women were once again shut out by a Chinese-North Korean sweep, and April had plenty to say when it was over.

"As some of you know," she explained, "each Olympic venue has a doping control station. As soon as an athlete finishes an event, he or she goes in for testing with an escort to make sure that the results are valid. They let the athlete drink liquids, but only the ones they provide, and once the athlete produces a sample, the staff divides it into A and B vials. The A sample is tested immediately, whereas the B sample is sealed and refrigerated. If the A sample tests negative, that's the end of it; but if it comes up positive for steroids or other drugs, the lab notifies the IOC Medical Commission Chairman, and the athlete and their coach can be present at the testing of the B sample."

"How long does all this take?" asked Gregory.

"Not long—if the results are negative." She picked up a piece of paper and looked at it. "Generally twenty-four to thirty-six hours; but if they're positive, well, that's a different matter. So I say all that just to bring up the results from tests done on the Chinese medalists from last Saturday, *which have just come in.*"

Bramble raised an eyebrow.

Reading from the page, she said, "It seems that Li Xiaoyang—I hope I'm pronouncing that correctly—the Chinese swimmer who won the 100-meter freestyle, had traces of ephedrine in her urine."

"Now, that's not a steroid," Bramble explained to the audience, "but it has been used as a masking agent for athletes taking Dianabol or other drugs."

"That's right," said April, "and her coach announced in a statement today that the vitamins she was taking contained ephedrine. Of course there's no law against vitamins in the Olympics, but since"—she looked at the sheet—"four other Chinese swimmers have been found either with ephedrine, probenecid, or esters of testosterone, all of which are also masking agents, it begins to look a little suspicious. Not only that, but many Chinese swimmers are suspected of using dehydrotestosterone or DHT, which comes in the form of a cream rubbed on the skin; but because it's extremely hard to detect, test results can't be conclusive."

"Certainly no one suspects the U.S. women of doping," Bramble put in with a laugh. "Otherwise their results might have been better in competition. But April, have any other positive tests come back—say, for the North Koreans?"

She shook her head. "No North Korean swimmers have shown up with either steroids or masking agents, but look at Hyun Chung-sun, who shattered the Olympic 50-meter freestyle record tonight with a time of 24.46 seconds." As she spoke, an instant replay of the competition ran across the screen, followed by scenes of Hyun at the awards ceremony. "Now, she's certainly larger than most Asian women, but she doesn't look at all like the typical steroid user."

"No mustache," Bramble quipped as the picture returned to the two of them.

"Well, of course swimmers always shave off any excess body hair to cut down on water resistance," April pointed out. "Still, she definitely doesn't look like a man—or, for that matter, sound like one. But let's just run that one clip over for a second and look at something. Okay, you see here how big her hands and feet look in proportion to her body? She's only 5'2", but she wears size 11 shoes, usually made for women a foot taller. Also, notice the prominent bone structure on her face."

"So what does all this tell us?" asked Gregory.

April shrugged. "I couldn't say." It wasn't that she didn't know the answer to the question, but to offer her opinion would expose her and NBC to charges of slander.

The print media also avoided any direct accusation of doping on the part of the North Korean swimmers, but they did make inferences and ask leading questions. One newspaper featured an article on the newest, most effective (and least detectable) form of doping available, called human growth hormone or hGH. Secreted by the pituitary gland, hGH stimulates growth and promotes lean body mass, particularly at puberty. Since the time it was isolated a few decades before, doctors had been prescribing it for undersized children and overweight adults. Athletes saw something else in it: neither hGH nor steroids nor any other drug can actually make someone run or swim faster, but they can help him or her build the muscles necessary to do so, and unlike steroids, hGH could not yet be detected through drug testing because it is naturally produced by the body.

But this "miracle growth drug" had its costs. A supply of hGH went for about $150 a week, making it extremely expensive for an individual athlete, though not for a country—even a poor one, assuming it put a premium on winning Olympic medals. More importantly, it took a costly toll on athletes themselves in the form of acromegaly, the tendency of some body parts (especially the hands and feet) to grow more rapidly than others. The ears and eyes do not grow at all, which leads to a further distortion of features; to illustrate this, the paper ran a close-up shot of a Korean swimmer who looked like the proverbial sideshow freak.

At weightlifting and rowing events on Friday, commentators approached the subject of Chinese and Korean doping with delicacy. If they could have made outright accusations, maybe it would have increased ratings; but as it was, NBC announcers' technical questions concerning athletes whose names most Americans couldn't even pronounce made for much less accessible entertainment than the bombing melodrama.

The end of Friday marked a good point to assess the Games to date. Swimming had ended, athletics (track and field) had begun, and a week's worth of competition had yielded medals in almost 100 of the Centennial Olympics' 264 events. As in Barcelona, more than fifty percent of the medals went to the top five countries, but otherwise the old Olympic order had altered greatly.

Fifth place belonged to a complete newcomer, North Korea, which had earned only twenty-one medals in all other Olympiads put together. In just seven days its swimmers, rowers, weightlifters, and other athletes had accumulated seventeen medals, representing one of the most dramatic improvements of any country in Olympic history.

The other four countries on the list had at least been there before, but they'd changed rankings. Ever since the U.S. and Soviet teams began vying for the top two slots in 1952, Germans could usually be found at number three, and in 1988, East Germany did something no other country had managed to do, taking second place from the U.S. But a few things had changed for the German people since then, and now the unified Federal Republic of Germany placed fourth.

The Germans had an excuse for their slump, given the difficulty of organizing an entirely new national team. And the Russians could feel good about second place, since they'd lost the fourteen nations that had helped the U.S.S.R. and Unified Team win in the past. But the U.S. had no such consolation in third place. Formerly it had rounded out its medal totals in less well-known sports such as synchronized swimming, rowing, and cycling, but now most of these medals went to other nations. This hurt America, though not as much as the drubbing it took in the swimming pools and gymnasiums.

The top slot went to the biggest surprise of all, the country that had promised big things in Barcelona and now exceeded all predictions: the Peoples' Republic of China, whose athletes received seventeen gold, fourteen silver, and eleven bronze medals during the first week. In women's swimming alone, they had taken fully a third of the medals, and together with the North Koreans, they left all competitors far behind.

On Saturday afternoon, the Bosnian handball team suffered a resounding 28-0 defeat by the Portuguese, themselves not known as a great power in the sport. The NBC commentator on the scene shoved a mike into the face of Bosnian coach Hakija Drabeznic and asked for his thoughts after suffering one of the worst routs of the entire Olympic Games. "We have never been the same after the lamentable bus accident in May, which took our best players from us," said a forlorn-looking Drabeznic. "We will go back to Sarajevo on August 4 without a medal, but"—he brightened and smiled at the U.S. reporter—"it is not over for us."

"Bosnian handball coach Hakija Drabeznic," said the commentator to the camera, "showing the true Olympic spirit."

The scene shifted to the decathlon, where Joe Bob Sweeney and Curly Rogers were getting ready to begin. Either man could win, and either way it would be a gold medal for the United States; but European commentators couldn't resist saying that the best decathlete in the world would not get to compete.

"Mike, tickets to this fight have sold out a long time ago," said Alf Stallings, surveying the throngs of people at Alexander Memorial Coliseum on Sunday night, "but I believe there's a few black-market entrepreneurs who've made small fortunes on hawking seats."

"Yeah, I've heard the going rate is three times the cost of admittance to the Opening Ceremonies," Mike Ameche replied with a smile. "There have actually been people flying in without tickets, just hoping for a seat."

Christiann Vervoerden's Danish opponent in the quarterfinals did not show up, so Vervoerden had won by default. Tonight the superstar would fight his semifinal match with Tyrone Bennett, an African-American.

But the racial overtones were not what made this fight special, at least not to true boxing fans. Because of boxing's strange rules, this semifinal would be *the* match of the Olympics. Whoever won would fight Hungary's Georg Molnar, who had defeated a Russian on a technicality in the other super-heavyweight semifinal earlier that day, but it was really a question of whether Bennett or Vervoerden would be the one to beat Molnar's brains out. In any other sport, the Hungarian would have taken the bronze, while Vervoerden and Bennett—clearly the best contenders—battled for the gold. But boxing and judo, alone among Olympic sports, offer two bronze medals: the Russian had earned one of them, and the other would go to the loser of tonight's fight.

"That means Molnar is assured of a silver just for showing up on Tuesday," said Alf with a chuckle. "And I believe if I were him, that's all I'd do—show up."

Bennett emerged from the dressing area with his trainers, raising his fists high and shouting, his words lost in the deafening roar.

A few seconds later Vervoerden came out, along with his attorney, John Shapiro, and his trainer. "I don't have an applause meter handy," said Stallings, "but I'd guess it's about fifty-fifty here tonight, Vervoerden fans to Bennett fans."

After making the introductions, the referee gave the customary signal for the two men to move into center-ring and touch gloves. Bennett and Vervoerden glared at one another, and then as though on cue, both turned their backs with disdain and walked to their corners to wait for the starting bell.

"Did you see that look, Alf? Makes you wish you were a mind-reader." As he said those words, the bell clanged. "Vervoerden is surprisingly silent as he emerges from his corner. This is the first time I've known him to come out without what U.S. journalists are calling his 'rebel yell.'"

Inside the ring, Vervoerden let his eyes and not his voice do the talking, staring poison arrows at his opponent.

"Maybe he's afraid of becoming a parody of himself," said Stallings. "But look at how he's moving—instead of bounding across the ring like he usually does, he's marching straight for Tyrone Bennett, who I think may be wishing that Vervoerden would pull his usual antics. At least then he'd know what to expect."

Up until then, Bennett had seemed cool and unfazed, but then he'd never stood this close to Christiann Vervoerden. "We see Tyrone going into his fighter's stance a little slowly," said Ameche, "and look! I'd swear he's glancing back at his trainer."

"I hope you're wrong, Mike," Stallings replied, "because that's the kiss of death for any fighter."

"Finally Tyrone is moving in," said Ameche, "cautiously, weaving and bobbing, no doubt preparing for the onslaught that's coming."

"Meanwhile Christiann continues to move forward," reported Stallings, "not wasting one ounce of energy and not taking his eyes off Bennett."

The two fighters looked like participants in a ridiculous dance, Bennett moving back and forth quickly while Vervoerden kept on coming with all the grace of a sumo wrestler. Then Bennett surprised everyone by striking the first blow.

"Look at that!" shouted Ameche. "He's showing some real spunk! I don't know if he's hoping to catch Vervoerden off-guard or if he's just trying to psyche himself up. . . ."

"Whatever the case, he's not getting through Vervoerden's screen," Stallings pointed out. "He's moving from side to side, but not forward. And look at how Christiann is pressing in now, fending off the punches like they were swats from a child."

"You're right, Alf. He's like a tank moving across a mine field—there are little mini-explosions popping up here and there, but they're not doing any damage. Tyrone is scoring lots of punches to Vervoerden's stomach and arms, but he's not getting him in the face where it really counts. Here we are thirty seconds into Round One, and Christiann Vervoerden so far hasn't swung once at Tyrone Bennett, yet he seems to have the advantage. It's eerie."

"Mike, nobody accuses Vervoerden of being a mental giant outside the ring, but inside it I believe he's got a mind that works like a computer, photographing his opponent dozens of times a second, analyzing his every move, looking for the hole in his defenses. Something's bound to happen at any second."

And it did. Vervoerden's internal computer found the hole it was looking for, and when the precise moment arrived for maximum impact, he smashed directly into the center of the other man's chin.

"Good God!" shouted Ameche. "With one blow, Vervoerden has literally lifted Bennett off the mat and into the air." Bennett bounced onto his back and did not rise.

"Now Vervoerden is standing over Bennett," said Stallings. "It's as though he's begging him to get back up so he can give him another punishing blow."

"I don't think that's gonna happen, Alf. . . . The referee has pushed Vervoerden back into his corner, and now he's counting Bennett down. Everyone is wondering if Vervoerden has managed to knock Bennett out with a single punch. . . . Look—the ref is raising Christiann's hand in victory to a tremendous roar of applause from the crowd here at Alexander Memorial Coliseum!"

A few minutes after this stunning defeat, Ameche was saying, "I believe we may have a future world heavyweight champion in Christiann Vervoerden. He's big, he's powerful, he's frightening. . . . And I think frightening is the word many African-Americans would use to describe him. Alf, I can see people in the crowd actually weeping over the results of tonight's fight."

"People have called Atlanta 'a city divided'," said Stallings, "but I believe the mixed reaction to this is more evidence of a whole country divided. It's safe to predict that as a result of this, there will be more controversy, more anger—and perhaps even more violence."

"Like I said, it's frightening," Ameche agreed. "And somebody else who might have cause for fright is Georg Molnar, who faces Vervoerden in the ring for the gold on Tuesday."

Fortunately for Molnar, he was watching the fight from the Village on the world feed, which carries no commentary, and he hadn't heard this. He had turned on the fight because he thought he might learn something about the tactics of his opponent, but he knew less now than he had before the fight began.

Suddenly he wished Vlasky, his Russian opponent on Saturday, had won their match. Unlike the Bennett-Vervoerden fight, theirs had begun with a hands-down favorite, and that had been Vlasky; but the Russian had hit him below the belt and gotten himself disqualified.

Now Molnar wondered what he should do on Tuesday. Should he enter the ring and simply fall down? He could never show his face in Budapest if he did that. Maybe he could take only one punch, and then fall. But that could be dangerous—he'd seen what had happened to a much better fighter with a single blow. Perhaps he could feign illness and forfeit the match, in which case he would automatically earn the silver medal, something well beyond his expectations before the Games.

He thought about gorging himself on greasy food from McDonald's, so that he would get diarrhea and have to go to the polyclinic.

Or perhaps some unforeseen event would save him.

"I think we have reason for a little cautious optimism," said Greg Robbins, beginning the security briefing on Monday morning, July 29. His face—the face of a man who had gotten three nights' worth of sleep in the preceding ten days—belied his upbeat tone, but he took another sip of coffee and kept talking. "We are now down to exactly one week left," he continued, making a nonsensical mark on the chalkboard beside him to emphasize the point, "and thanks in part to all the tension that followed the bombing, incident levels are now lower than we'd ever anticipated."

Around him sat the usual briefing attendees, a group Thomas Mason had dubbed the "Friendly Village Coffee Club." All the local jurisdictions had one representative each, led by Red Anderson of the Atlanta Police; so did the federal agencies and departments from Secret Service to Immigration to the FBI. Steve Kirk was there, too, as he had been ever since the bombing.

Michelle Hinton, as usual, had most of the men stealing glances at her—but Kirk was not one of them. Mason had taken note of that fact, because this pretense of disinterest was even more conspicuous than the awkward, shy glances he'd seen those two exchanging for months. He smiled to himself. Maybe they wanted to keep the fact from him, thinking he wouldn't approve. But Kirk wasn't in Michelle's chain of command, and as far as he was concerned, what they did on their own time was their business as long as it didn't interfere with the job they had to do.

Red Anderson, in a voice strained by too many cigarettes, spoke up. "Look here, Greg—I don't know about you, but my men are tired! We've been working eighteen- to twenty-hour days, and we're 'bout near falling asleep on the job." He looked around at the others, many of whom nodded in agreement. "I know you gotta keep us all on alert, but shit—we need some rest around here! Like you yourself say, everything's running smoother than a Texas whorehouse, so why not let us get back to a more routine schedule—say, ten-hour days for the remainder of the Games? And maybe we could have these meetings every other day, so we wouldn't have to be here at 5:30 every morning."

"Fine," Robbins said. "I'm just as tired as you are, Red, and I know the worst thing we can do is have worn-out personnel running our

security. Okay, we can cut back to ten hours a day on a staggered schedule so we'll have enough men on duty at any given time, but I'm afraid
we're gonna have to keep having these meetings every morning."

A few people groaned, but Mason silenced them. "The fact is," he
announced, "that if there was ever an ideal time for a terrorist to perpe-
trate something, it's now. They've had a chance to watch how we work,
they know our routines, and what's more they've got to know we're
tired." Everyone's eyes turned to him. "If you think I'm trying to scare
you, I am. Remember, a terrorist attack is not some little test to keep
you on your toes so you're prepared for the big one. It's the real thing,
and it comes only one time: *when* you least expect it, and *where* you
least expect it."

"Sure, Tom, sure," said Anderson irritably, turning around in his
chair, "but unless we get some replacements—and I don't see anyone
sending more troops in—we just can't keep this up."

The Dutch team occupied the second floor of Building D, at the
northwest corner of University Apartments. At noontime that Monday,
July 29, most of the team members were away at training sites or at
lunch, but the chef de mission had stayed in to finish some paperwork.
A knock came at the front door, and he was surprised to open it and find
a work crew of six wearing the uniforms of the Georgia Tech Plant
Operations Department.

"We're here to repair the leak in the wall," said a tall blond-haired
man with a deep drawl, obviously the foreman. He was the only Anglo
in the group; the rest of the crew looked like they might be Mexicans.

"I'm sorry, I don't understand," said the chef.

The foreman flourished a work order from his hip pocket. "One of
our crews found a leak in your wall, so we're gonna see if we can get it
patched up before tonight."

"Oh?" The chef scanned the work order, then handed it back. "Well,
I haven't noticed any leak. . . ."

"Just be glad we got here before you did!" laughed the foreman,
motioning the other men into the room with their equipment. "Now,
we're gonna have to cut into the wall, and so we can do it without damaging any of y'all's stuff, we'll move all the furniture out of this room
and into the next one." At the chef's look of dismay, he added, "Don't
worry, we'll get it all moved back nice and neat. It's gonna get pretty
noisy and messy here for a little while, so I'm gonna need you to vacate

the premises and put out a sign for your team members to stay out of here until—oh, say 4:00 p.m."

"Well. . . alright then," said the chef, gathering up his papers and preparing to exit.

By the time the Dutchman had taped a sign on the door and left, the crew had begun moving the lounge furniture out of the room. After that, one man cut into the 5/8" sheetrock with a utility knife, making a 4' x 5' section which two others tore out to reveal the inner structure of reinforced concrete block. Next, another man with a masonry saw, exercising considerably greater strain and making much more noise, cut a smaller square out of the concrete, and two men gingerly removed the section of block he had loosened. Then the crew stopped to look.

Instead of the pipe they'd supposedly come to repair, they saw an open shaft that ran from the first floor to the roof. Called a vertical chase, one of these had been designed into each corner of the building and at other strategic locations to allow for ease in running conduit or electrical cabling in the future. But this particular vertical chase already had something in it; the men stared at the blue thirty-gallon drum, then glanced at one another and smiled. "Y'all boys done good," said the foreman, addressing two of the men in the crew. "It's the mother lode, just like you left it."

The drum sat on a metal platform, and above it they could see the bottom of another container. In fact there were fifteen in all, stacked one on top of the other to the fourth floor. While the man with the masonry saw increased the size of the opening to three feet by five, two of the men went downstairs and returned with a large hydraulic jacking mechanism, which they placed on the floor and strapped onto the second container. They jacked it up a few inches, pushing the others above it higher into the chase, thus relaxing the downward weight and allowing them to slide the bottom container out. After that, they lowered the stack to the base level, attached the jack to the next container, and so on, repeating the process until they'd pulled out all fifteen drums.

Meanwhile, two other men cleaned up the plaster, mortar, and broken block, and with the drums removed, they dumped all the debris into the empty chase. The man who'd operated the masonry saw mixed a small application of mortar, and together he and two other men reinserted the portion of block they'd removed. After that, they cut a piece of 5/8" sheetrock to match the hole in the wall, taped it, and applied sheetrock mud to the edges.

"Alright, that's it," said the foreman after they'd moved the furniture back in. He grabbed a piece of paper off of a desk and scrawled a note to the chef de mission. *Dear Sir*, it read. *Your leak is fixed, and another crew will come tomorrow to sand and paint the patch on the wall. Sorry about the trouble we caused you.* He did not sign his name.

Using hand trucks, two of the men had been removing the containers via elevator to the first floor, then by means of a second elevator into the underground parking garage. There they loaded them into a Plant Operations van in which sat a seventh crew member.

Long before their promised departure at 4:00, the men left Building D. Three of them struck out on foot while the other four took the van north on Techwood, then west across campus to Fitten Residence Hall on McMillan Street near Northside Drive. No one paid any attention to the uniformed workers as they moved fourteen of the drums into the basement of Fitten, temporary home of the Puerto Rican team. Nor did anyone notice that two of them stayed behind to guard the cache while the others rode away in the van with the remaining drum.

PART FOUR

A MESSAGE TO THE WORLD

17

Mason's hand fumbled through the darkness toward the ringing telephone. *I swear that 5:00 a.m. wake-up call comes earlier every day*, he thought as he squinted at the illuminated red digits of the clock radio on the hotel room nightstand. It was 3:08. *What the. . . .* He felt a sudden shudder of alarm.

"Yeah?" he said into the receiver, his voice thick with sleep.

"Tom, it's Robbins. We've got an emergency."

The word *emergency* hit him like a triple shot of caffeine. Fully awake now, he swung his feet to the floor and switched on the bedside lamp. "What is it, Greg?"

"A break-in. At the German quarters. Some female athletes have been kidnapped."

"Break-in?" Mason snapped. "Someone got in through the fence?"

"No. Worse than that. None of the sensors on the perimeter detected anything. These people had to come from inside."

Inside: it was what Mason had feared from the beginning.

Placing the receiver between his cheek and shoulder, he grabbed the pair of pants he'd slung over a chair only a few hours before. He threw them on and listened as Robbins gave the details of the break-in.

"One of the girls managed to escape. She alerted a security officer, and they're en route now." Robbins's voice was strangely calm, but Mason knew it was experience talking, not emotion. "I called you first since this is Code Red, beyond Village Security protocol."

"You did right." Mason knocked the base of the phone onto the floor as he stretched the cord to reach the dresser. "Okay. Here's the drill. Number one, batten down the Village—completely. All gates, every damn thing. No one—I mean not one person unless he's with security—enters or leaves."

"Got it."

Mason flung open the dresser drawer, balancing first on one foot and then the other as he put on his socks. "Number two," he went on, "using the red band frequency, alert all security in the Village." He considered for a fraction of a second whether he should mobilize the Special Weapons and Tactics (SWAT) unit of Navy SEALs. Unlike Olympic basketball fans who couldn't wait to see Shaquille O'Neal and the rest of the "Dream Team" perform, Mason had hoped security's Dream Team would never see action. For weeks now, Lt. Boyd and the other twenty-seven men had maintained their cover as athletes living in Burge Apartments on North Avenue, but now it was time to call in the world's most advanced fighting force. "And alert Boyd," Mason said. "Have the SWAT team report to HQ ASAP."

"Roger that. Hey Tom, here comes the officer with the girl who escaped."

"Put him on the radio, secure frequency." Mason dropped the phone and grabbed his handheld two-way radio off the dresser. He switched it on and punched in his security code as he slipped an undershirt over his head.

"Big Wolf, Foxfire 23."

"Foxfire 23, report situation," Mason replied, pulling a fresh shirt out of the closet. He knew there wasn't time to put on deodorant, to shave or even brush his teeth; those luxuries could wait till he arrived at HQ, where he kept a kit for emergencies.

"Conducting routine foot patrol with partner in vicinity of Couch Field at McMillan and Sixth," the officer's voice crackled through the radio. "At approximately 0250, Caucasian female wearing only bra and athletic shorts ran from rear of Hemphill Residence Hall. Subject obviously frightened, screaming in German. Initially unable to understand a word. Attempted to calm her, and ascertained that three males had entered German quarters and forced her and roommates out through window at gunpoint. Subject took advantage of confusion when girl in front of her fell, and escaped."

"You got a description of the intruders?"

The officer paused to question the girl, and Mason sat down on the bed beside the nightstand to put on his shoes. In the momentary silence, he heard a voice behind him—*inside his room.* With a slow, measured nonchalance, he slid open the drawer of the bedside table, lifted the Gideon's Bible, and pulled something out from under it. A split-second later, he wheeled around with his Beretta pointed at the source of the noise. Then with a long exhale of relief, he looked down at the phone, still lying on the floor where he'd dropped it. ". . . Please hang up and try again," the mechanical voice chanted. "If you need help. . . ." Mason slammed the receiver back in its cradle just as the officer returned to the air.

"Negative on description. Intruders wore masks and gloves. Subject heard one man's voice, could not identify accent."

Pistol still in hand, Mason checked the clip before holstering it, then grabbed his mobile phone, keys, and identification. "How many persons abducted?"

"Seven," answered the officer. "Six females and one male."

"A *male*? In the female quarters?" Mason shut his room door and began striding down the hallway. "Have you verified this?"

"Negative. Did not have back-up. Partner remained on scene while subject was brought to HQ."

"Ten-four," Mason replied, pushing the button for the elevator and hearing it begin its slow rise through the fifteen silent floors below him. "Sit tight, keep her calm, and return security commander to radio."

"Have called Boyd," Robbins reported. "SWAT team will deploy from Burge in approximately ninety seconds. Security personnel are alerting Army, FBI, Central Intelligence, and local law enforcement."

Mason glanced at his watch. "Alright. Arriving at gate in two minutes. Have a vehicle waiting. Assuming two more minutes to get to HQ, I should be there in four."

"Roger that."

The elevator still hadn't arrived, and he tapped his foot impatiently, wondering if he should take the stairs. Fifteen flights would cost him at least a minute, but he was almost ready to make a break for it when the bell dinged and the doors opened. Stepping inside, he jammed the button for the garage level. The door took five precious seconds to close. "Come on, come on!" he shouted.

After an agonizingly long ride, he raced out into the garage, past a row of parked cars, and through the back door onto Spring Street. The early morning air was muggy, and with no breeze to take away the smells of the street, it reeked of oil and car fumes. It promised to be another Atlanta day in the 90s: he could already feel a fine mist of sweat that would soon paste his undershirt to his back.

Running at full gait, he glanced up the one-way street, rushed across it, and cut the corner of North Avenue across from the Varsity. Several cars were parked in front of the BP station to his left, and the place was packed with late-night Olympic partygoers stopping on their way home from the bars. Inside, a dozen or more waited in line to buy cigarettes or snacks, and plenty of others stood outside pumping gas, talking and laughing. No one even looked up as he ran by.

Once he rounded the front of the gas station onto North Avenue, he could see the Village gate a block away, just over the bridge across the Downtown Connector. Half a dozen security officers stood around the guard shack, their shapes bathed in the blinding perimeter lights that shone twenty-four hours a day.

Behind him Mason could hear the voices and laughter from the gas station, in front of him the occasional *whoosh!* of a car or an eighteen-wheeler passing under the bridge on the interstate. In between, there was only the sound of his running footsteps and his beating heart.

Then a loud, sharp blast of noise ripped through the predawn stillness. It wasn't a backfire or even a gunshot: this thing sounded like someone had driven a truck out of a ten-story window. The guards at the gate wheeled around to look down North Avenue toward the source of the noise.

As he sprinted across the bridge, a frantic voice called out to Mason from his radio. "Big Wolf, Baby Sitter!" It was Lt. Boyd. "We have a 10-33—emergency—10-33!"

"Baby Sitter!" Mason yelled into his radio. He was breathing hard, not slowing down a step. "Report situation!"

"Explosion outside door!" Boyd shouted. "Casualties on ground!" In the background Mason could hear sounds of crazed confusion, a mix of fast footsteps, gasps, and groans. "Smoke everywhere! Shattered glass, concrete. . . looks like five—no, six men down."

Mason could see smoke billowing into the sky from the direction of the SEALs' quarters.

"Dispatched first squad to HQ while remainder dressed," Boyd went on. "They stepped right into blast area of antipersonnel mine. . . could be Claymore." He was fighting hard to swallow his shock, and Mason could imagine the man's jaw muscle tightening as his fine dark face contorted with horror. Boyd had killed men and seen men killed, but this was different. This was a massacre.

Through the radio came the piercing echo of an ambulance siren. Seconds later, Mason could hear it coming down the street.

"Check the area," he ordered Boyd, "then report to HQ with one squad. Keep the remainder in quarters until otherwise directed." He almost added "and be careful," but that seemed ridiculous now.

He could picture the scene outside of Burge Apartments; he'd seen it enough times before, back in Vietnam. The Claymore mine was like a metal skunk, but instead of throwing a scent, it sprayed 700 steel pellets over an arc wider than a baseball diamond and deeper than the outfield. They had used it in two ways during the war: either a man could wire it to a pressure mat hidden on the jungle floor, or he could detonate it manually when he saw a Viet Cong coming. Manual detonation meant that you were certain you killed the enemy and not another American or a villager's child, but many units preferred using the booby-trap because it allowed them to set the mine and move on.

It made sense to guess that whoever had killed the SEALs at Burge had wired the mine and left the scene—except for the fact that Boyd had a guard on duty at all times observing the front, back, and sides of the building through concealed miniature TV monitors. There was simply no way anyone could have gotten past the guard to set the booby-trap. But if someone had hidden the Claymore nearby, pointed at Burge, then waited and triggered it at just the right moment. . . .

Mason felt a chill run up his back as he began to grasp the enormous sophistication of the force that had infiltrated the Village. Only a handful of people at the top echelons of security knew that the SEALs were even here, let alone where they were staying. But whoever had done this knew, and they knew that security would deploy the first squad as soon as word of the break-in at the German quarters got out.

"Papa Bear, Big Wolf," Mason said into his radio as he reached the gate and glanced down the street at the ambulance in front of Burge. Under the flashing lights, medics were loading in stretchers.

"Go ahead, Big Wolf." The calm in Robbins's voice sounded more forced than before, and the background noise at security HQ had increased dramatically after Boyd's radio call.

"Instruct personnel to apprehend anyone seen on foot in the Village." A security officer motioned him to a waiting car. "I mean *anyone*. . . . I don't care who their I.D. says they are, grab 'em and hold them at HQ for questioning."

"Ten-four, Big Wolf."

He could hear more sirens as Village fire trucks rushed toward Burge. He took one last look down the street at the site of the pandemonium, and in his mind he heard some long-forgotten words from the Book of Job: *The thing I have feared has come upon me.* Then he jumped in the car and raced to headquarters.

Dozens of phones were ringing at once inside the Naval Reserve building. Mason brushed past several people toward the gymnasium straight down the hall, where Village maps had suddenly appeared on the walls and an emergency command center had sprung up complete with telephones, fax machines, and a dispatcher's desk. He assembled the members of his own team (except Adam, who was on duty at the Bosnian quarters) and gave them assignments.

Michelle and Julio would call Adam and the rest of the operatives assigned to watch the teams that posed a possible security threat. If they couldn't locate one of these "hospitality clerks," Mason ordered, they should talk to the chef de mission. "Tell them. . . ." He thought for a second. "I don't know, tell 'em the electricity went out and you don't want their alarm clocks to shut off."

He grabbed Lamont and Aaron, and pointing to Couch Field on one of the wall maps, said, "Okay, we need to call every chef in this northwest area and have them check on their athletes. There's about forty different teams here, so you guys grab two other folks, and each of you call ten apiece. Lamont, I want you to report back to me in fifteen minutes."

"What are we gonna tell them?" Lamont asked.

"Just tell them there's an emergency, and that they're not to leave their residence halls until instructed otherwise." He thought a moment. "And tell them not to turn on any lights or go near the windows. That'll either piss them off or scare them or both, but it's what we've got to do."

Just then, Boyd arrived with a squad of six men. The SEALs, each equipped with a headset radio, a Heckler & Koch MP5 submachine gun, and night vision goggles, wore grayish-black combat fatigues with black vests and lightweight black hoods. They had the hoods pulled up to show their chins; their faces, blackened with grease, were devoid of expression.

"Allan, I'm sorry about your men," Mason began.

"Thanks," said Boyd calmly. "We confirmed that it was a Claymore, M-18A1, detonated as our first squad left the building."

"Manually, then?" Mason asked.

Boyd nodded. "Obviously, whoever set it had vacated, but they had clearly observed our activities well enough to know that we would be making that exit from the building." With an embarrassed, even helpless tone, he added, "Sir, this indicates sophisticated surveillance techniques, because normally we know if we're being watched from a mile away, and it shows that they planned carefully. I think it's safe to say that their objective was first of all to knock out some of our team—they killed four and left two severely wounded—and also to slow us down, which they sure as hell did. It took us eight minutes to secure the area."

Robbins walked in now, surrounded by security officers asking questions and handing him papers faster than he could take them. "I've contacted the National Guard and Reserves," he said. "They'll be sending in units by 0400, and we're gonna hold them at Bobby Dodd Stadium until we get a clearer picture. Also, the FBI and CIA are dispatching observers, but they're gonna keep a low profile and let you run the show." He paused. "The British contacted us to tell us there's been a break-in at their quarters in the Center Street Residence Hall, and eight of their females are missing, plus there are four Canadian females AWOL from Fulmer dorm."

"Have you apprehended anyone?" Mason asked.

"Tons. There's people everywhere, and believe me, every one of them is screaming bloody hell. We've begun holding them over at the main dining hall with armed guards, but so far they all check out."

"What do you mean, they check out?"

"We're verifying that the badges match the person, then running them through the scanner to make sure they're valid."

"What makes you so certain our guy isn't accredited himself?"

"Oh, shit."

"'Oh shit' is right. Besides, those people are safer in the dining hall than they are in the Village if there's some psycho wandering around." Mason glanced up at the map. "The question is, where do we find him—or *them*—and where are the hostages?"

"Unless they got out before you gave the order to shut the Village down, they've got to be here somewhere," Robbins pointed out.

"They had more than fifteen minutes after they took the hostages—plenty of time to escape."

"Yeah, but we've checked the gates," said Robbins, "and there hasn't been any traffic through there that can't be accounted for since a little after 1:30."

Mason thought for a second. "Let's get as many personnel as we can out on the streets in vehicles, including the Atlanta and Fulton County units we already have in the Village—not just to apprehend suspects but to look for suspicious activity of any kind. We need to show our presence here. But hey, if they come across any large groups of people, have them call for backup—nobody needs to engage terrorists on their own." From the look on Robbins's face, Mason realized he'd been the first to say the word on everyone's mind. "And don't go inside any residence halls either. My suspicion is that these guys are holed up in one of them. We need to find out where our intruders are without putting any of our people in danger."

A fiftyish man in the uniform of Village Security approached Mason and introduced himself as the officer who had found the German girl. She was in an office down the hall, the man said, if Mason wanted to talk to her.

"You bet I do."

Mason followed the man to the small office, where he found the young woman, an attractive gymnast with short brown hair and bright blue eyes, wrapped in a blanket and drinking a cup of coffee. He could see that the terror and shock of what she'd just experienced had only begun to set in. Beside her sat the German envoy, called in to translate.

Mason questioned her briefly, but he didn't get much more than what he'd learned from the officer's report on the radio: at around 2:30 or 2:45, three masked and armed men had entered her first-floor room and ordered her and her roommates out through the window. Mason noticed that she kept saying the word *München*, and he asked the envoy what this was all about.

"She says," the man replied with a somber expression, "'I kept telling myself, this is Munich all over again—Munich, Munich!'"

Mason thanked the two, ordered the officer to transport the girl to the polyclinic across the street, and returned to the gymnasium, where Lamont was waiting with a report on his calls to the delegations in the area surrounding the German team.

"You were right," said Lamont, running a hand through his thick, closely cropped black hair. "They were pissed—but once we explained the situation, they changed their tone. We left them with instructions to call us back if any of their athletes come up AWOL, or if they see anything else suspicious."

Aaron suggested that they go ahead and notify the rest of the teams. "Good idea," said Mason, as Michelle appeared at his side.

She and Julio had contacted all the observers assigned to the sensitive teams, she reported, and all of them checked out except for the Bosnians. "It's not like Adam not to answer," Michelle said, worried.

"You can't get anybody else with their team, not even the chef?"

She shook her head.

"Okay," said Mason, "Get two guys over to their dorm ASAP, and have them call me on the radio when they get there."

A crackle came over his radio a moment later. "Big Wolf, Foxfire 68, over." It was one of the units already out on patrol.

"Foxfire 68, give me your 10-20." Mason held the radio close to his ear to hear over the noise in the gym's makeshift command center.

"Big Wolf, 10-20 is Fitten Residence Hall, building one-one-nine on McMillan Street. Be advised of suspicious activity on premises."

"Foxfire 68, clarify suspicious activity?"

"Conducting patrol as directed, observed lights coming on in all other buildings, people moving about. But one-one-nine completely dark except for blue flashes through windows on first floor—flashes like from a welding torch."

"*Blue flashes?*"

"Affirmative. There's another one! Coming from several windows."

"Foxfire 68, set up surveillance in immediate vicinity. Will send assistance." Mason turned to Julio. "Get the floor plans for Fitten dorm," he ordered, "plus a map of the area around it."

While Julio went off to do as he was told, Mason said to Boyd, "Now, I don't want you to engage, you got it? We may have hostages in there, and we don't want anyone else to get hurt. Stand by for further instructions."

"Yes, sir," said Boyd. He looked like he had ideas of his own, but for now he would have to subordinate his plans to the commander's.

It took a few minutes to get the floor plans and maps, and as Boyd and his team left for Fitten dorm, they passed Michelle coming back in with a clipboard in her hand. "Michelle," Mason ordered, "have the dispatcher route ten cars, plus some lighting, to the street in front of Building 119, Fitten. Who's housed there?"

She glanced down at her clipboard. "That would be the Puerto Ricans."

Mason thought for a moment. Puerto Rican separatist groups had perpetrated fully a third of all the domestic terrorist acts in the 1980s. "Gimme the chef's name and number," he said, picking up his cellular phone, which he had strapped to his belt.

As soon as he had the information, he dialed. After three rings, a heavily accented voice answered, "Comité Olímpico de Puerto Rico."

"I'm sorry to disturb you," Mason said. "I'm trying to reach Geraldo Martinez, *por favor.*"

"*Si*, this is Geraldo Martinez. May I help you?"

"Well, I hope so, Mr. Martinez. This is Thomas Mason, Village

Security, and I realize that one of my people already called you, but I'm just following up. Is everything okay over there?"

The voice laughed politely. "Yes, we are fine, thank you. All team members are accounted for, except for those who I know are somewhere celebrating—but there is no danger in that."

"No, of course not." In spite of the chef's easy tone, something felt amiss, and Mason threw out a piece of bait: "I suppose your people are all awake now?"

"Oh, you mean because of all the noise outside? No, I have sent them back to bed. We cannot afford to lose our sleep—we have competition in a few hours."

"Of course, sir, and I won't keep you." Mason hesitated before saying, "Oh, by the way, don't I remember you from the '84 Olympics, Geraldo? Weren't you a pole vaulter in Los Angeles?"

The voice paused for a second, then laughed again in the same polite manner. "No, that was not me."

"Oh, well, just thought I'd ask. Sorry to bother you."

Robbins had come back in, and Mason told him about the conversation. "I don't know, Greg." Mason shook his head. "I thought I'd trap the bastard with that pole vaulter stuff, but he was too slick. One thing's for sure, though: the guy ain't no Puerto Rican—sounded more like a Mexican in an old Western. My guess is that if we're dealing with a hostage situation, the whole Puerto Rican team is being held along with whoever else they've captured." He glanced at the floor plan. "But we don't know, so that means we need to go knock on their door. Shit, I hate to do that! We don't know what we're getting our guys into."

He waited for a moment, hoping Robbins would offer an opinion, but he knew the final decision rested with him, and he would have to take action. "I'm going over there," he said, taking the cellular phone with him and grabbing a pair of ITT Night Mariner field glasses.

18

McMillan Street was little more than a one-way alley connecting Sixth and Eighth streets. On the west side sat the ancient Couch Building, once an elementary school. Its brick exterior was mellowed with time; but the Undergraduate Residence Hall, a vast complex behind and beside it (portions of which had been completed just in time for the Olympics), still looked very fresh. Most of the structures on the east side, clustered around Fitten Residence Hall, were of red brick with tinted windows that reflected a late 1970s design.

There was Fulmer dorm on the north, beyond it the Commander Commons Building and Armstrong and Hefner dormitories. On the south were Montag and Freeman residence halls. Though it was barely 4:00 a.m., all of these, along with Caldwell and Folk residence halls to the northwest, were abuzz with activity, their lights burning and people looking out the windows. In spite of instructions from Village Security, most of the residents had decided to find out what all the commotion was about, and the rest were busy beginning their day as though it were an ordinary one. Athletes showered and dressed, some joking amongst themselves and others doing stretching exercises, a few of them preparing for events set to take place later that morning.

Only Fitten Residence Hall, separated from Fulmer by a small parking lot with dumpsters behind it, and from Montag by a stretch of yard with scattered trees, stood dark and silent.

Fitten lay further back from the street than its neighbors, and its height of four stories made it taller than the other, three-story buildings. At the rear an additional floor, the basement mechanical area, faced the open expanse of Couch Field down a steep twenty-foot slope. A walkway ran between Fitten and Fulmer across the field, a temporary training site for the throwing events of track and field competitions. Fitten offered a commanding view, the perfect location for the fortress it had apparently become. The nearest building with a higher elevation was the giant Fuller E. Callaway, Jr., Manufacturing Research Center or

MARC, several hundred yards away beyond the screen of pine trees that separated Couch Field from Ferst Drive.

The only spots for concealment at the back were the dumpsters to the north and a tree lined with a semicircular brick wall along the slope to the southeast. Boyd had already stationed three men apiece in these two areas. The trees along the front provided cover as well for the ten cars on the street and the many officers in the uniforms of Village Security, the Atlanta Police, and the Fulton County Sheriff's Department who sat in them. The lamps Mason had requested hadn't arrived yet, and Robbins had ordered everyone to keep their headlights and emergency lightbars off for now; but even in the darkness and silence, this force of two dozen would have attracted the notice of anyone who happened to peek out between the blinds in Fitten dorm.

Lieutenant Boyd met Mason beside the Undergraduate Residence Hall across from Montag. On either side they could see lights on and people standing in the windows looking out, so Mason motioned Boyd into the shadows.

"I don't know what makes less sense," Boyd said, "these folks making a target of themselves in front of the windows when they've been advised to take shelter, or the ones in there, pretending to be asleep." He pointed to Fitten. "Assuming there are people in there."

"Oh, there are," said Mason. "I talked to the chef—or a guy who claims to be, anyway."

"Then they're definitely laying low," the SWAT team leader observed. "We haven't seen a sign of those blue flashes the officer reported. If I might offer a suggestion—"

Their conversation was interrupted by the crackle of Mason's radio. "Big Wolf, this is Foxfire 47."

"Ten-twelve, Foxfire," said Mason, then turning back to Boyd, he asked, "What's your suggestion?"

"I advise that we send a couple of men up close to the building to hook a micro-audio receiver to the wall. Maybe that way we can get a better idea of what's happening inside."

"Good plan," Mason replied, "but let's hold off for a minute." He returned to his radio and told the officer to give his report.

"Have arrived third floor, Building C, University Apartments, to inspect Bosnian quarters. Have knocked repeatedly on door and received no answer. Advised by Accreditation that three players and two coaches have returned to nation of origin, but records indicate sixteen players, four coaches, and one chef still on premises."

"Foxfire, proceed using master key, announce presence, then enter quarters, over."

Fifteen seconds later, the officer came back on. "Big Wolf, first suite is empty."

Mason told the officer to have his partner check the closets and drawers, and the officer reported that they were empty. As the men proceeded from one suite to another, each time with the same results, Mason's suspicions grew. According to their records, the suites belonged to the handball team, who should still be in the Village. Then in the fourth suite, the officer broke the discipline of radio language: "Oh my God!" he shouted.

"Foxfire, come in, over."

Boyd, who stood by tapping his foot, eager to take action, stopped and listened.

"Big Wolf, have located a body on the premises. Subject is Caucasian male, approximately forty-five years of age. Throat appears to be slit, body stuffed into closet. . . ." Mason and Boyd exchanged glances. "Subject appears to be approximately six feet tall, dark hair with mustache, dark brown or black eyes, dressed in business suit. No wallet or other identification on body; but have located invitation to chef meeting at 0800 this morning, addressed to Borsloff Helvinca, Chef de Mission, Bosnian NOC."

Before he had a chance to respond, the officer reported another body, and this time as he listened, Mason had a sick feeling he knew who it was. "Subject is Caucasian male, approximately thirty years of age. Appears to have been strangled. Thin rope around neck, signs of struggle. Checking identification. No driver's license, Village credentials, or other picture I.D. Does not appear to be routine robbery: wallet contains gas credit card and MasterCard, plus seventy-seven dollars cash."

"Give name on credit cards, over," said Mason, wanting to add *Hurry up, dammit!*

"Adam Stabler, over."

Mason's voice betrayed no emotion when he said, "Foxfire, subject was one of ours. Stand by for instructions. . . ." He paused a moment. "Foxfire, inspect remainder of premises, including adjoining apartments. Clear the area, then seal it off, over."

"Roger."

Boyd continued to wait while Mason radioed Robbins. Robbins confirmed that the Bosnian chef's name was Borsloff Helvinca, and yes, his I.D. picture fit the description given by the officer inspecting the team's quarters. Regarding Adam, who Mason considered a member of his family just like the rest of his task force, all Mason could do was report his death and ask Robbins to let the others know.

Robbins had more news about missing athletes. Not all delegations had yet accounted for all their members, but it appeared that four French women were missing from the Center Street Apartments—along with six U.S. females from the Eighth Street Apartments.

So now there were Americans involved. Boyd looked ready to storm Fitten at any moment. And of course these weren't the only U.S. citizens held captive: seventy-six athletes and forty-nine officials of the Puerto Rican team, officially billeted in Fitten Residence Hall, remained completely unaccounted for.

Remembering all his old suspicions about the Bosnian handball team, Mason asked Robbins for the name of their coach. He had to wait a few seconds while Robbins retrieved the information from his computer. "Individual's name is Hakija Drabeznic."

"What a mouthful." Mason had Robbins repeat it, and he wrote it down phonetically on his floor plan of Fitten dorm: *ha-KEE-zhah drah-BEZH-nick*. Mason dialed the number of the Puerto Rican delegation on his cellular phone.

This time it took eight rings until the same voice as before answered, sounding more peeved than on the previous occasion.

"Comité Olímpico de Puerto Rico—we are trying to sleep."

"Oh, I'm sorry, Mr. Drabeznic," said Mason coolly. He glanced at Boyd, who cracked a smile.

"You must have the wrong number, señor. This is Geraldo Martinez of the Puerto Rican team."

"Mr. Martinez, this is Thomas Mason. I called you a few minutes ago. Sir, you are probably aware by now that something is going on in the Village, and I would like to advise you of the danger to your team, but I need to do so in person because this isn't a secure phone line. Could you meet me at your front door?"

There was a pause of three or four seconds, then the alleged Martinez said, "I certainly would be happy to do that, señor, but I do not want to disturb my team members, who as I told you before need their rest for competition today. I could meet you at 7:30, just before the 8:00 chef meeting."

"Right. I'll be at your front door at 7:30."

Mason hung up the phone and looked at Boyd. "That lying bastard. Nobody could sleep through this."

Boyd shrugged. "I'm ready to send in my men as soon as you're ready to give the order, sir."

"Look, Boyd," sighed Mason, "you've already lost six of your men—four of them permanently. I can't be ordering them in until we have a better grasp of the situation."

"You don't have to force anybody to do it," said Boyd. "I can guarantee you, I've got volunteers lining up to do the job. There's two things we can't stand: to be caught off-guard, and to lose one of our own. This SOB has done both, and now everybody wants a crack at him."

Mason considered this for a moment. "Well, *if* I were to let them go in, what would your guys do?"

Boyd folded out his area map across his arm, switched on a penlight, and pointed to the spot where half his team had taken up a position beside the tree on the southeast corner. "Okay, there's only a twenty-five-yard gap between 119 and 118"—Fitten and Montag. "We've done a little recon, and we've located what looks like a blind spot along that approach coming in from the field below. I can move two men with M-60s from behind the dumpster to here and here"—he pointed to the northeast and northwest corners of Montag. "Then two men can move into that corner, using the shadows for concealment, and one of 'em can plant a mike on the outer wall while the other guy covers him."

Mason shook his head. "But those two guys are still gonna be in the open for twenty-five feet, and we don't have any idea what kind of defensive set-up they've got in there."

"You haven't seen how these guys can run," said Boyd. "I mean, they're like lightning bolts. We're looking at sixty, ninety seconds tops, meaning they can be back in a safe position before the man inside even knows what's going on, and once the mike is planted, he won't be able to disable it without exposing himself."

"Well, it's your call," Mason said. "I can't send your men into something like this, but if you want to do it, go for it."

"Alright," said Boyd. "Of course, this plan is calculated to avoid an engagement, but what are our orders if they do engage?"

"That's a problem, because we've most likely got hostages inside, plus we don't want to unduly scare any of these people in the nearby buildings." Mason thought for a moment, his better judgment telling him that they should hold off on any such operation until they got a better understanding of the situation. "Okay," he said. "You're only to fire if fired upon, and then only at the position from which you're being fired at. You got that?"

Mason called Robbins on the radio to remind the security officers not to venture any closer to Fitten dorm, but he did not say why, and when the lights arrived, he told the men delivering them not to hook them up just yet. He stayed in the shadows across from Montag to view the operation through his infrared field glasses.

Night still hung over the Village, and the moon was covered by clouds; Mason himself, watching from 100 yards away with vision enhancement and magnification, couldn't have seen what was happening if he hadn't known. The M-60 gunner on the northwest of Montag took up his position, then the two SEALs crept toward Fitten from the playing field. Slowly, very slowly, they crawled to the edge of the shadows; in a moment they would leap up and sprint to the side of the building.

Suddenly through his field glasses, Mason saw the unmistakable red light of a laser beam making a needle-fine point on the back of one man. In a panic, he reached for the radio, but even as he did he heard the *whoosh!* of a silenced weapon, then the cry of the man who'd been hit. The second one turned to look at his comrade writhing in pain, and in an instant he knew that there could be no help for him. He jumped up and started to sprint back into the darkness, but he got no more than two steps when the back of his head was illuminated by another laser light.

This time no one heard the almost-silent weapon, but they all saw the SEAL tumble over, dead in his tracks. Thinking quickly, Mason glanced at the gunner beside Montag, and he could see the man looking for a target. But there was none; only the dark mass of Fitten dorm, as quiet as it had been a minute before. "Baby Sitter, Big Wolf," he commanded over his radio. "Hold your fire, and withdraw to McMillan Street!"

"Damn it," he muttered aloud, looking up at the windows of Montag to see if any of the people inside realized what had happened. It didn't appear that they did. He knew he should have allowed time to set up negotiations with the men inside, but he'd given in to an impulse to take action as quickly as possible. The men holding Fitten, whoever they were, didn't behave like crazies or passionate zealots who might undo themselves at any moment with a sloppy mistake; they had all the markings of cold, calculating professionals with a clearly defined game plan.

He picked up the phone and dialed. Still maintaining the Puerto Rican ruse, the man who answered sounded more irate than ever.

Mason tried to stay calm in spite of everything. "Sir, this is Thomas Mason again," he said. "I am with Village Security," he lied, not about to disclose his actual role, "assigned to protect you and your athletes, and I'm afraid there's been a tragic mistake."

Now the man at the other end of the line laughed coldly. "Well, Mr. Village Security, I don't think you've done too good of a job, do you? My people certainly do not feel secure. As a matter of fact, it looks like some men were shot just a moment ago—what kind of Village is this?"

Mason gritted his teeth. "What can we do to put you at ease?"

"That's the language I like to hear," answered the other man. "Alright, to begin with, I suggest you keep your toy soldiers from trying to come where they are not invited."

"Sir, again, we are only trying to ensure safety in our area. That was the mission of the men who were shot, and like I say, it was a tragic mistake."

"A tragic mistake for you," the man said. "And if you persist in these activities, it will be a tragic mistake for the guests I have here under my protection. Don't insult my intelligence, Mr. Mason—we know what you were doing. So stay away from my territory."

"And what is your territory?"

"Our territory is this dormitory, the two surrounding buildings, and everything within 100 feet of them. I expect you to pull back your troops immediately, and to empty these two adjacent buildings within the hour. You have my permission to transport the athletes on buses or whatever conveyance you find, then you will send two men into each building. I want every curtain opened and every light left on, so that there will be no surprises."

"Alright, but—"

"Hold on, I'm not finished. You see the trees on the street in front of this building?"

"I see them."

"These are inside the boundaries of my territory as well, and here is what I want you to do. You are to send a crew of no more than eight men with chain saws to remove those trees immediately in front of Fitten, and any trees within fifteen meters of the building on all sides. I mean remove them completely, so that nothing is left but stumps."

"But there must be a dozen of those trees, and they're fifty years old or more!"

"Listen," said the man with growing impatience, "I know that you Americans care more for plants than you do for humans, but if you do not do what I say, there will be painful consequences for our guests. How do you think they will feel if they learn that the man charged with protecting them does not think enough of their lives to chop down a few trees?"

"By guests, I assume you mean hostages?"

"I will not argue over language with you," said the other man.

"And just how many 'guests' do you have, Mr.—?"

"If you do your homework, you'll figure that out; as for my name, that's not important."

"Is it Drabeznic?"

"If you want it to be."

From the tone of the answer, Mason knew he was right. Or at least, he had identified the name which the man had used when he entered the Village as coach of the Bosnian handball team. The strange facts about the team itself made plenty of sense now: the bus crash, the replacement of the players who qualified with others who could never have won a championship. . . .

"You need to get busy," Drabeznic was saying. "It is now twenty minutes to five—let's see. . . . Until 6:00 a.m., we will see to it that no one is hurt. That includes our guests, the men cutting down the trees, the men clearing the buildings, and the athletes being removed—provided you proceed immediately to fulfill these requests. Is that clear?"

"That's clear," said Mason. "Let me give you my cellular phone number so you can contact me."

As soon as the man who went by the name of Drabeznic had the number, the line went dead. Mason wondered if his men had a surprise waiting for them inside one of the buildings; after what had just happened with the SEALs, he couldn't afford the same mistake again.

With the four remaining men of his six-man squad, Boyd showed up, his face drawn. Mason explained the plan of action to him, then added an idea of his own: "I've got something else for your guys to do while they're busy opening curtains and blinds. . . ."

Boyd liked Mason's idea when he heard it, and asked, "Why don't we go ahead and cut off electricity and phone lines to Fitten for good measure?"

"Hold your horses." As capable as Boyd had proven himself in his career, Mason was glad this hothead wasn't in command now. "First of all, we need the phone lines because right now that's the only way we've got to communicate with them, and the electricity would just piss them off. So don't do anything until I tell you!" Boyd nodded his head.

After he'd dismissed Boyd, Mason called Robbins on the radio with a list of requests. First of all, he should have Plant Operations dispatch an eight-man crew to take down the trees, and order the security officers on McMillan to move out. Then he should put enough buses on Sixth and Eighth streets to hold all the people billeted in Montag and Fulmer, with a contingent of security personnel to help them make their way safely to the buses, and then to the main dining hall—which would mean clearing it of all the detainees they'd picked up earlier and removing them to a place of Robbins's choosing. After that, he needed to set up a temporary security command post in a building close to Fitten; Mason suggested the Manufacturing Research Center, or MARC. And finally, he should obtain any information in the Village Security files on Hakija Drabeznic of the Bosnian handball team.

All of this had to be arranged in the next seventy-five minutes, at the end of which Robbins would meet him in front of Montag with the file on Drabeznic; in the meantime, Mason himself had plenty to do.

He called Aaron on his radio and ordered him to report for instructions on clearing Fulmer Residence Hall while he did the same in Montag. Then he thought of Steve Kirk, who had most likely been advised by someone at Village Security about the ongoing events on McMillan Street. Now he dialed the Village Managing Director's number and gave him an update. As they spoke, he remembered their conversation in Barcelona when they'd discussed the possibility of this very thing happening in the Atlanta Olympic Village. Now the thing had come.

"I'm sure the media will get wind of this any minute," Mason continued, "if they haven't already."

"I was in the middle of preparing a statement for them when you called. Blanchot's been informed, of course, and—"

"I hope someone has informed the President by now."

"The President. . . ? Of the United States?"

"Yeah, Steve," said Mason with a sigh, "that's how serious this thing is."

19

By the time Aaron arrived and Mason gave him his instructions for clearing Fulmer, activity in the area had picked up considerably.

First, the ten security cars had started a slow migration up McMillan, east on Eighth, and south on Hemphill toward the MARC. Then Plant Operations had arrived with four trucks. Working swiftly, the workers unloaded saws, ropes, and other equipment, and moved the unused lighting equipment across the street to the edge of the Couch Building. Their foreman began calculating how to bring down the trees without damaging any power lines or adjacent buildings: it was the kind of operation that would normally take all day, and Drabeznic expected it done in little more than an hour.

Mason felt a twinge when he heard the first chain saw crank up and begin eating into an ancient tree, but it surprised him that Drabeznic hadn't required a perimeter larger than 100 feet, which would have entailed cutting four more. Maybe he realized how much more time this would take, and didn't have the patience to wait it out.

As the buses began to pull up Sixth and Eighth streets, out of sight from Fitten but visible at either end of McMillan, Mason walked across the street to Montag. From the sidewalk he could see faces pressed against the door and windows. Any one of them could be a terrorist. *There's only one way to find out*, he thought as he walked up the steps and pushed the door open.

The many athletes and officials in the brightly lit lobby parted to let him enter, but as soon as he'd managed to squeeze in, dozens of people began shouting questions at him. He put two fingers between his lips and whistled shrilly. The room fell silent. "Where is the chef de mission?" he demanded.

A man came forward and introduced himself as the chief official for the Swiss team. "Are you going to explain to us what is going on, sir?" he asked, with a tone of authority in his voice.

The last thing Mason wanted was a panic, which was exactly what he would create if he announced that a group of heavily armed terrorists had taken control of the building next door. "That will all be explained later," he said calmly. "What's important now is to evacuate this building in an orderly fashion. Could I have your assistance in getting this done?"

The man nodded his head.

"Alright, then, I want you to move everyone quietly to the southwest windows here on the first floor, and have them climb out single-file through the two windows. Please do not attempt to bring any of your personal belongings or allow any of your people to: just leave the building in as quick but as orderly a fashion as you can." The other people in the lobby, many of them dressed in running suits and some in ordinary clothes, pressed in around Mason and the chef, listening intently.

"There will be personnel on the ground to help everyone out and lead them past Freeman dorm to Sixth Street, where they will begin boarding buses. They should proceed single-file into the first one, with the first person in line taking the next-to-last seat on the right and the next person sitting beside them, then the next two on the left and so on—only two people to a seat. They are to sit with their heads down so that they cannot be seen from the outside. When that bus is filled, it will leave for the main dining hall while the next bus pulls up and begins boarding."

The chef, who had taken out a pad and begun writing down these instructions, looked up at him. "And what will we do when we get to the dining hall?"

"Then you'll await further word." With that he left the Swiss chef de mission to do his job while he climbed the stairs to the top floor and began checking the area. He passed a number of athletes on the way, but nothing about them or the area seemed amiss, so he got back on the radio to Boyd and told him to send in two men.

Nearly an hour remained until sunrise. The Plant Operations men had removed the trees directly in front of Fitten and started on the others close by, the sounds of their equipment loudly buzzing in the morning air. Montag and Fulmer were now vacant, their windows open and their lights on as Drabeznic had instructed, but the other nearby dorms remained full with restless athletes waiting to be moved to safety.

The people removed from Montag and Fulmer had gathered at the main dining hall a few blocks away on Ferst, where NBC had already set up cameras. For once, they would have the scoop on their competitors. Steve Kirk arrived and announced that he'd arranged the relocation of the teams to Emory University until he could locate facilities to house them; then he allowed a short question-and-answer session. It didn't surprise him when the first athlete asked about the morning's competition schedule.

"I have spoken with Jason Blanchot of the IOC," he said as the cameras rolled, "and he has instructed me to announce that all Olympic events have been postponed, pending further notification." This set off a barrage of murmurs and more questions, most of which Kirk either couldn't or wouldn't answer.

Blanchot, Hans Bliecher, and other officials of the IOC, USOC, and ACOG had assembled in a central "war room" command center at ACOG Headquarters less than two miles away. They had established a direct line for communicating with the Vice President of the United States, to whom the President had assigned the task of acting as Olympic liaison.

The group that had gathered in the Cabinet Room of the White House West Wing went by the official name of "Vice President's Terrorist Response Team," but the President had taken charge himself. The Attorney General was prepared to send a unit of the FBI Hostage Rescue Team to Atlanta, but the Pentagon maintained that with Mason and the SEALs already on hand, it was the job of Defense to coordinate security activities. Mason's commander, General Norbert Helms, would communicate with him via a secure phone at the MARC—secure, that is, from everyone except Defense Intelligence, which would tap all lines, including Mason's cellular.

At the MARC, teams of analysts and technicians had arrived with the first wave of security personnel, and were setting up to tap the phone lines at Fitten dorm. They also prepared to do thermography readings on the building to indicate the movement of bodies inside, but so far they didn't have anything conclusive.

Mason met Robbins at the corner of Sixth Street beside Freeman. Dozens of athletes peered out at them through the windows, some of them knocking on the glass for their attention. Though he couldn't do anything for them right now, Mason planned to announce to Drabeznic that they were going to empty the other dorms near Fitten, Fulmer, and Montag.

The two men walked around to the southeast side of Freeman, beyond the ring of pine trees that surrounded Couch Field on the south and east sides. Robbins told him that Gen. Helms expected to talk to him as soon as he'd had his 6:00 conversation with Drabeznic, then gave him a hostage count: so far, the tally included six Americans, four Canadians, eight British, four French, and seven Germans—all female, except for the one German male.

"You ever figure out what the male was doing in the female quarters?" Mason asked.

In spite of the tense moment, Robbins could not help smiling just a bit. "No, but I think I can guess. Anyway, just before I left the MARC to come over here, I got a call from the Russians—two more girls missing. That makes thirty-one people, all athletes as far as we know." He sighed. "And of course we've got seventy-six athletes and forty-nine officials for Puerto Rico, who are all still presumably in Fitten, making another 125: a total of 156 people."

"One hundred fifty-six!" Mason shook his head slowly.

"And we still haven't heard back from all the teams," Robbins said.

"Alright," replied Mason resolutely. "What you got for me on our guy?"

Robbins handed him a folder containing various routine forms filled out by the Bosnian NOC before any of its team members entered the Village, an official biography of Drabeznic, and a 5x8 photograph of a man with handsome dark features, a mustache, a prominent nose, black hair, and a slight smile that showed his gleaming teeth.

"This is it?" Mason asked after looking at the picture for a moment. He scanned down the bio sheet with Robbins's flashlight. "Let's see. . . born Srebrenica, 10/16/55. . . blah blah blah. . . handball team, University of Sarajevo, '73 to—" He looked up at Robbins. "This is just pure bullshit."

"'Fiction' might be a nicer way of putting it," said Robbins.

Mason looked at his watch. "Time for another chat."

This time there was no pretense of maintaining the Geraldo Martinez ruse; the voice at the other end of the line simply purred, "Yes, Mason?"

Mason reported on the clearing of the nearby buildings and the street, then added, "The men are still trying to get all the trees removed—I think we're going to need a little more time for that."

"Yes, I can see. Very well, but they must be finished by 8:00 a.m., because at that time I intend to hold a press conference."

"Oh, really?" said Mason, trying to hide his irritation at this latest development.

"Yes. You'd be amazed how busy I've been in the past hour, taking calls from those nice media personnel. I've told CNN, ABC, CBS, and the BBC that each of them can put one cameraman and one reporter on the east side of the field behind this building at precisely 8:00 a.m." He chuckled. "That is, if it's alright with you. I've told them I will allow only those four—no more, no less—and they have to share their wealth with others through a media pool."

Mason knew better than to oppose him on this. "That's fine," he said, "but a press conference is going to take more time, and don't you want to get this thing resolved as quickly as possible? I can start arranging to meet your demands whenever you let me know what they are."

"Oh, no, no, no!" said Drabeznic with a little laugh. "Before I ask anything of you, I want to give you a little present when we hold the press conference."

"You mean you're going to release your guests?" Mason asked coolly.

"Some, perhaps—if you behave yourselves. But I do have one demand now. Of course I cannot invite the media into my temporary home, so I must address them from a great distance, and in order to do this, I need someone to place an amplifier and speaker at the eastern edge of the field and bring me a microphone."

"Just a mike, nothing else?"

"That's all. If you will send someone carrying only a white flag and the microphone to the back of the building from across the field, we will let down a rope on which he can place the equipment. As long as your man does nothing foolish, this will take place without incident."

"Alright," said Mason. "Someone will bring it at 7:30. In the meantime, we've got people holed up in all these dorms around you. Do you mind if we let them leave, using the same game plan as before?"

"That would be fine. And I assume you'd like to send medics to pick up your fallen comrades as well."

"Yes. . . ."

"You are amazed by my civility, are you not, Mr. Mason? You will find that not only are we men of honor, but we are men of our word as well, so I can assure your safety and that of your medics as long as you don't try anything."

Your word doesn't mean a whole lot to me, Mason thought as he asked, "But tell me, who's 'we'?"

"I don't have time to discuss that," said Drabeznic shortly. "As you can guess, I've been up all night, and I intend to get a little rest so that I will look my best before I appear on camera. But do not make any dangerous assumptions—there is one thing you should know about my men and me. We are as vigilant as we are ruthless about protecting our safety."

With that, Drabeznic hung up, and Mason turned to Robbins. "Alright, we're gonna need an ambulance to get the bodies of those SEALs." He pulled his area map from his back pocket, held it open, and circled the vicinity of Fitten with his flashlight. "Then let's start evacuating all these dorms within a one-block radius."

Robbins took out a pad and began scrawling down names of buildings, then he looked up. "That's gotta be fifteen hundred people or more! Where are we gonna put them all?"

"That's Kirk's problem. Just call him and let him know what you're doing, then start hauling 'em over to the dining hall or wherever you want to take them—but get them out of here."

A few minutes later, the ambulance drove up to the front of Fitten and two medics jumped out. Moving stealthily, they ran over and put out a stretcher for the first casualty, and when they had carried the body to the ambulance, they returned for the second one. Within less than a minute, they had completed their work and driven away.

Meanwhile, Robbins and Mason walked across Couch Field to the MARC, which had by now become a busy command center.

The four-story building offered not only a good view of Fitten but a spacious layout, making it an ideal—if a bit bizarre—command post. A catwalk from Ferst Drive approached the red metal and tinted glass structure, and inside it looked like a cross between a factory, a prison, and a dance club. At the center was a large vertical open area with catwalks on either side, which reminded Mason of the setting in *Jailhouse Rock* where Elvis Presley sang his famous hit.

By now, the process of claiming the building for security's purposes had begun: desks were moved around; extra phone lines connected; conference rooms established for coordinating between Village, city, state, and federal forces; secure areas found for storing weapons; and surveillance equipment installed. Everywhere there were people, some in Village Security or local law-enforcement uniforms, some in combat fatigues or SWAT gear, some in the business suits of plainclothes agents.

Down a hall to the left, three Village Security officers were busy setting up an office for Mason's use across from the Rapid Prototyping and Manufacturing Lab, where Michelle and the others on his team had already set up shop. Besides a desk and PC, he would have a tape recorder, a fax machine, and six TVs. Three of these would be on cable, for following the media reports; and three others would be hooked up to closed-circuit cameras on buildings around Fitten. But security hadn't had an opportunity to mount the cameras, nor had any of this equipment been installed in the room except for the desk, which had already been there. "Sounds great," said Mason after a Village Security officer gave him a quick briefing on the plans. "Where's the coffee machine?"

"We'll have one in within the hour, sir," said the officer, even though Mason had only been joking. He pointed toward a phone on the desk with a yellow stick-on labeled *Washington*. "We'll also be installing more phone lines, but for now, you've got your direct link."

"The red telephone," said Mason, sitting down at the desk and looking at it, even though it was black. He picked it up, and instead of a dial tone he heard men speaking in low voices.

"Mason?" said a voice, its muffled tone indicating that he was on speaker phone.

"Yes, sir."

"Norbert Helms here. How are you, Tom?"

"Fine, sir. Were you able to get that last conversation with Drabeznic?"

"Loud and clear. Sounds like he's trying to stall for time."

"It does, sir."

"Well, you just keep trying to find out what his demands are. We need all the information we can get on these bastards."

Steve Kirk set up a speaker-phone conversation of his own with the commanding generals of the Centennial Olympic Games, but before he did, he spoke to someone who'd been much on his mind of late: Michelle. As usual in their short relationship—which, other than that one dream-like night, had consisted of stolen glances and guarded interchanges in the presence of others—she made the first move by calling him from the MARC. She was reporting on the evacuation of the dorms, she said, but they both knew this was a pretext since he'd already spoken with Robbins about that.

"So how are you holding up?" he asked. He could have put the same question to any of his other coworkers and not thought about it, but in this case he felt uncertain if he should even ask it.

"I'm just looking forward to when this is all over," she said. Then after a pause she added, "So I can get on with my life."

He wondered what that meant. Did she mean so that she could move on, and forget about everything that had happened in the Village—*everything*—or did she mean. . . .

"Yeah, I feel the same way," he replied. "You know, if there's anything I can do for you, just tell me."

"It's enough just to hear your voice, and to know you're there," she said.

He carried the good feeling her words had given him when he spoke to Blanchot and Bliecher, a fortunate thing because they were even harder to deal with than usual in the present situation.

"Gentlemen," he began, "there are certain decisions that need to be made very quickly. As we speak, Village Security is evacuating approximately 1,500 athletes from the vicinity of Fitten Residence Hall, to be moved to the main dining hall, and from there to Emory University. However, that is a temporary solution, and we need to find more permanent accommodations. Given that the city's hotels, motels, and other facilities are taxed beyond capacity at present, that won't be an easy task, and though I have a few ideas of my own, I need to discuss them with you before I take action."

He could hear Blanchot starting to speak, but Hans Bliecher interrupted in his thick, accented growl. "Steve, I don't see why they couldn't have just stayed where they were. The only building in danger is Fitten and maybe the ones on either side, and security has already evacuated those."

Kirk grimaced. "Hans, with all due respect, it would be out of the question to leave the athletes where they are. Security needs room to maneuver, and what would we do if an athlete got hit by a stray bullet?"

"I see your point, Steve," said Blanchot's voice.

They discussed various possible sites for temporary housing, including the Clark-Atlanta University Center, Fort McPherson in East Point, and other locations further outside the city limits. Since Blanchot proved so cooperative, Kirk addressed his next—and much more explosive—item of business to him. "But you may have a larger question to deal with, Mr. Blanchot." Crossing his legs and leaning back in his desk chair, Kirk tapped his foot nervously. "We have almost 12,000 more athletes and officials in the Village, and though they don't appear to be in any danger right now, I would suggest that we evacuate them to min-imize the confusion here."

"Wait a minute!" Bliecher yelled. "What are you going to do, start emptying out hotels so you can put them up? You might as well just put out a bulletin over NBC: 'That's it, the Olympics are finished!' No way, Steve—the thing to do now is to deal with this situation as quickly as possible and get on with the Games."

Kirk ignored Bliecher. In the eight months since "the Butcher" had assumed the helm of ACOG, he'd had to put up with his dictatorial ways; but in just a few days, his tenure would be over. "Mr. Blanchot," said Kirk, "the best possible way to bring a quick and safe ending to the present crisis is to do everything we can to make the job of security eas-ier. For that reason I can only give my strongest recommendation that we clear the Village of any non-essential personnel." He paused. "Failing that, I'd say for sure we need to empty out the Blue Zone," the western portion of the Village.

"Steve, I understand your concern," said Blanchot soothingly, "but let's give it a little more time. If I'm not mistaken, the Blue Zone hous-es over 4,000 athletes." He gave a nervous little laugh. "We don't have any place to put them, you know, and if we start moving them now, it's just as Hans says—the Games might as well be over."

Recognizing this condescending tone, Kirk wanted to slam the phone down, but instead he said, "Yes, sir."

"Anyway," Blanchot added, "I believe this problem will be taken care of within the day. Now, you want to talk about a really serious con-cern, think about me—I'm the one that has to deal with Ira Greenberg of NBC, and is he pissed!"

20

Plant Operations finished up their work as best they could, leaving a yard strewn with leaves and twigs. They had to back down McMillan on their way out, because Eighth Street was clogged with buses moving hundreds upon hundreds of athletes out of the danger zone.

At 7:30, Boyd sent a man named Miller from his unit to take the microphone across Couch Field as instructed, holding a white flag aloft. Mason watched by means of a telescopic TV camera that the CIA technicians had installed on the roof of the MARC, which relayed its image instantaneously via satellite to a secure listening post in the Pentagon basement, and from there to Gen. Helms at the White House.

The basement of Fitten had no windows or outside doors, but when the camera zoomed in closer, Mason could see that every portal on the first floor above was covered with what looked like wide strips of metal. He thought of the welding torches now—but what about the metal itself? Had they brought that with them too?

The barrel of a rifle poked out between two of the slats on a second-floor window to the left, and to the right he saw the same. Then a hand emerged from the middle window and lowered a rope. "As soon as this rope reaches eye level," said a voice from the floor above, audible through a button-sized listening device in Miller's vest, "tie the microphone firmly to it as quickly as possible."

Mason glanced at the top of his screen to see the source of the voice, which sounded like the one he'd heard on the phone. For a moment he glimpsed a face hidden behind a ski mask, and from the position of the hands he could tell it was not the man lowering the rope. Mason knew instinctively that he had just seen the man called Drabeznic.

Miller knew better than to waste any time, and as soon as the rope came down to him he wrapped it around the microphone several times and tied it firmly. "Okay," he said, but by then the rope had begun its journey back up.

Twenty minutes later, four vans pulled slowly up Ferst Drive to the east of the ball field, and from them emerged eight people, four with notepads and pens and the other four with camera equipment. The live feeds had already been brought over from the Village Press Center, some 400 yards to the east, and the cameramen quickly set up their equipment while the four commentators waited patiently without speaking. Everyone looked nervous, well aware that as the designated media pool, they would serve as the eyes and ears of the entire planet. The men and women of the press glanced continuously in the direction of Fitten dorm 250 feet away, wondering what the next few minutes would bring.

By now Robbins, a couple dozen Village Security officers, and a small contingent of FBI agents had gathered alongside the media. Boyd and the SEALs had taken up a position behind the Main Electric Substation a few yards away, and all along the ring of trees surrounding Couch Field on the Sixth Street and Ferst Drive sides stood National Guardsmen and Village Security officers. Mason watched the telecast from inside the MARC, communicating periodically with Robbins and Boyd by radio.

At five minutes to eight, the newscasters stepped forward and began speaking before the cameras; then, at precisely 8:00 a.m., a short blast from what sounded like a foghorn announced the beginning of the press conference.

"Ladies and gentlemen of the world," said Drabeznic's amplified voice, "as you probably know by now, there is trouble at these Olympic Games. The nature of that trouble, and of the humble requests we are making in order to end it, will be revealed to you in greater detail at a later time. What you are about to see is an unsolicited gift to the Commonwealth of Puerto Rico and the Federal Republic of Germany, and should serve for all nations of the world as a demonstration of our good faith and our ability to negotiate a peaceful conclusion to what we know is a discomfort to us all."

A rope ladder dropped out of a second-floor window, bouncing in the air three feet above the ground before coming to a stop. The back of a man clad in the red, white, and blue of the Puerto Rican team, with a sheet of paper bearing a large numeral *1*, emerged at the window, and he began a cautious climb down. As he came into view, it looked like he had a rope or chain around his neck, connecting him to the next figure, identified with a *2* taped to his back, who stepped out onto the ladder as the first man continued to descend.

One by one they came out, all tethered and numbered like runners in a marathon, moving slowly. When the seventh man emerged from the window, four others were standing below him while the other two stretched across the field in the direction of the press and security forces on the other side; once No. 7 made it to the ground, they moved ahead another five feet.

It looked like No. 1 had something else around his neck besides the rope, an olive-green bag the size of a baseball. Wires from it wound around the length of rope that stretched to numbers 2 and 3, but neither of them had this goiter-like object around their necks. Number 4 did, though, and so did No. 7 and No. 10, and so on with every third person.

Still more came, a seemingly endless procession of men and a few women. Out of place at the middle, but still numbered like the others, was a young man in the red, gold, and black of the German team. He stood out still more as the Puerto Ricans continued to emerge: 62. . . 63. . . 64. . . . By now No. 1 had long made it to the other side of the field, but he stood at a distance from the newspeople and security personnel, waiting for instructions from the man inside Fitten Hall. Meanwhile the others lined up beside him, shoulder-to-shoulder.

Finally a man with white streaks in his hair, bearing the number 109, stepped out onto the ladder. As he reached the ground, first one and then another large laundry basket fell out the window, and he reached down to pick them up.

Mason counted ninety male athletes and officials of the Puerto Rican contingent, eighteen females, and the one German. That left eighteen more Puerto Rican women inside. *Gift, hell!* he thought. *He just had too many hostages on his hands.*

As the last man joined his compatriots on the other side of the field, the voice from Fitten called out: "Is Mr. Mason present?" No one moved, and Mason held his breath. After fifteen seconds Drabeznic said, "Alright, then—someone else do the honors: please approach No. 109 and disarm the device around his neck."

Robbins started to do it, but one of the FBI agents stepped forward first. As the camera focused in on No. 109, Mason instantly knew that this must be the real Geraldo Martinez, Chef de Mission of the Puerto Rican team. He also saw the unique detonating mechanism Martinez wore around his neck.

Ashen-faced, Martinez stood watching the agent. *Hopefully this guy can defuse it*, Mason thought. Only his suspicion of Drabeznic's tactics told him that nothing would happen when the wires were cut. A dramatic moment like this one would serve Drabeznic's purposes with the media; blowing up 110 people wouldn't.

Without any outward appearance of hesitation, the agent brought out a pair of wire cutters, snipped the wires—and as Mason had hoped, nothing happened.

"Very good," Drabeznic called out over the microphone. "Now, take the baskets from No. 109 and set them on the ground. Excellent, excellent. Alright, then: you and two other men can cut loose these devices from our former guests' necks, and place them in the baskets."

Two other agents came forward with wire cutters, and as the three men worked, Drabeznic continued speaking. "Ever since they came under our care here, our guests have worn these antipersonnel devices, similar to a small satchel charge, which can be detonated by electrical impulse. As soon as these men complete their work, I would like No. 1 and No. 109 to bring these baskets over to us, as per instructions they have already received."

The athletes who'd had the explosive weights around their necks sighed with relief when they came off, even though the ropes remained. When the operation had finished, Drabeznic ordered that numbers 1 and 109 have their ropes cut, then each walked across the field to Fitten with the baskets. Two more ropes dropped out of the window, and they tied the baskets firmly to them. The men inside the building began pulling them up as the two turned around and walked rapidly back.

"I hope," Drabeznic continued, "that none of the men who cut the wires—FBI agents, I suppose?—have seen fit to slip one of our little toys into their pockets. We can count, and if we find even one of these missing, there will be severe consequences. As you may have guessed, we still have a few women staying with us, and they need jewelry of their own."

By now the two Puerto Ricans had made it back across the field, and Drabeznic instructed the first FBI agent to remove a single Polaroid photograph from the right front pocket of No. 109's warmup suit. The man walked up to Martinez and reached into his pocket.

"Now, sir, would you please approach the members of the press and let them see this picture?"

The agent glanced at it himself, and from his expression Mason could tell that the world was in for an ugly sight. Moving to within three feet of the cameras, he held it up. It showed two dozen or more women, all dressed in the warm-ups of their national teams, huddled together in a communal shower. They didn't have gags, but there were ropes tied around their hands and necks, and many of them had on incendiary devices like the ones just removed from the released hostages.

"Now, before you become too alarmed," Drabeznic went on, "know that these women are perfectly safe, and will remain so on two conditions. First of all, no one is to breach our security perimeter unless invited to do so; secondly, we will soon be making requests of certain nations, and we expect them to honor these. Otherwise, the consequences for our guests could be dire: any one of my men is capable of setting off these explosives with remote detonators."

He waited for these words to sink in, then continued. "We don't expect to do anything like that, for we believe that the authorities will prove themselves as reasonable as we are. Our next press conference will be at 10:00 a.m., and at that time we will discuss some of our requirements; in the meantime, I must request that you ladies and gentlemen of the media vacate the premises. You may continue to film the exterior of this dormitory building, but you must do so from a distance; or you can leave your camera equipment on site until you return at precisely 9:55. I'm sure it will be safe with all these security personnel around. That is all."

The CNN correspondent raised a hand.

"There will be no questions at this time," growled the voice of Drabeznic, then more softly he added, "However, you will find me at all times more than willing to assist you with any information I can reasonably provide. Governments will no doubt attempt to label us as 'terrorists,' and my wish is to provide twenty-four hour news coverage of these events, which should show the falsehood of such claims. Good day."

The Puerto Ricans trotted off through the thick pine trees toward ambulances that had now pulled along Ferst Drive. When they realized they were safe, many of them—strong athletes accustomed to putting their bodies through stress beyond the capacity of most ordinary people—collapsed to the ground. The ropes still holding them together made this awkward for the ones who remained standing, but a group of medics waiting on the other side of the trees ran forward and began untying them.

On instructions from Mason via his headset, Robbins walked up hurriedly behind Martinez and touched his arm. "Mr. Martinez?" he asked.

The older man nodded tiredly.

"Could you please come with me? Our operations commander would like to ask you some questions."

Martinez, a dignified man who would have looked as comfortable in a three-piece suit as the warm-ups he wore, rubbed the spot around his neck where the rope had chafed his skin and said, "Gladly."

As he watched the two men walking toward the MARC with a cordon of security officers around them to protect them from the media, Mason's cellular phone rang.

"Mr. Mason," said Drabeznic's voice into the phone, "I was sorry not to see you at the press conference." He laughed. "Then again, maybe you were there, and you just look a bit. . . different from what I'd imagined. At any rate, I have two more requests of you."

"Go ahead."

"First of all, I would like you to arrange for me to speak directly with the Chancellor of the Federal Republic of Germany. Can you do that for me?"

"Well, I—"

"I'm sure your contact at the Pentagon can take care of it."

"My what?"

"Mr. Mason, I'm not a fool! I know that this phone is being tapped, and that every word we speak is being relayed instantly to Washington. Hello, generals!" he added more loudly. "Hello, Mr. President!"

Now how would he know that? Mason asked himself. *Lucky guess, probably.* "Alright, I'll see what I can do. What else?"

"I would like a firmer commitment than that."

"Look, Drabeznic, in case you haven't figured it out, I'm willing to do whatever's necessary to end this thing as quickly as we can. If that means you need to talk to Michael Jackson, I'll do whatever's in my power—"

"That won't be necessary at present," said Drabeznic with a dry tone, "but I'll keep it in mind. Alright then, here is the other thing. Now that we've gotten all these buses and athletes out of here, I want to get a look inside these two adjacent buildings, and for that purpose I am sending two men to inspect each. I expect them to find everything as we discussed previously, and I expect them to return unscathed. For every one of them that is apprehended or otherwise harmed, two of these lovely young ladies in our care will pay for your indiscretion—and trust me, I make a very broad interpretation of the phrase *apprehended or otherwise harmed.* I don't think I even need to ask you if you understand."

Once again Drabeznic hung up without saying anything more. Mason called Boyd on his radio with orders to let the two men enter Montag and Fulmer.

They spoke on secure Motorola models, but Mason had instructed everyone to use code language as much as possible just in case Drabeznic managed to tap into their transmissions. For this reason, Boyd asked, "Request permission to turn up radios." On Mason's orders, when his men had swept the two residence halls, they'd installed wireless listening devices on each floor, which could be activated and deactivated upon command from the receiving unit located in the MARC; now the SEAL team leader wanted to make use of this equipment.

"Negative," Mason answered. If the terrorists were as well-prepared as they seemed to be, they would be sweeping the buildings for bugs, and it wouldn't do for them to pick up a strange signal inside Fulmer or Montag.

After signing off with Boyd, Mason checked with Gen. Helms to make sure that Washington had gotten Drabeznic's request about the Germans, and to inform him that he would be interviewing Martinez. Next he instructed Michelle to post two guards outside his door and keep everyone out, and he gave her his cellular phone just in case Drabeznic should call. Then he turned off his radio, and re-routed all the phones on his desk except the "red telephone" so he could speak to the Puerto Rican chef in peace.

Robbins escorted Martinez in, then left to join a team who would interview the released hostages before they went to Emory. Mason had a blanket brought to Martinez while another assistant poured the chef a cup of coffee, after which the door was shut and they were alone. They chatted for a minute, then Mason took out a notepad and pen, and asked permission to start the tape recorder on his desk while Martinez described the events of the preceding night and morning.

"At a little after 1:30 this morning," Martinez began, "I was awakened suddenly by someone entering my room on the first floor of our quarters. My first thought was that one of our celebrating team members had gotten drunk and been locked up in jail somewhere, and that my assistant was waking me to take care of it. This was quickly dispelled when someone shone a light straight into my eyes, put a gun up to my cheekbone, and said, 'If you do not say anything, you will not be hurt.' "

"Did you get a look at your captors, then or later?"

Martinez shook his head. "They were all wearing black ski masks, and every man I saw had the same uniform: some sort of military outfit, all black, with black sneakers, and of course the ski mask. I can't even say how many of them there were."

"Okay, go on."

"Of course I was terribly frightened," Martinez continued, "and though my first reaction would have been to scream, I held my tongue and stood up while they began to put duct tape over my mouth. Then they placed my hands behind my back, and taped those as well. I was left in my room with one man guarding me, and I watched as more and more of our male athletes and officials were brought in two at a time, bound and gagged. As each pair came in, the guards pushed them to the floor while I remained standing.

"I began to lose track of time. This process lasted maybe thirty or forty-five minutes, making it 2:00 or 2:15 by then. When the room was more or less full—say, twenty men or so—we and the remainder of the males on our floor were taken into the latrines at the center of the building. One of our captors told us that the same thing was happening to the other men on the second and third floors, and to the women on the fourth floor."

Mason had planned to ask questions, but Martinez gave such a thorough report that he didn't want to distract him with interruptions.

"Now, I don't know how long we spent in the showers, though I suppose it must have been three hours or more. It seemed like an eternity. We were instructed to sit down on the damp tile—some men leaned up against the walls, others against one another—and they taped our feet as well and began stringing that rope with the explosive devices around our necks. There were two doors on either end of the bathroom, one of which was closed and locked, we were told, and the other one open, with a guard sitting outside it.

"Hours passed, and they changed the guards several times. Finally, I think it must have been the man who spoke to the press this morning, he walked in and explained to us about the bombs, then said, 'If one of you attempts to escape—any single one of you—all of you will instantaneously die.' From then until the wire was cut, that sentence was all I could think of, Mr. Mason. I myself have lived a good life, but as I looked about at my team members, some of them no more than eighteen years old, it frightened me that they might end up just like those Israelis in Munich."

Mason waited while Martinez collected himself. "After awhile they took the tape off our mouths in order that we could drink some water they passed around. Having the tape peeled off was extremely painful, but we were instructed not to say anything, and of course no one did. Then they asked if we had any questions. At first the men were afraid to speak, but finally one young man said that he had to use the toilet. Then the lead terrorist—the one who spoke to the press—told him he'd just have to do it right there. By the time we were released, some of the men had been forced to foul their own pants. It was a degrading experience, and soon the stench became unbearable."

"But you all came out in fresh uniforms," said Mason.

"Well, they went through our rooms, and gave everyone a set of the warm-ups that Adidas had provided. They untied each man long enough for him to clean himself up if necessary and put on his clothes—there were two armed men watching, so there was no chance of escape. I suppose they wanted us to look as good as possible in front of the TV cameras."

"What do you know about the female athletes that are still in there?"

"I was told as we were leaving that the female athletes were treated in a like manner, and then the photographs were put into my pocket." He pulled back the blanket and tapped it. "I haven't even looked at them yet."

"Could I see them?"

Martinez pulled them out, and Mason walked around and glanced over his shoulder at them. Like the one he'd already seen on TV, they showed groups of women, bound but not gagged, dressed in warm-up clothes and sitting on the floor of a large white-tiled shower. Again, every other one had a bag tied around her neck. "Does this look like the same type of facility the men were held in?"

Martinez studied the pictures for a moment, then said, "Yes, all the floors are the same."

"Can you identify any of these athletes?"

"Some. There's Rodriguez, there's Colon and Barros—they're ours, but there are others that I don't know who they are. It's good they let them wear their uniforms, so we can identify the countries."

Mason thought the same thing. Even though Drabeznic wouldn't admit the number of athletes he had in captivity, he clearly wanted the nations involved to know that they had *some* people in there.

"Now, how about the German male who came out with you? Do you know anything about him?"

Martinez shook his head. "We'd never seen him until they threw him in with us."

They chatted a while longer, but Martinez seemed to have come to the end of his recollections. After all he'd been through, he needed food and sleep, so Mason informed him that the two guards outside the door would escort him down to the front desk and arrange a ride for him to join his team. Later, when he'd had a chance to rest, someone else would interview him and the other team members in case he remembered anything else of importance.

As Martinez prepared to go, he said, "Mr. Mason, I know you're doing all you can, but please in the name of God, get those women out of there."

"I will," Mason said. "I will." Then he thought of something. "Oh, by the way, there were reports of flashing blue lights in the middle of the night there, like someone was using a welding torch or something. Do your recall anything like that?"

Martinez brightened. "Yes, I could see the flashes from down the hall, and could smell—it smelled like acetylene, though I'm not the best judge of that. They were banging around in some of the rooms like they were tearing things apart or knocking equipment around. Then as we were marched out, I noticed that it looked like our bed rails were stuck up against the windows down there. On the first floor, they had some washing machines and dryers stacked up in front of the windows, which they had to move aside before they let us out. Even then there were bars in front of the windows, and I'm sure they were the slats from our beds."

Mason smiled. So he'd guessed right about the welding torches. *These are some resourceful bastards,* he thought. They had created a formidable barrier at the first floor, making any kind of assault on the building extremely difficult.

21

As Mason handed Martinez off to the guard outside the room, he switched his radio back on, and soon he had a message from Boyd. "Be advised of activities by tangos sent to inspect adjoining buildings," said the SWAT team leader, using SEAL jargon for terrorists. "Appear to have some form of gear attached to their backs."

"Baby Sitter, are you able to identify gear?"

"Negative. Resemble rucksacks."

"Roger, Baby Sitter, over."

Mason sat down at the desk, routed the phones back to him, and switched on his mobile. One of the stationary phones rang, and when he picked it up it was Robbins, who gave a report on the interviews with the released hostages in the Naval Reserve Building. The information didn't add much to what Mason had already learned from Martinez, except that Robbins had confirmed his suspicion as to how the German male came to be among the female captives. The youth had been visiting his girlfriend, and both had been taken hostage; now he was free and she remained captive.

"Alright," said Mason. "As soon as you get finished over there, report back to MARC. I need you to help my people figure out how these Bosnians—or whoever they really are—managed to get their weapons through access control."

"Will do. Listen, I think we've heard from all the teams now. Looks like we've got seven more girls in there."

"Who?"

"North Korea. They waited till after the press conference, then they called in to tell us that seven of their females were abducted from Hefner Residence Hall."

"Alright. Have you compiled a list of names, so we'll know exactly who we've got inside?"

"Just about. I'll have one by lunchtime."

"Speaking of which—"

"Yeah, I know," said Robbins. "I've already made arrangements so that whenever the man inside orders food, we can get it to him pronto. Talk to Michelle."

"Excellent."

Like clockwork, the cellular phone rang after he'd hung up with Robbins.

"Mr. Mason," said Drabeznic's voice, "what have you heard from the Germans?"

Mason looked at his watch: it was a quarter past nine, just forty-five minutes until the next press conference. "I expected you should have gotten a call by now," he said, genuinely surprised.

"I have not. Perhaps they don't understand the seriousness of the situation."

"I'll put in another call to Washington right now," Mason replied. "By the way, I didn't get a chance to tell you last time we talked, but I appreciate your gesture of letting the males depart."

"Certainly. It was an act of good faith on our part, and I'm sure you can see that we are reasonable men."

"Of course." Negotiating with a terrorist required diplomacy at all times. "But how about the rest of the women?"

"How about them?"

"Well, for starters, are they being treated well?"

Drabeznic sounded offended. "Sir, we are professionals on a mission, not rapists. These women are being treated with the same dignity with which we have treated our male guests—perhaps even a bit better since they are females—and they will be perfectly fine as long as you do nothing foolish."

"I'd like to know how we can help you get what you want, so that they can be released and you can be on your way wherever you're going."

"You're getting ahead of the script, Mason," said Drabeznic with a laugh. "All in good time—you'll just have to wait until 10:00 like the rest of the world."

"Alright then. Say, was everything okay in the other two dorms when your men inspected?"

"I don't know, was it? You should know the answer to that."

"I just wondered," said Mason coolly, "because we noticed they had some kind of backpacks on. What were those for, if I might ask?"

"Oh, I don't know, Mr. Mason. You may have to go into those

buildings to find out, though of course they're off-limits to you, and you know what that means, don't you?" *Click.*

Mason picked up the Pentagon line. "General Helms?"

"Right here, Tom."

"Sir, I'm concerned because—"

"I know, I know, we heard. The moment we got Drabeznic's request, we relayed it directly to the Secretary of State, and as far as I know, he got on the horn to Berlin immediately."

"Well, I just hope the Germans call back soon, sir. I don't think this guy intends to play around."

Jason Blanchot and Hans Bliecher had shut themselves up in Blanchot's office, away from the ACOG war room. "Look, Jason," said Bliecher, "we've been on hold for competitions all morning. Tell me what I'm supposed to do about the Games for the rest of today."

"What do you mean?" asked Blanchot sharply.

Bliecher shrugged. "In Munich, they went on during the day of the terrorist attack."

"Yes, and then they canceled them that night. No, we've got the world reaction to think about. If we get this thing over with tonight, we'll re-schedule over the remaining time."

Bliecher was incredulous. "Re-schedule? That would be like re-scheduling a dozen World Cups."

Blanchot waved a hand. "Start running simulations on your computer. Do one with the assumption that we start back tomorrow, another if we have to postpone until Thursday, the first of August." He narrowed his eyes at Bliecher. "And tell me something, Hans. Why in the hell did you cancel the Games insurance?"

"Because," Bliecher sputtered, "it was costing us another damn $20 million, that's why."

"And now we'll probably end up losing $200 or $300 million— you're quite the financial wizard."

Bliecher folded his arms. "You were aware of that decision, Jason. I did not make it in a vacuum. If you're looking for a scapegoat, sue the U.S. government—they're the ones who had the overall responsibility for this security."

"I might as well try to sue the Pope." Blanchot glanced up at a bank of televisions lining the walls. "Speaking of lawsuits, Ira Greenberg's secretary informed me that he should be calling any minute, so you'd better get busy running your simulations. It's a good thing we've already got them committed for Winter and Summer through 2008—"

"Don't be so damned confident," said Bliecher with a spiteful smile. "I believe those bastards worked some kind of loophole into the contracts so that they can nullify everything if we don't prove we're able to secure the Games. If I had to bet on their attorneys versus our security people, I'd say—"

"Why are you still standing around in my office?" Just then, the phone rang. As Bliecher turned to go, Blanchot called after him, "Let's just finish these Games any way we can, get the hell out of this damned country, and never come back—oh, hello, Ira."

He listened as Greenberg fumed on the other end of the line, saying things by now very familiar to him, and ending with a new twist: "To top it off, Blanchot, we're even being shut out of coverage on this hostage situation."

"Ira, you know I don't control—"

"But what you *do* control," Greenberg's voice hissed, "or at least what you *did* control before you screwed it up, is access to this Village. Now you listen to me, and you listen good: get those damn terrorists out of there, no matter what it costs, and get on with these Games."

"How can I get them out of there if we don't even know what the hell they want?"

"That's not my problem. And by the way, Blanchot, if you think you've got us by the balls for the next twelve years, read the damn contract."

The Secretary of State had just put in another call to Berlin, and reported that he'd been told for the third time that morning that the German Chancellor was in a meeting and couldn't be reached. Everyone in the Cabinet Room looked at him, dumbfounded. "What the hell could he be doing that's so damned important?" demanded the Secretary of Defense.

The President ran his hands through his hair and drawled, "Well, hell, I guess I'll have to call him myself."

"What if he refuses to speak to you, too?" the First Lady snapped.

Her husband looked at her. "I hadn't thought of that." He glanced around at the others. "Alright, that leaves us with our situation back in the Olympic Village. What can we do?"

"We can't do anything until we know what their demands are, sir," said the Secretary of Defense. "We've got Defense analysts working with the people in the Village to figure out who they are so we can make our own educated guess as to their desires, but so far—"

"We're going on the assumption that they're some kind of Muslim fundamentalists," broke in the Director of Central Intelligence, or DCI. "That seems reasonable, assuming they really are from Bosnia. From that we can deduce that their agenda would include diversion of our peacekeeping forces in that country to the side of the Muslims."

"Which would go over like a lead balloon at the U.N.," the Secretary of State pointed out.

"And they'll probably want weapons too," the DCI added.

"Well, let's think about this," said the President, tapping his fingers on the table and looking up at the ceiling as he worked the situation out in his mind. "What could we offer them preemptively?"

"You mean an inducement of some kind?" asked the Attorney General. "Mr. President, it's always been the position of previous Administrations that the United States does not negotiate with terrorists."

"It'll look a lot worse if we let anybody get killed, I'll tell you that," the President replied. "Besides, even though that's been the stated position, it's hardly been the case in the past. Look at Reagan and Iran-Contra—now *that* was negotiating, and when it was all said and done, the people were more behind him than ever."

The Secretary of State cleared his throat. "Well, there's a perceived difference between negotiating with a country that supports terrorism, as in the case of Iran, versus actually negotiating with terrorists in a situation where they have hostages. If we're seen as giving in now, we open ourselves to all kinds of demands in the future."

"Another difference," said the First Lady, "was Reagan's popularity before it ever happened—not to mention that he put across an impression as a strong President." Several of the advisors exchanged glances: they'd had the same thought, but only the President's wife would have dared express it.

The President threw up his hands. "What the hell can we do? We've got foreign nationals under our protection, and if they're harmed, our credibility turns to crap anyway."

"It's definitely damned if you, damned if you don't," the Secretary of State agreed.

The President looked at his Attorney General. "Janice, what are your thoughts on a surprise attack with stun bombs—like the French did in '94 with that hijacked jet?"

She shook her head cautiously. "We're assessing that possibility, but keep in mind that we're facing some obstacles they didn't have on that Air France plane. There, the terrorists isolated themselves in the cockpit and made an easy target, but here the terrorists and hostages are in the same location, and most of the hostages have been wired with explosives. Before we could attack we'd have to be able to disarm the transmitters for those bombs, which would mean knowing how many there are, where they're located, and most of all how they function. We don't know any of that."

The President rubbed his eyes. "Well, shit. Now I know how Jimmy Carter felt back in '79, when those bastards in Teheran had our hostages." He looked around at the men and women gathered in the conference room. "It's times like this that I wish I weren't President."

He was certainly not the only person in the United States who had that thought.

"Welcome again, my friends," announced Drabeznic over the microphone as he began his second press conference at 10:00 a.m. sharp. "First let me introduce myself." On his TV screen, Thomas Mason saw several reporters lean forward, expecting him to divulge his true identity. "Our individual names are unimportant"—a collective sigh of disappointment—"but our cause is. Although we have arrived here in the uniforms of the Bosnian team, we represent not only the nation of Bosnia, but all the peace-loving Muslim peoples of the world. Therefore you may know us as *al-Ansar*, which means 'helpers'. As anyone who knows the true religion is aware, this refers to those who stood by the Prophet Mohammed in his hour of betrayal by the hypocrites of Mecca.

"In the same way, we are standing by the innocent victims of the hypocritical Western nations, whose double standard against Islam is literally killing the people of Bosnia. Throughout the years, you have been more than willing to demonize Islamic leaders—Arafat, Qaddafi, Saddam Hussein—when it suited your purposes. But when you see Muslims suffering at the hands of so-called Christian Serb forces, your moral outrage is suddenly not so great. The most you will do is support a U.N. 'peacekeeping' force, which treats both sides as equally culpable for the atrocities. Genocidal acts which led you into a world war when they were committed against the Jews are now dismissed as merely a part of the fighting."

The press and the security officers stood motionless, listening to every word. Mason folded his arms and listened, too, leaning back in his chair. *So that's what it's all about*, he thought. *Or at least, that's the script for now—we'll see what this guy really wants when it comes time to talk turkey.*

"Many of you no doubt think that I am overstating my case," Drabeznic continued, "but I assure you I am not. The actions which are taking place now in the Olympic Village were necessary to draw the world's attention away from fun and games to the question of a people's fate. And to prove that what I say about your Western leaders is accurate, listen to this.

"Following our last conference, I requested to speak with the Chancellor of the Federal Republic of Germany, several of whose citizens are presently under our care. Not only did I have certain requests to make, I wanted to pass on important information regarding the status of the German athletes. One would have assumed that he would be very interested in speaking with us. . . ." Drabeznic paused for ten seconds. "But so far he has refused to return our phone calls because, according to one of his aides, he does not negotiate with 'terrorists'."

A gasp went up from the members of the media and even the security officers, many of whom looked at each other in disbelief.

"These are foolish words," Drabeznic continued. "If he were sincere in his claims, he would immediately cut off all diplomatic relations with the terrorist state of Israel, and he would gladly speak with the freedom fighters of al-Ansar. Unfortunately for all of us, however, he may not be the one who has to pay for his lack of judgment. To illustrate what I mean, please look to the roof of this building."

Up to now, the cameras had focused on the second-floor window from which Drabeznic's voice emanated. But now they zoomed skyward, five stories above the concrete walkway below, and came to rest on three figures nearing the edge. Again there was a gasp, this time more pronounced. In the middle, between two masked men in black, stood a girl dressed in the German colors with her arms bound behind her. The telephoto lenses narrowed in on her youthful face, contorted with terror as she tried not to look at the fifty-foot drop that lay just over the edge of the building.

Mason nearly jumped in the air when a voice crackled over his radio earphone. "Big Wolf, Baby Sitter. Request that you advise: we have tangos on rooftop in our sights, can drop them. Repeat, request that you advise."

There had been almost no radio traffic since the press conference began, and now he hissed into his headset mike, "Back down!" *Trigger-happy fool*, he thought as he looked out at the Main Electric Substation where the SWAT team hid. Boyd would take any chance he could to avenge the deaths of his six men, and his cowboy tactics could very easily end up killing the hostages too.

"The young woman you see," Drabeznic continued, "is named Heidi Hirsch. She is very frightened, and her fear has nothing to do with the treatment she has received from us." He stopped while every eye watched the trembling girl, then he raised his voice. "This is a message to you, Mr. Chancellor! If I do not receive a phone call by 10:30 a.m. Eastern Daylight Time, precisely twenty-four minutes from now, this young lady will die. Her fate is in your hands: please do the right thing."

Mason picked up the Pentagon line the moment the conference ended. "Look, Tom," said Gen. Helms, "the President is trying to get through to the chancellor even as we speak."

"Sir, with all due respect—"

"I know, I know," sighed the general. "It's out of our hands. Listen, as soon as you get a breather down there, I want to have a conference call with you and Robbins. We want to find out what you know about these people, how they got their weapons in, and what possibilities you see for an assault."

"Sir, I can tell you right now what we know, and that's nothing, zip, nada. All that I know has already been passed on to you in the regular reports we've been filing with you since the athletes arrived in the Village." He ran a hand across the stubble on his face, which he hadn't yet had time to shave. "As for the assault plan, those explosives on the hostages are keeping our hands tied. If we had to go in right now, my estimate would be close to a hundred percent casualties for the hostages, not to mention a significant number of our own men. And as far as how they got the explosive material and weapons in, with all due respect, it doesn't really make a shit now, but there's simply no conceivable way they could have managed it since the time the Village was secured."

He left the general to draw his own conclusions, and he did: "Are you implying that it could have entered the Village before it was secured?"

"That's the only possibility available, sir."

"Dammit, Tom, we're under a hell of a lot of pressure to wrap this thing up as quick as we can. I want you to use every opportunity available to find out what he wants, because it's looking like negotiating is gonna be our only way out."

"Yes, sir. I'll get back to you as soon as we have anything more."

The door of his office was shut, closing out the pandemonium in the hallway and the adjacent offices of the MARC. Mason wished he could stay put here behind his desk: he needed time to think, but time was in short supply.

Outside his window he could see the rooftop of Fitten dorm and the three figures still standing there. He picked up one of the TV remotes on his desk and clicked on the volume long enough to hear a CNN reporter say, "We have just located the family of Heidi Hirsch in Berlin, and we take you now to—"

He muted it again and left the office, heading down the corridor to the northwest stairwell, which offered a clear, full view of Couch Field and the dormitory building on the other side of it.

The phone on his belt rang.

"Mr. Mason, perhaps you have figured out by now that I'm trying to run up your cellular bill."

"If that's all you want, Mr. Drabeznic, I'd be happy to oblige you."

"I'm glad you're maintaining your sense of humor."

"I have to." He put his hand on the railing and gazed at the tiny figure of Heidi Hirsch flanked by her two guards. "Look, we're willing to do whatever's necessary—"

Drabeznic cut him off. "That is in the chancellor's hands, not yours. Now, while we're waiting for him, I want to make sure your people know better than to get any foolish ideas about those two men I've left exposed. Let me make myself clear: we subscribe to the notion of an eye for an eye, but we apply a four-to-one ratio. Do you understand?"

Mason sighed. "All too well. Now is there anything else I can do for you to expedite matters?"

Drabeznic yawned. "We may be wanting some lunch later, but not yet—we're still busy working up an appetite."

Ten-thirty came and went, and still the three figures stood on the roof of Fitten Residence Hall. By now the July sun had begun to beat down, forcing most of the people on Couch Field to roll up their sleeves and fan their faces, yet Heidi Hirsch shivered uncontrollably.

On the muted TV screens of his office in the MARC, Mason could see scenes of rioting in front of the Reichstag building in Berlin and outside the chancellor's offices.

By the time Drabeznic's voice again blasted forth, it was nearly eleven. "Ladies and gentlemen," he announced, "I have just gotten off the telephone with the Chancellor of Germany." This brought a collective sigh of relief, and one of the reporters almost began to clap.

"But before I explain the outcome of our conversation," he continued, "I must tell you what I requested. First, I asked that certain persons currently held in German jails on charges of terroristic acts in the name of Islam—a total of fourteen names which I read to him—be released within four hours and placed on a chartered jet to be flown to a location which I would disclose later. Second, I requested that within twenty-four hours he send the first of six C-147s, fully loaded with weapons and ammunition, to Sarajevo to aid the soldiers of Bosnia-Herzegovina. In return for this, I said we would release all our German guests in exactly twenty-four hours."

He paused. "That is what I asked for, and now I will tell you what I did not request. I did not require that a single German soldier be deployed on the side of the Muslim forces, nor did I make any demands concerning the internal politics of Germany—unlike the Western leaders who have attempted to manipulate events in Bosnia to their advantage. My objective was purely this: that Germany should use its considerable economic and military power to assist the beleaguered Muslim peoples of Bosnia in equalizing the conflict. And now I will tell you the outcome of our conversation."

Everyone present, voluntarily or not, held his breath.

"Unfortunately, the Chancellor of Germany rejected our request out of hand." The crowd remained silent. "What you are about to see is the consequence of his actions, or rather his inaction, and you have only him to blame."

The men beside the girl on the rooftop moved forward with her, and she let out a cry of terror as they approached the side. She struggled with them for a moment, but they were much stronger. Her left leg and arm were over the edge of the building, flailing wildly, and it took only the slightest additional push from the men to nudge her a few inches further, so that her body's center of gravity hovered in the air five stories above the cement sidewalk. For a few seconds the three of them performed this dance of death in silence, then she let out another scream as she began falling, and the scream did not die until her body hit the sidewalk with a loud crack.

Most of the media there had spent time in war zones, yet several of them now had to fight back the urge to gag at the sound and sight of the woman's cracked skull. Otherwise the crowd on the east side of Couch Field was as silent as the lifeless body of Heidi Hirsch on the pavement.

"Ladies and gentlemen," Drabeznic shouted into the stillness, "this woman died heroically for a country whose leader did not care whether or not she lived! Do his sentiments reflect those of the German people? I hope not! At noon we will have an opportunity to know, for at that time another German athlete's fate will be weighed in the balance. People of Germany, pray that the value of her life, and those of the four other athletes you have left here, will not be found wanting!"

Again the foghorn, then total silence on Couch Field. Not even the most smooth-tongued journalist had anything to say.

Mason dialed Drabeznic's number furiously, but he forced his voice to sound calm when he said, "I'm sure you'll allow us to retrieve the body?"

"Of course. And how about some lunch? All this activity has made me very hungry."

22

Drabeznic claimed the food was for his captives, but his choice of cuisine had a distinctly Middle Eastern flavor. He ordered a five-gallon container each of cooked rice and couscous, five pounds of hummus, twenty pounds of roasted lamb, fifteen loaves of naan bread, fifty pounds of assorted fruit, eighty servings of baklava, and thirty gallons of sealed bottled water.

Michelle had already contacted Aramark, the company that provided meals within the Village, and Mason gave her instructions on how the meal should be delivered. "They'll come up McMillan," he said, "then back their truck up to the side entry. One person will approach the nearest window, and someone from inside will throw down a rope with a bushel-sized basket. That person will put as much food as he can into the basket, then they'll raise it, empty it, lower the basket, and so on. This whole process needs to be done as quickly as possible, so they don't get nervous inside. No one else is to go anywhere near the building unless instructed, got it?" He thought for a second. "And tell the Aramark people not to use disposable plates or flatware—have them provide the nicest china they've got, plus their best silverware."

Michelle said she would, and if she thought Mason was crazy, she didn't say so. It was a time-honored tactic of hostage negotiators: the fine table settings helped create a subtle atmosphere of civility to which terrorists might respond on a subconscious level.

The President had his own bank of televisions in the White House Cabinet Room, and he watched the screens while he waited for the German Chancellor to come on the line. He also had a running State Department report, which came out in reams over one of the room's six fax machines. There was rioting from Hamburg to Munich to Bonn to Dresden. In major cities such as Frankfurt, large-screen TVs had been set up in open plazas—originally so that crowds could cheer their

Olympic teams—but now these places had become scenes of pandemonium as the screen replayed the image of Fraulein Hirsch falling to her death. Throughout the nation's small towns, particularly in the east, gangs of skinheads went on rampages. They smashed up mosques, attacked families of Turks and anyone else of Middle Eastern appearance, and burned copies of the Koran. Now, as the television showed, the angry rabble around the chancellor's offices had begun to storm the building.

The chancellor, who had gathered with his cabinet in a secure room deep inside the building, finally got on the phone. He spoke flawless English, so he did not need an interpreter, and he came straight to the point: "Mr. President, the world is blaming me for the death of Fraulein Hirsch, but we entrusted the security for our athletes to you and your forces, and you failed to protect them."

The President gritted his teeth. "Herr Chancellor, we have an expression in English, 'Hindsight is twenty-twenty.' I understand what you're saying, but the question is, what can we do now?"

"Sir, I think we all know what our friends the Israelis would do. They refused to negotiate with Black September in 1972, and every time since then when their citizens have been taken hostage, Tel Aviv has treated them as soldiers in a battlefield. As they did in Entebbe, they would storm Fitten Hall at the first opportunity with the assumption that everyone would die; therefore any survivors would be considered a victory."

"I understand the emotional desire for actions like that," the President replied, "but the United States is not Israel."

"It certainly isn't," the chancellor replied sharply. "If this situation isn't resolved, my government will probably collapse overnight, yet I'm in no position to do anything except give in to the demands of al-Ansar, which I don't want to do." He paused, then said in desperation, "By God, why won't you attack?"

There was silence on the other end of the line for fully five seconds, then the American Commander-in-Chief said, "We can't do that at the moment. I need you to give in to his demands in order to buy us a little more time to evaluate the situation."

The chancellor sighed. "Okay, Mr. President," he said resolutely, "I will consider your request, but I remind you that once they run out of Germans and the others, the American hostages will have their turn."

As the press assembled in their place at the east end of the ball field five minutes before the noon conference, Mason noticed that one of the cameramen had been replaced. *Poor bastard*, he thought. *He just couldn't take it.*

Just before the sounding of the foghorn, three figures emerged on the roof—two terrorists with a tall, blonde-haired woman between them. "People of the world," Drabeznic's voice announced, "allow me to introduce to you Fraulein Katarina Heindrich, late of Dresden, who you may recall just this last Saturday won the bronze medal for her country in the 200-meter sprint. This was a special victory for her, because she was not expected to compete again after a car accident two years ago. Now she faces an even greater challenge: will her country's leader save her life, or will he allow her to die like our Muslim brothers and sisters who are dying every day in Bosnia?"

Around the world, a billion prayers centered on Fitten dorm in Atlanta. In Germany, where virtually every one of the nation's 31 million television sets was tuned in to the broadcast from the Olympic Village, the prayers mixed with curses; but in Tripoli, Damascus, Baghdad, Teheran, and Kabul, people prayed for the heroic defenders of Islam known as al-Ansar.

Drabeznic launched into a lengthy diatribe restating the offenses against the Muslims of Bosnia and the humble requests he had made to the German Chancellor on their behalf. The fear in the spectators mounted. Why would he speak so long and so methodically if he planned to spare the young girl's life?

This thought occurred to Mason, now on the edge of his seat before the television screen like the rest of the world. But he also knew that Drabeznic—like any other terrorist—loved to hear himself talk.

Katarina Heindrich, who seemed to be made of stronger stuff than her predecessor, struggled with her captors. But her arms were bound so tightly behind her that she could hardly move, so she finally settled down and stared straight ahead without sobbing, without trembling, without even blinking.

". . . And therefore," Drabeznic concluded, "we are forced to face uncomfortable choices." A gasp went up from the crowd. Women began to cry, and men shook with anger; everywhere, people continued to pray, and many others tensed themselves for what they feared would follow.

"But. . . the Chancellor of Germany has. . ."

What was it going to be?

". . .made a wise decision."

A sigh of relief rippled through the crowd, and Katarina Heindrich broke into sobs.

"Yes, the chancellor has granted our requests, and therefore his athletes will be freed in twenty-four hours, provided we receive confirmation that he has freed the political prisoners and delivered the first of the six C-147s loaded with weapons to the freedom fighters in Bosnia."

With these words, a cheer rose up at the far end of Couch Field, and it spread over the entire United States and across the ocean to Germany, where crowds of people sobbed and hugged and thanked God. Drabeznic waited a moment, then added, "And as evidence of our good faith and our recognition of the emotional duress she has suffered, we will release Fraulein Heindrich immediately." With that, the girl's hands were untied in full view of the audience.

"But," he went on in a grave tone, "let us not pretend that this episode is concluded. Although the chancellor has agreed to our requests, it will take time to fulfill them, and I urge the security forces here in the Olympic Village to take me seriously when I say that any threat to our safety will be dealt with very harshly.

"Our next formal meeting with you, the press, will take place at 6:00 p.m. Eastern Daylight Time. In the meantime, we will be arranging to converse with several world leaders, and at that time we will report the results. Now, before I go, I will take one question—and one question only—from each of the news services represented here, starting with CBS."

The reporter picked up her microphone and said, "Sir," but her voice cracked, and in embarrassment she cleared her throat. "Sir," she began again, "would you tell us your true name and what you want?"

"First of all," Drabeznic replied sharply, "I said there would be one question each. You have asked two, so I will only answer your first: the answer is no, I will not tell you my true name. Next question, from ABC."

The ABC reporter sounded as frightened as his colleague from CBS. "Who is the next world leader you intend to call, and what requests are you making?"

This made Drabeznic even more irritable. "To be people who talk all the time, you're not very good listeners. Again, you have asked two questions, and this time I won't answer either except to say that if I wanted to give you that information, I would have already. Now, BBC, let's see if you can follow orders better than the Americans."

"Yes, tell us, please sir," the British reporter asked, "what you hope to accomplish?"

"My mission, as I have said, is to win a small battle in the war of oppression against the Muslim peoples of this world. Finally, CNN."

"Do you expect to leave this country alive?"

Drabeznic laughed. "Let's just say that I'm not worried. Our cause is just, and if we die fighting, we are prepared to meet our God."

By the time Katarina Heindrich reached the other side of the field, Mason was on the phone with the physician assigned to attend to her.

"I know she's in shock," he said, "but we need to speak with her immediately."

"Yes, but——"

"No buts," he ordered. "The safety of the other people inside will depend on it. I'll give you a couple minutes, because I'm expecting a call from the man inside, then I want you to turn her over to one of my people."

A second after he hung up the phone, it rang.

"Mr. Mason, I have another mission for you, if you care to accept. This time I'd like to talk to the President of France. Perhaps you can do better than you did with the German Chancellor."

"I'll do anything I can to expedite things."

"But, my friend, this is a dramatic situation. Let's not spoil the drama. I have been planning this event for some time, and we must savor the moment. And speaking of 'savor,' where's our food?"

Rather than bring Katarina Heindrich around the intense security environment of the MARC, Mason elected to send her over to the relatively subdued Naval Reserve Building, where this morning's hostages had been interviewed. Most of them had departed for Emory, but when she arrived surrounded by guards, she had a surprise waiting for her.

It was her boyfriend, the male who'd been taken captive with the females in the predawn raid on their quarters. The two embraced and exchanged soft words in German while the security personnel pulled back and gave them their space. Though the young man spoke excellent English, the German envoy had been called in to speak with him earlier and had remained to await Katarina. It was a good thing, because her command of the language—especially in her state of shock—failed her.

Before going to interview her in the same office where he'd spoken to her teammate this morning (though it seemed like months ago),

Mason spoke to Robbins. The press would probably want to record running footage of Fitten dorm, he said, and he intended to preempt them by having security operate a single camera atop a nearby building. That way they would control the feed that went to the media pool at all times other than press conferences, with a special touch: they would run it on two-second delay, routed past a team of CIA technicians inside the MARC who would monitor the footage to make sure it didn't contain anything the media—and the rest of the world—didn't need to see.

After that, he walked down the hall to the room where Katarina sat flanked by the envoy and her boyfriend. Unlike the Puerto Rican chef, she offered only a very confused report as to how they'd been taken hostage, but she had much more to say about the conditions of their captivity. "They, uh. . . ." She looked at the envoy nervously, and asked him how to say the verb *absondern* in English.

"Segregate," the envoy translated.

She nodded her head. "They segregate us into groups that are very small."

Mason found this interesting, because it indicated a change in operations since the time of Martinez's captivity and the photographs of the women tied together in the showers. As the interview continued, he determined that although the explosive devices had remained on them, the girls had been put in individual rooms, and the ropes were replaced with handcuffs fastened in front of them. The change allowed more freedom of movement—for eating and for reading magazines and newspapers, which they'd been allowed to look at to alleviate some of the boredom—without the danger of an unguarded athlete escaping her bonds.

The girl also said that they were often moved from room to room, which indicated preparations for a long siege. Prisoners were more easily controlled if segregated as much as possible, not to mention that this made a hostage rescue operation much more difficult.

One thing about her report intrigued him: periodically, in the process of moving them about, the terrorists brought the hostages together in larger groups and ordered them to separate first according to nationality, then race, then medal status. This created smaller groups that were then further subdivided into rooms, but that alone did not explain why they did this, because the terrorists could have divided them arbitrarily. What it suggested to him was a technique pioneered by the North Koreans and Chinese with American POWs during the Korean War: by emphasizing differences in status and ethnicity, they encouraged disunity among their captives, making them more easily controlled. Between the black, white, and Hispanic American captives, the terrorists hoped to play on subtle resentments, as well as between those who'd earned gold, silver, bronze, or no medals at all during competition at the Games.

As for their treatment, she reported that the terrorists had been very solicitous of their comfort—aside from the fact that they weren't allowed to talk, watch TV, listen to the radio, or go to the bathroom unaccompanied. Mason's next question was a sensitive one, and he'd thought of asking her boyfriend to wait outside during the interview, but he elected to keep the young man there because his presence seemed to put Katarina at ease. Had any of the terrorists made any sexual advances toward her or any of the other girls?

She shook her head emphatically. "They are very. . . gentleman," she said. "Even when we to the toilets go, they remain outside with the opened doors." Mason had been inclined to believe Drabeznic's claim that none of the girls had been threatened in any sexual way. It would be disastrous for a terrorist commander to allow such fraternization, because it would take his men off of their true objective—whatever that was.

He had one last question for the girl, another sensitive one. How close had she been to the late Heidi Hirsch?

"Oh, Heidi is my friend," said Katarina with a smile. "I know her since two years, and I am so glad that she is released."

The envoy and the boyfriend both looked startled.

"Released?" Mason repeated.

"Yes, they have told to us that she is freed. When can I see her?"

While the occupants of Fitten received their lunch, many thousands more—their former neighbors until the evacuation earlier that morning—ate at various dining halls around Emory University, where they had been temporarily relocated.

One athlete finished his meal quickly, and afterward found a spot in front of the TV in a crowded dayroom. Instead of the scheduled events, the screen showed the rear view of Fitten dorm, with a commentator's voice saying, "We have received word from the office of Jason Blanchot of the International Olympic Committee that the Games may resume tomorrow if the present situation is resolved by then; however. . . ."

The shadow of a smile crossed the athlete's face. He was Georg Molnar, the Hungarian super-heavyweight boxer scheduled to fight Christiann Vervoerden that night. Now there would be no fight, and it didn't look likely that the Olympic planners would manage to re-schedule it. That meant he could go back to Hungary without the embarrassment of the default he would have taken by feigning illness—and just maybe the judges would see fit to award both Vervoerden and him the gold medal.

In another building, his would-be competitor lay in bed with a young equestrian who had often exhibited her aptitude at the sport in which they'd just engaged. Sex as a form of career advancement had always come naturally to JoEllen Cunningham, and from the moment she first saw the newspaper headlines billing Christiann Vervoerden as the future heavyweight champion of the world, she had known where to direct her energies. Now she pretended to be asleep with her head on his chest, her mind racing with thoughts of her future. As for Christiann, he was awake too, but if there was anything going on in that giant head of his, his face did not show it.

A cellular phone beside the bed rang. Christiann's lawyer, John Shapiro, had given it to him so that they could maintain constant communication, and Shapiro called him nearly every hour. Christiann had become tired of these lengthy conversations, but JoEllen kept telling him he had to put up with Shapiro because it could mean a lot of money for him.

The phone rang three more times, and she raised her head. "Don't keep John waiting," she said.

Christiann grunted and picked up the phone. "Yeah?"

"Christiann," said Shapiro's voice, "we need to talk. There's been a huge amount of activity, and I'm getting all kinds of offers."

JoEllen had meanwhile switched on the TV and flipped around the channels. Virtually every one of them featured the Olympic crisis—even MTV, where an environmentally conscious rock star was telling a reporter that people should be just as concerned about the trees cut down that morning as they were about the hostages. But she didn't care about that. In her mind she was watching another TV show, one that would run six months or a year from now, when Christiann won the heavyweight title. And there she would be beside him—once she'd edged Shapiro out—planning how he would spend every dime. From the corner of her eye she glanced at her new amour's giant, dumb face. He needed someone like her.

"Yeah," said Christiann sleepily into the phone, "but you know I can't have any serious talks with anyone until the Games are over."

"Forget the Games," said Shapiro with a laugh. "They're history. Let's talk about what you're gonna do in the pros."

The nationwide audience for the Olympic drama had become the largest in the history of United States television. Because of its reputation for covering such events, CNN got most of the viewers, but ABC and CBS did not fare poorly. NBC continued its feeble news broadcast with commentators in the *Today Show* studios at the center of the Village, but well away from the action, trying to speculate on what was happening. The network took a poor fourth share in a whopping combined 93.9 rating, and its executives found little comfort in the fact that this figure would never become official because of the non-commercial, multi-network nature of the event.

Still, an after-lunch program in which Gregory Bramble profiled the U.S. captives drew in a few viewers. As each athlete's picture appeared on the screen, Bramble gave her vital statistics, including medals earned in the past two weeks, followed by short interviews with relatives or coaches.

At the end of the list were two names that particularly stood out, the first of which was Melody Johnson. In three days of competition that had concluded on Monday, the eighteen-year-old gymnast had earned an impressive total of two golds and two silvers. "That's quite an accomplishment," as Bramble said, "for someone who didn't even qualify in Barcelona. Yet along the way, Melody did something equally impressive, which was to win the love of millions of fans. Like Cathy Rigby and Mary Lou Retton before her, she has become America's sweetheart, and now that sweetheart is held captive in Fitten dorm along with twenty-three of her fellow Americans."

NBC had tried to interview her parents in Concordia, Kansas, but the Johnsons had announced in a statement made earlier that day that they were too distraught to talk. As for the cereal company that had contracted to run her picture on their box, they had rushed production to put the item on the shelves so that—as Bramble said gravely—"Americans can show their support for the hostages in Fitten dorm."

The last girl profiled had gained notoriety not just for the bronze she'd earned in the 200-meter backstroke, one of the few swimming medals won by Americans against tough Chinese and North Korean competitors, but also because she was the only athlete participating in the 1996 Games whose father worked with ACOG. Across the screen flashed a photograph from *The Atlanta Constitution* taken more than a year before, which showed a smiling Elizabeth Taggart at the edge of a pool. Next to her sat her father, Ben Taggart, Director of Protocol for the Olympic Village.

In the picture Taggart was beaming with pride, but when the NBC cameras caught him for an interview, his face looked drawn. His wife, Susan, refused to speak to the media, and Taggart himself had little to say. "Elizabeth, if you're able to hear this," he said, "your mother and I love you very much, we're praying for you, and we know you'll be coming home soon." He struggled to find more words, but the reporter interrupted him.

"What do you know about the efforts, if any, to secure the release of the hostages?"

"Nothing," he said truthfully. He'd gotten a call from Greg Robbins early that morning, of course, and Steve Kirk had asked him to help with relocating the athletes; but he'd been privy to little inside information, and what he had he wasn't about to share.

By 2:00 p.m. Eastern Daylight Time, the U.S. State Department had initiated a conference call between the American President and the other leaders who had citizens captive in Fitten dorm: the Chancellor of Germany, the prime ministers of Great Britain and Canada, and the presidents of Russia and France. The First Lady had advised her husband that it would be a wise gesture to include the Governor of Puerto Rico, who would listen but not comment. As for the North Koreans, officials from the U.S. had tried to contact them several times, but Pyongyang refused to participate in what it condemned as "power-jockeying by imperialists."

The French President reported on the demands his government had received from al-Ansar: the release within four hours of eighteen Iranian, Syrian, and Lebanese extremists held in French jails; and the delivery, in twenty-four hours, of the first of five C-147s loaded with weapons to Sarajevo. Only the numbers of prisoners and planes were different from the requests made to Germany, and once again Drabeznic promised the release of all four French captives within twenty-four hours if his demands were met.

The French President (who, like his Russian counterpart, used a simultaneous interpreter) reiterated what the German Chancellor had said a few hours before: the U.S. had to do something. The American President tried to respond, but before he could, the Frenchman went on: "You saw how we handled a similar situation two years ago, when one of our Air France jets was hijacked in Algiers. We knew we were risking those 171 passengers, but the terrorists had already killed three hostages, so we went in with our commandos, and in the end they managed the rescue without a single additional casualty, except of course for the four terrorists. If you do not take similar action now, I will hold you accountable for our losses—including any of our athletes who may be harmed in the meantime."

Again the U.S. President tried to speak, but the Russian leader cut him off. "I both agree and disagree," he said. "You must attack, as these men say, but if and when my government is approached by these Bosnians with their demands, we will refuse! Any government which submits to terrorists is a weak one, no matter how many of its people are in jeopardy."

"We have a different system from yours," said the German Chancellor, obviously offended. "Unlike you, we can't just cut off the television service so that no one sees our athletes being thrown off a roof."

"You are living in the past, Mr. Chancellor!" the Russian thundered back. "It is true that we don't thrive on live carnage as you do in the West, but we care what happens. And we will care if our new allies show themselves ineffectual in dealing with these Bosnians!"

"Well, I think it's clear where our colleague in Moscow stands," said the American President nervously. "Anyone else?"

Even though the Puerto Rican Governor wasn't supposed to speak, he did. "I'm afraid the situation does not appear as clear-cut to me as it does to you heads of state," he said. "We have no power to make any decisions, yet if you attack, we will suffer the greatest losses because we have the largest proportion of athletes held hostage. We're at the mercy of our federal government, and Mr. President, I urge you to do everything you can to buy off these terrorists so that no one else is harmed."

"Leave it to an American citizen to suggest that," said the Russian President.

Just then an aide slipped a note to the U.S. President, who hastily read it and then said, "Gentlemen, I've just received word from a diplomatic intermediary between the United States and the Democratic People's Republic of Korea, which states that the government in Pyongyang supports the 'requests' made by the 'freedom fighters' from Bosnia, and that we should give in. They've threatened action against South Korea if their athletes are killed and ours are somehow spared."

"Oh, that's poppycock!" said the Canadian leader. "They know we're all in the same boat. It's just posturing on their part."

"North Korea!" said the Russian leader with contempt. "Stalin's last great legacy to us. Forget about them, Mr. President—what are *you* going to do?"

"The United States does not support negotiations with terrorists any more than any of the other governments represented here," the U.S. leader replied, "but we all know that theory and reality aren't always the same. My predecessors negotiated with Iranian terrorists for the release of hostages, and we have not been the only government to do so."

He cited examples from his colleagues' governments. The British had shied away from searching the baggage of Libyan "diplomats" they expelled in 1984, even though it probably contained the weapons they'd used to kill eleven British subjects outside the Libyan embassy in London. The Germans had refused to extradite one of the TWA Flight 847 hijackers, who killed a Navy SEAL in June 1985, because two Germans had been taken hostage by the group responsible for the hijacking. And then there was France, which had bent over backwards to maintain good relations with its trading partners in Teheran. In 1990 President Mitterrand had pardoned the man who tried to assassinate the Shah's former prime minister in Paris; a second murder attempt succeeded a year later, while relations with Iran improved and France released two more suspected Iranian killers. Even the Soviet Union in its waning days had negotiated with bank robbers.

"I do recognize the fact that someone over here dropped the ball," the President continued, "and I'm not shirking that responsibility. We intend to take the building, to which end I have instructed my military advisors to develop a plan that will minimize the number of casualties. But we need to buy as much time as we can to ascertain strengths and weaknesses of the terrorists, and that's where I need you to help by making concessions to them. Keep in mind that some of these can be retrieved once we have the advantage."

"So you're saying," the British Prime Minster asked, "that you will attack only after we have given up prisoners and arms and made major changes in national policy?"

"What he's saying," the French President put in, this time speaking in English, "is that while he figures out what to do, the rest of us are being held hostage by him, just like those young women in the dormitory building are being held hostage by al-Ansar."

"I cannot agree with your over-simplification of the problem, sir," said the U.S. President indignantly.

The French leader, disgruntled that an American would dare accuse a Frenchman of over-simplifying, responded just as indignantly. "We made an appropriate and timely response in Marseilles, and I believe you can do the same in Atlanta. If it had been American citizens on that jet, you would have been screaming for us to take action then."

The American lost his cool. "You seem to have a fixation with the Air France incident, sir—perhaps that's because it was the only time your government dealt effectively with terrorists."

"Gentlemen!" put in the Canadian Prime Minister. "While we argue, the clock is ticking. I for one say that we should get behind our colleague in Washington—but I believe I speak for all the other leaders when I say that we expect the United States to reimburse us for any material losses we incur in meeting the terrorists' demands."

"Good point!" echoed the British Prime Minister. "Well said!"

"Alright," said the U.S. President, "you have my word on it."

"Very well," said the Frenchman, "but let it be known that I for one am dissatisfied with the way you have handled this situation up to now. Publicly, of course, I will support you because we have to present a united front to the rest of the world. But this is my honest opinion between the seven of us."

"I hear what you're saying, and I feel your pain," the American answered in a measured tone. "I'll keep you all informed of the progress."

"Then I'd suggest you get busy," said the Brit.

23

"Are you buying this 'savor the moment' crap?" asked Gen. Helms.

"No, sir," said Mason. He sat with Robbins, Michelle, Julio, Lamont, and Aaron around his desk as the general's voice boomed out over the speaker phone. "Clearly he's trying to use time to his advantage, and I think he sees the media as his accomplices—willing or not. If he can keep exciting the kind of pandemonium he did in Germany, he'll be able to tell any world leader to jump and they'll say 'How high?'"

"Alright," said the general, "the key is to figure out what he really wants, and to do that we have to know who we're dealing with. Central Intelligence doesn't have a clue, because these guys entered the country under the auspices of the Olympics, which is about as good a cover as any terrorist could hope for. And Sarajevo has made a statement, but it's just what you'd expect from politicians: they deny all knowledge of these people, and have declared this an act of piracy on the part of a renegade group with no relation to them."

"Sir, if I might," said Robbins, leaning forward in his chair as he spoke to the phone on Mason's desk, "there's no reason to believe that they're involved in any way. From what we know, Drabeznic financed the whole handball team, and given the situation in Bosnia, we can figure the government was just glad to have some competitors they could send without having to foot the bill themselves. He appeared to be offering them something for nothing, and they jumped at it."

"They didn't even check him out?"

"Well, sir, their national Olympic committee is less than three years old, and it's really little more than a shell. Because of the split between all the countries of the old Yugoslavia, and the conditions ever since then, records are virtually impossible to come by—whatever there might be is either somewhere in the old capital of Belgrade, or has been destroyed. And even if they'd had access to the proper records, from what we can see, they'd have come up empty-handed."

"It's damned eerie," said the general. "It's like they just came out of thin air."

Mason reminded the general about the suspicions he'd had following the mysterious bus accident in the spring. "But there wasn't much I could do," he said. "Given the situation, everybody felt sorry for the poor Bosnian handball team, and nobody at the IOC or the international team handball federation bothered to ask many questions, nor was I at liberty to."

They talked about the handball team's miserable defeat by the Portuguese the preceding Saturday. "So it was obvious they weren't real handball players," said the general.

"Sir," Robbins replied, "there are plenty of athletes here who aren't world-class, and we all know that. But the Bosnians all had Olympic credentials, and we're required to allow credentialed athletes into the Village—unless of course they are known terrorists, which these guys weren't. Other than the handball team, with sixteen players and four officials including Drabeznic, everyone else in the Bosnian delegation appears to have been clean: there was the chef de mission, who as you know was found dead, and they only had three other athletes and two other officials, all of whom have gone home."

"Sixteen players and four officials," the general repeated. "Twenty men—a hell of a lot of firepower. Which brings me back around to what I asked before: how the hell did they get all those weapons through your access-control setup there?"

Aaron spoke up. "Sir, we might have a lead on that. As we were checking with the various chefs to inventory their team members, we asked if they'd noticed any unusual activity. The chef of the Dutch team in University Apartments reported that yesterday afternoon, a crew from Plant Operations came to repair a leak in his wall which he didn't even know was there. We checked with Plant Operations, but we found no corresponding work order, so we investigated the area where the repair took place."

As Aaron reported, they found that a five-foot-high opening had been knocked into the wall and hastily patched. Inside there weren't any water pipes, but they did locate a vertical chase or air shaft—with a metal platform welded into its bottom. There were blue scrape marks on the concrete blocks surrounding the hole, and after taking samples of this to a lab, they discovered that the scrapes came from a medium-density polyethylene such as one would find in a plastic barrel or container. They also found traces of a wax-like substance, and something particularly bizarre: cayenne pepper.

"Interesting," said the general. "Any idea of how many containers?"

"Well, sir, the chase is two feet square and five stores high—"

"Great!"

"—But we've had a crew make an opening from the roof to inspect the chase, and they haven't found any blue scrape marks above the fourth floor."

The general sighed. "Alright, so there was something inside some plastic containers, enough to fill approximately—what, eighty cubic feet? Assuming that they did get materials out of there, how did they transport it?"

Lamont jumped in. "Checking the motor pool, sir, we discovered that one of the people there had authorized the sign-out of a van to go to the Dutch team quarters at University Apartments to repair a water leak. The individual who signed out the van used the name and identification of a Henry Billings, and we've determined that there is no such employee at Georgia Tech."

"Didn't that raise any red flags?"

"No, sir, the motor pool doesn't have the time or the manpower to run checks on I.D.s that appear valid."

"Keep in mind, sir," Robbins pointed out, "that they sign fifty or a hundred of these authorizations a day, and there's not much reason to check on the vans as long as they're returned, which this one was. This was all taking place within a secure Village, and since the men weren't attempting to take the van off-site, and their work order appeared to be valid, there was no cause for suspicion."

"According to the person I spoke with at motor pool," Lamont continued, "the van was signed out by a white male, more than six feet tall with blond hair."

"And that fits the description of the foreman given to us by the Dutch chef de mission," Aaron interjected. "He reported that there were also five other men, who he assumed to be Hispanic. I asked him if they could have been Middle Eastern, and he said possibly. But the only one who did any talking was the foreman."

"Okay," said the general. "I assume you looked at the van?"

"Yes, sir," said Lamont. "It was returned relatively clean, but we were able to find microscopic remnants of gray duct tape with traces of the same blue polyethylene material on it that was found in the vertical chase. There was also evidence of sheetrock particles that matched what was on the walls, and we found metal scrapes that may have been from tools."

"So you have this vertical chase, and you have the van—what then?"

"Several of the Puerto Rican team members I interviewed," said Robbins, "reported that yesterday afternoon they saw a Georgia Tech van pull up to the side of Fitten, and several men unloaded blue drums of some kind."

"Well, that part seems pretty clear," said the general, "but you still haven't told me how the hell these blue drums got into University Apartments in the first place."

Robbins sighed. "Sir, our only guess is that the placement of these containers happened some time during the construction of the University Apartments."

"*What?*"

"Well, three years ago, when various contractors bid on the project, it would have been fairly easy to steal or purchase a copy of the plans from an unsuccessful bidder. We're checking with the various companies involved, but we believe it was probably a theft. From the blueprints, it would have been easy to know about the vertical chase, and how to take advantage of the possibilities it offered."

"But you would have still had to have men on the construction crew."

"Yes, sir, and it's literally beyond the scope of our abilities to check out all the personnel who worked on the project," Robbins admitted. "But it's reasonable to assume that one or more members of al-Ansar or their advance team could have gotten jobs on the construction crew, and from that position taken the steps necessary to weld in the platform and even insert the drums. Obviously it would have had to take place at a fairly early stage, and then—"

"Shit!" the general thundered. "I know you people did some kind of inspection on those buildings!"

Lamont looked at Robbins and held up a hand to indicate that he wanted to respond. "Sir," he said, "we did, and I was present earlier this month when the dog teams went through Building D, where the materials were apparently secreted."

"Well?"

"Well, even though the dogs were there for the purpose of inspecting only the mechanical areas such as storage closets and the like, I remember that when they got to Building D, they began to go wild, scratching and sniffing at the walls. So we brought in a Plant

Operations crew to break into the concrete in a few places, but we couldn't find anything. So finally we took some paint samples to the lab, and. . . ."

"And what? Spit it out!"

"And there appeared to be traces of gunpowder in the paint, sir."

"Jeez Louise," said the general.

"By that point," Robbins explained, "we were five days away from opening the Village, and we had a choice of either proceeding on the assumption that there was some aberration in the paint used—or condemning the building and tearing it apart. There was really no choice. Obviously it appears now that the gunpowder—as well as the wax and the cayenne pepper—was used as a masking agent, but at the time there was no reason to suspect. . . ."

"If I'm not mistaken, the Bosnian team's quarters are also in the University Apartments complex, right? How'd they swing that—and don't tell me the luck of the draw?"

"No, sir," Robbins replied. "Some months prior to the opening of the Village, they requested that location."

"Again, no red flags for any of your people there?"

"No sir," said Robbins. "Most all of the teams made special requests—for instance, the Italians asked to be put on Tenth Street because that was the one area where they could have a private dining facility to cook their own pasta. Village staff attempted as much as possible to match all teams with the areas they requested, and in fact as I understand it, they had some difficulty finding teams who wanted the University Apartments because they were high-rises overlooking the expressway. Therefore when the Bosnians put in a request for the second floor of Building D—"

"Wait a minute—you're saying they asked for the spot where the Dutch team was? Where you found the vertical chase?"

"Yes, sir, but the Dutch had already selected D. So the Bosnians were put as close as possible, in Building C."

"I suppose you've checked out that building."

"With a fine-tooth comb, sir. It's pretty much the same as Building D, and they share an underground parking garage, which is used primarily for team storage during the Games. There's all kinds of equipment, mostly stored in forty-foot-long shipping containers—saddles, kayaks, shoes, uniforms, you name it—plus, the French team brought in their own wine, and the Australians have their beer. But none of that was contraband."

"Well, shit," said the general. "Why couldn't they have brought in their weapons that way?"

"Because, sir, not only did the containers have to clear customs, but we inspected them with ordnance-sniffing dogs."

The general brought up the subject of Adam, and the members of Mason's team exchanged glances. With all that had happened in the preceding hours, they hadn't had much time to think about him. After discussing how he'd died, Helms asked about the information he'd collected.

"Well, sir," said Michelle, "he and the other two resident hall clerks reported that from time to time the team members would enter with bags of what looked like electronic items, including hand-held radios, that they'd purchased at Radio Shack. But we don't have any exact inventory, because the minders weren't authorized to inspect packages, and even if we'd tried to conduct a covert search of their quarters, there was always at least one member of the Bosnian team present. But one minder who delivered a routine message to them from Village Management said that he saw what appeared to be a cage with canaries in it, located in one of their apartments."

"You're putting me on."

"No, sir."

After they got off the phone, Mason turned to the rest of the group. "There's a missing link here, and we've got to figure out who it is."

"Missing link?" asked Robbins.

Reading her chief's thoughts, Michelle explained, "Even though the work order that Plant Operations supplied to the Dutch was bogus, it indicates some kind of inside knowledge—you don't just walk in off the street and pull off a job like that."

Mason nodded his head. "They've got some kind of insider, a person or persons who would have intricate knowledge of the construction of these buildings, the Georgia Tech facilities, and the inner workings of the Village." He looked at Lamont and Stein. "Most likely it's this six-foot, blond-haired foreman of yours."

Lamont's face had a strange expression. "The guy repairing the wall!" he said suddenly.

"What?"

"The day of the lockdown—I'm sure it was the same guy. Same

description. I remember how he acted, kind of smug, singing some old song while he patched up the wall . . . . "

"You think he's a real Georgia Tech employee?" asked Robbins. "Keep in mind, though, all Tech employees hired in the past two years—not to mention volunteers and temporary Village employees— have had complete FBI checks. The same goes for any professors or administrators entering the Village area."

"I know," said Mason. "If I recall correctly, there were three professors from the Middle East, one from Algeria and two from Lebanon, who were denied security clearances because they had past records of sympathy for terrorist organizations in their countries, even though they didn't have any record of actual participation. They had to be sent on sabbatical for the time being, even though we were facing a big stink over discrimination."

"But they're not Plant Operations anyway," said Michelle. "I say the guy we're looking for is the real thing."

"And," Mason added, "I'll bet you he was hired more than two years ago."

"Again, I'm telling you," said Robbins, "everyone working in the Village has had a security check. I mean, the long-term employees didn't go through as intensive a one as the others, but still, they were checked out."

"Just humor me on this one, Greg," said Mason tiredly. "I'd like you to run a computer check of all Plant Operations employees hired since the date Atlanta was awarded the Games: September 18, 1990. I'll put Julio and Aaron on the job with you."

"Okay." Robbins closed his notebook. "We can get something back to you by about suppertime. But say we do find him—"

"Oh, you won't find *him*, just his name." Mason glanced out his window in the direction of Fitten dorm. "If he exists, he's over there with them, which brings their numbers up to twenty-one."

"If we had provided proper defense for the Village," said the Secretary of State, looking at the President across the table from him in the Cabinet Room but clearly speaking to his counterpart in the Department of Defense, "we wouldn't be screwed the way we are now."

"Then again," said the Defense Secretary, "if our illustrious colleagues at State had provided proper information on our guests from

Bosnia, we might have been able to anticipate this type of thing and headed it off."

"Alright, calm down!" said the First Lady. "We've got two major things to consider here, and we need to keep our focus on them."

"That's right," said the President, "how to deal with the terrorists and how to secure the release of those hostages."

"No," she said, "how to appease our allies and how to make the best impression with the public."

"Right, right." The President glanced at the Secretary of State. "Walter?"

"Well, sir," said the Secretary, nervously running his finger under his shirt collar, "you heard the consensus of our allies, and I'd have to say I understand their concerns. They've put a lot of pressure on us to act, but they in turn are feeling pressured as far as meeting the terrorists' demands."

DCI, the Director of Central Intelligence, spoke up. "Now, when we're talking about allies," he pointed out, "we have to consider gradations here. At the far end of the spectrum you've got Canada and Britain which, in spite of the prime minister's comments today, have historically lined up solidly with American interests. Further down the scale you've got Germany, and further still France, who are likely to support our interests so long as they see a benefit to themselves. Then there's your wild card, which is Russia, with whom we've had only limited experience as an ally. They're not used to being on the receiving end of terrorism—part of the price they're paying for democracy. And finally there's North Korea, which ranks right up there with Iraq as an enemy of the U.S. and friend of terrorism."

"Yeah, it's more than a little odd how they came to be messed up in this," the Secretary of State observed. "It could just be a red herring on the part of the terrorists to make it impossible for us to guess where they're coming from, or more likely it's to put additional pressure on us by involving a country that hates our guts."

"Pressure to do what, though?" asked the President.

DCI answered the question. "I'd suspect that before it's over with, this al-Ansar is going to demand a large sum of money. But in the short term, I think we can extrapolate from the experience of the French and Germans, and assume they'll expect us to release the World Trade Center bombers and various other Islamic extremists incarcerated over here, then send planes loaded with arms to the Bosnian Muslims." The Director of Central Intelligence had a pipe, which he hadn't yet dared to light in the room, but now he took it out and tapped it on the table in a way that made several people jump. "Of course, I would imagine the numbers of prisoners and planes will be much higher, and I think we'll be called on to give al-Ansar safe passage either to Iraq or some other country friendly to them."

"That raises a possibility," put in the Secretary of State. "At the moment no nation—not even Iraq or Iran—has claimed any connection to the group." The President raised his eyebrows, and the Secretary went on: "In fact, we've had informal conversations with both Baghdad and Teheran today, and they say they're willing to support our efforts to apprehend the criminals if they should try to seek refuge over there."

"What's their angle?" asked the President.

The Secretary rubbed his thumb and first two fingers against each other. "Follow the money. I think both of them would see this as good P.R. with the world community so that they can get better distribution on their oil. That's not to say that anyone's seen the light—I would imagine both governments secretly wish these SOBs well, and they may have even provided some funds, but we're not likely to know because it would have been done in secret. The point is that in public and for the whole world to see, I believe we're going to have full cooperation from both governments, especially Iraq. In my conversations with their foreign minister, he was at great pains to assure me that the Iraqi government would provide us with all possible assistance in tracking them down."

"What a world!" said the President. "Iraq, Russia, and maybe even North Korea on the same side as the United States. All we need's Cuba now."

"Keep in mind, sir," said DCI, "those 'assurances' of theirs are no guarantee. Even if we were talking about a friendly nation, which we're not, we'd be looking at the likelihood of losing a good portion of the released prisoners." He stared at his Chief to make sure the meaning was getting through. "They'll be caught, of course—eventually, maybe—after they've had a chance to blow up a couple more embassies, a couple more planes filled with tourists."

The First Lady put a hand on her husband's wrist. "Before we do anything," she said, "we need to consult with Larry."

The President turned to his "Dream Team" of political consultants. Up to now, they had stayed quiet, sitting on the opposite side of the room from the Cabinet members, the two sides exchanging suspicious glances. Now Larry, the chief pollster, spoke up.

Of course things had happened so fast, Larry said, that they hadn't had much opportunity to collect conclusive polling data, but that night more results would come in, and they would be holding focus groups. But he could say in advance what he expected to find: that the public wanted their President to act decisively and quickly to clear out the terrorists—without any casualties.

"What the hell kind of answer is that? They might as well say they want me to take a piss without anything getting wet."

Jimmy, his re-election campaign manager, said, "As long as all of the Americans come out alive and no more of our U.S. personnel on the rescue team are harmed, I think you're fine. I hate to sound insensitive here, but I think the people could give a crap about any of the other hostages."

"But," said the First Lady, "I'm thinking about the raid on the Branch Davidians in Waco back in '93. A lot of people supposedly didn't give a crap about them either, but look at all the trouble that caused. How's this different?"

"There are some similarities," Jimmy admitted, "but I think far worse than a few casualties in an assault would be the sight of more hostages being thrown off the roof. Just think of the photos that would come from that, and how devastating they'd be. Remember that one from Vietnam, with the naked girl running down the road in flames? Or the shots of those students in Teheran torching the American flag? Even the patriotic ones, like the fireman carrying the baby out of the rubble in Oklahoma City, can look bad for us if we're considered the cause of the problem in the first place."

"How about if we negotiate, what's the damage there?" asked the President.

"Considering that most of our allies are willing to," said Jimmy, "that might not be too bad if it's handled right. We know Russia's not gonna play ball, but we can always blame that on historic ties between them and Serbia going all the way back to the czars. And I doubt the North Koreans will negotiate—they're much more likely to use those athletes as sacrificial pawns to get at us—but who really gives a shit about North Korea anyway? Not the voters. If you do negotiate, I recommend that you string these SOBs out as long as you can, not only because that wears them down and buys time for the rescue team, but also because it gives you an opportunity for some good sound bites. You go on TV, explain what's going on to the nation, ask for their support and prayers. . . you know what kind of stuff you have to say. It can look real good if it's handled right, and as for the terms of the negotiations themselves, that'll hardly matter as long as you can take back whatever concessions you've made once we have the upper hand."

"What if we attack and half the hostages are killed, but none of them are Americans? How would that look?"

"I think that would be okay—not great, but at least recoverable," Jimmy answered. "Basically, your worst danger is in letting any more people, Americans or not, be thrown off the building in broad daylight, because it will be perceived that you let them die without doing anything. Second-worst is an attack where everyone's killed, and third would be if we were to negotiate and not be able to recoup our losses."

"Sir," said the Secretary of State, who along with his counterpart in Defense had listened to all this with distaste, "I must say that I find this Machiavellian discussion appalling. We should be making our decisions based on the long-term interests of our country and our allies, not percentage points!"

"Wrong, Mr. Secretary," said the First Lady. "If we don't get re-elected, everything we've done for this country will go down the drain, and that's a hell of a lot more important than punishing a bunch of terrorists."

The Secretary of State slumped back into his chair.

"The fact of the matter is," said the President, "this may be the defining moment in this Administration. We need to rise above it all, and make the tough decisions. The American people want to see leadership."

The campaign manager watched his Chief's face, and he smiled to himself. This Administration needed a well-handled crisis to pull itself out of its mire in the polls.

"Sir," said the Secretary of Defense, "I may be able to help you with that. My staff at the Pentagon have been working on some plans, and though I can't guarantee that their idea will work, it would definitely be a case of taking decisive action without too much exposure."

The President leaned forward. "What kind of plans?"

PART FIVE

STORMING THE GATES

24

Drabeznic held an uneventful press conference at 6:00 p.m. in which he announced the "requests" he'd presented to the French President, and his apparent willingness to fulfill them. Therefore the French athletes would be released on the following day. He allowed a few questions from the reporters, most of which he answered coyly if at all. He would hold the rest of the hostages, he said, "As long as it takes." But he seemed to be in an upbeat mood.

Afterward, he called Mason to request two things: supper, to be delivered at 7:30, and a phone link with the Russian President. Mason said he would take care of it. Then he informed Drabeznic that he intended to evict the media from the Village until 6:45 a.m. on Wednesday, just before the next scheduled press conference.

As they spoke, the kitchens of Aramark at the center of the Village buzzed with preparations for the meal to be delivered to Fitten. The menu was much the same as it had been at lunchtime, and Greg Robbins had ordered a sampling of standard American fare—roast beef and mashed potatoes, etc.—for the thousands of security officers. The chefs at Aramark had a great talent for serving up delectable food in large quantities, not always an easy combination, and they enthusiastically fell to the task of feeding the security forces.

At the same time, a courier was speeding down I-75 from Dobbins Air Base in Marietta, carrying a special sealed package. Upon arriving at the Aramark kitchens, he would present the head chef with signed orders from the Department of Defense stating that Drabeznic had requested a special variety of curry-like spice, which had been rushed from the only available U.S. supplier in New York City. The orders directed the chefs to apply liberal doses of it to all food destined for Fitten Hall—and *only* food destined for Fitten—and they advised strongly against tasting the spice or the food once they'd applied it. "This is an extremely strong substance," the memo concluded, "and has not passed through ordinary U.S. Customs channels. We supply it only upon the request of Mr. Drabeznic."

When he received it, the head chef took the package into his office and opened it. He found a zip-locked plastic bag containing perhaps eight ounces of the brownish-yellow powder, an enormous amount even for this quantity of food. Skeptical, he looked around, then opened the bag. It smelled like ordinary curry powder, or perhaps cumin. Checking again to see that no one was watching him through the window from the kitchen, he wet his finger and tasted it. It *tasted* like ordinary curry, and he waited a moment for a burning blast to hit his taste buds, but the sensation was only a mild one. He tasted it again, then did so a third time before shaking his head, closing up the bag, and returning to the kitchen to do as he'd been ordered.

Mason had received word via Gen. Helms of a plan which had the President's strongest approval. When he heard the idea, Mason told the general he didn't like the sound of it, but Helms abruptly informed him that when Washington wanted his input, they would ask for it. "Look, Tom," said the general, "the President's all for this thing, so nothing else matters."

After he passed on instructions to Boyd, Mason informed Michelle of the details, and while they waited for the plan to coalesce, the two sat in his office and debated the wisdom of Washington's plan. "I know from our own terrorist simulation," she said, "that withholding food isn't a good practice in these kinds of situations, but this is different."

"I wish I could agree with you," said Mason, rubbing his eyes with exhaustion. He knew he had a long night ahead of him. "But it's just too James Bond for me. It's exactly the kind of notion you'd expect from a bunch of CIA wanna-be's in the Defense Department—the same folks who've come up with brainy ideas in the past like consulting psychics to find kidnapped diplomats." He sighed. "I'm really not excited to see how this thing plays itself out."

At about the same time, the head chef at Aramark once more retreated to his office away from the hustle and bustle of the kitchen. The sight of all that activity at the stoves made him drowsy, and he wanted nothing so much as to just sit in his swivel chair and relax.

By 7:45 p.m., the food had still not been delivered, and an irate Drabeznic called Mason to ask when it would be coming.

"Well, you know, these things take time," said Mason blandly.

"Why didn't you just call me back?"

"I apologize, Mr. Drabeznic—I've had a lot of things on my mind, as you can imagine. But I think we should have it to you in the next fifteen minutes."

The food was soon delivered by the same method employed at lunchtime. Mason's phone again rang. "Mason," said Drabeznic, "make a note to send along some hot peppers next time." *Click.*

"What the hell kind of humor is that?" Mason asked aloud.

"I beg your pardon?" asked Michelle, coming into the room with a sheaf of papers in hand.

"Nothing."

Their own meals soon arrived, but Mason only picked at the food in the styrofoam tray on his desk. He looked at his watch. They would be eating by now, he thought, and soon it would be time.

As for the spice on the food now entering the mouths of the people inside Fitten, the head chef had been half-right in guessing that it was mere curry powder of the type available in any grocery store. But that was only half of what the zip-locked bag had contained: carefully mixed in with the curry was an odorless and tasteless powder, whitish-yellow in color. No recipe in the world called for this ingredient.

The "spice" didn't come from the Middle East at all, but from Colombia, where the Bogotá underworld and its unwitting victims knew it as *Burundanga*. It came from a plant nicknamed "the tree that drives people mad," which contained scopolamine, a powerful sedative used legitimately in small doses to prevent motion sickness. The "madness" came from neurotransmitter blockages caused by the scopolamine, which resulted in dizziness, blurred vision, memory loss, hallucinations, convulsions—and great suggestibility.

Burundanga was a concoction of chemists working for the drug cartels, yet this was a drug for the use of the cartels and assorted criminals, not for recreation. Sometimes cartel hit men would take it to help them murder without feelings of guilt, but more often gangsters administered it to innocent victims.

A person under the hypnotic influence of Burundanga appeared alert and awake, but as the U.S. State Department warned, "disoriented and powerless to resist the criminal." Women allowed themselves to be raped, and victims of either sex willingly gave up their car keys and other valuables, made multiple ATM withdrawals and handed over the money, or acted as drug-smuggling "mules" for the cartels. Later they would find themselves unable to remember anything after the moment they'd been offered a drink—or a meal or a cigarette—by a stranger.

At 8:41, the sun went down, and twilight gathered over the Village. Forty-five minutes later, two groups of four SEALs apiece, equipped with radio receivers and earphones for communicating with their home base behind the Main Electric Substation, began slowly and stealthily taking up positions at the rear of Fulmer and Montag residence halls.

Mason waited another hour, till 10:15, to dial the number of Fitten dorm. The phone rang once, twice, five times—the longest Drabeznic had ever waited before picking up—fifteen times, twenty times. Mason hadn't counted on this, and though it might mean that everyone inside had fallen asleep or simply become too incapacitated to answer, the evidence wasn't conclusive. He radioed Boyd using the code phrase "Don't go on break just yet," walked across the hall, and ordered Julio to call Plant Operations and have them shut down electricity on the grid that contained Fitten, but not the MARC.

Within three minutes, Fitten Residence Hall and the buildings around it went dark. Mason waited for his phone to ring, and finally he tried calling again. No answer.

He still didn't feel good about proceeding, but he went ahead and radioed Boyd to "take his break," whereupon the SWAT team leader sent a similarly coded message to each of the two groups at the south of Fulmer and the north of Montag. Now two advance men sprinted the hundred feet or so between the two buildings and Fitten. The one from Montag, Ensign Santiago, took the southeast corner while his counterpart, Petty Officer Jackson, reached the northwest corner from Fulmer. Each crouched in his position for several minutes, waiting for any signs of activity. But the building remained so dark and quiet that it could have been empty.

Taking a portable TV monitor with him, Mason and Michelle moved onto the roof of the MARC and behind one of the raised skylight-dormers that ran down the middle of it. He glanced up toward the Centennial Research Building at the corner of Tenth and Dalney to the northeast, where a camera trained on Fitten provided an uneventful feed to the media.

Mason scanned Fitten dorm with his ITT Night Mariners, battery-powered binoculars which amplified available light by a factor of 2,000; everything looked okay and so, again using code, he reported to Boyd on his headset radio. A minute later he heard the SWAT team leader give orders to Santiago and Jackson to "smoke 'em if you got 'em."

Mason and Michelle watched as Santiago began scaling the wall, moving like a spider without benefit of rope or ladder—and like a spider trailing a "web" of long black wire behind him, connected to a hastily assembled listening post hidden behind Montag. "How do they do that?" Mason said to Michelle with a sense of awe. He spoke at a whisper, hardly audible over the roar of the air conditioner vents nearby. Rock climbers who moved up sheer rock faces with the aid only of their fingertips and toes had always amazed him, and he was just as impressed as he watched this commando make his ascent up the brick side of Fitten dorm.

The two SEALs would climb all the way up to the fourth floor, then begin making their way down, installing a small black chip (an electronic listening device developed by the KGB and often used by their competitors in the CIA) on the wall at each floor. Through the extremely thin but durable wires attached to the listening posts on the other side of the neighboring buildings to the north and south, the teams on the ground could hear any noise on the interior of Fitten, including voices and footsteps. Once Santiago and Jackson had completed their task and reached bottom, the assault teams would determine when the coast was clear, then rush the building.

Mason waited and watched. In the gathering darkness, he could see through the infrared vision enhancement of the field glasses the greenish figure of Santiago stopping beside the fourth-floor window, then reaching into his backpack to extract a listening device. Everything seemed to be going well—perhaps just a bit too well.

As Santiago retrieved the chip from his rucksack, Mason saw something move in the window to the man's left, but before he could say anything into his radio, gunfire from a Cobray M-11 submachine pistol ripped the air. The lightweight weapon could fire 1,200 rounds a minute, which had made it a favorite among both the drug gangs and the secret services of the world; within seconds it poured enough lead into Santiago to kill half a dozen men. His limp body fell the four floors to the ground.

On the other side of the building, Jackson began rapidly descending after hearing the gunfire. As soon as he got to the third floor, he sprang out from the wall, landing like a cat on the grass below, and began running across the parking lot toward Fulmer. But he had gone no more than ten steps when a burst from a machine gun on the second floor began to rip into the asphalt on his left. He stopped in mid-stride and cut right, only a split-second before another unseen sniper, this one on the third floor, began hitting the pavement to the right side with another burst of fire. What they had done to Santiago seemed downright merciful compared to this. Mason could feel the bewilderment of the hapless Jackson, who spun around for a moment before running straight forward. Now both streams of fire converged on his back and tore into him like a sewing machine on a piece of cloth.

The echoes of the shooting rang in the air, which had suddenly become dead quiet. Both Mason and Michelle, crouching behind the row of elevated skylights, jumped when his cellular phone rang. They exchanged glances as he picked it up and switched it on.

"Foolish," the voice hissed. "Foolish indeed. Did you really think we would eat the food you provided? Did you really think men on a mission such as ours need to eat? You have only made it easier for us to control our guests!"

Mason said nothing. Of course "men on a mission" had to eat, but anyone who'd prepared as carefully as al-Ansar would have thought to bring in their own food and water.

"What did you put in these girls' food?" Drabeznic asked. "They're all acting like zombies, and if my men were not honorable . . . ." He didn't finish the thought, but the implication was clear. "Whatever it was, you have broken the rules like a wayward child, and like a child you will have to pay the penalty. Now, turn our lights back on, and remove the troops behind Fulmer and Montag that were prepared to charge in here once you'd determined we were off-guard—just consider yourself lucky that I convinced my men not to shoot at them, too. Then, have your President call me."

"Would you repeat that?"

"My English is very good, and I enunciate clearly: I want to speak to your President in thirty—no, make that fifteen minutes. You've got my phone number. Have him call me back immediately."

Mason had by now sat down against the air conditioner vent, and he stayed there even after he hung up the phone. "What'd he say?" Michelle asked, leaning over him.

He would have liked not to have to speak, not to have to do anything, but he had to go downstairs now and get on the phone with Helms, who would have just witnessed the same scene via satellite from 600 miles away. For a moment he let his head rest in his hands, trying to block out the image of those two SEALs dying.

The plan to drug the food hadn't been his. He'd opposed it as best he could. But he felt responsible anyway, because he had known that the Pentagon's crazy scheme wouldn't work. Now two more men were dead.

The troops pulled back and the lights came on almost instantly, but it was past eleven o'clock before the Secretary of State got on the line with Drabeznic. "I apologize," said the diplomat in a cordial tone, "but the President is occupied at the moment, and he gives his regrets. He's asked me to speak for him." The Secretary waited through several seconds of silence. "Mr. Drabeznic . . . hello?"

A moment later, the Secretary pulled the phone away from his ear at the sound of a loud crashing as Drabeznic smashed his receiver against a wall. "Listen to me," said the terrorist leader after he'd made his point, "get off the damned phone and tell that weasel you work for that if he does not speak to me within five minutes, you will soon see one of your star divers performing the last dive of her career. *Is that clear, Mr. Secretary?*"

"Sir, if you would just—"

"You have taxed my patience beyond what I can endure. Watch for the next victim."

It didn't take two minutes before the President, furious but trying to hide his anger under an accommodating veneer, came on the line. "Mr. Drabeznic," he said. "I understand you want to talk to me."

"Sir," said Drabeznic coolly, "clearly you don't understand this, but the property my men and I occupy is for the moment a de facto sovereign nation, and as such, you have violated our boundaries. Do you know what happens in such situations?" He didn't wait for a reply. "This is not merely a war, but a holy war, a jihad, in which we are quite willing to give our lives for what we believe in. You must be willing to do the same, though like all heads of state in time of war, the life you sacrifice will not be your own. But it is your job to pick one."

"What do you mean, pick one?"

"We have people here from the United States and its territory of Puerto Rico, as well as citizens of Great Britain, Canada, and North Korea. There are Russians as well, whose President has so far chosen to play hardball—to use an Americanism—by not speaking with us, so I'll offer you his citizens as well. However, out of respect for their efforts to comply with our requests, I won't include the French or German athletes on the roster."

"To be released?"

Again, Drabeznic slammed the receiver against the wall, then said to the startled President: "I warn you not to play the fool with me, sir! You know damned well what I'm talking about."

Determined to stall, the President said, "But you killed two of ours, and we didn't injure any of your people."

"If a man breaks into your house without harming you, and you manage to shoot him, do you therefore drop the charges against him?"

"Well, to use your analogy, I wouldn't be so quick to shoot anyone, but—"

"Enough! Choose one, or I'll choose for you. How about one of your African-American citizens under our care?"

"God, no!"

"Oh, so you prefer a white, then, or one of these Hispanic Puerto Ricans?"

"No, I didn't say that."

"Ah!" said Drabeznic. "You don't have many Orientals in your country, and your blacks and whites both resent them for their great financial success and intelligence, don't they? So how about an Oriental—but not just any Oriental—a North Korean, the sworn enemy of the United States? Your people would enjoy that, wouldn't they?"

"Can't we negotiate, and end this thing?" asked the Commander-in-Chief weakly.

"Oh, we will negotiate, Mr. President, and you will meet your requirements in the same way that your allies in Berlin and Paris have already done . . . in time. But your actions have delayed the solution for now, and what we want at the moment is mere justice." He chuckled. "To put it in terms a capitalist would understand, you want to go straight to paying the principal, but you have to pay some interest first."

"Mr. Drabeznic, if you refuse to negotiate, I have nothing further to say."

"Very well, then. So that means you want the North Korean. Good-bye."

"Wait—"

But by now the President of the United States, the most powerful man in the world, was talking to himself.

Phone taps of Fitten made from the MARC revealed that Drabeznic had called CNN before he even spoke to the President, and now one of the network's helicopters, its familiar logo barely visible in the darkness, came to a hover over Twelfth and State streets about a mile to the northeast.

Mason switched on the TV. CNN had preempted a panel of analysts discussing the hostage crisis to show the live telecast, and CNN Headline News on another channel had interrupted its regular report as well. The screen, with the word "LIVE" in the upper right-hand corner, showed the well-lit dormitory building, and across the bottom scrolled a two-second-delay transcript of a phone call from Drabeznic to the reporter in the chopper.

"We now see below this building," read the transcript as Drabeznic's voice spoke over the fuzzy phone connection, "the bodies of two brave soldiers, killed when their merciless leaders sent them in to take advantage of the fact that our forces were supposedly incapacitated with narcotics. My sympathy is with the families of these men, who served their country well but were sacrificed by fools in the Pentagon Military-Industrial Complex.

"Unfortunately, as I made clear to the President of the United States on the telephone just a moment ago, these men did not pay the full price of their leader's transgressions. Therefore I asked him which athlete he would select to pay that price, and this was his choice. I direct your attention to the fourth-floor window on the northeast side of the building."

The world watched as two sets of hands placed a smiling and sleepy-looking girl on the window sill. "The President indicated to me," Drabeznic went on, "that he was unwilling to sacrifice any more American lives, and that therefore I should select an athlete from the Democratic People's Republic of Korea, one of the few nations in the world community brave enough to oppose U.S. aggression through puppet dictatorships such as the one in Seoul. In fact, he instructed me to pick the smallest, most defenseless-looking of the Korean athletes as a statement of Washington's sentiments toward Pyongyang.

"I protested that this was an act of cowardice on his part, and that we have no quarrel with the peace-loving peoples of North Korea. But he insisted, and I have complied with his wishes to the letter." The camera zoomed in on the frail figure at the window, her head drooping to the side as she stared ahead dully. "The remainder of the Korean athletes in our care are of the hardiest stock imaginable, some of them as big as men. They might have given us a struggle, even under the influence of these drugs the American government so foolishly employed against us, but this one will not.

"This, ladies and gentlemen, is Lee Chin of Chongjin, who I understand fulfilled a promise to her family and her country by helping to win the gold medal in the women's table tennis finals just yesterday. It is sad that this is how the President of the United States chooses to recognize her performance."

Unlike Heidi Hirsch or Katarina Heindrich, this girl looked positively peaceful as she contemplated the great depth below her. Perhaps her captors had told her that what she did, she did for her country's "Dear Leader"; perhaps they told her she would land on her feet and walk away. Whatever the case, on a word from one of the men beside her, Lee Chin jumped of her own accord. An instant later she hit the asphalt, snapping her neck.

As the CNN commentator came on and began his recap of what had just happened, the President himself grabbed the remote control lying on the table before him and muted the wide-screen TV. Then he stood and looked around at his Cabinet and aides with a menacing glare.

"That son of a bitch will die!" he shouted. "Do you hear me?" No one said anything. "And heads are gonna roll here too, starting now." He pointed at the Secretary of Defense, who looked up at him in terror. "You first, Al. I want your resignation, and I mean now! And I expect you to take everyone who had anything to do with security for the Olympic Games with you."

Without giving the Secretary a chance to reply, he wheeled on the others. "All right, damn it," he said, "you people are supposed to be my 'panel of experts,' so tell me how we're gonna clean this thing up and come out smelling good. Give me some answers—now!"

The group sat in respectful silence except for the red-faced Secretary of Defense, who closed his briefcase and left the room. He tried to catch the eye of the Secretary of State, who pretended not to see him as he spoke up: "Sir, considering that the Carter Center is in Atlanta—"

"Don't mention that bumpkin's name around here," said the President, raising an angry finger. "I can just hear the media right now—'Send Jimmy Carter in! Send Jimmy Carter in! He'll negotiate it for us!' Yeah, right! If he was such a damn negotiator, why in the hell did the Iranians keep our hostages for 500 days? Sure, he manages to look good now that he's not President, but I'm not about to have him waltz in and take all the credit while we get all the risk."

He glanced at his Chief of Staff. "Hank, it's time for damage control mode. Who else is to blame for this mess besides the Secretary of Defense, huh? Who was the idiot?"

"Mr. President," said the Secretary of State, "you approved the plan."

"Don't get smart with me," said the President sourly. "You know I didn't come up with that bullshit." He turned to the Deputy Secretary of Defense, now the de facto Secretary. "What's the name of the guy in the field? Mason? Is that his name?"

"Yes, sir," said the Deputy Secretary, "but if you recall, General Helms communicated to us that Mason had strong reservations about the plan."

"Yeah, well, somebody has to be the fall guy," said the First Lady.

"Yes, ma'am, but I wouldn't suggest that we take Mason out of the picture at this time. He's the one person on the ground that seems to know what's going on, better than anyone except Drabeznic himself, and it would be a mistake to change negotiators now." He turned to the President. "I would advise that we see how things transpire, and if all goes well from here, we'll take the credit; on the other hand, if the shit hits the fan, then it's all Mason's fault."

"Hm," said the President. "I think we have an excellent new Secretary of Defense in our midst."

25

By midnight, all but a small graveyard shift of security officers had taken to beds and cots, their radios and cellular phones handy in case they had to be summoned quickly. Most of the forces already posted to the Village simply returned to their quarters, and Steve Kirk somehow managed to find places for the rest. Mason ordered a cot placed in an office on the top floor of the MARC, away from the noise of the skeleton night crew, and he hoped he could force himself to sleep for a few hours.

But before he could rest, he arranged for the removal of the two SEALs' bodies, and that of Lee Chin. Then he listened to a recording of a tapped phone call from Fitten dorm to Moscow, the second attempt, made at 11:16 p.m. Apparently Drabeznic spoke fluent Russian, because the call proceeded without any delays except the normal ones involved in a transatlantic connection. Mason knew a smattering of the language from earlier Defense Department training, enough to recognize from the tone of the conversation what he already knew, and what a faxed translation from the State Department confirmed a few minutes later: the Russians were refusing to talk.

One part of the interchange struck him as significant: "Your accent," said the Russian diplomat, "it sounds familiar. Are you from the Caucasus?" Drabeznic replied curtly that, as everyone on the planet knew by now, he was a Bosnian.

By the time Mason finally stretched out at midnight, he'd been going for twenty-one hours without a break. Still, he found it nearly impossible to turn off his mind. Only by sheer willpower did he finally drift into a light, dreamless sleep a few minutes before 2:00 a.m. At a quarter after 4:00, the handheld radio of the security officer checking his floor woke him up, and he never got back to sleep.

With nearly three hours to go before the morning press conference, he decided to get up and start Day Two of the hostage crisis. By the time he'd shaved and performed the rest of his morning ablutions, he felt amazingly renewed.

Aramark sent over breakfast at 5:30, and he ate everything on his plate. Drabeznic didn't call to order any food, and he wondered if the residents of Fitten would be skipping this meal; more likely al-Ansar would eat their canned rations, and make the girls wait until after the press conference.

The sun came up at 6:48, just a few minutes after the four sets of reporters and cameramen arrived and set up their equipment. Mason, meanwhile, had taken up the same position as before on the roof of the MARC to watch through binoculars. From where he stood, he couldn't see the blotch on the pavement at the northeast corner of Fitten, which was all that remained of Lee Chin after her body had been driven away in an ambulance and handed over to the North Korean officials at Emory.

Drabeznic sounded oddly cheerful when, after a blast from the foghorn at 7:00, he came on the loudspeaker and said, "Ladies and gentlemen of the press, I trust you are fit and well-rested for another day of the Olympic drama." *He's trying to play their game,* Mason thought as he listened. *And doing a pretty good job of it, too.* The leader of al-Ansar made no reference to the incidents of the previous evening, and reminded the world of his intention to release the French and German hostages later that day. Everything seemed to be going well; but then—

"Just a few minutes ago, I made my fourth attempt to speak with the President of the Russian Federation by telephone to Moscow, where it is now a few minutes after 3:00 in the afternoon. Through intermediaries I was informed that he refuses to hear our requests." Mason scanned the faces of the media: they looked strangely eager to see what Drabeznic would do in retaliation.

"Apparently," Drabeznic continued, "the Russian President is the only person in the world who still does not understand the price to be paid for such a show of stubbornness."

With that, two men thrust a very awake and struggling Olga Shcharansky onto the sill of the same fourth-story window from which Lee Chin had jumped nine hours before. Sounding like an NBC color man, Drabeznic introduced her and went on to say, "Olga came to Atlanta with modest hopes: to reach a level of success in gymnastics that would guarantee a better apartment for her family in St. Petersburg. Unfortunately, she was overshadowed by her competitor Melody Johnson of the United States—also under our care—and only won the bronze in the individual all-around competition last Thursday." He sighed. "Today she takes the last tumble of her life."

A moment later, arms and legs flailing in mid-air, her body went sailing earthward. As it hit, Drabeznic bellowed, "This is a message to the President of the Russian Federation: you have fifteen minutes to contact us! Your swimmer Christina Rostov is eagerly awaiting your answer."

Though many local affiliates refused to show the carnage, millions of Americans saw this gruesome spectacle, and billions more throughout the world watched the media-pool broadcast. Only in Russia did the government, reverting to the tactics of its predecessor, cut off coverage. Of course the president and his staff in Moscow had satellite access, and so did a few wealthy citizens, but most other Russian viewers had to settle for what their national networks and local stations served up for them: archival footage and documentaries about past Soviet Olympic triumphs. Therefore very few Russians heard Drabeznic's announcement, exactly fifteen minutes later, that Moscow had again refused to speak with him.

"Now poor Christina Rostov," he said as the trembling girl stood at the fourth-floor window, "will die for the mistakes of her so-called leaders. You think this is a terrible thing, and it is, but how many Muslim children of Bosnia have died in the last four years without your noticing? How many Muslim children in the city of Grozny in Chechnya have been slaughtered by the Russians, and how many more in Afghanistan during the ten-year war of aggression there? Does the world care about them? No, the world is upset with us for interrupting the Olympic Games. But I warn you, people of the world, that until these injustices are addressed, more innocent victims will die on both sides.

"This may sound like a threat, and if so, treat it as such—especially you people in the United States, who no longer find yourselves in the splendid isolation you've enjoyed forever. We are now on your shores, and we will not be silenced." He paused for a moment. "Once again, I direct your attention to the fourth-floor window . . . ."

"Listen to this crap!" An aide muted the TV while the President of the United States fumed. "Does he really think the world cares about children in Grozny?"

"No," said the Secretary of State, taking off his glasses and rubbing his eyes. "And that's just it—the world doesn't seem to care, which makes him seem justified in his cause."

The President looked at the man scornfully. "You picked a fine time to get a case of the Stockholm Syndrome," he said, referring to the tendency of some hostages to sympathize with their captors, as had happened during a 1973 bank robbery in the Swedish capital. "Anybody got anything positive to say?"

The Vice President, who acted as the Administration's Olympic liaison, had spent most of the hostage crisis on the phone, and now he spoke up: "Mr. President, I'm getting calls from everywhere, demanding action. Every major corporation that has sponsored any part of the Olympic Games, especially NBC, is pressuring us to do something. The stock market has also dropped ninety-three points today." He gazed without blinking at his Commander-in-Chief. "This thing is literally costing the nation hundreds of billions of dollars, and everybody's looking to us for action."

"This is positive?" asked the President with irritation.

Ignoring the question, the Vice President went on: "I've also had some interesting conversations with Jason Blanchot at the IOC. He of course thinks we should be financially liable for any losses they might suffer, but there is a bright side." All eyes turned to him. "Blanchot expressed a willingness to put up IOC money—a loan, if you will—to get the terrorists out of there. Of course he didn't relish the idea, but he said he knows that traditional U.S. policy prohibits us from making a direct payoff to terrorists, whereas he's not under those same guidelines."

"That's good to know," answered the President. "Very good to know."

"But," the Vice President continued, taking advantage of the fact that for once he had the President's ear, "whether we take that option—Plan B—or we storm the building, the last thing we want is a protracted hostage situation. And as for Plan B, I don't think we want to put ourselves in the situation of being beholden to the IOC."

The acting Defense Secretary saw his chance to enter the conversation, and he took it. "Mr. President, we're working on another hostage rescue plan—"

"Is it as good as the last one?" asked the First Lady sarcastically.

"Hold on a minute," said the President. "Let's hear him out. How far along are you?"

"Well . . . ."

"Be prepared to present your plan by 7:00 p.m," the President ordered, suddenly raising his voice. "Got that? No later than 7:00 tonight! It's only a matter of time before this guy starts negotiating with the British and Canadians, and I'd be willing to bet he'll strike some kind of sweet deal with North Korea to piss us off. After that, you know who's next." He pointed a finger at the acting Secretary of Defense. "If we don't get him flushed out of there one way or another before he starts throwing U.S. citizens off the roof, this country will be in chaos and everybody in this room will be out of a job next January."

After the morning's executions and the cleanup that followed, Mason had a surprisingly uneventful day. There was time for a catnap, time to call his wife and tell her he was okay.

He spoke only twice with Drabeznic. The first call came in the morning, when the leader of al-Ansar arranged a tete-a-tete with the Canadian Prime Minister, as well as breakfast for his hostages. "And need I say," Drabeznic added, "that we expect their meal to be drug-free? By the way, I do appreciate your use of fine china and silver-ware—perhaps you missed your calling in life, Mason. You would have made a good maitre d'."

Later, Mason and Gen. Helms listened in on the conversation with Ottawa. Again, Drabeznic demanded more planes and more released prisoners, and the prime minister, who had guessed the requests in advance, didn't put up a fight.

Because breakfast came late, Drabeznic ordered a late lunch, and with it a request for a hook-up with London. At 6:00 p.m. he would hold another press conference, no doubt to announce the results and—Mason hoped—keep his word about freeing the French and German hostages. Then a team could debrief them, from which they might discover some new information about the equipment and operations of al-Ansar.

Robbins had promised to give Mason the results of his search for the presumed "mole" in Georgia Tech Plant Operations by suppertime on Tuesday, but with the events since then, the news didn't come until early Wednesday afternoon. As Robbins explained, Plant Operations had taken on more than 120 new-hires from September 18, 1990 until July 1994, when Village Security began running heightened security checks on all new applicants.

"The FBI ran checks on all of them before they were hired," Robbins said, "and they came up clean or they wouldn't have been let in. Some stayed for periods of time and left, but about eighty are still here, so we did a more detailed check on them. It was surprising how many felony convictions we found that the feds didn't seem to have caught—"

"Felony convictions?" Mason asked.

"Nothing that would indicate terrorist activities," Robbins answered. "Anyway, we interviewed as many out of those eighty that we could locate by telephone. A good portion of them were told to stay home because of the situation in the Village, but they're all supposed to call in an hour before their shift is scheduled to begin, then remain on call until it ends, so it was easy to locate them—all but three. We researched those three thoroughly, and out of those, one candidate emerged."

He handed Mason a black-and-white I.D. photograph that showed a man in his late thirties with blond hair and a handsome, rugged face. While Mason studied the picture, Robbins read from his notes. "He goes by the name of Jonathan Dewberry, hired January 15, 1991. He's routinely gotten excellent evaluations, and was promoted to foreman last year over several others with more seniority—but he didn't call in either yesterday or today. We ran a check with the Social Security Administration, and while we were waiting for the results to come back, we called the one past employer he gave on his prior employment record."

"Only one?"

"He claimed he'd worked with the Gateway Construction Company of Springfield, Missouri, for twelve years from 1978 to 1990, and because of the tenure, Tech didn't require him to submit any information on jobs before that. The record indicates that the school's personnel department called Gateway in late January 1991 and got a glowing reference for him, so we called the number ourselves. It turns out to belong to a private citizen who's had the number since early in 1992, but the phone company shows that the number was in service with Gateway Construction Company only during the month of January 1991. We checked with the Springfield Police, as well as their chamber of commerce, and no one had any record that the company ever existed."

"Looks like he kept the number just long enough for personnel to verify his employment," said Mason thoughtfully.

"Meanwhile," Robbins continued, drawing a breath, "Social Security called us back and reported that they did have a Jonathan Dewberry under the same I.D. number as this guy used, but they show him as being born on May 12, 1938, whereas this guy's records at Tech list a birthdate of May 12, 1956—a difference of eighteen years. Not only that, but they show Jonathan Dewberry as residing in Dallas in 1990, but prior to that he hadn't filed a tax return for eight years. So we checked with the Dallas Police, etc., and it turns out he was a drifter who mainly did odd jobs—last seen in December of '90."

"Just a month before 'Dewberry' showed up here!"

"You got it," Robbins replied.

"That's great work, Greg," said Mason. "I don't know what good it does us right now, but it's good to know."

Just then his "red telephone" buzzed, and he picked it up, waving to Robbins.

"Listen, I want to give you a heads-up," said Gen. Helms. "I've got a team of technicians en route to Dobbins, and they should be arriving later this afternoon. They'll proceed to the Village to conduct a reconnaissance mission."

"Technicians? Reconnaissance?" The two words didn't seem to go together.

"It's a little unusual," conceded Helms, "but they're on orders directly from the acting Secretary of Defense."

Steve Kirk had a much busier time than Mason that Wednesday. With the crisis showing no signs of ending any time soon and the administration at Emory pressuring him to do something about the sudden and unwelcome population explosion on their campus, he'd put in repeated calls to Jason Blanchot without getting any definitive go-ahead to take action. Finally in the early afternoon, Blanchot's secretary called and said that the IOC President had ordered all athletes who had been eliminated to go home, as well as those who'd had finals on Tuesday and Wednesday.

This solved at least part of the problem, and Kirk hastily dispatched a crew of aides to Emory to organize the confused exodus to the airport. Within an hour, that confusion spread to Hartsfield International Airport, where ticketing agents fought to rearrange seating for the unexpected stampede. Some of the wealthier NOCs chartered flights, but delegations from such out-of-the-way spots as Burundi and Nepal had a long wait ahead of them.

NBC had sent a crew to interview the departing athletes, and they were disappointed to find that Christiann Vervoerden wasn't among them. But they did at least catch Vervoerden's would-be competitor Georg Molnar, who smiled bravely at the cameras and lamented the lost opportunity to compete for the gold: "It's unfortunate that things had to happen this way," said Molnar in passable English, "but as a Hungarian I sympathize with the cause of peace in Bosnia, and I am willing to make this sacrifice."

There still remained thousands of athletes at Emory, many of them hoping that they would still have a chance to compete on Thursday. But quite a few—especially the coaches and officials—could see the end coming, and they were only waiting for the word from Jason Blanchot.

As for Blanchot himself, he spent one of the worst days of his long life ensconced in his office at ACOG Headquarters, taking more angry calls from Ira Greenberg and other irate sponsors, presidents of international sports federations and national Olympic committees, and anyone else who managed to get past his secretary. As for Hans Bliecher, who had become the focus of the wrath Blanchot couldn't afford to turn against his callers, he kept as low a profile as he could manage.

Late in the afternoon, Kirk took his golf cart over to the MARC for a briefing. As he sat in the meeting, he couldn't help noticing how exhausted—even defeated—Michelle looked, and when it was over he pulled her aside. "You need a break," he whispered.

"Are you kidding?" she asked, glancing at Mason, who was walking by.

Mason looked up at her. "Take fifteen," he said. "You need it."

So Kirk and Michelle walked outside, hopped into his golf cart, and motored several blocks to Junior's Grill. She hadn't been outside the MARC all day, and now she saw how the formerly vibrant Village was deserted except for security forces. Junior's, the only commercial eating establishment in the entire place, had been there for Tech professors continuing their research projects during the Games; but they had all gone home after the governor declared a state of emergency. The restaurant would have shut its doors if it hadn't been for a few security and Olympic officials who came to get away from the tension for a few minutes.

Kirk ordered two chocolate malts, and they sat down next to each other at a table for four. He smiled at her. Michelle looked miserable, and the smile she gave him in return was nothing like her usual sunny expression.

He reached out and touched her hand, but she looked away. "This morning I saw the bodies of the two Russian girls," she said, straining to hold back the emotion. "They looked so young, so innocent . . . . They were just here because they wanted to come to the Games and do their best, and now . . . ." She looked back at him, her lip trembling slightly.

He shook his head. In all the time he'd known her, he'd never seen her this vulnerable.

"I've seen people die," she said, drawing a breath. "A couple times. But never anyone just murdered like that, not something so senseless." With a deep sigh, she took a drink of her malt and said, "It's all been easy before: the planning, the simulations, the infiltrations. Those were games. But this is different, and . . . I wonder if I'm right for the job anymore."

He put his arm around her, and she rested her head on his shoulder. "We're all tired," he said. "Stressed and pushed to the limit. That's the only reason you're questioning yourself like this."

"Think so?" she asked.

"I know so. Look, Tom believes in you, and he's one hell of a pragmatic guy. He wouldn't give you so much responsibility if he didn't know you could do it." He smiled again. "Once this thing is all over, you'll be back to your old ball-busting self."

"Yeah, I guess."

He took her chin in his hand and looked at her, raising his eyebrows.

"Okay," she said, trying to laugh. "I *know*."

As she once again rested her head against him, he said something he'd wanted to say for awhile. "You know, I had the most amazing dream about ten days ago, and I don't want it to end."

"Dream?"

"About a beautiful woman, who—"

She looked up at him. "You don't have to worry about it ending. Not all dreams do, you know." The color was coming back to her face, and a flash of her old confident smile returned.

"Then think about this," he said. "After this ends, I'm gonna take you to a friend's house on Ambergris Cay, and you're not gonna have any responsibility but to eat and sleep and run your toes through the sand."

"Mm, sounds lovely. Where's Ambergris Cay?"

"In Belize."

"Belize," she repeated. "I wish I was there now."

The CNN reporter stood in front of the camera with the hulking mass of Fitten dorm clearly visible across Couch Field behind him, performing the media task of explaining to viewers what they'd just seen and heard. "Hakija Drabeznic, leader of the shadowy Bosnian faction known as al-Ansar, whose siege of Fitten Residence Hall is now entering its fortieth hour, has just completed his scheduled 6:00 p.m. news conference. He announced the successful commencement of negotiations with the British and Canadian governments toward the release of their hostages, a total of twelve young women."

The camera panned to show eight female athletes, half of them wearing the colors of the German team and the other half in the French tricolor, surrounded by medics who escorted them to waiting ambulances on Hemphill Avenue. "More significantly," the correspondent went on, "he has fulfilled a promise made yesterday to release the hostages from France and Germany. This came upon confirmation that their governments have met his demands of arms shipments to Bosnia and the release of some thirty-two 'political prisoners' to an undisclosed third country."

There followed a report from Sarajevo, where it was midnight. At a military airport under Bosnian government control, enthusiastic groups of soldiers were busy unloading crates of munitions from the French and German planes. A colonel who consented to speak with the CNN reporter on the scene said through a translator, "As a military man, I cannot say I agree with the illegal methods of these men in Atlanta— whoever they are—but I would be most ungrateful if I did not profess to appreciate what they have done for us." Misty-eyed, the colonel added, "These weapons and the others on the way could make all the difference in our fight for survival."

As for the undisclosed destination of the released prisoners, panels of experts around the television dial and in newspapers all over the world offered endless speculation. Some suggested Libya, and the name of Syria came up more than once, but most of them concluded that it had to be either Iran or Iraq, probably Iraq.

Washington wouldn't comment on this, or much of anything else. In fact, the President had been strangely incommunicado since Tuesday morning, and even through his White House Communications Director he had released information to the press at only three briefings. Scenes of protesters along Pennsylvania Avenue holding up signs that said *Free Our Olympic Athletes* and *Mr. President, Why Won't You Do Something?* blended eerily with footage of "spontaneous demonstrations" in support of al-Ansar taking place on the streets of Cairo, Damascus, and Teheran even into the wee hours of the morning.

26

The President's 7:00 p.m. meeting did not convene until 7:30. This time the group in the Cabinet Room was joined by Gen. Helms in person and Thomas Mason through a phone link.

Mason gave a report on interviews his people had just conducted with the released French and German hostages, which confirmed much of what he'd heard from Katarina Heindrich the day before. On the one hand, the girls said, they were kept apart, handcuffed, equipped with explosive devices, and forbidden to watch TV or listen to the radio; on the other hand, they did have permission to read magazines and books, and generally received polite treatment from their captors.

"Tom," asked Helms, "has al-Ansar tried to establish rapport by explaining to the hostages, from their perspective at least, why this is happening?"

"Yes, sir, they have. The version of events they gave is basically the same we've been hearing from Drabeznic in the press conferences. The hostages are not permitted to listen in on these conferences, of course, and none of them knew what had actually happened to the four young women who have so far been killed. Most assumed—probably because they wanted to believe—that these four had been released. Clearly the objective of the terrorists is to keep the captives calm, and therefore more easily controlled; it's interesting to note that only after they found out that their colleagues had been killed did the girls cease to make statements that I can only call sympathetic to the terrorists."

"Sympathetic?" the President demanded.

"Yes, sir. From their perspective, the men didn't hurt them, and they acted as gentlemen. Clearly Drabeznic had an ironclad rule against any touching or sexual advances, because there's been none of that in the reports we've gotten. One of the Germans said, 'This situation has been an inconvenience, but what is a few hours of discomfort in light of what those poor people in Bosnia have suffered?' Then I told her about Lee Chin, the two Russians, and her own compatriot Heidi Hirsch. At first she refused to believe me, but when I showed her a newspaper with the

Hirsch story on page one, it started to dawn on her that she didn't fully understand the situation. She began to cry and curse, and at that point the delayed shock of the incident came over her so violently that I concluded our interview.

"As for the terrorists themselves, the girls all reported that they didn't seem nervous at all—in fact, *casual* was the word used by one athlete. In spite of that appearance, though, they are heavily armed with automatic weapons, hand grenades, and extra ammunition, which they keep with them at all times. The girls have also confirmed that they appear to have welded bed frames onto the windows of the lower floors, and stacked heavy equipment such as washing machines and dryers against these. On most of the upper-floor windows, they have placed aluminum foil, which we know to be a means of protecting against laser listening devices.

"They have radios, but use has been limited, which may explain why we have been able to detect few of their conversations through the surveillance equipment in the MARC. It seems there are hard-wire communication devices between each floor and throughout the building, along with TV monitors, which suggests that they have established a closed-circuit TV system to communicate without using radios. And of course it's likely they have regular TVs too—for themselves but not the hostages—so they know everything that's happening from our perspective."

"Damn well-prepared, aren't they?" asked the acting Defense Secretary.

"Sir, I'd say that's an understatement. As we surmised from our, uh, difficulty last night," Mason went on, choosing his words carefully, "they have plenty of food as well. One hostage told us she could smell them cooking their own food. This was before we sent in the first meal at lunchtime yesterday, and she asked to be fed, but was told, 'This food is not for guests.' Another said she saw a man drinking from a bottle of Crystal Springs, so presumably they brought that in, too. God knows there was plenty of bottled water around the Village. How many days' worth of provisions they have is anybody's guess, but I would suppose that they're prepared for a week-long siege, at least."

"A week!" gasped the President.

"How about protective masks, Tom?" asked Helms.

"No, sir, not that anybody's mentioned, but—"

"Alright, Tom," said the President. "Excellent report. Now I believe

General Helms has a plan to present to us, so let's all listen—you too, Mason."

"Mr. President," said the general hesitantly, "this is not *my* plan per se, and even if it were, I'd want to make sure that all concerned parties understand that we've had minimal time to prepare for this mission, and don't necessarily recommend this assault option."

"What exactly are you saying?" asked the Chief of Staff.

"Sir, I'm only pointing out that this plan is frothing with risk, that's all. As far as I'm concerned, it can only be talked about responsibly in an academic sense. In other words, this is what we'd do if we had more time and resources for planning."

"Let's skip all that for now," said the President. "Give us the plan, and we'll get back to the risk issue."

With a resolute sigh, Helms began to speak: "We have made an intensive study of the nearby campus layout, including communication lines and other infrastructure. In the course of this, we discovered a six-foot sewer servicing the west side of campus. It's a trunk line, fed by the run-off of nearby dorms through various conduits, and it runs just ten feet below and thirty-seven feet from the east wall of Fitten dormitory."

"How does that help?"

"We have sent men in on a reconnaissance mission, and we believe a properly equipped team can go in with the type of equipment normally used to inspect and photograph the insides of pipes in factories. They would run a flexible tube called a borescope through the plumbing system, entering the central bathroom area through the valve of a commode, and releasing a gas such as nitrous oxide, which would immobilize both terrorists and hostages and make it possible for a scout team wearing protective masks to enter the building. Upon a successful reconnaissance mission by the scouts, an assault team would go in and—if all goes well—take out the terrorists and disarm the explosives."

Several of the Cabinet members exchanged optimistic glances, some of them giving low whistles of amazement. The acting Defense Secretary beamed with pride at "his plan," but the Vice President spoke up and said, "Now about this pipe—this borescope—how does it work?"

The general began to explain the mechanism, similar to the type of tube used in highly sophisticated arthroscopic surgery, utilized by plumbing engineers to examine pipes in areas difficult or impossible to reach without disturbing the surrounding structure. A keypad operated by an engineer at the end of the tube acted as a sort of remote control to move it around corners and through intersections of pipes. In this case, however, the probe would be attached to a hose through which nitrous oxide would be released.

"And exactly how does nitrous oxide work?" the First Lady asked.

"Common name is laughing gas, ma'am," explained Helms. "It is not known to be lethal in any quantities, but produces reactions similar to the effects of a hallucinogenic drug. In general, it induces in the subject an overwhelming sense of well-being and of disconnectedness with his body, and in larger doses leads to unconsciousness—which is why it makes a good anaesthetic for dentists and doctors."

"The proverbial 'chill pill'," said the President, obviously fascinated.

"You could call it that, sir."

"But I fail to see how this is substantively different from what we did before with the food," the Vice President said. "Either way the idea is to knock out the terrorists and go in, so why should this plan work any better than the other one?"

"Well, sir, the difference would be that they didn't have to eat the food, whereas given the fact that to our knowledge they do not possess protective masks, they will have no choice but to breathe the air."

"Sir," Mason said from the speaker phone, "if I may clarify, we haven't been told that they do possess protective masks, but that certainly doesn't rule out the possibility."

"True," Helms agreed, turning back to the Vice President. "However, this isn't like CS—what you call tear gas. There's no coughing, no smell, no visible sign of the vapor; therefore presumably they'd be knocked out before anyone realized any gas had been released."

"Has this been tested yet?" the Vice President wanted to know.

"Not on site, sir. Before we do this, I would request approximately four hours' time to conduct a test in the area of Armstrong dorm, on the other side of Fulmer from Fitten. I believe we're going to find that this operation becomes increasingly difficult the higher up in the building we go, and the more turns we make. The test would also allow us to measure noise levels, which is one of our chief areas of concern."

"Mm-hm," mumbled the President. He knew he didn't have time for a four-hour delay.

"What if the nitrous oxide doesn't knock out all the terrorists?" asked the Vice President. "Or what if they have masks?"

"Then, sir, I'd say our scout team would be on a suicide mission."

"But the hostages would be okay, wouldn't they?" the President asked.

Mason jumped in. "Sir, given the fact that Drabeznic has already demonstrated his willingness to kill hostages, you'd definitely be looking at some casualties there, too. If it came to a death struggle between him and our forces, he'd likely set off all the detonating devices."

"Bottom line," said the President, "What do you think of our chances for success?"

"I couldn't put a number on it, sir," Helms answered gravely. "The problem is that you have to factor in hostages; otherwise, we could have just started lobbing tear gas and grenades in there and blown the terrorists out thirty-six hours ago."

"Then let me re-phrase the President's question, if I may," said the Vice President. "What do you see as our biggest chances for failure?"

"Sir, I would say the biggest liability is the noise we might make with the pipes. If they heard us, it might lead to the terrorists setting off their trip mechanisms to detonate the explosives on the hostages. Secondly, as I said, there's the chance they have protective gas masks, and would be waiting for our troops. And thirdly, even if there's only one man standing, the existence of the trip wires makes that one person quite capable of killing all the hostages single-handedly. Given all these possibilities, I can't recommend that we go forward without testing this plan, and even then—"

"Shit," said the President irritably. "If there are that many risks, why'd you bring me this plan?"

The general looked at the acting Secretary of Defense, who tried to avert his eyes but finally had to reply: "Because you said you wanted one, sir."

"Mason," said the President into the speaker phone, "what do you think of all this?"

"Mr. President, I am in full agreement with General Helms. I can't in good conscience recommend any attack on these terrorists, not with the casualties we've already sustained between the four hostages and the eight members of Lt. Boyd's SEAL team. I didn't feel good about our last attack from the beginning, and this one appears even more problematic. Of course I will do whatever I am ordered, but—"

The President sighed. "Alright. We'll confer. In the meantime, prepare your people there, and I'll have General Helms call you with specific directives. We'll make a final decision by 10:00 tonight."

As an aide flipped off the speaker phone, the others in the room looked to the President, hoping beyond hope for some inspiration.

But instead of saying anything, he simply stared into space. His advisors glanced at one another, and everyone had the same thought: *He's losing control.*

He took several steps before turning back, as though he'd forgotten that the rest of them were even in the room. "Alright," he said quietly. "Ten o'clock. In the meantime, I'm going to confer with the First Lady." He glanced at her, and she stood up to go. Just before leaving, he announced to the others in the room, "We're gonna *pray* over this decision."

These last words struck the assembled Cabinet members, advisors, and aides as particularly bizarre. They'd all heard their Chief wax sentimental with religious rhetoric on the campaign trail, showing up at churches for photo ops and reciting Scripture in a majestic voice at political rallies, and none of them had taken any of it seriously. These were merely the motions any Presidential candidate, whether he was religious or not, had to go through in order to attract the votes of the great uneducated mass of Americans. Perhaps his words now were only a figure of speech, or perhaps they proved that in a time of crisis, almost anyone believes in a God.

When Helms called, he had Mason instruct the sewer technicians to make all preparations short of actually entering the Fitten dorm secondary line. The National Guard units in the Village, who had seen little action since Tuesday morning aside from creating a heightened security presence at press conferences, would provide cover for Boyd's SWAT team. Therefore the general relayed orders to the National Guard commander to assemble seventy-five of his best marksmen, as well as three squads of machine gunners, and report to the first floor of the library for a briefing by Lt. Boyd at 10:30.

Lastly, Helms asked Mason if the CIA technicians viewing the media's video feed of the Fitten dorm exterior had taped the footage, and Mason said that as far as he knew, they had. Whatever the case, the general said, they should begin taping at about ninety minutes after sundown, and collect several hours' worth of video footage. "Anything you say, sir," Mason replied, not sure where Helms was going with the idea; but when he had it explained to him, he broke out in one of the few genuine laughs he'd had in a long, long while. It was brilliant, he said.

The technicians, or "Sewer Rats," a tactical unit from the 4th Psychological Operations (Psyop) Group at Fort Bragg, set up a temporary operating post on the north side of Armstrong Residence Hall, well out of sight from Fitten. The entire Georgia Tech plumbing and drainage network had been drawn some years before on a Computer Aided Design system, and the men possessed data on the exact footage, within certain tolerances, of each length of pipe between joints. Yet pipes in several of the nearby buildings had undergone repairs and replacements since their installation in the 1970s, calling into question the old plans and highlighting the need for a test run on another dorm, as Gen. Helms had suggested. But there was no time for that.

Eight of the sixteen Sewer Rats would remain above ground to guide the maneuvering of the borescope, a job that would become increasingly tedious once the flexible pipe entered the secondary line, with its twists and turns. But their work was recreation compared to that of the other eight, who would make a 500-foot trek through the sewer to the opening of the secondary line, where they would provide manual support in guiding the borescope.

It was a journey into a foul-smelling hell. They would walk through a concrete tunnel too small for a six-foot man to stand up in without hitting his head, knee-deep in sludge and excrement, surrounded by vile creatures—including *real* sewer rats. Besides that, there were the many threats that make sewage and waste-water one of the most dangerous industries in the world: falls, electrocution, cave-ins, and poisonous or flammable gases.

To protect themselves, the team ventilated the space with a mechanical blower, and each man wore a decontamination suit and gloves, waterproof boots, a hard hat, and a self-contained breathing apparatus. Such precautions had become standard fare for those who dared to venture into sewer pipes; but due to the covert nature of their mission, these men faced additional dangers, the greatest of which was noise as the pipe moved along the secondary line. The borescope had a casing of stainless steel braid with polyurethane to reduce scraping, and as an additional precaution, the Sewer Rats wrapped the probe in thick rubber tape.

The borescope itself represented decades of enhancement in computers, robotics, and polymer plastics since the 1940s. At its business end were a tiny light, a camera chip, a condenser mike, and an electronic signalling device behind a glass window etched with a razor-thin line. The line cast a shadow on objects in front of it, which made it possible to determine the distance from the tip of the probe to the object ahead by applying the known geometric relationship between the positions of the camera, the light source, and the line. The signalling device converted images from the camera and transmitted them to the operating station above ground, where a technician in a 3-D video helmet would use virtual technology to guide the probe.

Inside, along its polyvinyl chloride core, was a custom feature that made this particular borescope quite different from the ones used by industry to inspect difficult-to-reach spots inside airplane engines, cooling systems, and piping networks. A high-pressure gas line a quarter of an inch in diameter ran the length of this mechanical serpent, and opened at the far end. When the time came, it would release a vapor pumped through it from cylinders in the "Rat Hole," as the Sewer Rats called their area of operations.

A mournful quiet, much like that in the Olympic Village, reigned over the White House. While the President sought the counsel of his wife and an even higher power, the rest of his staff retired to their offices for a few stolen minutes of rest, or strolled down to the commissary in the West Wing. Everyone knew it would be a long, long night.

A Secret Service man overheard a conversation from the study next to the Yellow Oval Room on the second floor. The talk was all one-way: "How about showing some damn backbone?" a female voice commanded. "Our only possible hope now is a lucky break," she said, and "This *could* get us re-elected, if you don't screw things up!"

Then at 10:00 p.m. the President emerged from his quarters, looking refreshed and ready for another round.

Five minutes later, he stood in the Cabinet Room and gave his decision: the hostage-rescue operation in the Olympic Village would proceed according to the plan outlined earlier. "In difficult times," he said, "leaders must make difficult decisions, but I believe that the fact that we're in the right, and will press on toward our goal with vigor, will ensure our victory."

The reassembled group exchanged glances. A few of them were thinking that planning, not Kennedyesque rhetoric, would ensure the victory—and planning was one thing in short supply. "I'm willing to lay this Administration on the line for the sake of innocent lives," the

President went on. "If I am wrong, I will certainly take the responsibility."

He turned to Gen. Helms. "I want you to shelve anybody, including yourself, who is not able to commit one hundred percent to this assault. Nobody's being punished, it's just that we can't afford to have anybody on the team who's not gung-ho. Are you in or out, general?"

"I'm in, Mr. President," said Helms, though he wasn't anywhere near one hundred percent convinced. Still, he felt safer about the operation with himself in charge than with anyone else.

"Good. Now, it's clear that Mason has some hesitation, so here are your orders for him: he remains in charge of field operations down there, of course, but in this attack he's acting only in the capacity of your liaison. The entire SEAL attack group will be removed from his command and report directly to you. Is that clear?"

"Yes, sir."

"Alright, give me a time frame for this operation."

"Well, Mr. President, I—"

The President held up a hand. "*Minimum* time, general."

"Sir, right now it's 2215 . . . or rather, 10:15. I believe it would be safe to shoot for an entry time of 2:00 a.m. That would give them almost four hours to get the borescope lines in, and still put the SEALs into the building well before sunrise at 6:49."

"Okay. Go to it." The President, who had not sat down, now turned to go. "I'm going to get a little sleep. Wake me up when the assault begins."

27

Mason didn't have much to do in the next few hours, having been relieved of all responsibility except coordinating the assault. He wanted to believe that the mission would succeed, but his gut feeling went against that hope. It looked to him as though Washington would willingly sacrifice men for political expediency, just as he'd seen another Administration do in Southeast Asia thirty years before. He wanted no part of it this time. Still, he didn't feel entirely good about seeing the operation turned over to Lt. Allan Boyd, not just because of the danger but because he had doubts that the officer could approach the mission rationally, given the high toll of casualties Drabeznic's men had exacted on his team.

At 10:30 p.m., having prepared his own men in anticipation of Washington's orders, Boyd walked over to the Georgia Tech Library to brief the National Guardsmen. As he explained to the troops, if all went as planned, at around 2:00 a.m. on Thursday, the electricity would be cut to the area surrounding Fitten. At that time, they would divide into three groups to take up positions in the three surrounding buildings: Montag, Fulmer, and Couch.

Of course Drabeznic had declared Montag and Fulmer off-limits to anyone but al-Ansar, and his men might have installed explosive devices inside, but under the circumstances the security forces had to take the chance. Only a few people in Washington and Atlanta knew of the plan; Boyd told the Guardsmen that they would be providing cover for a possible reconnaissance mission.

Each sniper was given a photocopied plan of the floor and building to which he was assigned, with the location of the specific room where he would take up a position, highlighted alongside a notation of the window of Fitten at which he was to aim. If they saw any movement at that window *of a hostile nature*—no one wanted to see a hostage get killed by friendly fire—they were to take out the target. The machine gunners, stationed on the rooftops with M-60s, would provide additional firepower. Even if one of the terrorists tried to shoot at them, he'd likely be taken out by a sniper before he got off more than a couple rounds.

Finally, Boyd said, if anything should go wrong, a red flare would signal cease-fire and retreat. "But," he added with a nervous smile, "nothing's going to go wrong."

The slow-motion slalom of the borescope proceeded with relative ease on straightaways or when the tube reached an elbow joint and had no option but to take a ninety-degree turn; the hard part came when the plan required a turn into a T-section. The probe would want to follow the main pipe forward, forcing the operator to coax it into making the turn instead.

Below ground, the Sewer Rats operated the machinery that pushed the borescope forward, provided manual assistance by keeping the probe away from obstructions, and watched a video monitor which displayed the position of the snaking device relative to its destination. There wasn't much to do but stand around knee-deep in muck and check the operations of the insertion machinery from time to time.

It took almost thirty minutes and sixty-five feet of tubing before the borescope entered a plumbing stack leading directly upward through Fitten dormitory's four central bathrooms. It followed this stack all the way to the fourth floor, at which point the technician operating the probe from above ground had to make an excruciating ninety-degree turn toward the toilets. As he began one last turn before the point of penetration, the men in the operating center outside Armstrong Residence Hall sent word to headquarters that they were prepared for the final thrust.

As the probe crept closer to home, the risk of making noise increased. Thus, on a command from the operating center, a helicopter parked near the MARC cranked up its engines and rose slowly into the air before making a loud, leisurely spin over Hemphill Avenue and Eighth Street. It made a wide berth around the area of Fitten, then turned slowly southward toward the Georgia Dome a mile away, where it set down in the parking lot three minutes after lift-off.

In those 180 seconds, the technicians had time to push through the drain and penetrate a toilet. As the probe neared the surface, the operator's assistant at the ground station turned off the light at the end—and then suddenly, with a thrill of exhilaration, they realized that they were now looking out of the number one toilet bowl on the fourth floor of Fitten Dorm. The operator pushed the end up just above the surface of the water, and the assistant switched on the microphone. The radio technician listened, but he could hear nothing other than the drip of a water faucet from the basin directly across the way.

"The eagle has landed," the technicians' commander said into his radio. At these words, the order went out to the Sewer Rats to turn on the gas line.

But this was only the first probe. It had taken nearly an hour and a half to put it into place, and at the rate they were going, it would be 4:30 a.m. before they installed the fourth one—much too late to begin the assault. Of course each successive probe would be shorter, and having one in place might make the others easier to follow. Or it might not. Whatever the case, they had to work faster.

Mason had waited tensely through the chopper's short flight, expecting an irate Drabeznic to call at any moment. As with the previous evening's raid, he had a cover story; yet the phone did not ring, and he didn't know whether to feel worried or relieved.

Boyd came into the office to wait for a three-way call with Gen. Helms and a chemical specialist at Fort Sill, Oklahoma, on the "red telephone." While he waited, he paced the floor, his face gaunt with stress.

Mason watched him from the corner of his eye, then cleared his throat. "You know, Allan," he said, "it seems to me that this mission requires a commander at the rear, to have some perspective."

Boyd stopped pacing in front of the coffee maker, where a pot at least an hour old sat half-empty. "This any good?" he asked over his shoulder, pouring himself a cup.

"Yeah, if you like battery acid," said Mason.

Boyd sat down, sniffing the coffee before setting it aside and responding to Mason's comment. "In other circumstances I might agree with you, Tom, but here the perspective is all at the front."

"I respect what you're saying," said Mason, choosing his words carefully, "but this is not some battle in ancient Greece or the Middle Ages, when the king would lead his men right into the thick of things. This is post-Gulf War, almost the twenty-first century that we're talking about here—battles run by staff officers in dress uniforms."

Boyd cleared his throat. "I don't think you believe that. Sure, it's post-Gulf War, but it's also post-Munich, post-Desert One, post-Desert Storm—the age of special operations, counterterrorism—you know, the way you and me both earn a paycheck?" He was right about that: without men like Boyd to go in first, the series of high-tech engagements that made the front pages in the Gulf War would have gone quite differently. "Besides," he added, "it's a good plan, and I trust Helms."

"Hell, I trust Helms too—it's you I don't trust."

"Me?" asked Boyd indignantly.

"You know the old saying," said Mason. "'Revenge is a dish best served cold.' You just want to get even, and while I can't blame you for feeling that, I think—"

"I'm not under any illusions that this is going to bring back any of those guys who went down," said Boyd, who in spite of his disdain now took a sip of the thick black coffee. "Remember the SEAL motto: 'The only easy day was yesterday.' I know we can take these bastards out, and then we'll prove we're worth our salt."

"But you don't have anything to prove! No one blames you for the losses your unit has suffered, and I still say that the best way for you to lead is from here."

"No," said Boyd. "I'm going in. All seven of the guys I'm taking with me are volunteers, and we can't wait to get started. I'm not about to shrink back from this mission now. I feel . . . ." He glanced up at the ceiling, then back at Mason. "I feel like it's my destiny."

Mason looked both with pride and sadness at the man he'd come to appreciate and admire during the weeks they'd worked together. "Allan, I wish I'd had ten men like you in my unit in 'Nam."

Putting in the second probe was an exercise in mind-numbing tedium, and the commander at the station outside Armstrong switched operator-assistant teams at thirty-minute intervals to keep fresh, alert minds on the mission. Likewise the Sewer Rat leader allowed two men at a time to take half-hour breaks and return to the surface, and though the slow process of wading to and from the opening reduced their above-ground time to only ten or fifteen minutes, it was a welcome relief from the Rat Hole.

Unfortunately, the second borescope line took just as long to move in as the first, because the obstruction created by the first probe in the narrow pipes cancelled out the advantage of having it there as a guide. They got the probe all the way to the third-floor entry before realizing that the tubing that led to the fourth floor was blocking the way. That meant that they could either pull out of the fourth floor and try to reinsert, which was out of the question because of the time and energy it would take, or they could skip the third floor altogether and go straight to the second. Under the circumstances, they had no choice but to do the latter.

It was now 1:30 in the morning, just half an hour away from the originally scheduled assault time.

As the second probe reached its destination, the chopper returned from the Dome on a reverse of the path it had made before, and once again Mason's phone failed to ring. He felt a crazy urge to dial up Drabeznic and ask him why he was keeping so quiet. Outside he saw the great silent hulk of Fitten dorm, only a few lights on at this hour, and he radioed the man operating the camera on the Centennial Research Building to ask how it looked from there. "Boring" was the reply.

After receiving the unpleasant news of the delay, Boyd consulted with Helms and the officer at Fort Sill over the "red telephone." The chemical-agent specialist estimated that the first gas line had, in ninety minutes of operation, achieved nearly one hundred percent coverage on the fourth floor, a figure that dropped drastically for each successive floor below. If they turned on the second-floor line now, within two hours it would raise the overall figure to about eighty; still, the officer at Fort Sill warned that there would still be limited coverage of the first floor. But if the last probe were in place for at least one hour, that would raise their coverage level to about ninety-four percent.

"So we should move our assault time back to 0330, sir?" asked Boyd hopefully.

"For now, yes," said the general in a non-committal tone that told the lieutenant that his superior had second thoughts about the mission.

Another hour passed.

Boyd waited with Mason in his office, eager for word from below. Periodically, Mason would doze off in a half-sleep, but the SWAT team leader stayed wide awake, fueled by adrenalin.

At 2:27 a.m., their radios crackled with a transmission from the technicians to the relay team in the MARC. "Making final turn," a voice said, and Boyd sat forward to listen. "Ten more feet . . . . Crank up the noisemaker." As the order went out to the chopper pilot to stand by, the lieutenant broke into a big grin, but his face fell a moment later when the voice on the radio said, "Hold last order! Toilet flushing . . . ." There followed several subdued curses, then another breach of radio discipline: "We damn near stuck that probe up somebody's ass . . . . Tower One, hold for five."

"Roger, Tech One."

Five minutes passed before Boyd and Mason heard: "Tower One, Tech One. All clear. Proceed to fly."

As the chopper outside began to lift off, Boyd picked up the "red telephone" and spoke to Helms, who like Mason had been dozing. Within two minutes the SEAL commander was off the phone and on the radio to his assistant squad leader. "Commence at exactly T-plus sixty minutes. I have 0236 and 25 seconds. Mark. We begin at 0336."

Boyd stood up. "Well," he said to Mason with a nervous laugh, "it's like they say in jump school: 'Stand in the door'."

"Good luck, partner." Mason stood up too. "We'll have breakfast waiting for you when you get back."

"I'll be starving—see you then."

Boyd made a smart turn on his heels and exited the office, looking as though he actually believed the confident sound of his words.

The President was having a nightmare. He saw himself being pushed through a long thin pipe, the metal sides contracting, pinning his arms to his sides and squeezing him forward like so much toothpaste toward a destination he couldn't see. He began to choke and gasp for air, and just at the point of fainting he heard a voice telling him to hold on just a little longer—it would be easier when he got to the end of the pipeline.

But the voice was a liar, and he knew that the pipe would spit him out somewhere he didn't want to be: into the middle of a crowd of hungry reporters; into a seat on a plane returning to his home state on January 21 of the next year; into a leather chair behind a desk in some center for international studies where ex-Presidents went to die. He could hear people saying, *He's an expert on terrorism, in spite of . . . you know. He's well on his way to becoming the next Jimmy Carter!*

The President awoke with a start, and it took him a few moments to realize where he was. Around him he saw spartan decorations—spartan, at least, for the White House—not the plush curtains and furnishings of his official bedroom on the second floor. He was on the third floor, in a little cubbyhole of a room nestled among the rafters of the mansion. Of late he had found this a comforting place to get away—away from the toughest job in the world and the toughest wife in the world.

His eyes focused on a painting that depicted one of those forgotten Presidents between Jackson and Lincoln, moved to this remote White House wall to make way for the greater men whose pictures lined the halls below. It bore no inscription, and he'd never wanted to admit his ignorance by asking who it was: Fillmore? Buchanan? Franklin Pierce? The sound of the names frightened him with images of his own future. Who the hell was Franklin Pierce, and would they stick *his own* picture up here next to the forgotten Presidents fifty years from now?

He glanced at his watch: three-thirty a.m.

"Damn it!" he said, grabbing one of five phones beside his bed, this one without any buttons.

An aide answered instantly. "Yes, Mr. President?"

"Chuck? It's damn 3:30, and nobody's called me! What in hell's going on down in Atlanta?"

"Sir, just two minutes ago, General Helms sent word that the SEALs would be going in within the next ten minutes."

The President sat up in bed. "I thought they were going in at 2:00."

"Yes, sir, but apparently they had some kind of problem with the probes."

"Ah, hell," the President sighed. "Okay, tell Helms to make sure those bastards down there let us know when the SEALs get in—and I mean *the second* they get in that sucker."

"Yes, sir."

The President glanced again at the picture on the wall before rising to dress. At least he had some things Franklin Pierce never dreamed of: closed-circuit TV, satellite transmissions, fiber optics on a secure line to relay the radio messages from the MARC and Fitten dorm once the SEALs got in—and best of all, the most highly trained and well-equipped commandos the world had ever known.

At the very same moment, Lt. Allan Boyd and the six other men of his point team prepared to go in. Because of the delay in getting started, he had modified the earlier plan with Helms's wary acceptance: instead of sending in a pair of scouts, the point team led by Boyd would go in first. That left ten other SEALs, positioned in two groups to the north of Fulmer and the south of Montag, to await word from inside before coming in as a secondary force of "barracks sweepers."

The point team, grouped on the west side of the Couch Building, would split into two squads for entry, one of them commanded by Boyd, the other by his assistant team leader. Each of the two groups would also have a point man, a machine gunner, and a bomb-diffusion specialist. Those at least were their specialties, though in difficult circumstances any one of them could do the jobs of his teammates.

They all wore night-insertion dress, every item of their gear either black or dull, dark gray. All of them had customized protective masks with night-vision goggles and secure Motorola walkie-talkie headsets for coordinating between themselves if and when they got separated, but Boyd and the assistant team leader had radios for communicating with headquarters as well. To their backs the two gunners, "stoners" in SEAL jargon, each had a Heckler & Koch MP5N 9-mm submachine gun strapped on, as well as Remington 870 12-gauge shotguns, a favorite weapon for close-order combat.

But due to the presence of hostages, these would be secondary options, the 9-mm guns to be fired only in small bursts of three shots, and the Remingtons to be used only in cases of high certainty that no hostages were in the area of operations. The men would rely first of all on knives, not normally an item of importance in such operations, and secondly on their sidearms: either the Beretta M9 9-mm or the .45-caliber Offensive Handgun System. Each man also carried several smoke grenades.

A slight chill hovered over the morning—though *chill*, of course, was a relative term. It was seventy degrees, the coolest it would get today in Atlanta, so when Boyd felt a cold shiver run down his spine, he knew it came from something besides the weather.

At precisely 3:36 a.m., Montag and Fulmer residence halls—a moment before still brightly lit, with their air-conditioners humming in the morning quiet—went dark and deadly silent. So did Couch, and everything was still except for the faint rustlings made by the seventy-five National Guard sharpshooters assembling in these three buildings.

Boyd radioed the leaders of his two backup teams, each of whom sent a man carrying a lightweight aluminum ladder to prop against the north and south walls of Fitten. In planning the mission, unit pride had made Boyd reluctant to use the ladders: SEALs spent hours a day working out on bench-press machines, developing enormous upper-body strength to climb ropes or sheer walls, just as the two doomed men had done the night before. Ladders seemed downright sissified, but under the circumstances, they made the most sense because securing a rope to the building would take longer and put the man securing it in an exposed position. Still, Boyd and several other men in the point team carried lengths of rope in tight rolls attached to their web gear, just in case they needed them.

The lead man on each ladder would carry with him a diamond cutter, with which he would make a tiny hole in the glass of the second-floor window. A shard about the size of a quarter would land on the floor inside, and with this removed, he would slip in his gloved finger and hold the pane in place while he cut a hole the size of a salad plate. Once he had this larger piece loose, he would slide it toward him so that it came out into his hands, then pass it down to the next man and so on to the ground, where it would be quietly laid aside. Meanwhile the lead man would have reached his arm through and flipped the latch on the window. The trick was to do all this as quickly but as silently as possible: hopefully when the first tiny shard hit the floor, it wouldn't be loud enough to alert anyone who might not have yet succumbed to the nitrous oxide.

Boyd waited till both of the other squad leaders had radioed him that the ladders were in place. Then he turned to his men. "Alright, gentlemen," he said. "Time to rock 'n roll."

The videotape plan that Helms had explained to Mason earlier that evening, which required recording several hours' worth of footage showing the exterior of Fitten dorm, now came to fruition. The camera that provided the media feed from atop the Centennial Research Building had ceased to operate, and in its place the videotape was running, complete with a phony time-display programmed in by the CIA technicians. Instead of showing what was really happening—the lights going off in the buildings around Fitten, and a heavily armed SWAT team preparing to go in—it would show the same bland view of the dormitories as before. The only eventful occurrences the cameras had recorded this evening were the three sorties flown by the helicopter to mask the sound of the borescope penetration, and these had been carefully edited out. Only a very observant astronomer would notice that the angle of the moonlight was wrong for this time of the morning. The networks would access the footage, run continuously on news reports and updates with titles like *Olympic Crisis: Hour 50*, and no one would realize they'd been duped until it was too late—not even in Europe, where it was mid-morning and millions of people were watching "live" telecasts.

"Dear God, let them succeed," Mason prayed under his breath as he surveyed Fitten through his Night Mariners.

"Did you say something?" asked Michelle.

They were standing on the roof of the MARC as they had the night before, except that this time there were others around them.

"Nothing," he said gruffly.

Mason watched half the squad move up the ladder on the southeast while the screen of the closed-circuit TV showed the northwest team doing the same. It all seemed like déjà vu, and for a moment he pictured Santiago and Jackson going up by the very same route twenty-nine hours before. *If I were a superstitious man . . .* he said to himself, but he didn't finish the thought. From the ground to the opening of the window took thirteen seconds; in another eight, the men on the southeast ladder were in, a fact confirmed by Boyd over the radio: "This bird has flown."

In such tense moments, even a mind as disciplined as Mason's had a capacity to wander. *This bird has flown*, he repeated to himself, and then he thought of what Michelle had reported to Helms yesterday in their speaker-phone conference. One of the men watching the Bosnian team said he saw what appeared to be a cage full of canaries in the handball team's quarters . . . .

Suddenly, Mason's mind leapt to the present. "The canaries!" he said. "Damn! I can't believe I didn't figure that out!"

But before he could speak into his radio, he heard the assistant squad leader reporting from the northwest that his team was in as well.

Mason groaned. "I can't believe I didn't think of it."

"Think of what?" Michelle asked.

He shook his head.

Ninety seconds later, Boyd reported: "Have located and waxed two tangos."

"My God," said Michelle, realizing that the two terrorists had most likely been killed in their sleep.

Mason shrugged as though to say "War is hell." There was no time to tie up any of the terrorists, and it wouldn't have done to fire a weapon during the insertion phase. What were they going to do, wake them up and then kill them? Still, he felt a slight wave of revulsion.

Word came in from the other team that they had likewise taken out two of the terrorists, and after that came Boyd's report: "Entering latrine. Six hostages, possibly Puerto Rican, all unconscious and tied together in the showers. EOD"—his bomb diffusion specialist—"will begin disengaging explosives."

Tied together? Mason asked himself. *But Katarina and all the other girls who were released said they'd been—*

At that moment he heard a sound that sent a chill right to the bottom of his heart: the ringing of his cellular phone.

28

No one on his side would be calling him now.

As Michelle watched him with a look of shock on her face, he picked up the receiver and waited.

"Mason," said a muffled voice. After several seconds of dead quiet on the other end of the line, the voice said, "Turn on CNN." Then the line went dead.

"You stay here!" he ordered Michelle as he rushed for the stairs.

On the top floor was a makeshift break room with a TV, and he sprinted toward it, thrusting the door open to find a Village Security officer stealing a few minutes of sleep on the couch. The man jumped up, but Mason brushed past him to the television and flipped it on. It was a late-night infomercial for an exercise machine.

"Quick, switch to CNN."

The sleepy security man scratched his head. "Sir, I—"

"Never mind." Mason grabbed the remote and frantically flipped through the channels until he saw something that stopped him cold.

"Boyd," he shouted into his radio, dispensing with communication protocol, "*get the hell out of there!*"

"Repeat?" A man on the TV screen who might be Boyd—though the protective mask made it hard to tell—was standing in the bathroom before a group of six unconscious athletes while his bomb-diffusion specialist knelt beside him, gingerly deactivating the explosive devices.

Mason knew this because he could see him—and so could everyone else in the world who happened to be watching CNN at that moment.

"They've got you on the frigging TV—don't ask me how—just get out now!"

Behind Boyd sat two girls with their heads propped against the wall; even as Mason spoke these words, their skulls vaporized in a bright flash of light—there was no sound to go with the picture—and a moment later there were only two decapitated corpses gushing blood from their severed necks. Instantly there followed another blast, and the heads of two more women suddenly evaporated, leaving the floor awash in blood and pieces of flesh and bone.

Frantically, Mason punched in Drabeznic's number on his cellular phone while the security man he'd awakened looked on in speechless astonishment. "Come on, dammit!" he shouted as the phone rang lazily: once, twice, three times, five times, eight times, and still no answer.

"Big Wolf!" shouted Boyd into his radio. The other man crouched beside him, trying desperately to cut the wires of the two women remaining.

Still the phone rang without any answer.

There came a third flash, and the body of the bomb specialist—who had just pulled the devices off of the two girls—went hurling backward against the ceramic tile wall. The last two female athletes, alive but unconscious, slumped down into the pool of gore that dripped into the shower drain.

Boyd disappeared from view and the screen went blank, but when the picture reappeared a few seconds later, it had switched to a camera following him and the two remaining men of his squad down the hall.

"How are they sending this signal out?" Mason asked himself aloud. Then it hit him: Drabeznic must have called CNN and set up a phone line to transmit the images, just like reporters in Baghdad had done during the Gulf War. He turned to the security man. "Run downstairs and tell them to cut the phone lines into Fitten—now! Go!"

The man scurried away while the cellular phone in Mason's left hand kept on ringing.

The scene on the TV switched to the four men of the other squad, who had heard the explosions and set up a defensive perimeter on the other side of the building. Facing opposite directions with pistols at the ready, they moved cautiously backward toward an interior doorway. Suddenly, between them and the camera, came an enormous explosion, much larger than the ones that had preceded it. The four men went flying against the wall, their blood smearing it like some grotesque form of graffiti.

Claymore, thought Mason with disgust. *Caught by the same damn booby-trap.*

"Eagle 2!" shouted Boyd into his radio. "Eagle 2!" It was no use, and now he called Mason.

Just then, someone finally picked up the phone. "Eagle 1, hold," Mason ordered.

"What the hell?" came Boyd's shocked reply. "Big Wolf—"

"You better tell those men to get out now," said Drabeznic, his voice still muffled by a protective mask. The camera returned to Boyd, moving slowly down the hallway along with his point man and Petty Officer Miller, who had delivered the microphone to Fitten Tuesday morning. "And the ones in the building across the way—yes, we see them. Pull back, or none of these athletes are going to get out alive."

"Then let those men out!" Mason yelled.

"It is too late for that, Mason."

As the three men on the screen passed by a closed door, a hand emerged and dropped something, then the door slammed shut an instant later. At their feet, spinning like a top on the hard surface of the floor, was a grenade. The point man, seeing that he had no place to flee, jumped down on top of it. It exploded a second later, killing him in a flash; but his sacrifice saved his two comrades' lives.

On a signal from Boyd, Miller took one side of a doorway while Boyd kicked open the door and pulled back before cautiously pointing a pistol in. The room was empty, and Boyd ordered Miller into it, then he pushed open the door across the hall and jumped into that room.

Mason watched all this with a mingled sense of helplessness and disgust. It had seemed like a bad omen when they cut those sleeping men's throats, a product of Boyd's single-minded determination to get the job done at all costs; now it looked like it would indeed cost him everything—including the hostages' lives.

Mason called Michelle on his radio and ordered her to fire off the flare.

On receiving the signal, the troops inside Couch—unaware of what had happened and frustrated that they hadn't gotten to see any action after such a long wait—began to make an orderly retreat out the back, forming up on the west side. But Drabeznic had a surprise for the snipers and gunners inside and atop the two buildings on either side of Fitten.

As the men inside Fulmer started down the stairs, moving single-file and as quietly as possible, a device attached to a light fixture on the third-floor landing suddenly erupted, leaving four men dead and three others wounded. The ones on the steps above and below stopped in their tracks, and a first sergeant called out, "Everybody stand fast!"

The same thing happened simultaneously in Montag, this time killing two and wounding five.

Frantically the COs of the two contingents radioed their unit commander in an office inside Fitten. He ordered them not to move, and then he called Mason.

"They've walked into a booby-trap," the National Guard commander growled over the radio. "Tell that son of a bitch to let my men get out of the building!"

Mason's mind flashed back to the reconnaissance mission the two men from al-Ansar had conducted yesterday morning. Montag and Fulmer should have been swept for explosives before the Guardsmen went in, but like everything else about this mission, there hadn't been time.

Suddenly the television screen went blank just as he got a call confirming that the telephone lines had been cut, and he instantly cursed his haste in giving that order. Not only could he no longer communicate with Drabeznic, but the TV feed had given him a visual on Boyd that might have made it possible for Mason to help him escape alive.

Not that it would have likely made any difference—the terrorists controlled the cameras, and they wouldn't have allowed any useful information to get out. It all made sense now: the bags from Radio Shack that the operatives in Building C had noticed, the reports from the released hostages of TVs and cameras set up throughout the building . . . . And somewhere in the middle of Fitten, operating a control center, was the elusive Drabeznic.

This son of a bitch just keeps outdoing himself, Mason thought. Had the leader of al-Ansar been a fanatic or a romantic, he might have commenced a battle he couldn't win, but he was neither of these: he had planned his every step like Boris Spassky predicting a checkmate fourteen moves away, and it looked like a battle he couldn't lose. For every action Mason took, Drabeznic negated it with an opposing action, opening up new and dangerous possibilities and always maintaining control over the agenda.

"Eagle 1," Mason said into his radio. "Give me your situation."

"They've got us pinned in here," said Boyd, and behind him Mason could hear sounds of gunfire. "We're getting heavy fire from every side. Jump back!" These last words were followed quickly by a loud explosion.

"Eagle 1, Eagle 1!"

"Yeah, I'm still here," said Boyd after a moment. "They're tossing grenades down the hall, but unless they can throw a curve ball, we're gonna keep firing from the doorway." Mason heard the sound of firing close by—Boyd's own pistol—and then his voice returned: "Listen, Tom, they're probably picking up our signal at this point, so I advise we discontinue relaying specific plans over the air."

"Roger that, Eagle 1."

"Oh, don't stop now!" said Drabeznic's voice over the same frequency. "This is such fine drama, which calls to mind the final scene of *Butch Cassidy and the Sundance Kid*. Do you remember how Robert Redford and Paul Newman end up all alone, facing hundreds of—"

"You bastard," said Boyd with disgust.

"Ah, well," said Drabeznic. "Yes, you are right: once you were inside our building, it was easy enough to scan the signals and pick you up. I thought you SEALs were invincible? I suppose not. Now, since our entertainment is drawing to a close, let me say one thing to you, Mr. Boyd, or should I say Lieutenant Boyd, who will never live to rise above that rank. Lieutenant Boyd, whose name will go down in the annals of military history as the leader of yet another doomed last stand, like your Davy Crockett at the Alamo, your General Custer at the Little Big Horn . . . and now you, a black man, fighting for the white man and his religion. A Buffalo Soldier indeed, or rather a Buffalo Sailor. And speaking of which, I have a few of your sisters from the African diaspora here: British, Canadians, and yes, Americans. I suppose that when I retaliate for this foolishness, in honor of you, I will choose one of these sisters to pay the price."

Mason hadn't tried to interrupt Drabeznic because he saw no need to bait him at this point. But Boyd had nothing to lose: "Come and get me," he said now. "I'm waiting for you down here."

"I would not trust someone who slits the throats of sleeping men to fight an honest fight," said Drabeznic coolly. "But nonetheless, if you surrender now, all will be forgotten. We'll take care of you—is not Islam the truth faith of our black American brothers?"

"Screw you, Drabeznic. Mason, I'm out."

"Roger that, Eagle 1—and . . . ." But Mason could think of nothing more to say to his friend.

Boyd switched off the radio, his last link to the life outside the walls of Fitten dormitory. He didn't know how he would survive what lay ahead, but one thing was for sure: they wouldn't take him alive. Over that, at least, he still had some control.

He looked across the hallway at Miller, the two of them facing in opposite directions, both firing with their right hands. "Better to die on your feet than on your knees, ain't it, Jeff?" he shouted. He forced himself to grin, though it hardly mattered because they both had masks on.

"I thought that was *live* on your knees," said Miller as he fired off a shot down the hall.

The terrorists continued to shoot down the hallway, from time to time lobbing yet another grenade from what seemed like a bottomless stash. They had nearly succeeded in destroying the floor between the doorways, but still the two SEALs fought on.

Looking behind him toward the window, Boyd spied a large wooden headboard, no doubt left there after the terrorists removed the metal bed rails. He pulled the rope off his belt. "You're gonna have to work both sides for a minute, Jeff," he yelled to Miller, then proceeded to tie one end of the rope to the headboard and drag the heavy piece of wood toward the window.

He returned to the doorway and pulled out two smoke grenades from his web belt. "On ten, I want you to jump over here," he ordered Miller.

Miller glanced down at the space between them, no longer a floor but a gaping wound of concrete and rebar with exposed pipes and wires.

"You can make it," Boyd said. With that, he pulled the pins of both smoke grenades and threw them, one to his left and one to his right down the hall. "One . . . two . . . three . . . ." Within seconds, the corridor was completely engulfed in a thick, inky vapor. "Seven . . . eight . . . nine . . . ." Boyd fired down the hallway, first in one direction and then the other. Miller took a running start and leapt across the corridor, rolling past Boyd and into the room. In one smooth motion he jumped to his feet, changed clips on his pistol, and charged to the doorway, firing down the hall in the opposite direction from his commander.

"Okay," said Boyd over his shoulder, "Get by the window. I'm going to slam the door and lock it, and the moment I do, I want you to throw the rope out and be at the bottom in three seconds while I cover the door. You got it?"

"No, sir," said Miller. "You go first."

"This is not a discussion, Miller," said Boyd through clenched teeth. "You have an order—get your ass over by that window now! And leave whatever clips you have, plus your weapon."

Boyd continued firing, shooting ten rounds in each direction and counting down for Miller. The moment he'd fired the twentieth bullet, he slammed the door and threw the bolt while Miller hurled the rope out the window and slid down.

Miller's plan was to slide to the first floor, then jump the last ten feet and run as fast he could toward the southeast corner of Montag. As he scrambled down the rope, he saw something moving behind the slats on the barricaded first floor; suddenly, before he could react, he realized he was looking into the barrel of a submachine gun. Miller moved quickly, letting go of the rope and dropping the rest of the way, but the man with the gun was faster. *Brrrrpppp!* The automatic weapon sent the SEAL's flailing body backward, landing with a thud on the ground.

Boyd heard the shooting and sensed what had happened, but he couldn't think about that now: the terrorists in the hallway were shooting at the handle of his door, trying to blow off the lock. Grabbing Miller's weapon, he returned fire through the heavy door panel, which forced the men outside to pull back.

Having bought himself a few precious seconds, Boyd threw down his weapon and his mask, grabbed the rope, and started down in a serpentine slide, swinging first to the left and then the right, avoiding the open window directly below the one from which he'd just emerged. It was a wonderful, beautifully acrobatic maneuver, and those few who witnessed it would call it the greatest display of athletic prowess at the 1996 Summer Olympics.

He dropped off about five more feet, finding himself barely eight feet off the ground. He let go of the rope and landed gracefully in stride. With his next step, he was virtually at the peak of acceleration.

Though the sun would not rise for more than an hour, the National Guardsmen trapped in Montag could clearly see the lone figure as he sprinted toward the safety of the building's corner. They'd been ordered not to fire on the terrorists' building for fear of another explosion inside their own, yet when they saw him running for his life just ahead of a stream of automatic fire from the first floor, three sharpshooters answered it with fire of their own. The terrorist operating the automatic weapon slumped forward into the metal bed slats, dead from two rounds in the head.

Boyd raced closer and closer to freedom, and a cry of applause started to go up from the Guardsmen, only to be stifled by the crack of a single shot from a fourth-floor window of Fitten dorm. Suddenly Boyd lurched to his knees. The bullet had ripped through his back and severed his spinal cord. Still alive, he slumped and began to crawl forward just as another shot tore into his right shoulder.

Again, the National Guards opened fire, this time not only at the window from which the shots had come but at every window on that side of the building. Mason spoke into his radio. "Cease fire, cease fire." Still one of the snipers on the third floor of Montag continued shooting until an officer took his M-16 by force.

Boyd crawled the last five feet to the edge of Montag, and two medics rushed forward with a stretcher just as he passed out. By now every window on the south side of Fitten had been shot out and many of the bed rails on the first floor were ripped up. The building once again became quiet.

In the confusion, the Guardsmen in Fulmer and Montag escaped out the second-floor windows. Mason didn't waste any time getting the phone lines restored, and he oversaw the mop-up operation from his office, which had filled up with people asking him questions. Steve Kirk was there, too, waiting for a report on the hostage deaths so he could call the chefs de mission of the countries involved. But before Mason could give him the exact toll, he'd have to talk to Drabeznic, and the sun had just begun to rise when the mobile phone rang. Mason walked down the hall to answer it.

"Mason," said Drabeznic in a silky voice, "you're not very adept at games of strategy, are you? But then again, I suspect you weren't the one who ordered such an unwise attack. You're much too smart for that. It was your President, wasn't it? He must be getting very desperate." Drabeznic paused. "You have nothing to say to this? Then let's review the price both sides have paid for this most recent example of foolishness. It appears that you have lost eight of your men, plus who knows how many of those soldiers in the adjacent buildings. Then there are the four young ladies whose deaths the SEALs caused by tampering with our wires, not to mention the woman killed in your indiscriminate firing at our windows."

"What?"

"Yes, another of our guests from the Democratic People's Republic of Korea was dispatched by your own soldiers. Also, there are two others who seem to be suffering the effects of over-inhalation of whatever gas it was you pumped in here. I would have given them protective masks, but we didn't have quite enough to go around. And you killed our birds, too! Our pet canaries are all dead from asphyxiation. At least they died for a good cause, in the line of duty as it were, so that we would know what you were doing and don our masks." Once again, Mason had guessed correctly about their tactics, but he'd guessed too late.

"Let's see . . . oh yes, you have severely wounded another young lady—one of your Americans, by the way, a swimmer. She seems to have been hit in an artery, and is bleeding profusely, for which she needs medical care that we're incapable of providing."

"Then why don't you let her out?"

Suddenly Drabeznic's tone changed from the lazy drawl it had been a moment before. "The time for talk of mercy is past, Mr. Mason. Do you not know the words of your own Bible? 'Touch not God's anointed.' You have slain men doing the work of God, slain them in cold blood, and now the blood will flow—it will gush like a mighty river out of this place, gathering power and force as it rushes up even to the steps of your nation's capital." He laughed. "I know you are recording our conversations, and I expect your President to hear what was just said, and to mark its meaning. I want no more foolishness, and if this happens one more time, everyone will die—one giant blast, which will obliterate everyone. Do you understand?"

But Mason kept his cool. "Be careful that you don't paint yourself into a corner."

"Meaning?"

"I assume you understand the expression, since you speak excellent English." Drabeznic said nothing, so Mason went on, knowing that the President would hear what he said next but hoping he'd understand his reasons for saying it. "You have probably caused the President to lose this next election, and if he's going to go down, he'll likely take you with him. Think about that."

"Don't bluff me, Mason."

"I assure you that I'm in no position to bluff you, sir. I don't have anything to do with what can be negotiated. I am only the messenger."

From the long silence on the other end of the line, Mason could sense that for the first time yet, he had gotten to his adversary—if only a little.

Finally the other man spoke. "Enough of this, Mason. Let me tell you where we go from here." He sounded as though he'd recovered his sense of assurance, but Mason knew he'd rattled the man. "I want some large fans brought over here immediately in order to remove the last traces of the gases in our little hotel, and I also want breakfast for our guests right now—no tricks, or you know the consequences. Lastly, I want the direct feed to the networks restored in time for us to hold another news conference at exactly 9:00 a.m. Have you got all this, Mason?"

"Yeah, but how about the injured woman?"

"As quickly as you are killing our hostages, and you want us to release one?"

"She's of no value to you if she dies. It would only put more pressure on us to react."

"We have several qualified medics here. Send over medical supplies, including sutures and morphine, and we will sew her up."

"It makes sense to release her. She can't do you any more good, and if she stays there, she'll die. Not to mention that she's in shock . . . . What's her name, anyway?"

"I told you, she's a swimmer. She's tall, she won a bronze medal—"

Oh my God, Mason thought. "You mean Elizabeth Taggart?"

"Yes, I believe that is her name, now that you mention it."

Mason didn't think anything could upset him more in his present state of agitation, but this did. It was one thing to have hostages in harm's way, whatever their nationality, and even worse to know that they included one's compatriots—but worst of all was the knowledge that his friend's daughter might die if he couldn't do anything for her quickly.

As he set the phone down, he could hear Ben Taggart's words from just three weeks before: *You know, it's funny*, the Protocol Director had said. *We sit here and we talk about dangers in the Village . . . but I can't look at this quite as objectively as y'all do, not when my own daughter is going to be—*

"From the look on your face," said Steve Kirk, entering the room, "it looks like bad has just gotten worse."

"You don't even know." Mason sighed. "Steve, it looks like Elizabeth Taggart is wounded, and that bastard in there won't release her."

Kirk leaned up against the wall of Mason's office. He'd cared about the victims up to now, just like everyone else, but partly because it was his job to care. This was different. He had been in Elizabeth's home, had spent time with her family and followed her progress for four years. When she'd come to his Village to compete, he'd felt like an uncle entrusted with the care of a niece.

"Someone's gonna have to tell Ben," Mason was saying.

"I'll do it," said Kirk hurriedly. "I wouldn't want anyone else to."

"Thanks. Now I've got to figure out what we can do to get his daughter out of there."

PART SIX

MOVING OUT

29

When it was 8:00 a.m. in Atlanta, it was already 9:00 in Puerto Rico, where videotapes showing the deaths of the commonwealth's four athletes had run nonstop ever since the feed went out over CNN several hours before. A radical separatist group, quickly taking advantage of the situation, organized demonstrations in the towns of Ceiba, Salinas, Sabana, and Guaynabo, where they urged crowds to rush on the gates of nearby Army or Navy bases. In San Juan, students and intellectuals addressed mobs from loudspeakers, calling on them to unleash the "creative force of violence" against North American business and government offices; the mobs obliged, and soon parts of the capital devolved into a morass of broken glass and burning buildings. On the radio, the archbishop and governor pleaded for peace, but it was too late. A general advisory throughout the island warned all Anglos to stay indoors until police could quell the unrest.

Half a world away, at a remote spot in the Iraqi desert just west of Ar Ruṭbah near the border with Jordan, it was 4:00 p.m. and well over 110°F. A contingent of U.S. Special Forces warily eyed a group of Saddam Hussein's Republican Guards through telescopic lenses across miles of sand that separated their two temporary encampments. The Americans had been posted there almost twenty-four hours before, to await the arrival of several small planes from Baghdad ferrying the "political prisoners" released from Germany and France to the remote drop-off point. The convicted terrorists, many of whom hadn't seen the outside of a prison cell in years, had arrived early that morning to find groups of comrades there to meet them. Helplessly, the American soldiers had watched them drive away across the desert in Humvees, unable to pursue them because to do so might mean the deaths of more hostages in Atlanta.

On the Korean peninsula, it was 10:00 p.m. on that Thursday. The leadership of the Democratic People's Republic of Korea, having learned that another of their athletes had died in Fitten Hall, appeared ready to use the Olympic crisis as a pretext to invade their southern neighbor. Satellite photos and radio intercepts indicated that Pyongyang had placed the entire People's Army on a state of alert, and had called on pro-North students in Seoul to riot. News reports from the South Korean capital showed fierce street battles with police bearing shields and clubs, and early dispatches indicated that two U.S. servicemen on leave in Seoul had been killed in the skirmishes. Following this announcement, all U.S. military personnel had been ordered to return to their barracks or ships, where they would await further orders.

And in Washington, more bad news came in. On Wednesday night, small groups of twelve men and women apiece, segregated by demographic factors, particularly race, had gathered in cities all over the nation—any place where that elusive creature known as the "ordinary American" could be found. These were not juries in the traditional sense, but focus groups: people of average intelligence and education, paid to offer sometimes ill-informed and often poorly expressed opinions while analysts with master's degrees sat behind two-way mirrors and followed their every word. The central question was, "How do you rate the President's handling of the hostage situation in Atlanta?" The consensus was not good for the Administration.

Early on Thursday morning, the President's chief pollster called his assistant at home. In a raspy voice, he explained to his subordinate that he'd caught a twenty-four hour flu virus, and wouldn't be going to work that day. The assistant, amazed at the transparency of this ploy and cursing his boss for making him deliver the bad news himself, told his wife not to wait up for him that night.

There was not a single smile to be seen in the Cabinet Room that morning, nor was there any talking, so that when a White House steward came in with a fresh pot of coffee, the sound of it pouring into each person's cup was like the gush of a waterfall. On the screen of the muted television set, an announcer at CNN headquarters was talking; in the upper-right hand corner was a map of the Korean peninsula with an icon representing an explosion.

A few minutes after the group had assembled, the President walked in with slumped shoulders and a look of profound disgust on his face. As he sat down, his eyes scanned the others around the table until they fell on the still-unofficial Secretary of Defense, sitting with Gen. Helms.

"I have one question for you gentlemen," the President said in a sullen tone, then suddenly raised his voice. "Why in the hell did you let them stop the attack? Those men were in there, and the next wave could have come in and wiped out the terrorists."

The acting Secretary did not offer any answer, so Helms spoke up. "Sir, those men went in on the understanding that if they discovered that the gas had not had an effect on the terrorists, they would retreat. There should have been an initial entry by two scouts, but against my better judgment I allowed Lieutenant Boyd to bring in his point team first, which—"

"Against your better judgment," the President repeated sourly. "Well, then, once those guys were screwed anyway, there was no good reason not to go in with both barrels blazing."

"If we'd done that, Mr. President, all the hostages would have been killed."

The President looked around for Larry, his pollster, but saw only Brian, the assistant. "Yeah, well," he continued, "it's one thing to lose hostages when you're trying to free them, quite another when all you're doing is getting your ass kicked by a bunch of terrorists. It may be the same amount of casualties, but the perception makes all the difference." He eyed the Defense Secretary and, speaking to an aide on his left, said, "Karen, check and see what's the shortest tenure in U.S. history for a Cabinet official."

"Sir?"

"Mr. President," said his second-in-command, standing now and looking out over the Rose Garden, "I think we could be doing something more constructive right now than assigning blame for past mistakes. We need to be planning our next step, even if we've got no other choice but to negotiate our way out of this—and we need the military as much for Plan B as we did for Plan A."

The President glanced up at one of the muted news reports, which showed a group of protesters on Pennsylvania Avenue a few hundred yards from where they sat, holding a banner that read *Mr. President, If You Can't Free Our Hostages, Find Someone Who Can.*

"Yeah, I suppose you're right," said the President tiredly, "but we definitely need a strong sense of civilian control here, like Truman and MacArthur." He stared straight at Helms.

The Director of Central Intelligence reported on the situations in

Puerto Rico, Iraq, and Korea, all of which (as the Vice President said again) pointed to the need to commence serious negotiations with al-Ansar.

"I guess the whole world saw that damn CNN tape from inside the dormitory," said the President with a sigh.

"Most of Europe, anyway," answered a National Security advisor.

"I'd be willing to lay down money that Drabeznic runs it again at his press conference," the Director of Central Intelligence suggested.

"Yeah, and that brings up the whole P.R. nightmare of U.S. troops killing men in their sleep," the White House Director of Communications pointed out. "If the audio from the SEALs' assault were to be leaked to the media—"

"That happened in the middle of a terrorist intervention," DCI replied, lighting his pipe in spite of a no-smoking policy enforced by the First Lady, who had not shown up for this meeting.

"Yeah, but handcuffs would have looked a lot better," said the Communications Director. "I mean, *tape*, for God's sake—hasn't anybody ever heard of taping someone's wrists instead of slitting his throat?"

"Not to mention that killing a man in his sleep is a violation of the Geneva Convention," the Secretary of State observed.

The President glanced at the pollster's assistant. "Brian, what have you got for me? Say, where the hell is Larry?"

"Sir, he's—" Brian's voice starting to crack, and a few of the others snickered until the President glared at them. "He's not feeling well, so—"

"Alright, whatever. Gimme the numbers."

Brian cleared his throat. "Sir, you know how the public is in these times of crisis. They tend to overreact, and this polling data is not necessarily valid for the long term, particularly with the election still three months away."

"Don't give me that horseshit. What are the damn numbers?"

Brian looked at the papers before him. "Well, sir, your negative rating is . . . fairly substantial. But again, I don't think—"

"Spit it out! Give me the positive first."

"The positive is . . . ."

"What's that? I didn't hear you."

"Sir, the positive is nine percent."

"Nine percent!" the President yelled, looking around at the others.

But no one wanted to catch his eye. "Nine percent! Single frigging digits?"

"Yes, sir," said the pollster meekly.

"Has that ever happened before?"

"No, not to my knowledge, sir."

"Well . . . alright," said the President, straightening his shoulders and trying to make the best of the situation. "This has all happened so quickly—I'm sure there are a lot of undecideds." Lowering his head slightly as though to dodge a blow, he ordered, "Give me those numbers."

"Sir, I'm afraid to say we had only seven percent who answered as undecided."

The President sat back heavily. "Seven plus nine is sixteen—you mean *eighty-four percent* are unfavorable?"

The young man nodded.

"Brian," said the President with a look that could drill through steel, "neither you nor your boss Larry are worthy of the title of pollster. Your methodology is screwed, and until you can figure out what you did wrong, you are excused from this room."

The young man scurried out, taking his briefcase and his piles of printouts with him and thinking that perhaps he'd spoken in haste when he told his wife not to wait up.

"Damn pollsters!" said the President irritably. "What are they doing taking polls in the middle of a crisis?"

"While we're in the damage-assessment mode," said the Vice President, "let me tell you about a phone call I got from Ira Greenberg of NBC about an hour ago. The man's frantic. He says that unless we get control of this situation, they may not survive the financial setback it will cause them."

"So what?" asked the President testily. "I'm worried about the whole country going to hell, and you're talking about whether *Saturday Night Live* will run next season?"

The Vice President kept his cool. "Sir, it's a little bigger problem than that. Even with cable, they're still a major player, and if they go down, it could have massive repercussions in the economy. But here's the point: Greenberg says that Jason Blanchot of the IOC has tentative-ly agreed not to file suit against us if—"

"File suit? That aristocratic shit is talking about taking legal pro-ceedings against the United States government?"

"Yes, Mr. President, and if there were ever an entity with the financial resources to do it, it's the IOC. But Blanchot has reiterated the terms of an earlier discussion with me, which I reported to you before: if we can put an end to this thing today, they'll help us meet any financial demands Drabeznic might make. He understands that we might be prevented for political reasons from buying off terrorists, and he's willing to put up the necessary funds."

"Hm," said the President. "That's looking better and better, but I'm still not sure I want to put us in a position of being indebted to any private international organization yet." He pointed to an aide. "Get Mason on the phone."

"Mr. President, I really don't see that we have a lot of options at this point," said the Vice President.

"Just one." The President held up a finger. "And that's to push Drabeznic over the edge."

DCI, who had now snuffed out his pipe in deference to the protests of his colleagues, asked calmly, "What are you saying, sir?"

"All I'm saying is that if he were to go nuts and start slaughtering hostages, we'd have no choice but to storm the building."

No one said anything for several seconds; then Gen. Helms spoke up. "And I suppose all the hostages would die."

"Yeah, but they're going to anyway, aren't they?"

"We can't know that for sure, sir."

"Well, one thing's certain—we're all going down in flames if we don't do something quick." The aide motioned to the President that Mason was on the phone, then brought it to him and pushed the speaker button. "Look here, Mason," said the President. "I've got to know if you're getting any indication that Drabeznic is going to start killing the rest of the hostages."

"Why, no, sir," said Mason at the other end, a little puzzled by the question. "Only if his demands aren't met."

"But you're still set up to assault the building?"

"Of course, sir. We have the troops, and we've got tanks and armored personnel carriers at the other end of the Village that could be brought in within minutes—plus helicopters and all the other equipment—*if* that was what we were going to do. But of course none of the hostages would survive."

"Not one?"

"I doubt it, Mr. President. Our other two attempts were going to be surgical, and look how they turned out. Not only that, but if Drabeznic is really who he claims to be—a Muslim fanatic waging a jihad—then he doesn't mind dying in a siege on the building. In fact, being a 'martyr' would be the greatest honor imaginable, and guarantee him a free ticket straight to heaven."

"You make an interesting point," said the President. "In other words, the worst possible thing in his mind would be for us to capture him and incarcerate him for years, wouldn't it?"

"Yes sir, I suppose so."

"Alright, well, thanks for the tip."

When he got off the phone, the Chief seemed excited. "We are definitely not going to kill the SOB, uh-uh, no. We're taking Drabeznic alive at all costs."

This didn't seem like the language of someone concerned about the hostages, and the Vice President said in a calm voice, "Mr. President, I think our objective right now should be to preserve the long-term best interests of the United States."

"But don't you see? Punishing him and preserving our interests are the same thing: we negotiate to get him out of there, then take him when he gets to Iraq."

"*If* he's going there—and *if* we can do anything about it when he does," Gen. Helms pointed out. "Those are two big *ifs*, and so far we haven't had a lot of success in the area of second-guessing."

As the U.S. Director of Central Intelligence had predicted, Drabeznic did attempt to show the videotape in its fullest, most gory detail, having arranged a feed to the media pool just prior to his 9:00 a.m. news conference. He introduced it with his own lengthy version of the failed attack, including a chilling description of the ruthlessness with which the American forces had slit the throats of sleeping guards. Then with a ceremonial flourish, he announced, "If you do not believe me, watch this."

Unbeknownst to him, however, the members of the pool had agreed not to show the video, and in its place ran a still image of Fitten dorm with the words *The Olympic Crisis: Day Three* beneath it. It took him half a minute to realize this, and when he did, he railed at the sudden impulse for delicacy on the part of the U.S. media.

"But then," he added with a bitter laugh, "this alone should show you, peace-loving peoples of the world, just how gruesome this action on the part of the U.S. government was. If these purveyors of violence will not show it to you, it must be awful indeed. However, there are no doubt many copies of this tape by now, and I encourage any media directors who love the truth as I do to run it constantly on their stations.

"Now, this has naturally affected our hostage negotiations, and though I have received word that the British and Canadian governments have begun meeting our requests, I am afraid I will have to continue to keep their guests under my care. This is a particularly unfortunate situation for these two governments, because in addition to the four Puerto Rican girls and the one Korean, two others—one British and one Canadian—died from an overdose of nitrous oxide."

After this, he allowed stretcher-bearers to come forward and receive the bodies of the seven slain young women, who were taken out the front door under the eyes of four heavily armed terrorists. But the would-be attackers received no such respect: in full view of the cameras, Drabeznic's men on the third floor dropped the bodies of the six SEALs who had died inside Fitten the night before. One by one, they hit the ground and smashed with a hideous pulpy noise as the cameras rolled.

After further ranting on the lessons Washington should draw from its failed attack, Drabeznic said, "Oh, yes, I almost forgot this when I said that no Americans had been killed. It does appear that indiscriminate machine gun fire from the U.S. forces last night severely wounded one of their own athletes, and despite our best efforts, we cannot guarantee that she will survive."

At the whisper of shock from the reporters, Drabeznic hastened to add, "But we do not wish anyone to die needlessly, even if that's what your government wants. Therefore to show our good faith, we will consider a one-for-one swap with someone of the authorities' choosing. However, that person must be female, and she must submit to a complete search to make certain that she is not bringing in a weapon or any other device which might threaten our security. If this is to happen, it will take place at precisely 9:30 a.m."

"Mason, let me affirm the details of my offer," said Drabeznic over the phone a minute after he'd finished speaking to the press. "I will accept only a female, and she must carry neither a recording device nor a weapon of any kind—not even a fingernail clipper—and you know we will check. By my watch, you have precisely eighteen minutes to put someone on-site."

"We need more time." Mason looked around at the people sitting in his office with him: Steve Kirk, Greg Robbins, the three remaining male members of his Response Support Team—and Michelle.

"Why? So you can develop another one of your bizarre plans?" Drabeznic laughed. "I can just imagine the discussions: 'Do we have any transsexuals or 300-pound lesbians? Could we recruit one of those Chinese swimmers?' No, if you want this deal, you have to go with what you have . . . . I seem to recall observing a very fine-looking brunette at the other end of the field during some of my press conferences. Is she one of yours?"

Mason glanced at Michelle. She was leaning forward, knowing full well what was being said. He looked away. "That's her decision to make."

"Very well. You have my terms, and remember: the offer expires at 9:30 a.m. Period. After that time, the wounded swimmer will be on her own as far as medical attention goes."

Gen. Helms was on speaker phone, listening to the call through a headset. When Drabeznic hung up, he started to say something, but Kirk beat him to it. "That murdering bastard!" he yelled, for once losing his usual cool. He slammed his fist down on the desk.

"Steve." Mason held up a hand. Again, his eyes—along with everyone else's except Kirk's—fell on Michelle. He would have taken her place in a minute, and he knew any of the others would have as well. But that wasn't an option.

Helms was saying something, but Mason wasn't listening. As bad as everything had been up to now, this was worse, a complete no-win situation. Did he let his best operative, someone he thought of almost as a daughter, go into a rapidly deteriorating situation unarmed, or did he allow an innocent seventeen-year-old to bleed to death?

"Tom, I'm gonna let you make the call on this," said Helms.

"Yes, sir." Mason knew his commander too well to think he would avoid responsibility, but no one was going to make this decision for Michelle. He turned to her. "Michelle, you know, I—"

"Tom, stop," she cut him off abruptly. "I know you wouldn't ask me to do this, but this is what I'm paid to do—it comes with the territory." She smiled. "Remember that coffee cup I used to have, the one that said on the side, *Sometimes the Best Man For the Job Is a Woman*?" She laughed, obviously psyching herself up. "This is one of those times, so quit being such a sexist, huh? I've got a job to do, and I want to get on with it."

Tom Mason never got choked up over the sappy romance movies his wife sometimes subjected him to. He hadn't even allowed himself to feel the emotion brought on by the deaths of Adam or Allan Boyd. But now he felt himself experiencing what an old Army buddy of his, an Airborne Ranger, had euphemistically called "sweaty eyes."

He started to speak, and swallowed hard. "Michelle," he said, gesturing to the other men, who looked on somberly, "it's an honor to serve with someone like you."

"Thanks, Chief, same to you." She got up, walked over to where he sat, and bent down to embrace him. By unspoken rule, they had both always considered it unprofessional to touch, but now they held each other for several seconds, each of them patting one another on the back and feeling the warmth of the other's face on their shoulders.

"And I'll tell you another thing," he said, releasing her and regaining his composure. "I think I speak for all of us when I say that it's personal as hell now." The other men nodded. "Drabeznic's a dead man as far as we're concerned."

Helms was not as emotional, but he did wish Michelle luck, and said she was an example to everyone.

"Thank you, sir," she replied, then looked at Mason. "I'd better go."

"You're not armed, are you?" Robbins asked.

"Oh, thanks for reminding me." Usually she dressed like the men, in khakis, a cotton button-down, and hiking boots; but this morning she had changed into a skirt. She put her left foot up on a chair and, with unconscious sensuality, slowly pulled the hemline back eight inches above the knee to reveal her smooth, tanned thigh—and a .30-calibre, two-slot Derringer in a holster. At other times (out of Mason's earshot), her comrades on the Response Support Team had joked with her in a mildly flirtatious, off-color way, but now no one said anything. Yet even in this tense moment, each of them felt a slight tingle of reaction to her sensuous movements.

Handing the weapon to Robbins, she started for the door, patting Aaron, Julio, and Lamont on the shoulder as she passed them. Then she turned and looked back at Kirk, smiling that familiar smile of hers. "Steve," she said, "would you walk with me to the edge of the field?"

The other men—all except Mason, who didn't bat an eye—exchanged glances.

The two walked out of the MARC in silence and made their way across the catwalk toward Ferst Drive. Not until they'd gotten to the edge of Couch Field did she speak. "Steve, I know you don't want me to do this," she said, "but I also know you respect my decision enough not to question it." She took his hand and squeezed it. "Tom always taught us to think about something good if things get bad, so whatever happens, just know I'll be thinking about you."

She started to let go and begin the long walk across the field, but he squeezed tighter. "Michelle," he said slowly, "I'm gonna pray that you get back safely, and . . . ." *Say it now or you'll regret it forever*, he thought. "And I want you to know one thing: I love you."

"I love you too." She looked into his eyes, then dabbed at her own. "I don't want that joker in Fitten to see me crying, so you'd better let me go."

They kissed. Then, at 9:28 a.m., Michelle Hinton started her solitary trek across the open field toward the dungeon called Fitten Residence Hall.

30

As soon as she reached the window, two men pulled her in while Drabeznic announced over his microphone that the new guest was being treated with the utmost care and respect. They threw her against the wall, and while one man held an automatic rifle on her, two others conducted a rough search of her clothes and her person, even looking into her ears and mouth for any microscopic recording device she might have hidden. She had expected this; she just hoped they wouldn't make her strip. They didn't, but they did run a hand-held magnetometer over her, as well as a device for detecting electronic listening equipment; then they took her shoes and handcuffed her.

A second later, they wheeled her around, and she became the first person from outside Fitten Dorm to look at Drabeznic up close since the crisis began. He was not tall—5'6" or maybe even 5'5"—and he had a handsome face, with wavy black hair, a mustache, and deep-set, piercing, almost hypnotic eyes. "Glad to have you aboard, madam," he said, as though welcoming a guest onto his boat for a Sunday afternoon sail.

Michelle looked around her. They appeared to be standing in a day-room of some sort, with all the chairs and couches pushed up against the walls and two industrial-sized fans blowing air out the windows. At the far side of the room stood a large console TV showing the exterior of Fitten dorm on the screen, with the CNN logo in the lower right-hand corner and the word *LIVE* above it. There were three smaller television sets besides, showing views from the inside of Fitten that switched periodically from camera to camera. On one of them she saw two men carrying a girl who looked like Elizabeth Taggart, then the camera switched to an empty hallway.

In the room with Michelle, there was Drabeznic, another man adjusting the controls on the public-address equipment, the two standing guard over her, and two more lounging on chairs with AK-47s slung across their laps. Most of them appeared to be Middle Eastern or at least Eastern European, but one of the two seated men looked like an

American. He had blond hair, and appeared to be quite tall, though he was sitting; when he saw Michelle looking at him, he grinned and said, "Hey, darlin', wanna share my room? I'll make sure no one else bothers you."

"Not if your dick isn't any bigger than your brain," she shot back.

"We got a live one!" he laughed, then his expression became sour. "You better watch yourself, bitch."

Drabeznic silenced the man with a sharp look, then said something in a foreign language to Michelle's guards, who led her away.

Just after the 9:00 a.m. press conference began, Mason had gotten a fax from the White House informing him that as soon as the conference was over, the media would be ordered out of the Village and not allowed to return until the situation in Fitten was resolved. Of course that meant that Washington would now have two enemies to deal with, al-Ansar and the press corps; but that was their problem, not his.

He had also received word of the President's intention to speak with Drabeznic, and after the conference ended, he dialed into Fitten Dorm.

"The President has instructed me to patch him through on a phone call to you," Mason said when he had Drabeznic on the line, "so that we can bring this thing to closure."

"And what makes you think I'm ready for closure?"

"I'm not saying you are, just that the time might be opportune."

"Okay," said Drabeznic in an indulgent tone. "Put him through in ten minutes."

"Will do."

"You haven't asked, but I will see to it that the woman—Michelle, I believe it is?—is unharmed as long as you respect our boundaries. And please keep me informed on the young swimmer's condition."

"Alright . . . I will."

"You sound surprised that I would care," said Drabeznic, assuming a hurt tone. "That only shows how little you understand of me and my motives. Poor girl, it was her own government's bullets that wounded her. She was a mere pawn, like that commando leader of yours, Boyd— a brave man. By the way, I hope he was given proper medical care, and is recovering?"

"Yes, he's just fine," Mason lied, not wanting to give his opponent any further satisfaction. The SEAL leader had been given proper care, alright, but he had died on the way to the hospital.

"In any case, we fighting men understand how it is to be controlled by forces we can't see or even understand, don't we, Mason?"

"Yes," said Mason, surprised at Drabeznic's chattiness. Perhaps if he kept the man talking, he might learn something useful. "Yes, that's true, and I can tell that you speak from experience. Did you ever serve in a regular army like I did, or have you been an independent freedom fighter all your life? Your methods tell me that you're a man with extensive training—either that or you're a genius when it comes to counterintelligence and guerrilla warfare."

Drabeznic laughed. "This is one situation where the American expression, 'flattery will get you nowhere,' is particularly appropriate. You know we can't get into those little details, but let's just say that my men and I are experienced."

"No, I'm serious. It was brilliant, having the handball team qualify for the Olympics, planning this operation nearly six years in advance, even putting someone on your payroll in deep cover—you're a mastermind. And by the way, how is Dewberry?"

"I will determine the direction of the conversation, thank you," said Drabeznic in a tone that was firm but not unpleasant. "Isn't your President waiting to speak with me?"

"Mr. Drabeznic, this is the President of the United States."

Drabeznic yawned. "Okay. What do you want?"

The man on the other end of the line worked hard to keep rage and desperation from creeping into his voice. "I'm ready to conclude the matter at hand."

"And how do you propose to do that?"

"To be honest with you, Mr. Drabeznic, the fact that you haven't told us precisely what you want makes it difficult for me to propose anything. At least you've made things clear to our allies, and they've now released their prisoners at Ar Ruṭbah—even the Canadians and British have done that, though you haven't so far seen fit to honor their compliance."

"And speaking of honoring agreements, Mr. President, how successful have your forces been in recapturing these men?"

The President didn't respond.

"But that is not my concern. I have only fulfilled my promises to my brothers by securing their release, and it is up to them to outwit you as

I have done. Be that as it may, how do you know I want anything from you?"

"Come on, Mr. Drabeznic," said the President impatiently, "everybody wants something, so why don't you go ahead and tell me what it is? Then we can end this thing one way or another."

"What do you mean, 'one way or another'? Is that a threat?"

"Take it any way you want. There aren't going to be any more press conferences. I have ordered the media removed from the Village, and if you start throwing more prisoners from the roof, don't expect anyone to film it or photograph it. The only response you'll get will be from us, and it won't be one you like. And in answer to your question, no, this is not a threat—it's a promise."

"I see. Well, perhaps I'll just have to wait you out, then. I wonder how long your media will allow that to happen."

"I don't think my message is getting through to you. Tonight, this thing will be over with—one way or another."

"And you would kill innocent people just to get at me?"

"I'm trying to save them, Mr. Drabeznic. So tell me what you want, and we'll see what we can do."

"Alright," said Drabeznic resolutely. "Call back in thirty minutes, and I'll give you my requests. But if the media are not outside to hear my announcement following your phone call, someone will take a dive. Do you understand that?"

"I don't hear anything, Mr. Drabeznic. The media are gone. You have been cut off from the world, and this is your only communication link left."

Hanging up the line, Drabeznic reached over and grabbed a cellular phone to dial the special line to CNN that he'd been given. But he got nothing, and when he looked down at his phone, it was flashing *Call Blocked.*

"Damn," he said aloud, looking around him. Then he ordered one of his guards to bring the newest prisoner to him.

Drabeznic sat in his command center on the interior of the second floor, at the furthest possible remove from any listening posts the authorities might have trained on the building. Until Tuesday morning, it had been a storage room, and upon taking the building, he'd had his men remove the contents to a bedroom across the hall, whereupon they installed the equipment for controlling the closed-circuit TVs. Like his counterpart Thomas Mason, he had regular televisions as well, for which the electricians on his team had strung cable lines to the nearest connection, and several phone lines.

When Michelle, still handcuffed, appeared in the company of two guards, Drabeznic had the cuffs removed and offered her a seat. Then he came straight to the point: "I would like to hear your opinion of your President."

"Uh . . . alright," said Michelle, not sure of the purpose for this. "He's a good leader, very decisive, who sticks by what he has said he'll do."

Drabeznic, finishing a soft drink in several giant gulps, silenced her with a loud, very unpleasant-sounding belch. "My dear, you're a terrible liar, and to help you understand the gravity of the situation, let me tell you that I've just informed your President I may have to throw one of his citizens off the roof if we can't reach some kind of understanding." He stared at Michelle. "I hope it won't have to be you, but with answers like that one, I can't give you any guarantees. Now, I will not insult you by speaking to you as a woman, but as a soldier. I understand that you people in the armed services have very little respect for a man so lacking in understanding of military matters."

"Yeah, but he's still the Commander-in-Chief."

"Perhaps you would agree with the impression of him that I have garnered from magazines and television: that he is a weak, undisciplined man—one who in a situation such as this one might give in to desperation?"

"Maybe," said Michelle, "but never underestimate a desperate man. Looks like to me you've spoiled any chances he might have at getting re-elected, so don't be surprised if he takes his anger out on you."

That was the second time this morning Drabeznic had heard this idea. "I suppose you're just repeating what Mason told you to say?"

"He didn't tell me to say anything."

"Never mind. So you're saying he might decide to storm the building?" Drabeznic looked amused. "I find that hard to imagine, if Jimmy Carter's performance in Teheran serves as any guide. He didn't make any attempt to free the hostages until many months into the crisis, and when he did, it was an enormous failure. Americans don't have the heart to conduct an operation like the Israelis made at Entebbe, or the Soviets did to anyone foolish enough to hijack one of their planes—certainly Carter didn't have the heart, and this man seems similar in many ways."

"But he's not Carter, and this is 1996, not 1980," answered Michelle.

"Like I said, you can't predict what someone will do in a desperate situation—especially this guy."

"You're not much help, madam," said Drabeznic, sounding irritated, "and as I have work to do, I'm afraid I'm going to have to send you back to your quarters." He motioned to a guard, who slapped the cuffs back on her. "By the way," he said in a gentler tone as she stood at the door with her captors, "let me know if any of the men tries to bother you again, and I will deal with him severely."

"I can take care of myself," she shot back.

"I'm sure you can, my dear. I'm sure you can."

Drabeznic's demands to the President began with a long list—longer than those he'd presented to the other heads of state combined—of "political prisoners" to be released from U.S. prisons and flown to the rendezvous point in Ar Rutbah. As U.S. intelligence had predicted, it included Sheikh Abdel Rahman and the others convicted in the World Trade Center bombing, along with assorted Libyans, Palestinians, and Syrians indicted by the FBI in the past decade. But there were other, unexpected, names that the Director of Central Intelligence had said might be included as "a big *screw you*": members of Chicago's El Rukns gang, imprisoned for receiving funds from Qaddafi to conduct terrorist activities; various African-American criminals; Native American activists accused of bombings at reservations in the western U.S.; and the Unabomber. In all, this added up to almost 200 men and women whose combined sentences, if laid end-to-end, would stretch well past the year 6000 A.D.

Secondly, Drabeznic demanded 500 Stinger missiles, 1,500 other anti-aircraft weapons, 5,000 M-16s, and 2,000,000 rounds of ammunition to be delivered to Sarajevo via ten C-5A transport planes. "If you have any space left over," he added impishly, "fill it with medical supplies, food, uniforms, and boots."

Third was the matter of how to get Drabeznic, his men, and their "guests" out of the Village. To this end, he requested that a plywood corridor be constructed from the sidewalk on McMillan Street to the front door of Fitten Residence Hall. Then a bus, with all windows except for the driver's side of the windshield covered in black paint, would drive up directly in front of the corridor at 5:00 p.m. A large black canvas would be placed over the space between the walkway and the bus, and when all this was arranged, the group would depart. At

Hartsfield International Airport, he expected two L-1011s, fueled and prepared for a transatlantic flight, to be waiting on the runway beside the international concourse when they arrived at approximately 6:00 p.m. The planes should be placed a safe distance apart, and after he chose one of the two, it would be flown to Frankfurt, where it would refuel before going on to Iraq. At Ar Ruṭbah, assuming that all his demands had been met, he would release the hostages to the U.S. troops.

"Okay," said the President after he'd heard all the demands. "Is that it?"

"Just one more thing, Mr. President: immediately prior to the arrival of the bus, we want delivered to us here in the Olympic Village fifteen L-1011 cargo containers in which you will place a total of $500 million in gold: South African Krugerrands or coins of some similar denomination, such as the American Gold Eagle or the Canadian Maple Leaf. The particular coinage is not important, but it must be $500 million."

The President gasped. "What did you say?"

"I believe the request was clear, sir: $500 million in gold coins."

"Mr. Drabeznic, even if we had it to spare, which we don't, you know the government of the United States cannot pay ransom."

"I really am not concerned how the money is raised, Mr. President, but if you do not comply with this request, I shall consider our entire agreement null and void, and will take appropriate action."

"Alright. I can go ahead and agree to numbers one, two, and three, but I'll have to get back to you on four."

"Ten minutes, Mr. President. No more."

The group in the Cabinet Room had listened to this on speaker phone, and the moment the Vice President heard the ransom figure, he was on the line to Jason Blanchot while an aide rushed to obtain figures for the exact value of gold on Wall Street that morning. After preparing the way for his Chief, the second-in-command turned Blanchot over to him.

"Five hundred million dollars?" said the IOC President. "That is virtually all the money we will have left in our bank accounts after our losses from the Atlanta Games!"

"Apparently, Mr. Blanchot," said the President, "Drabeznic has done his homework on this, just like with everything else. I'm sure if there had been more, he would have asked for it."

"Mr. President, need I remind you that it is the fault of your country that we're in this mess in the first—"

"Sir, we have no options left at this point. Besides, do you really think they'll be able to just disappear with five hundred million dollars' worth of gold? Do you have any idea how much that weighs?" He motioned to the aide with the Wall Street figures, who quickly ran the numbers on a calculator and wrote them down.

"No, Mr. President," said Blanchot icily. "How much does it weigh?"

The President, glad to have an answer to what had sounded like a rhetorical question, read from the paper his aide handed to him. "Roughly 90,000 pounds. Now, how in the hell would someone disappear with forty-five tons of gold?"

"Not too easily," Blanchot admitted.

"Okay," said the President, considering the deal done. "We deployed the Seventh Special Forces and the 160th Aviation Regiment to Iraq on Tuesday afternoon, and they're going to be on the scene when the plane lands. As soon as the hostages are released, they're gonna come in and wipe out al-Ansar. Your gold will be back in Switzerland by close of business Friday."

"Why do I have trouble believing that, Mr. President? The latest reports I've heard are that the prisoners released by France and Germany have disappeared."

"That was a different situation, because we still had the hostages to think about, whereas once they're released, all agreements will be off. And even if by some miracle the terrorists got past all the firepower aimed at them from both our side and the Iraqis', they'd have to figure out how to transport fifty tons of gold across the desert."

"If it's that easy, why don't you use your own gold?"

The President looked at his watch: they had already used up nearly four of the ten minutes Drabeznic had given him. "Look, we're running out of time here. You know it's impossible for me to place even one dollar from the U.S. Treasury at the disposal of terrorists—even if I know I can get it back. But you, as a private organization, are not prevented from taking such action . . . . And need I point out, Mr. Blanchot, that a significant portion of that money in your reserves has come from lucrative business relationships with American companies?"

"The Olympics will survive whether your companies are around to support them or not, Mr. President."

"Mr. Blanchot," the President said tiredly, "if we don't get this thing resolved now, the Atlanta Games could very well be the last Olympics."

Blanchot said nothing for a long moment while the seconds ticked away. Then he sighed and said, "Alright, Mr. President, I will give in— on one condition, relating to one of those American companies you referred to. I need assurances of full indemnification by the National Broadcasting Company for any repercussions resulting from the suspension or cancellation of the Olympic Games in Atlanta."

The President sighed too. "I don't think you quite understand how our legal system works here, but rest assured that we'll work with NBC to resolve this." Ever alert, the Vice President whispered to an aide to get Greenberg on the phone.

"I'm tired of your legal system, Mr. President. I want a firm assurance, in writing, that NBC is not going to hold us accountable for their losses. Once I have that assurance, then we will front the money—"

"Okay."

"—*with* the understanding from you that it's coming back."

"I'll guarantee it personally, Mr. Blanchot."

There followed a short, tense discussion between the President and Greenberg, and a few minutes later, he called back Blanchot and announced that NBC's counsel was drawing up the indemnification papers as they spoke.

Just thirty seconds short of the ten-minute mark, the President was on the line to Drabeznic again. "We're prepared to move forward," he said. "Your gold will be there at 3:00 this afternoon."

31

The President now had another problem on his hands: the media. It was a problem he could have avoided. If on Tuesday morning he had put a stop to Drabeznic's plans for a press conference and instead filtered information through spin doctors on the Administration's payroll, it would have given Mason and the rest of the security forces more freedom to end the crisis swiftly. The press would have criticized this, of course, but the euphoria following quick success would have stifled their complaints. But he didn't want to anger his friends in the media, so the cameras had stayed. By the time he realized that they were working to Drabeznic's advantage, not his, the electronic genie had escaped from its bottle, and it would be much harder to put it back in.

At a noon briefing in the White House, the President sent his hapless press secretary, Dotty Grayson, to do his dirty work. Clearly nervous as she approached the podium, her voice cracked as she read her prepared statement. Not only would all media personnel be denied access to the Olympic Village, she said, there would be no live camera coverage from nearby buildings or helicopters; in fact, the Administration intended to enforce a five-mile no-fly zone around Fitten dorm. Ignoring the gasp of disbelief that rippled through the assembled reporters, she went on to say that any further reports would be disseminated through her at briefings every two hours. She glanced up from the page for a moment and, seeing the stony looks that greeted her, skipped several paragraphs to her conclusion, then announced that she would take only two questions.

The room broke out into a screaming match, as every reporter began clamoring for recognition from Dotty Grayson. But she had orchestrated this carefully beforehand: ignoring a chorus of voices and a tumult of upraised hands, she pointed to Don Samuelson of ABC News.

Samuelson, an old Washington hand who had seen five Administrations, stood to his full six feet, four inches and launched into what amounted to a soothing oratory rather than a question. He praised the current Administration for its openness in providing information as events unfolded, and expressed his sympathy with their desire now to "have us step back a little, so that we can be part of the solution instead of part of the problem." He purred along in a slow, self-assured cadence, as though he had all the time in the world and there weren't a hundred other reporters in the room eager to ask their own questions. By now many of the hands had come down, and his disgruntled colleagues had begun to mumble angrily back and forth among themselves. Clearly the Administration had offered him some sort of quid pro quo, probably an exchange of inside information in return for a little P.R. work on their behalf. Those around him began to hiss and cat-call, partly from anger and partly out of jealousy.

Finally he came to his question: "The thing I'd like to know, Dotty, is given these parameters you've established, and given the fact that America doesn't just want to hear me talk"—he said this with a disparaging glance around the room, which brought a smile to Dotty Grayson's tired face—"how are we going to obtain pictures from the Village to go along with our audio?"

"Thank you, Don," said Dotty, as though his "question" were new to her. "That's a very good point, and I meant to cover it in my statement. You'll be receiving access to footage taken by military camera crews inside the Village, and though of course we'll have to clear all pictures to make sure they don't provide any information that would help the opposition forces, we intend to cooperate with you as much as we can."

Again, the hands burst up and people began yelling, but she looked straight at Elaine Clifton of *Newsweek*. An audible groan went up from the assembled reporters. The President had no more ardent supporter than Clifton, of whom the running joke in New York and Washington was, "If he shot someone on live TV, Elaine would say he did it to make a point about gun control."

But Elaine Clifton surprised everyone in the room, especially Dotty Grayson. "Dotty," she began, "I've done some research into the question about media access." Grayson looked at her notes. This didn't have anything to do with her scripted question concerning rumors that the President would soon bring the hostage crisis to an end. "It appears that whereas you can control what happens within the Olympic Village, it is unconstitutional for the United States government to demand that our cameras not be allowed to operate outside it—unless marshal law is declared. Is this Administration prepared to take that step, and if so, how do you reconcile this with the Constitution of the United States?"

Two things happened immediately: the room broke into applause, and Dotty Grayson's mouth fell open. "According to the Justice Department," she stammered, "our actions are in accordance with the Supreme Court's decision in *Schenck v. U.S.*, 1919: the First Amendment has to be constrained if its use constitutes a clear and present danger. Therefore, in the interests of protecting U.S. citizens, as well as international guests in this country—"

But Elaine Clifton did not relent. Looking directly into Grayson's eyes in the blinding glare of camera lights, she said, "Dotty, you and I go 'way back, and I want you to be straight with me now. What you're really saying is that the press has made you people look bad by reporting what's actually going on in the Village, and you want us to provide disinformation to the people of the United States. So screw the First Amendment, right?"

Another cheer went up from the press corps, and in the seconds that it took for the room to grow quiet again, Grayson went from defensiveness to anger. She picked up her papers in a wad. "You people are hiding behind the First Amendment like a bunch of pornographers!" she shouted over the din. "You don't care about the truth, you just want to show people being blown up and thrown off of buildings! You should be ashamed of yourselves!" Realizing she had completely lost control and would have a hard time ever facing the White House Press Corps again, she fled from the room as the cameras clicked.

By noon on Thursday, nearly fifty-seven hours had passed since Mason got that first phone call from Greg Robbins. Since then he'd slept a total of five hours, mostly while sitting at his desk. The rest of his task force had done a little better, but not much; Robbins and many of the others found that even when they tried to sleep, their nerves wouldn't let them.

The Sewer Rats and technicians of the 4th Psyop Group had long departed for Fort Bragg, their work here completed. It wasn't their fault that last night's painstaking operation had failed. The FBI and CIA operatives remained at the MARC, functioning in a role subordinate to Mason's, and the National Guard battalions—including the gunners and snipers released from Fulmer and Montag that morning—had finally gotten to see some action. But they weren't up against Drabeznic; their job was to maintain the Village perimeter, and ensure that the media and the public were kept at bay.

Meanwhile Mason and Robbins worked to meet their end of Drabeznic's demands, as per orders received from Gen. Helms. Plant Operations sent a crew to McMillan Street to construct stud walls along the walkway from the door of Fitten to the curb-cut in front, which was separated from the street by a small island. The walls ran about fifty feet, and the men covered them in plywood along the outside only; lastly, they would nail 4 x 8 plywood sheets over the top, completely enclosing the makeshift corridor. Thus Drabeznic and his men could come out when the bus arrived, free from the fear that a few well-placed snipers could hit them without hurting any of the hostages.

The Plant Operations workers, who'd been rushed there without the chance to eat lunch, watched hungrily as an Aramark van arrived and two people got out to deliver baskets by means of a rope lowered from a second-floor window. If everything went well, this would be the last meal served at Fitten Hall, because Helms and Mason had agreed that with the scheduled 5:00 p.m. departure, the delivery of supper would create too much confusion; therefore the hostages' evening meal would be served on the plane.

While this was happening, Mason discussed options with Julio, Aaron, and Lamont at the MARC. Clearly Drabeznic had covered all his bases as far as protecting the bus windows from snipers, and by keeping the hostages close at hand, he would ensure that the gold got with him to the airport. "Now, we can't count on Michelle to do anything," Mason said, "even if we wanted her to. She's to be treated as just a hostage now, and that leaves us with only one option." He thought for a minute. "Boys, I've got a job for you . . . ."

In the aftermath of Dotty Grayson's announcement, every major network flew its top negotiators to Washington to demand that the White House rescind its order and grant them access to the Village. When they found themselves rebuffed by their old friends, they filed lawsuits in D.C. and Atlanta district courts, an obvious bluff because the current situation would end long before these ever came before a judge.

Meanwhile, in lieu of live coverage, the networks brought out all their experts to speculate on events in the Village, re-ran the old footage, and waited for more word at the next White House briefing that afternoon. As always when there was no story to report, the media reported on themselves, or rather on their colleagues from the newspapers and wire services, as well as TV crews not invited to join the media pool. These other journalists had gathered as close to the Village as possible to report what stories they could, and had virtually taken over the Varsity on North Avenue. An ABC camera crew found plenty of angry reporters at the Varsity "media center" eager to denounce the President.

Throughout America, forces realigned in ways that were as odd as they were temporary. Members of the nation's minuscule conservative media found themselves joined by their liberal colleagues in criticizing the President; and the so-called Christian Right—no friends of this Administration—applauded it now for preventing the media from polluting American homes with more scenes of gore.

Meanwhile, something very disturbing was taking place in maximum-security prisons from New York to Oklahoma, and South Dakota to Alabama. Justice Department representatives had begun making phone calls to wardens, informing them of an order from the Chief Executive himself to release the persons listed by Drabeznic in his demands. This raised considerable protest over the legality of such an action in view of the separation of powers set forth in the Constitution, but like the networks' considerably less significant legal challenges, these were rendered moot by the fact that the prisoners had to be released today.

Therefore a motley crew of bombers, assassins, and robbers found themselves, to their great joy, removed from their homes behind bars—some in solitary and some on death row—and placed in holding cells. From there they would be escorted aboard heavily guarded planes chartered for Dobbins AFB, from whence they would depart for Frankfurt aboard two C-141s at the same time the L-1011s carrying al-Ansar left Hartsfield that evening.

Jason Blanchot held a lunchtime meeting with his executive committee at ACOG Headquarters in Atlanta, in which he informed them of his discussions with the President and Ira Greenberg. Following this, he placed a call to the President of the Premiere Bank d' Nationale in Lausanne. The banker in turn issued an irrevocable letter of credit to the U.S. government for $500 million, which was wired directly to the Americans. With that, the International Olympic Committee's coffers, full to overflowing for the past twelve opulent years, were virtually emptied.

So too was the coin portfolio of the Atlanta branch of the Federal Reserve Bank. At 1:30 p.m., five cargo trucks, each with three L-1011 containers, pulled up in front of the bank on Marietta Street downtown, and armed guards began loading in crates. As Drabeznic had ordered, these contained U.S. Gold Eagles, Canadian Maple Leafs, and South African Krugerrands—but only $350 million worth. An entity which handles as much gold as the federal government typically stores it in bars, which each have to be assayed to determine their value. Drabeznic had wanted coins precisely because they could be accepted on their appearance and weight, but his exorbitant demands had exceeded the easily obtainable reserves.

By 3:00 p.m. the trucks, each carrying three cargo containers holding roughly 6,300 pounds of gold worth about $33 million, pulled slowly up McMillan. The first driver got out, put up his hands to show that he was not armed, and carefully opened the side doors of the containers on his truck before stepping away. A moment later, three of Drabeznic's men emerged, and one climbed into the first container with a bag and an electronic scanning device in his hands while the other two covered him.

If the U.S. government had been foolish enough to plant a transmitter among its gold, the man with the scanning device would have detected it immediately. Instead, he found only a single layer of large wooden boxes, each of which weighed over 300 pounds and contained 5,000 coins separated into plastic tubes. Having satisfied himself that they were not being double-crossed, the man set down his detecting device, withdrew a small crowbar from his back pocket, and began to break open the tops of several boxes selected at random. From each of these he withdrew a handful of coins, poured them into the bag, and replaced the tops of the boxes. He went through this same process with the other two containers on that truck, then he repeated the entire drill six more times with the three containers on each of the next two trucks. When he entered the fourth truck, however, he began to turn up not only coins but gold bars. Ordering the driver to stand fast, he grabbed his bag full of coins and retreated through the plywood corridor while his two companions stood facing in opposite directions, their AK-47s at the ready.

Shortly afterward, Drabeznic was on the phone with Mason. "Are you playing games here, sir?" he demanded. "I said *gold coins*, and gold coins only—how clear do I have to make myself?"

"That would be fine," Mason replied calmly, "if you hadn't cleaned out all our gold coins. Now, I'm sure we could go to other Federal Reserve banks, or Fort Knox, but that would take a day or two."

Suppressing his fury, Drabeznic demanded, "How do I know that these bars are real?"

"Mr. Drabeznic, if you think that in the past few hours, the U.S. government has had enough time to concoct a scheme—"

"Governments do these things. They might have already had them set aside for just such a situation. I want you to send me a power drill so I can determine that these aren't just gold-plated lead."

A minute later, someone from Plant Operations ran over to Fitten with a Makita cordless. The terrorists' assayer entered the fourth truck and drilled through several bars at random, then did the same with the fifth truck until he was satisfied that they were indeed the genuine article.

Then Drabeznic, sounding pacified, called Mason and ordered him to have the five drivers wait in the Couch Building for further instructions. After they spoke, Mason called home. He hadn't had much chance to speak to Sandy in the past three days, and she'd be glad to hear his voice—until he told her, in very vague terms, where he planned to be that night.

At precisely 5:00 p.m., a red-and-blue transit coach drove up past the five cargo trucks full of gold and pulled into the curb cut before the makeshift corridor leading into Fitten dorm. Though spotlessly clean and virtually new, it didn't look quite as it had when the Tacoma, Washington, Transit Authority had loaned it to ACOG a few weeks before: all its windows except for the driver's side of the windshield had been painted black, and all the seats except for the driver's had been removed.

Two of Drabeznic's men, armed with submachine guns and carrying a piece of black canvas, stormed down the corridor to search the vehicle from end to end. Satisfied that the interior was free of bugs or bombs—a fact easily verified because the seats had been removed—they walked around the outside. They checked the mirrors, the gas tank, the license plate, and any other place where the authorities could have hidden a device; they scrambled underneath the vehicle and carefully inspected the underside; and lastly they examined the engine for intentional defects. Then they spread the canvas from the roof of the bus to the roof of the corridor, making it impossible for anyone entering to be seen.

While one of them guarded the driver, the other returned to the inside of Fitten, and shortly afterward, Mason's cellular phone rang.

"We're ready to load," said Drabeznic. "Have all your troops pull back out of sight, and keep in mind that all our guests have explosive devices that won't be deactivated until we reach our destination."

"Understood. Hey—one other thing."

"What is it?"

"I'd like to say a few words of encouragement to your guests."

Drabeznic considered this for a second, then said, "Alright. That can't hurt anything. Be standing near the front of the bus with a megaphone just before we leave. I'll call you and let you know when you can approach."

From half a block away, Mason pushed up the sunglasses he was wearing and scanned the bus through his binoculars. The terrorists had draped a Puerto Rican flag over the unpainted portion of the windshield, and only slight rustlings of the canvas between the hallway and the bus told him that the hostages were boarding. Further down the line, he saw groups of armed men milling around the five cargo trucks full of gold; it looked as though Drabeznic intended to leave the original drivers in Couch Hall, and replace them with his own men.

He turned around to look at his reflection in the window behind him and flashed a quick, toothy smile. *Good*, he thought as he saw himself. *You look like hell.*

Twelve minutes elapsed before the driver emerged from under the black canvas and ran toward him.

"They said they want to use their own driver," said the man, out of breath.

"That doesn't surprise me." Mason glanced at the bus, then at the obviously relieved driver. His phone rang.

"We're ready," said Drabeznic tiredly.

Mason walked to the front of the bus and lifted a small megaphone. "Ladies," he said loudly, "I am an agent of the federal government. I apologize for our inability to secure your release, and I understand the fear and discomfort you're experiencing right now, but please realize that it will all be over in a few hours." Then he added something as much for Drabeznic's ears as theirs: "Your security on this vehicle and on the airplane that will convey you from Hartsfield Airport will not be threatened by any of our forces, and according to the agreement between the President of the United States and your hosts, you will be released as soon as you reach your destination. At that time, you will be returned to your homes and families. That is all."

"That was nice, Mr. Mason," said Drabeznic over the phone when he had finished.

"Take a good look at me, Drabeznic," said Mason. He looked up at the flag and smiled broadly. "There's no place in this world where you can hide from this face. One day you'll turn around, and . . . ." He pointed his index finger like a pistol going off. A shadow pressed up against the windshield behind the red and white stripes of the Puerto Rican flag, and that was all he saw of Drabeznic.

But Drabeznic studied Mason's appearance carefully. He saw a man in his forties, of a heavyset build, with graying hair and a brownish mustache going gray. He had a strong jaw and a broad smile, marred somewhat by a gold cap on his left canine tooth; the only thing Drabeznic could not see were Mason's eyes, hidden behind dark glasses.

"Your dramatics fail to amuse me," said Drabeznic. "Let's get on with it."

"Alright," Mason replied, stepping backward but still facing the bus, "a police car is going to pull out in front of you on Eighth Street. Just follow him. He'll take you right to the expressway, which has been cleared except for an additional police escort of five vehicles. You'll see that all our people have been moved back several blocks, and there won't be any troops—or anyone else, for that matter—in your path."

Mason stepped back and watched as the bus and all five trucks started their engines. The bus pulled north on McMillan, then made a right turn off the narrow street onto Eighth, where the Atlanta Police escort waited. The bus driver ran up over the curb and knocked down a stop sign. *I guess that's the only time you'll ever see anybody do that right in front of a cop and get away with it*, Mason thought.

He stood there with his hands on his hips, watching them leave. But the moment they were out of sight, he sprinted back toward the MARC.

32

The multiple southbound and northbound lanes of the Downtown Connector were almost always busy, be it 4:00 in the morning, or Christmas Day, or the night in October 1995 when the city watched their Braves defeat the Cleveland Indians in Game Six of the World Series. To shut down this enormous motorway required monumental circumstances: a Presidential visit, a hazardous waste spill, or something like this.

Yet nothing like quite like this had ever happened in America. The Downtown Connector was deserted, as if a hard wind had simply swept everyone away. But of course it was the police, and not the wind, which had swept the highway, along with North Avenue, Spring Street, Courtland Street, and all the other thoroughfares that passed over it. The closest outsiders could get were the streets parallel to the Connector, and thousands of spectators lined the chain-link fences that looked out over the expressway below, many of them holding up signs that read *Let the Hostages Go* or something similar. The crowds bristled with patrolmen and National Guards, there to ensure that no one would try to shoot something more potent than an angry look at the strange motorcade.

Down the empty highway, moving at a rate of forty miles an hour, came the procession. The first three police cars were followed by two cargo trucks, which Drabeznic had ordered to pull out ahead of the bus as soon as they got on the Connector. The bus containing the thirty-five hostages was next, then the other three cargo trucks. Three more police cars brought up the rear, and five hundred feet above, three police choppers hovered.

These were the only aircraft along the route, since the area had been declared a no-fly zone. Though this made it harder for the media to cover the story, it didn't stop them. Every network in the world had a camera mounted on one or more buildings along the Connector, with commentators on-site or in the studio providing a running narration.

"We have just received word from an unidentified State Department source," said Margaret Winter on the network that had given the world *Atlanta: A City Divided,* which now seemed like something from the distant past. "The International Olympic Committee has agreed to pay al-Ansar $500 million in untraceable gold coins, and the Administration has released some 200 federal prisoners in exchange for the safe return of the remaining hostages."

As the motorcade moved beyond the range of their first camera, Margaret and her co-anchor Tim Barakoff speculated on the implications of the source's report. They were supposed to get pictures from a second camera on the Peachtree Summit Building further south, but there was a problem with the link. While technicians worked frantically to fix the hookup before the motorcade got within range of the third camera just south of the Olympic Stadium, Tim began to ramble.

"Margaret, all this raises a further question in my mind: what is the future of the Olympic Games? As negatives pile up on top of negatives, each of them burying the ideals the Olympics are supposed to symbolize, what city or nation would want to host the Games?"

The third camera was on now, showing nothing but an empty highway because the motorcade hadn't gotten there yet, so Barakoff went on talking. "We have accusations that a shoe company has allegedly perpetrated a felony to enhance the prospects of athletes it has sponsored . . . we have allegations that certain teams have consumed performance-enhancing drugs . . . we have racists spewing bigotry and hatred, and what does it all mean?"

"Tim, I—"

"It means ratings, that's what it means. Without controversy, no one is interested in the Olympics—no one, that is, except for terrorists such as the ones who tried to kill 85,000 people in the stadium two weeks ago, or the ones now taking their thirty-five hostages and their gold with them to the airport."

"That motorcade of terrorists and hostages that Tim refers to should be appearing on your screen momentarily," Margaret put in.

"It's my conclusion," Tim continued, "that the Games are no longer viable from a security standpoint unless a police state agrees to host them, and there are fewer and fewer of those around. Nor are the Olympics economically viable, not when there are so many good reasons for sponsors and TV networks to stay away—and not when the IOC has already had its pockets picked."

Now the convoy appeared on the screen, but Barakoff wasn't going to let Margaret interrupt him. "So take a good look at this," he concluded. "You are seeing the end of the 1996 Olympics—what may well be the last Olympics."

Mason had raced back to his office the moment the motorcade first departed, shed his oversized shirt and sport coat, along with the foam rubber padding that had added about forty pounds to his appearance, and rubbed off the makeup that had obscured the scar on his left cheek. Julio started up a set of shears and begun running them over his chief's head. Nervously Mason glanced at his watch as hunks of his hair fell on the floor. Even taking into account their slowed pace because of the cargo trucks, the trip from the Village to the airport wouldn't likely exceed twenty minutes because of the cleared motorways. He had to move quickly.

Once he'd shorn off all of Mason's hair, including his mustache, Julio lathered his head and began shaving it with a straight razor. "Stop fidgeting," said Julio. A minute later, Mason was looking in the mirror at a man with a head as smooth and shiny as a deodorant roll-on.

"How do I look?" he asked.

"All you need is a Tootsie Roll pop," Aaron said, trying not to laugh, "and you'd be a dead ringer for Telly Savalas."

Mason grinned, and when he did he saw the fake gold cap on his tooth. "Better get rid of this," he said. "It's amazing how people fixate on something like this—blinds them to most everything else."

Aaron brought him a Delta pilot's uniform tailored to his precise size, and Mason had started to get undressed when Lamont came in bearing a briefcase with a half-dozen sets of glasses. "Take your pick," he said, gesturing toward the briefcase. "I told Lenscrafters to get us the latest styles, all with clear-glass lenses, to keep your 20/20 vision."

"Good job." Pulling on his shirt, Mason selected a pair of circular gold-rimmed glasses and hooked them over his ears. "The sophisticated look," he said, surveying himself in the mirror. "How's this?"

"Mm," Lamont replied, grinning at Aaron. "Kojak as a Harvard graduate."

"Cut the crap."

"I'd have a hard time recognizing you myself," Lamont said in a more serious tone, "and I know you a lot better than he does."

"Not only that, he didn't see my eyes." Mason sat down and began slipping on the socks and shoes from the uniform. "They can be a real giveaway, and I didn't want to fool with colored contacts, so the shades seemed like a good idea. I'm just glad the bastard didn't tell me to take them off. Damn, these shoes are tight—are you sure they're ten and a half?"

Aaron shrugged. "That's what they gave us. Besides, I don't think you'll be doing a lot of walking."

Mason ran a belt through the loops in the pants, then he had Julio hold up the mirror for him while he tied his tie. With the coat that Aaron helped him into, he looked exactly like a very bald, very intelligent Delta Airlines pilot—and forty pounds lighter than when Drabeznic had seen him.

Lamont had placed a neutral gray screen against a wall, and now he had Mason stand against it while he snapped his picture several times with a Polaroid camera. He went next door, cropped the photos, pasted them onto a couple of badges on which information had already been typed, then ran them through a laminating machine. When he returned, he had a Georgia driver's license and a Delta pilot's I.D., complete with the Social Security Number and name of one Robert L. Brown.

Mason glanced at this material proof of his new identity—he'd selected Brown because his height, weight, age, and eye color matched his own—then checked the contents of a Delta carry-on bag sitting on his desk before grabbing it. "Okay," he said to Lamont, "let's go." He turned to the other two. "I'll see you back here . . . soon."

As the two walked swiftly toward the back of the MARC and the Jet Ranger waiting on the helipad, he checked his watch again: only eight minutes had passed since the terrorists and hostages had left. People who didn't know what was going on were looking at him, probably thinking that this bald pilot looked awfully familiar. He heard someone say, "Good luck, Tom," and he looked up to see Kirk, who stepped out the back door alongside him and Lamont.

The roar of the chopper filled the air, so Mason had to shout in Kirk's ear, "Don't worry—I'll bring her back." In spite of the tension he felt, he smiled. "But I oughta kick your ass."

"What?"

"You heard me. For ruining my best agent." Lamont got into the helicopter, and Mason turned around to Kirk. "She's done, I can tell from that look in her eyes. Pretty soon she'll be telling me she wants out." He put a hand on Kirk's shoulder. "But that's okay—I approve."

"Thanks, Dad!" Kirk yelled as Mason got into the chopper.

Mason and Lamont sailed over downtown in the helicopter, within two minutes flying past Lakewood Freeway on the south side. But the motorcade was still ahead of them, and they could see it making its way past the Stewart Avenue exit toward the airport. "There they are," Mason shouted to Lamont over the hum of the rotors, pointing at the procession hundreds of feet below. "We're not a minute too soon."

Mason ordered the pilot to put them down beside Concourse E. Moments later, he and Lamont scrambled out onto the tarmac and, crouching low, made their way toward the terminal while the Jet Ranger lifted off again.

Two FAA officials met them just inside the international terminal to escort them past security without going through the magnetometers. Mason didn't have any firearms, which could penetrate the skin of an airplane and cause rapid depressurization, but in the pilot's bag bearing the Robert L. Brown I.D. were two items that would have been seized from an ordinary passenger.

They were Tasers, small devices about the size of a flip phone that generated an electronic charge of approximately 250,000 volts, which made them particularly useful to law-enforcement officers in disabling dangerous suspects. All the operator had to do was point the Taser at the subject from as far as fifteen feet away and pull the trigger, then it would send out two razor-thin wires with tiny barbed probes at the end, which embedded themselves in the subject's body. This would immediately immobilize anyone, and depending on the size of the man, a thirty-second charge could knock him out for as long as fifteen minutes. Repeated applications could ensure that he stayed out.

There were only two hitches to the application of the Taser. Someone drugged up on PCP, as Rodney King had been when the LAPD used it on him in 1991, would not respond to it, and in King's case this had resulted in the infamous videotaped beating. Presumably, Mason didn't have to worry about any of Drabeznic's men being on angel dust, but the act of sending a quarter-million volts of numbing pain through a person's body had another effect: it caused the bowel muscles to relax, and when the victim awoke from his daze, he usually needed a change of pants.

The FAA men walked them down a series of hallways, past windows looking out onto the empty tarmac. As they rounded a corner, Mason heard a sound from Lamont's radio. Lamont spoke into it, then said, "Okay they're turning off the exit ramp, headed toward the south terminal."

"Here's the pilot's lounge," said one of the FAA men as they stopped before an inconspicuous-looking door.

Two dozen pilots, co-pilots, and engineers in the lounge were all watching the approach of al-Ansar on television, and it startled them when a bald man in a Delta uniform burst in. Standing alone in the doorway, he hastily shut the door behind him and said, "Listen up, everyone. I'm with the Department of Defense, and I'd like a moment of your time, if you don't mind."

If he had come a minute later, he would have found the room empty, because they would have all disappeared into the concourse to see the arrival of the motorcade for themselves. Walking rapidly to the front of the room and turning down the volume on the TV set, he announced, "I need two volunteers." No one blinked. "Now before anyone rushes forward," he added, "let me go ahead and tell you that I don't want anyone who's married or has children at home, because this mission has some risks. But if you're willing to do it, your country needs you—and so do those thirty-five hostages in the bus."

Still no one said anything, so Mason went on, speaking rapidly and glancing every few seconds at the TV. "I know you're all aware of what's taking place right now, but I have a hunch that the terrorists are going to skip both of the aircraft that are waiting for them out there and pick a third one. I need to be on that plane, and therefore I need two good people to help me fly it."

A distinguished-looking pilot with graying temples who appeared to be in his mid-fifties spoke up. "Sir," he said in a deep Southern drawl, "you say 'help' you fly the aircraft, but just how many hours of flight time do you have?"

Mason smiled. "I'll be honest with you: my flying experience is limited to being a passenger." This brought nervous snickers of derision from the pilots. "But I'm not going on that plane to fly, and that's why I need two of you."

"But from what we've seen on TV," reasoned the pilot with the drawl, "it's not hard to imagine the terrorists killing either the pilot or co-pilot or both, in which case the third person would have to help fly the aircraft."

"That's a fair appraisal," Mason admitted, "and you've got just the kind of cool head I want to have with me. Yes, I'd be in trouble if I had to fly by myself, and yes, this is a last-minute effort to save the hostages, but . . . . Are there any takers?"

As he looked around from face to face, each in turn avoided his eyes.

He knew better than to push them. "Alright, then," he said. "I certainly understand your apprehension, and I thank you for your time." With that, he turned and walked from the room.

The runways at Atlanta's international airport looked as strangely calm as the expressway running through the city. There were no planes taking off or landing, no fuel trucks, no baggage cars—only the two Lockheed L-1011s that Drabeznic had requested, sitting by themselves at the far end of the runway.

The terminal and concourses were quiet, much quieter than they had been during the sudden rush of athletes, officials, and guests who'd begun departing on the second day of the hostage crisis. But the silence came from the somber mood that had fallen over the entire city, not from any reduction in the number of passengers. On orders from the President, the FAA had postponed all incoming or outgoing flights from 5:00 to 7:00 p.m., leaving thousands of people waiting nervously for the boarding call they hoped would come later that evening.

To prevent overcrowding in the outer terminal, those awaiting re-scheduled flights, who would be the first to board after the regular schedule resumed, waited in the concourses. There were thousands upon thousands of them filling every seat and every aisle, and many more stood at the windows, watching the drama taking place outside. But they couldn't see much. Drabeznic had ordered the erection of a twenty-foot-high plywood fence reinforced with metal plates, which covered everything but the tops of the two aircraft.

A cordon of security guards were waiting for the caravan when it arrived, and they threw open a gate marked *Absolutely No Admittance*. As soon as the convoy was inside, Drabeznic radioed his police escort and told him to pull their vehicles to the side, then follow the airport guards into the terminal after they shut the gate. While the cargo trucks moved in the direction of the two planes as they'd been supposed to do, the bus departed from its predetermined route, and pulled slowly toward the long line of concourses.

A network of security cameras along the perimeter, inside the terminal and concourses, and at strategically hidden spots on the tarmac recorded every move of the motorcade. At the White House, the President and the rest of his staff in the Cabinet room watched this on a bank of television sets, and as the paths of the cargo trucks and the bus diverged, the President shouted, "What in the holy hell is he doing?" He glanced over his shoulder at the DCI. "You think he's figured it out already?"

Upon receiving Drabeznic's request for the two aircraft, DCI had arranged the installation of additional hidden transponders on each plane that would periodically send out electronic codes plotting their flight position. Not only that, the flight crew would all be CIA. Of these four pilots and two engineers, several of the older ones had flown with Air America during Vietnam, and all of them had experience with a more recent "proprietary company" or front operation called Aviation Tech Services. So they were used to posing as ordinary pilots providing a run-of-the-mill service which took them to places where business travellers seldom went—the jungles of Central America, or assorted hot spots in the Middle East.

"I doubt it, sir," said DCI.

"Then what the hell's he doing?" asked the President again.

When Mason came out of the pilots' lounge, Lamont told him what had happened. The two men stood for a second and watched as the bus approached the concourse, then turned and began pulling slowly alongside it, past one boarding gate after another.

"He's looking for another plane, just like I thought." Mason made a fist with his right hand and punched his left palm as he looked out at the bus passing by on the tarmac. "But damn! If I can't find anyone to fly for me, it doesn't do me any good."

"You mean—?" Lamont pointed toward the lounge.

He said the last words to Mason's back, because his boss had taken off running, keeping pace with the bus, thirty feet away on the other side of the plate-glass windows. Mason lost sight of it while passing a solid wall, then rushed to the next window and pushed a crowd of gawkers aside to see it. It was still moving.

He ran from gate to gate, glancing out at the bus from time to time. Just when he was nearly out of breath, he saw the vehicle stop before Gate 12, where Delta Flight No. 20 sat waiting for its 7:21 takeoff to Frankfurt. The passengers rushed to the window, blocking Mason's view, and he started to push through them when he heard the phone at the boarding desk ring.

When the attendant answered it, a worried scowl crossed her face. Hanging up, she immediately whispered something to her co-worker, who rushed through the boarding door and down the jetway to the plane. Mason knew what was happening. She'd gone to tell the pilots about Drabeznic's request, and in a minute or two, the people who had hoped to board Flight 20 would see their luggage being unloaded from the plane's cargo hold. Sure enough, even as the announcement of a change of plans came over the loudspeakers, he watched as the pilots and flight engineer jostled out through the door into the concourse with the Delta employee who'd gone to summon them.

Mason chuckled to himself as he watched the three men hurrying away into the crowd. Of course it was no coincidence at all that Drabeznic happened to have picked a flight going to the same destination as the other two planes, and for once Mason had managed to second-guess his opponent. The damn thing about it was that it didn't matter, because he had no way of getting himself from the concourse to the cockpit of that plane. For all he knew, Drabeznic had his own pilots among the entourage.

The Delta baggage carriers had begun unloading the luggage, and this caused as much stir from the would-be passengers in the gate area as the arrival of the bus. In the midst of this grumbling, Mason heard a voice speaking to him from behind. He turned around to see the distinguished-looking pilot who had questioned him, along with another man he recognized from the lounge. "Sir, we'd like a moment of your time, if we might," said the pilot in his heavy drawl.

Mason nodded toward a pillar in the middle of the concourse, out of sight from the bus. The three stepped over, then the first man introduced himself as Charlie Bass, and his friend as Rick Watson. Mason gave his name as Robert Brown, which brought a knowing look from the two— since both knew the real Brown—but he didn't see any reason to divulge his true identity when the knowledge of it could only endanger these men.

"After you left," said Bass, "Rick and I discussed it, and we decided we'd like to sign on with you for this mission."

"Sorry it took us so long," said Watson with a grin. "We've both got grown kids, but we needed to call our wives and tell them we'd be flying a little different kind of mission. But don't worry, we didn't tell them what."

Mason nodded and smiled with boundless gratitude. "Okay, great. Obviously neither of you guys were actually scheduled for Flight 20. The ones who were didn't wait around for the action."

"We can get on the flight, no problem," Watson said. "All we have to do is move ahead with purpose."

"Great. Okay, I need a sixty-second crash course here: where do you want me to sit?"

Bass chuckled. "You'll sit to the right of the flight officer—that's me—and Rick, being the engineer, will be sitting behind you facing starboard, or right as you might call it. As for everything else, we'll sort of talk you through as we go."

"Sounds like a plan." Mason tapped the bag beside him. "I've got a couple weapons—don't worry, they're not firearms, just something I might need to keep the peace. Is there a place in the cockpit where I can hide them?"

Bass said that could be arranged.

"Alright." Mason could see that the attendant at the desk was calling the pilots to report to the plane, and he turned to the two men. "Now, very quickly: I go by Robert, not Bob. You guys have met me before and we've chatted, but we've never flown together. I'm from Cairo, Georgia, and my wife Darlene and I don't have any kids."

"We know all that," said Watson, smiling. "We already know more about Robert Brown than you do."

"No doubt about that."

The three men began walking toward the door of the jetway. No one tried to stop them; on the contrary, everyone seemed to make a wide berth around the three pilots who had the guts to board this particular flight.

33

As soon as Drabeznic announced to the tower that he would need a third aircraft, he demanded an airport maintenance crew to expand the barrier around the first two. A dozen trucks scrambled onto the tarmac, and out of them piled a group of workers who hastily began erecting an extension of the plywood wall.

Also on his orders, another dozen catering trucks lined up parallel to the bus. One by one they pulled next to the door, where the same black canvas the terrorists had used to conceal their departure from the Village was spread between the bus and each truck, in succession. There were signs of movement under the cloth, which then would be pulled back. The truck would proceed toward the two planes, to be followed by another for a repetition of the process.

Lamont, who'd by now jostled through the disgruntled would-be passengers to look out the window, tried to interpret the moving shapes under the canvas. With sixteen terrorists and thirty-five hostages, logic would dictate that each truck contained one or two terrorists and two or three hostages; yet so far logic had been no guide to predicting the actions of al-Ansar, and they could just as easily be sending some trucks away empty and crowding people into others. Even when the catering trucks pulled away one by one, he couldn't see anything because they were fully enclosed.

After the last truck had been loaded, the bus followed it out onto the tarmac. That meant they had at least one terrorist left on the bus to drive, no doubt with another man guarding several hostages as security. When they loaded their cargo—human and monetary—onto the planes, they would be behind the plywood fence; but even there, Lamont thought, they'd probably conceal their actions. Just as the bus reached the fence, another dozen cargo trucks pulled out from the terminal in the direction of the aircraft.

The First Lady had a habit of disappearing whenever crises at the White House reached their lowest point, and this morning she'd maintained that perfect record by staying away from the damage assessment meeting. But now she slipped into the Cabinet Room just as DCI was explaining to the President that Drabeznic had ordered more empty cargo containers. "With all those identical containers behind the barrier," he said, "we can't tell which is loaded into which aircraft. He could either be dispersing the gold along with the empties, or maybe he's putting it all in one plane and empty containers in the other two." The Director of Central Intelligence threw up his hands in a helpless gesture. "Your guess is as good as mine."

"But at least now we're pretty sure he'll use all three planes, instead of the two like we agreed?" asked the President.

"Looks like it." The DCI chewed on his pipe, full but unlit. "If that's the case, we of course have our transponders on the first two planes, and the third one has its own transponder. If it's turned on and not disarmed, we're good to go—not only that, our two aircraft each have an additional transponder that will only come on after the plane's been in the air for an hour."

"Okay, so we've got your guys in two planes, but what about the third?"

"Sir," said Gen. Helms, "I've just learned from one of Thomas Mason's people that Mason has gone to the airport disguised as a member of the flight crew, and attempted to recruit a couple of Delta pilots to help him fly the third plane. It appears he's been successful in making the insertion."

The President nodded his head thoughtfully, but the First Lady said to the Attorney General, "Janice, has there been a complete check on this Mason?"

"I beg your pardon?"

"You heard me."

"If I may, ma'am," the general put in, "Mason has been with Defense for over twenty years, the last four of them on assignment to Atlanta for the Olympics. He's got top-secret clearance, and—"

The First Lady folded her arms. "But he seems to be just half a step behind the terrorists," she observed, "which puts him about three steps ahead of us. I smell a rat."

"That's a good point," said the President. "Especially because we have reason to believe this was an inside job."

"Sir, Mason himself was the one that advanced the idea about the mole at Georgia Tech," Helms pointed out.

"So how did he know they were going to take another aircraft," asked the President, "and once they did, that he'd be able to get on it?"

"He didn't know," said DCI judiciously. "It's just the kind of instinct that comes from years in the field."

"Or from inside knowledge."

"If you ask me," said the First Lady sharply, "I'd watch Mason."

"Now," said Watson as Mason settled into the seat in front of his and to Bass's right, "let me tell you a couple things you might want to know."

Leaning over Mason's shoulder, the flight engineer began explaining the bewildering array of dials and buttons before him. "Here you have your flight instruments," Watson was saying, pointing as he spoke. "Air speed, altitude, heading . . . . There's your inertial navigation system or INS, which is what we use to plug in a set of coordinates and point the plane in that direction. It's coupled to autopilot, which is what's physically holding the yoke in place."

As Mason listened, he felt like a first-grader in graduate school. He literally prayed he wouldn't be called on to use any of this information.

"And then, while you and Charlie are doing all that," Watson continued, "I'm back here with my own little set of gauges."

Mason nodded his head gravely. In the background he overheard Drabeznic on the radio ordering Bass to proceed toward the expanded plywood curtain. It seemed strange to hear the by now familiar voice in such unfamiliar surroundings.

"As soon as we finish inspecting the other two aircraft," said Drabeznic, "we will board yours."

"Roger," said the captain as the tow vehicle began the slow and arduous job of pushing the plane away from the jetway, then pulling it toward the other two aircraft.

Mason felt all of his muscles tensing, especially the ones around his shoulders and the back of his neck. If he could help it, he didn't intend to speak to Drabeznic on the radio, because his voice without his changed appearance might give him away.

The Delta plane edged forward and pulled behind the makeshift screen, where the crew saw the rows of cargo and catering trucks lining the sides of the planes. Men were everywhere, directing the unloading and loading. Two terrorists boarded each of the other two aircraft, no doubt checking out the pilots and searching for anyone else who might have secreted themselves in a hidden compartment, after which they would take the elevator down to the lower galley and inspect it and the cargo holds.

A few minutes later they came out, apparently satisfied with what they'd found. Then one of them entered the cockpit of Mason's plane. He was a gigantic fellow, big enough to be a wrestler, with club-like forearms and a chest the size of a steamer trunk. This was the closest Mason had yet come to any member of al-Ansar, and he looked up at the man without blinking. The terrorist didn't seem to speak much English. He glanced around the cockpit, grunted, then exited to search the cabin.

By the time the giant had completed his inspection of the entire plane, catering trucks had pulled next to the two other aircraft, and it looked like they were loading hostages into the cabins. Simultaneously, cargo trucks backed up onto conveyor ramps leading to the cargo holds on either side of the two aircraft, and began loading in containers. These could be the containers from the Village, laden with millions of dollars' worth of gold—or they could be the ones brought out a few minutes before, which carried an equal weight of lead so the load factors of each plane would be identical.

No one besides the leader of al-Ansar knew all this, or the reasoning behind it, but Mason could guess. *It's one big shell game*, he thought as he watched the loading process. *Only one guy knows exactly where all the gold is.*

Holding a .45 automatic, Drabeznic entered the cockpit of the first government-supplied aircraft, followed by an escort with a submachine gun. To the man in the pilot's seat he said, "So you are a Delta captain, correct?"

The man nodded his head.

Drabeznic smiled. "Delta, yes—more like Delta *Force*. Do you really expect me to believe that after I ordered the U.S. government to prepare these aircraft for me, that they wouldn't put their own operatives on them? Even they aren't that stupid!" He placed his pistol against the head of the co-pilot. "Now tell me who you really are."

"Okay, okay," said the pilot. "We're volunteers."

"From? And don't tell me Red Cross."

With a defeated look, the pilot admitted that they were CIA.

"All of you?"

"Yes," said the pilot. "Yes, all of us."

"Christians In Action." Drabeznic chuckled. "Pleased to meet you. Now, then, surrender your weapons."

The pilot swallowed hard. "We're not armed."

Drabeznic cocked his pistol while the co-pilot did his best to appear unfazed. "Shall I search for your weapons before or after I blow this man's brains all over the cabin? There won't be time to clean up the mess, and I warn you, it's a long flight, so the smell will—"

The co-pilot himself spoke up. "They're back there." With a thrust of his chin indicating the pilot, he added, "He'll show you."

Within two minutes, Drabeznic had rounded up three different pistols from various caches and given them to the other terrorist to carry. "Is this all?" he asked the pilot. "Keep in mind that if we find out otherwise later, you'll be the one who pays the price."

"That's all," said the pilot wearily.

"Good." Drabeznic nodded his head slowly, finally uncocked the .45, and shoved it into his belt. He pointed toward the guns. "Those wouldn't have done you much good anyway, as you yourself should know. Firing a pistol in a pressurized cabin would be . . . extremely unwise."

He motioned the pilot back to the cockpit, where he gave all three their instructions: "I've decided to keep you on, in spite of your dubious credentials, but let's make sure we understand each other. All three planes will take off together, and at that time, we will provide you with further instructions regarding your destination. There will be someone with you here in the cockpit at all times to ensure that you do as you are told, and if we detect any resistance, we will deal with it severely. Is that perfectly clear?"

The three men nodded their heads.

With the pilots in the second aircraft, he cut to the chase, informing them that he knew they were CIA and had weapons stowed on board. He went through the same drill with them as with their colleagues, and again netted three pistols: one behind the radio of the engineer's compartment, one stuck under the pilot's seat, and the third behind the towels in the toilet facility directly behind the cockpit.

The third and last aircraft remained for Drabeznic to inspect, and he expected this one to be "clean" since the government hadn't had a chance to tamper with it. He made his way toward it as Mason and his two crewmates waited anxiously.

"Alright, gentlemen," said the terrorist leader as he stepped into the cockpit. Three men looked up: a silver-haired pilot in the flight officer's seat, a somewhat younger flight engineer off to the right, and a man in the co-pilot's seat without a millimeter of hair on his head. Looking over his shoulder, Drabeznic said something in an Eastern European language to his armed guard just outside the cockpit door before shutting it. "I'm going to ignore the fact that you have on Delta uniforms," he continued, "because your colleagues in the other two planes have already revealed that you are all CIA. Now—"

"Sir," said Bass, "we were assigned to this flight before you commandeered it. They gave us the option of being replaced, but we agreed between the three of us that we should stay with our craft."

Drabeznic laughed. "Well, that's very noble of you, Mr.—let me look at your badge here." He unhooked it from Bass's jacket. "Ah yes, Mr. Charlie Bass, I see. And your Social Security number?"

Bass gave the correct number.

"How many years of service have you had with Delta?"

"Twenty-seven."

"Let's see if that's true." From his back pocket, Drabeznic retrieved a computer printout and scanned it. Mason took the opportunity to steal a glance at him. So here, after all this time, was Hakija Drabeznic in the flesh, looking shorter than he'd imagined.

"I have here a roster of all the Delta pilots," said Drabeznic, "so if you're lying, I will—ah, here we are, Charles A. Bass. Your birthplace, Mr. Bass?"

"Hartwell, Georgia."

"Correct—or you memorized this."

"Do you mind me asking where you got that roster?"

"It's not really any of your business, but let's just say that plenty of information can be obtained on the Internet if you know the proper codes and pay the proper people." *So that was how he knew where Flight 20 would be,* Mason thought.

Drabeznic went through the same drill with Watson, once again confirming his information on the roster. As Mason waited for his turn, he felt a lot like the way he had on the first morning of Army Basic

Training thirty years before when he'd shown up in formation without his headgear—only this was a hundred times worse.

"And the co-pilot here," Drabeznic was saying. "Is this Mister Clean?"

"No, sir," said Mason in a thick Southern drawl. "I'm Robert L. Brown, from Cairo, Georgia." He pronounced it as locals did, *KAY-row*.

"I see, Mr. Cairo." Drabeznic pronounced it like the name of the Egyptian capital. "Tell me how long you've been flying, and your Social Security Number."

With the barrel of the pistol now resting against his temple, Mason answered that he'd flown with Delta for twenty-three years, then gave the number he'd memorized. At that moment, he didn't think he could have given his real Social Security Number, because he'd so firmly embedded the Robert L. Brown identity in his consciousness.

"You've been a pilot almost as long as Captain Bass here," said Drabeznic as he flipped through the roster with one hand, keeping the pistol pointed at him with the other. "How come you're still only a co-pilot?"

"I fly captain on domestic," answered Mason, trying not to glance at the roster, "but I like these European flights because of the schedule, and my seniority only allows me the co-pilot seat."

Drabeznic looked up from the printout in his hand, straight into Mason's eyes. "That face—I've seen it somewhere before."

My God, Mason thought. *He's figured it out.*

Drabeznic let the printout drop to the floor as he cocked his pistol. "Why don't you go ahead and admit that you're CIA and disclose the location of your weapons before I—"

"Look here," said Bass. "I already told you who we are. We're a team, and if you don't like one of us, none of us is going."

"If you notice, Captain, I am the man making the rules here, and I understand that two of you can fly this plane."

"Maybe a newer model like a 757 or 767," Bass said calmly, "but this one needs a three-man crew."

"Hey," said Watson, and Drabeznic wheeled on him, pointing the pistol straight at his nose. "If you hurt any one of us, you might as well kill all three, because we're not flying your damn aircraft anywhere. If you want us to do our job, you're gonna have to leave us alone. Otherwise we'd be happy to get off right now and let you fly it your own damn self."

Drabeznic hesitated for a moment, then lowered the pistol. As he did, he looked Mason over again.

Before Drabeznic could say anything more, the cockpit door opened, and one of his guards was telling him that they'd begun boarding hostages onto the plane. The guard left the door standing wide open, and Mason moved imperceptibly in his seat to see past Drabeznic. The aisle stretching from the cockpit through first class and into tourist had filled up with the female athletes, their shoulders slumped and their faces haggard, making their way to seats guarded by terrorists. He wasn't sure, but he thought he saw Michelle, too.

"Alright, where was I?" said Drabeznic after he dismissed the other man. "Oh, yes—the familiar face." But the tension had passed now, and he chuckled derisively. "I've probably just got you confused with the bald-headed Mister Clean on the commercials. But I will be watching all three of you personally." He patted the pistol, which he'd shoved back into his belt. "Alright then, get busy making your flight preparations."

As Drabeznic stepped out into the cabin, Mason could see three more terrorists coming on board with six hostages. It looked like the bulk of the group, not to mention Drabeznic himself, would be on this plane. That meant that the gold would probably be—

"Hell, my butthole's tighter'n a lug nut on the Concorde," Watson said with a low chuckle.

"Try the Space Shuttle," Bass whispered.

"You guys handled yourselves like real pros," said Mason.

"Well," said Bass modestly, "we figured when we signed on, we signed on all the way. Now let's get this sucker airborne."

At 6:33 p.m., Drabeznic re-entered the cockpit and ordered Watson to hand him the radio microphone so that he could speak to the control tower. "Tower, this is Bosnian Air Force One."

The air traffic controller didn't miss a beat. "Bosnia-One, this is the tower."

Drabeznic designated the planes for communication purposes, assigning the numbers two and three to the other aircraft. Then he outlined their takeoff procedure. Bosnia-One and Bosnia-Two would take off simultaneously on parallel runways, immediately followed by Bosnia-Three, which would take off directly behind Bosnia-One.

Drabeznic had the tower repeat those instructions. Then he issued a stern warning against any use of chase planes by the authorities. "Be advised, and pass this on to your government," he said. "Since our radar only picks up objects to the front, we will periodically make 360° turns in flight for the purpose of ensuring that we are not being followed. Is that clear?"

"Roger, Bosnia-One."

Before leaving the cockpit, he gave the flight crew their orders. Once they were airborne, they would turn immediately on a heading of zero-four-seven degrees, climb to 30,000 feet, and maintain until he instructed otherwise.

"As always," said Drabeznic with a sigh, "I have to remind you that I'm no fool, and if you make any alteration in direction or altitude, I will know it." He glanced around at the three. "You all appear to be intelligent men, and I'm sure no such warnings are necessary; however, after my recent experiences in the Olympic Village, I've realized that some people do not understand that 'no' means 'no'. Carry on."

The Delta L-1011, designated at Bosnia-One, roared down the runway, bouncing clumsily on the tarmac. Even though they'd given him almost nothing to do, Mason performed each task with uncertainty, and at this point he couldn't rely on the other two to watch his every move because they had their hands full.

He grimaced. The runway was nearly two miles long, and yet they were chewing it up quickly. Glancing over at Bass, he saw a concerned look on the captain's face.

"Damn," the older man muttered. "Come on, come on, come on. You're using up almost the entire runway." Finally, he pulled back on the control yoke and the aircraft lumbered into the sky like a fat pigeon.

"Shit," said Watson. "What's in this damn plane?"

"You mean it wasn't something I did?" asked Mason with surprise.

Watson chuckled. "Buddy, you didn't *do* anything, 'cause we're not letting you."

"There aren't many passengers on board," Bass said, "so I thought we'd have no trouble getting this baby up, but hell!—whatever they put on here, it must be awfully damn heavy. This thing is moving like it's full of rocks."

"More like gold," Mason responded. "About forty-five tons' worth."

Bass glanced sideways in disbelief, then looked forward again as the airplane climbed at full throttle.

"What is that, fifty million dollars?" he asked finally.

"Try adding another zero."

"Five hundred million?" The captain let out a low whistle. "That's enough to tempt anyone."

"Yeah, if you wanted to join up with these guys."

"Nah, I don't think so. But that's a trip, ain't it? Five hundred million dollars!"

Watson had something else on his mind. "Ninety thousand pounds of cargo, you say?"

"About," said Mason. "Depends on what they put in the other plane, but my hunch is that most of it's here."

"Then our ramp weight card's all wrong . . . ." Watson didn't say anything for a few seconds as he added up figures. "If what you say's right," he concluded, "and if this bozo does what he says about making a few turns in flight and whatever other kind of acrobatics he might be up to, we could be more than a little tight on our fuel gettin' to Frankfurt."

"I wouldn't worry about Frankfurt," said Mason.

PART SEVEN

UP, UP, AND AWAY

34

Bosnia-One leveled off at 30,000 feet. A few minutes later, Drabeznic unlocked the cockpit door and entered with another man. Unlike the others Mason had seen, who had the swarthy complexions of Southeast Europeans or Middle Easterners, this one looked like an American. *Dewberry*, Mason thought. *So at last we meet.*

"A bit of a bumpy takeoff," said Drabeznic, "but regardless of that, we're in the air now, and at this point I don't think we'll need your flight engineer anymore."

Watson looked up at him sharply, and Drabeznic laughed. "Oh, no, no, I just want you to sit in the back while my friend here monitors the work of your colleagues. Come with me, Lieutenant, and enjoy the ride."

From the corner of his eye, Mason glanced at Bass. With Dewberry there, the captain couldn't whisper instructions to him, but Bass nodded his head slightly as though to say *I can manage it.*

"Now, as you may notice," Drabeznic was saying, "this gentleman is not of my homeland. Be assured that he will understand your every word, no matter how idiomatic, and because he also has flight experience, he'll know if you disobey my orders. As for your communications with the ground, there will be none until we make our approach some hours from now—unless I direct otherwise, of course." He glanced sideways at Watson. "Rest assured that your flight engineer will pay the price for any indiscretions on your part."

"Listen up," said Dewberry after Drabeznic and Watson had left. "You heard the man—we don't want any shit out of you. You got it?" Mason and Bass nodded. "Alright, just so you know, this same thing is happening right now on the other two planes, and once they're within two miles of us, I'm gonna be talking to them." He pointed to a hand-held radio strapped to his belt. "I want you to continue on at exactly the same altitude and course until we pass out of Uncle Sam's airspace, which should be in about . . . ." He looked at his watch. "About fifty-eight minutes."

Bass looked at Mason. Dewberry had calculated the figure exactly.

"Once we get about twenty miles out from D.C.," Dewberry continued, "the other two aircraft will fly parallel above and below us at an altitude differential of 200 feet."

"Two hundred feet?" said Bass. "You must be joking. That's nothing—if we get into turbulence, we'll smash against each other like three eggs."

"If we get into turbulence, I'll let you make some adjustments, but for now you do what I've told you."

By now they were on autopilot, and for the next hour Mason found it easy to pose as a co-pilot doing his job, which consisted largely of sitting in his seat and staring ahead. Dewberry made readings on the gauges and called out information to Bass; then Mason heard him speaking into his radio.

Holding altitude became more difficult as the two other planes maneuvered into position at the ninety-minute mark, and Bass kept busy. From time to time when he needed Mason to do something, he would point at the instrument panel and Mason would put his hand on it; then Bass would make subtle motions to indicate the direction he should move to the right or left or top or bottom, until he had his finger on the appropriate switch. This of course made the captain's job that much harder, but it prevented Dewberry, occupied on the radio, from noticing any awkward movements on the part of the "co-pilot".

Mason leaned forward to look out the front starboard window, and he saw an amazing sight: the white fuselage of another L-1011 a few hundred feet below and slightly to the front of their own, and many thousands of feet beneath it the dark waters of the Atlantic shallows as the ocean fell away from the North American continent. Dewberry ordered Bass to increase speed slightly while the bottom plane slowed a bit, and soon the aircraft were stacked one above the other, causing all three to shake with the turbulence.

By the time Bosnia-Three left the ground, it was 6:52 in Atlanta, and ten minutes later the "political prisoners" released by the United States followed. They flew in two planes, each with approximately 100 convicts and fifty armed federal agents. Many of the bombers and bank robbers, still in handcuffs and leg irons, had begun planning how they would resume their careers once they got off the plane at Ar Ruṭbah; but if the government had anything to do with it, they would all be back in prison by the weekend.

A Delta Force unit would be waiting for them at Flughafen Frankfurt-am-Main, the city's international airport, when they landed at 9:56 Friday morning. Failing a successful operation there, another Delta Force unit would board a C-5 chase plane at Rhein-Main Air Base and follow them to Iraq, where the Seventh Special Forces would be eagerly awaiting the prisoners' arrival.

In the meantime, the Air Force had placed on alert four Airborne Warning and Control squadrons at bases in the United States, Greenland, Germany, and Turkey. These contingents would shadow the L-1011s from seventy-five to 100 miles away on a parallel vector, each monitoring one-quarter of their flight from Atlanta to Frankfurt to Ar Ruṭbah.

The Boeing E-3 Sentry AWACS (Airborne Warning and Control System) aircraft possessed extremely sophisticated radar mounted on its fuselage, tracking devices so powerful they allowed the AWACS to stay as much as 150 miles behind the L-1011s, well out of their radar range. As the authorities had suspected, al-Ansar had deactivated the standard transponders on each L-1011 while they were still on the ground, but the additional government-installed transponders on board two of the planes would make tracking relatively easy.

The first AWACS, dispatched from Dobbins, cruised at 40,000 feet, somewhere over the Atlantic Ocean east of Norfolk. At 8:24 Atlanta time, one of its radar specialists began noticing something unusual on the screen, and she reported it to her commander.

The general bent down to see that the three green dots representing the aircraft had merged into a single blip. "What's going on?" he demanded.

"They must be very close together," she replied. "At this distance, we can't determine if they're actually on top of each other, but—"

"Is it possible one of them has left the formation?"

"No, sir," called a technician down the row. "I'm getting signals from both of our transponders, and I've positively identified them as coming from the same point."

"Any deviations from their course?" the general asked a major sitting beside the lieutenant.

"No, sir," said the major. "They're on a vector south of the conventional one, but they're holding that." As he showed the general on his screen, the normal Great Circle Route from the United States to Europe would put them over land masses until four hours into their flight, when they would have left North America near Gander, Newfoundland. But on the course they'd set, they wouldn't cross dry land until the coast of France.

"Very interesting," the general said. "I'm gonna get on the horn to the White House with this." He looked around at the computer screens in the windowless fuselage of the AWACS. Only the rumble of the aircraft served as a reminder that they were seven miles in the air. "Let me know if you see anything else suspicious—any of you."

Another ten minutes passed before the three terrorist-controlled aircraft had settled into a more or less comfortable flight pattern, in the process of which Dewberry had to order the upper plane to raise another 100 feet. Mason waited ten more minutes before turning around and saying, "Alright if I go take a leak?"

Dewberry looked him up and down for a second, then said irritably, "Lemme call someone up here."

He spoke into the intercom: "Could we have some help up front?" A few seconds later, a knock came on the cockpit door, and Dewberry opened it to let in the same coarse-looking giant who had inspected the cockpit in Atlanta, just before Drabeznic boarded the plane. Dewberry jerked his thumb in Mason's direction. "Tokai, he needs to take a leak." Tokai looked confused. "You know," Dewberry said with annoyance, "he's gotta piss—stick with him."

"Come." The man motioned Mason toward one of the two lavatories immediately behind the cockpit. Mason intentionally avoided the portside one where he'd hidden his Taser, instead taking the one to starboard, and he started to close the door when Tokai stopped him.

"Alright," said Mason, and unzipped. The floor shook with gentle turbulence under him. He looked down at the tiny airplane toilet, then back up at the man, who was watching him attentively through the half-open door. "Do you mind?"

Tokai looked away, and Mason relieved himself. *That's the most relaxing thirty seconds I've spent in a long time*, he thought to himself. He washed his hands and glanced at his guard. "Can I get some coffee?"

"Hm?" The man shook his head.

Mason made a motion of holding a cup with his left hand and stirring it with his right index finger, then drinking from the imaginary cup. "You know—coffee?"

"Oh." Tokai smiled. "Coffee!" Then he did exactly what Mason had hoped he'd do: instead of getting it for him, he motioned for Mason to walk to the food and beverage station between the cockpit and first class.

Mason's eyes took in everything. On the second row sat a guard with two captives; behind them on the fourth and last row of first class was Drabeznic, his head against the starboard wall and his eyes closed; and on the other side of the aisle was Michelle Hinton, who glanced up at Mason. Mason averted his eyes to look through the open curtain into tourist class, where he could see another two dozen hostages, including Watson, and ten or more captors.

As he poured his coffee, he glanced at Michelle, who stared back at him intently. Taking his time, Mason raised the cup to his lips, his nose telling him that it was freshly brewed. "Gotta have cream," he told the guard. He normally drank it black, but this would buy him a few more seconds at the food and beverage station.

Mason glanced at the sleeping Drabeznic, then back at his guard, then at Michelle again. He set down his cup, took off his glasses as though to rub his eyes, and then with a very subtle motion ran his index finger over the top of his lip to indicate a mustache. He winked at Michelle, and she smiled back. Mason knew she understood.

Tokai tapped him on the shoulder. "Back to cockpile."

"That's cock*pit*," Mason corrected, following him.

The hours went by like days for Mason. From time to time he glanced at his watch, still set on Atlanta time, almost 9:30 p.m. At approximately two and a half hours into their flight, they crossed a line parallel with the eastern tip of Maine, moving them into another time zone, where it was almost 10:30 p.m. Drabeznic's promise to the tower at Hartsfield that they would rotate the plane every once in awhile must have been a bluff, because they continued on a straight path.

Bass stared ahead, his face set, his mind obviously alert. Every once in awhile he would say something, but mostly he kept quiet, and Mason had little to do but look out into the pitch-black darkness.

He found the emptiness beyond the reflection of his shiny head in the front window slightly hypnotic, especially when combined with the semi-hallucinatory effects of limited sleep. Through his mind passed a parade of phantoms in those endless minutes and hours over the chilly north Atlantic, memories of the last three days . . . girls flying off the roof of Fitten Hall one by one, the two SEALs who'd climbed up the side of the dorm dying in a spray of bullets, the apparition of Boyd in a protective mask on a grainy telecast over CNN . . . . He felt once again the electric surge of adrenalin from Greg Robbins's initial call to him in his hotel room; then he tried to think of something peaceful: of Sandy and the kids, or of the long sleep he'd have if he made it through tonight and tomorrow alive . . . . Periodically his eyes would close, and his head would slip forward. Then he would catch himself, shrugging his shoulders and rubbing his eyes to stay awake, hoping Dewberry hadn't noticed.

One hundred eighty minutes into the flight, or approximately 10:00 p.m. Atlanta time, the three planes were about two hundred miles south of Halifax, Nova Scotia, on course for outlying Sable Island. Dewberry, who hadn't said anything for nearly an hour, suddenly spoke up. His voice startled both the pilot and the "co-pilot," who had once more drifted into a half-asleep, half-awake state.

Dewberry wasn't speaking to them, but to the other two planes on his handheld radio, and when Bass heard what he was saying, he glanced around in amazement. The moment Dewberry finished his transmission, the captain said, "Would you mind telling me what that's all about?"

"I was planning to," Dewberry replied. Yawning and stretching in his seat, he began giving coordinates and instructions. As Bass listened, his eyebrows raised higher and higher.

Mason tried to look surprised too, but he wasn't. He'd known something like this would happen; the only question had been when and where.

Michelle Hinton, her head against the portside window on the fourth row of first class, had drifted off to sleep. As the plane hit an air pocket, it jarred her awake, and for a moment she didn't know where she was; then she looked down at her handcuffs, the reminder that brought her back to the moment.

She leaned back against the headrest and stared at the lights and call buttons above her. Like her commander in the cockpit, she was trying to call up a good memory: that night with Steve Kirk. It had been the first time she could remember when she'd allowed emotions to get in the way of professionalism. She'd convinced herself that she'd felt compassion for him, that she'd only done it because he needed the emotional lift, but she knew that wasn't true. She had needed it as much as he did—*wanted* it as much. And now she wondered if she would ever see him again . . . .

Suddenly she became aware of someone standing over her seat, and she glanced up to see Drabeznic leering down.

"Ah, our heroine. How are you doing?"

Michelle sat up. "Fine."

"I apologize for interrupting your sleep. I thought we might chat for a few minutes."

"You're in charge," she said, but her tone was defiant.

As Drabeznic sat down beside her, he pressed the *Call Attendant* button.

"I didn't see any flight attendants on this plane," she mumbled.

"One of my men," said Drabeznic with a wave of his hand. "Perhaps not as attractive as some stewardesses—or present company, for that matter, but—would you care for a drink?" He gestured toward the food and beverage station from which she had seen a very familiar-looking pilot getting his coffee an hour or two before. "Delta very thoughtfully allocated all these fine provisions for their first-class passengers, and it would be a shame for it to go to waste. I've heard the Quail Ridge Chardonnay is good."

"Only if you'll have a drink with me," she said, with as inviting a tone as she could manage. She didn't want a glass of wine—or anything else, except maybe some peace and quiet—but she wanted to see what Drabeznic would say to that suggestion.

"Thank you, no," he replied. "I won't touch any until this mission is over."

The man from the back came up and stood beside them to find out what his leader wanted. Michelle said a cup of black coffee would be fine, and Drabeznic barked an order at his man.

"I thought alcohol was against your religion, mission or not?" she asked.

Drabeznic smiled and grunted, then sat in silence while Michelle received her coffee and began drinking it, a difficult task because of the handcuffs.

"I'm thinking of a comment you made back in the Village,"

Drabeznic said finally, "that I ruined your President's chances of being re-elected."

Michelle nodded her head. "Yeah, I'd say you've probably toppled the strongest government in the world."

"You flatter me, madam," said Drabeznic. "If so, that was certainly not my intent, but then, many an action has unintended consequences, does it not? Considering the attitude of military people such as yourself toward this Administration, I should be given a medal for this great act."

Michelle, shell-shocked from lack of sleep, chuckled. "The only thing they'll pin on you if they get a chance is a pair of these." She gestured toward her cuffed hands.

"Ah, well, it was a corrupt government anyway," Drabeznic declared with a shrug.

"Yeah, but we like to change our government by the ballot box, not with bombs, like some countries do."

Her comment seemed to set Drabeznic off. "In your arrogance and ignorance, you people castigate other nations for their revolutions or coups or what you call 'terrorism'," he said angrily, "but Americans have used a form of terror—assassination—to change their government more often than any nation in the world."

Michelle studied Drabeznic's face for a moment. Somehow his apparent passion for this subject had an unreal feeling to it, as though he'd rehearsed these words before. "So what's your point?"

"My point is that the world we live in today is a ruthless one, and there is no nation as ruthless as your own. You dare to become irate with the Chinese for what they did at Tienanmen Square, but what of your handling of the Branch Davidians in Waco? In both cases, governments quelled protests with superior firepower."

"Is that what this is all about, Drabeznic?" Michelle took a sip of her coffee, holding the cup in both hands. "Showing us how terrible we are?"

Drabeznic shook his head. "You know what this is about: it's about giving our people in Bosnia a chance, something America would never have done of its own accord because of its prejudice against the Muslim world."

Michelle nodded gravely, acting as though she'd seen the light. She had a feeling she was being set up, that Drabeznic was only spouting off all this nonsense so she would pass it on to someone else. Whatever the case, he might inadvertently reveal something of importance, so it would be a good idea to keep him talking, and the best way to do this would be by stroking the man's ego. "And you've certainly made an impressive showing," she said finally. "I mean, leaving the moral issue aside entirely, I can appreciate what you've done as a strictly military maneuver." She looked into his eyes. "And because it was so *daring*, so bold. Were you ever wrong about anything? If you were, I didn't notice it."

This psychology seemed to work on Drabeznic; either that or he felt chatty in the flush of victory. "Oh, we had a few deviations from our plan here and there, especially when that little Kraut escaped on Tuesday morning and alerted the authorities. We'd intended on inviting more guests into our hotel, and expanding the occupancy list to include some other countries, but she and her loud mouth forced us to take the people we had and lock ourselves inside Fitten." He sighed. "I didn't want to have to blow up your SWAT unit, but we had to create a delaying tactic, so in a sense the German girl could be blamed for those men's deaths."

"Then who do you blame for the other troops that got killed?" she asked, amazed at the man's glib avoidance of responsibility.

"Oh, you mean the ones that attacked us? Well, my dear, those men's deaths were a consequence of their own decisions, or decisions made for them. We'd planned to complete our mission without bloodshed, even though we knew that would be difficult. But your President decided to become violent, and I had to respond in kind even though—and I know you'll find this hard to believe—I hate violence!"

Michelle only half-listened. She wasn't sure, but it seemed as though their plane had entered a sharp turn toward the left. She set her paper coffee cup, now empty, on the armrest. It drifted toward the right until she stopped it, and when she set it back in place, it did it again.

She glanced up to see Drabeznic looking at her. "Turbulence," he said with a shrug.

35

At almost 10:30 Atlanta time, the technician at the radar screen of the AWACS called her commander over to her station. Instead of one flashing green dot as there had been for almost two hours, the dot had split like an amoeba, one part moving to the right and one to the left. At the same time, the major beside her reported that Bosnia-Three had shifted course on a north-by-northeast heading and dropped altitude sharply, moving toward the line of the Great Circle Route, while Bosnia-Two had begun moving south-by-southwest on a heading of two-zero-zero.

"South—?" the general demanded. "Where's the one without the transponder?"

The lieutenant at the radar screen shrugged. "Sir, it could be going either way."

The commanding officer grabbed his direct line to the White House and began reporting the latest development. "Request that you advise, sir," he told the President when he'd finished. "We can either follow the one to the north, or the one to the south."

"Shit," came the President's reply over the phone. "How long can you keep both of them on your screens?"

"Thirty minutes, maximum."

"So we've got one of our planes headed more or less in the right direction, and the other going toward God knows where . . . . What about the Delta flight?"

"We don't know, sir."

Clearly the President would have to make some kind of decision, but he stalled a little longer. "And you're saying you can only follow both blips for another half-hour?"

"Yes, sir," answered the general.

"Alright. Hold on."

After two minutes, a general from the Pentagon came on and informed the AWACS commander that an E-3 at Gander was already airborne, and would come east to pick up the northerly blip on the Great Circle Route. Meanwhile the first AWACS would veer southward toward Bosnia-Two.

There was just one problem: even if the Gander AWACS were on its way, the first AWACS would have lost contact with the northern plane before the Gander AWACS picked it up. Therefore the AWACS commander suggested deployment of reconnaissance aircraft to the south to track Bosnia-Two, while he followed Bosnia-Three until it came in range of the Gander AWACS.

"Yours *is* the southward aircraft," said his superior at the Pentagon. "We weren't planning on any of the L-10s going south, and we couldn't deploy an AWACS in that direction within a reasonable amount of time." He paused. "I tell you what, we'll direct the Gander AWACS onto an interception course with the northern craft."

Half an hour passed before the commander of the first AWACS sent another message to the Pentagon that he had the southbound Bosnia-Two on his screens, but he'd lost contact with Bosnia-Three, which had moved into the Great Circle Course of approximately zero-four-five at about 450 knots. Meanwhile the Gander AWACS predicted interception in twenty-one minutes. In between now and then, there would be no one to track Bosnia-Three.

"So," said Michelle finally after Drabeznic had not spoken for several minutes, "we're not going to Iraq, are we?"

Drabeznic shook his head. "No, but it will be warm where we're headed."

"I was plenty warm in Atlanta." She thought for a second. "I'm no expert, but if I had to guess, I'd say we're headed north."

"For now, yes."

"I didn't bring any winter clothes."

"I wouldn't worry about that."

"Where do you think you're going to hide?" asked Michelle. "I'll bet they've got a $25 million bounty on your head."

"Madam," said Drabeznic, his voice suddenly stern, "I remember reading in one of your newspapers how when someone would ask the Olympic marketing people about their sales of supplierships, they would say, 'Well, I could tell you, but then I'd have to shoot you.' Surely they meant this as a silly joke, but I'm saying it to you seriously.

Information is dangerous. I may answer your questions, but keep in mind that the more you know, the more danger you put yourself into."

"You started the conversation," she said coyly.

Drabeznic returned to his earlier friendly tone of voice. "True, and given the fact that I'm in the mood to talk, I will talk. But for your own good, do not press too far."

"Mr. Drabeznic," Michelle replied carefully, "my job is not just my job. It's something I'm willing to risk everything for, because I believe in what I'm doing." She gestured toward him, raising both hands. "You ought to understand that yourself. Here you are, risking your life, giving all and gaining nothing, to help the freedom fighters in your homeland." She waited for him to reply. "Isn't that true?"

In his eyes she saw a slight nervous twitch. She had seen this before in people confronted with a misdeed, just before they told a lie.

"Well, of course, madam," said Drabeznic, shifting in his seat. "Why else would I do this?"

The general aboard the first AWACS had another surprise at 11:30 Atlanta time, when his technicians tracked the southerly L-1011, Bosnia-Two, turning 180° and heading north again on a course of zero-two-zero degrees toward the line of the Great Circle Route. The aircraft had changed altitude to 30,000 feet and climbing, increasing speed as though attempting to catch up with Bosnia-Three, which was approaching the 40th parallel. Now the first AWACS turned around and began following Bosnia-Two northward.

The Gander AWACS had picked up Bosnia-Three at 35,000 feet from 200 miles out. Staying out of the L-1011's radar range, it began to follow it.

"Have you made a determination whether there's another aircraft with it?" asked the general at the Pentagon.

"No determination at this time," came the reply from the Gander AWACS. "We don't have an angle to do that from this distance."

At this point the authorities knew the exact locations and headings of the two planes equipped with government-installed transponders. As for Bosnia-One, the Delta jet, they simply could not be certain.

"I guess," said Michelle with a yawn, "that once this is all over, you'll be leading the Bosnian freedom fighters into battle?"

"I think not," said Drabeznic dryly. "No, after this, I will disappear from the face of the earth."

"As easily as that? You'll have your face plastered on the wall of every police precinct in the world."

"Yes, the face of Hakija Drabeznic, whoever he is. Do you really think you could recognize me a week from now? Do you think that what you see now is my true appearance"—he grinned—"as handsome as it is? But this hairstyle, this color of hair, this mustache . . . perhaps these eyes aren't really even brown—I could be wearing colored contacts, for all you know."

"Your voice—"

"Voices can change. As to where I'll live, well, who knows? The world is a big place, and it's easy to disappear. For that matter, Atlanta seemed quite nice. I might even live there—it's the last place they'd look for me."

"You might get your wish. Maybe they'll give you Al Capone's old room at the federal penitentiary there."

Drabeznic shook his head. "No, my dear. If they ever caught me, which they won't, they'd never bring me back alive."

"You just don't get it, do you?" Michelle was genuinely amazed at the man's arrogance. "You can go to the Andes, and they'll have a picture of you in the police precinct . . . China, and there'll be some Chinese agent looking for you . . . go to the Arctic and they'll be hunting you with sled dogs. And forget about plastic surgery. Once the price on your head comes out, they'll send your picture to every plastic surgeon's office in the world, and I doubt you'll offer the doctor the amount he or she could get for turning you in." Michelle laughed. "Of course, there might be some surgeon in India someplace that they might not reach, but are you sure you want to trust yourself under that guy's scalpel?"

It was Drabeznic's turn to yawn. "This is all speculation on your part. None of the authorities will ever . . . ." He paused. "But tell me about your boss Mason back in the Village. He's a dogged sort, isn't he?"

If only he knew, Michelle thought. "Yes," she said, keeping a straight face. "Yes, you ought to be concerned about him, Mr. Drabeznic. I'm sure he's back there in Atlanta trying to deal with his rage over the fact that you got past him, but he's an outstanding agent, and he'll figure out something eventually—a month down the road, a year, ten years, whenever you're comfortable and least expecting him to come along. I'm sure he'll be looking for you till the day he dies."

"I suppose he'll just have to die with his wish unfulfilled," said Drabeznic nonchalantly.

Michelle tried to keep the conversation going, just in case he might reveal any useful information. "Surely you know some of your men will get caught? Don't you think they'll talk?"

Drabeznic shrugged. "Oh, possibly. But all that they know of me is untrue, including my destination, so the police would have much to sift through."

Michelle lifted an eyebrow. "They're not going with you?"

"Of course not. We will all disperse, and where I go, I will go alone." He looked her up and down. "Or perhaps you might go with me—it would be a great lifestyle. But no, forget that. We wouldn't want to change *your* appearance. Anyway, before leaving, I will allow each man to take whatever gold coin he can carry. The smart ones will only take a light load, say fifteen or twenty kilos, which is two hundred or two hundred fifty thousand dollars, U.S. The greedy ones might not be so smart, and may weigh themselves down too much. But it doesn't matter to me if every one of them takes a million dollars. That's a drop in the bucket—the cost of doing business, as the capitalists say. And we have a pretty big bucket."

"You don't sound like you care if they get caught."

"Men foolish enough to get caught won't possess any information useful to the authorities. They'll only slow down the manhunt." He cast an amused eye on Michelle. "You're not taking notes?"

"You haven't offered me a pen and paper," she said, holding up her handcuffed wrists.

"No, nor am I likely to."

"Well, assuming you do get away, is there any statement you'd want to leave the world?"

Drabeznic seemed to think about this for a moment, then launched into an oration about Islam and jihad, about the poor defenseless people of Bosnia and the Great Satan in Washington who wanted to keep them that way, about the "right" to use the Olympics as a stage for sending a message to the world. It was the same stuff he'd preached to the press from his microphone in Fitten dorm, warmed over and more stale in the retelling.

"That's very moving," said Michelle with feigned seriousness. "But can I ask you one more thing?"

"Yes?"

"You talk about your devotion to the One True God, and as I

understand it, a devout Muslim is supposed to pray toward Mecca five times a day. But I've been with you since this morning, and I haven't seen any of you pray once."

"You think in a crisis like this, we would lower our heads and cover our eyes?" asked Drabeznic sharply, his eye again twitching. "No, we did enough praying before this mission, and we will resume our prayers when we have completed it." He looked at his watch, then stood up. "I need to get some rest." With a derisive smile he added, "And I promise you I'll say my prayers before I go to sleep."

As soon as Drabeznic returned to his seat, Michelle rested her head against the window and pretended to doze off. Half an hour later, she opened one eye slightly to see him hunched against the wall of the airplane, shoulders slowly rising and falling with his snores. She opened both eyes and glanced around. The terrorist and the girls with him in the seat up ahead were all asleep.

Slowly she lifted her two cuffed hands and searched carefully through the seat pocket in front of her until she found what she was looking for: the cardboard flight-safety instructions for the L-1011 aircraft. She flipped it open to see pictograms of people responding to various emergencies on the plane. Bearing down heavily with a fingernail, she carved a short note on a gray strip along the inside flap. When she'd finished, she carefully tore off the strip and worked it into her pocket, returned the card to the seat back, and attempted to fall asleep once again.

It was almost seven hours since the three terrorist-controlled planes had taken off from Atlanta. A third AWACS from Strategic Air Command in Thule, Greenland, reported that the two transponder-equipped L-1011s, one behind the other, had begun to slow their speed, and predicted landfall on the west coast of Ireland at 5:09 a.m. local time.

The general at the Pentagon asked if they had any reading on the third aircraft.

"Negative," came the reply. Presumably the authorities at Shannon Airport in Dublin would pick it up with ground radar once it entered Irish airspace.

As the L-1011s crossed the west coast of Ireland, the AWACS from Greenland picked up a transmission to Shannon tower: "Listen carefully and pass this on. At precisely 0748 GMT, this flight will land at

Flughafen Frankfurt-am-Main. All runways are to be kept clear at that time, and all three aircraft will land simultaneously. We will refuel for the rest of our journey. In the meantime, all our radios are being shut down, and there will be no further communications with the ground. Will you repeat that message, Shannon Airport?"

Shannon repeated the message, which would be heard by the White House, the Pentagon, and the tower in Frankfurt a few seconds later.

Meanwhile Dewberry's counterparts on Bosnia-Two and Bosnia-Three ordered the flight engineers returned to their stations. As soon as they had assembled the crews, they ordered that the planes begin to drop altitude to 5,000 feet and de-pressurize, after which Bosnia-Three would slow down and maintain a speed twenty minutes behind that of Bosnia-Two. They told the pilots to remain in the cockpit, and to make sure they did, they attached devices to the doors that would explode if anyone attempted to open them from the inside. As further insurance, they had installed an altimeter bomb next to a bulkhead and its strategic hydraulic lines, which would detonate if they dropped below 5,000 feet prior to the time when they should be making their approach to Frankfurt. They explained that the authorities on the ground would have no trouble disarming the devices on the cockpit door, as well as those on the hostages, two of whom sat in the cabins of each plane with their hands cuffed to the metal bases of their seats.

Then the terrorists smashed up the planes' radios and returned to the cabin, where they had stowed parachutes. Each man put on his chute, along with an extremely heavy rucksack that he strapped onto the front, and took the elevator to the galley.

As the planes dropped to 5,000 feet and de-pressurized, the aft cargo doors on both blew off. Through the gaping hole in the plane's side, the terrorists watched the swelling Irish Sea, then the patchwork farms of England, passing by underneath.

Somewhere over Normandy, the first two terrorists parachuted from Bosnia-Two, followed twenty minutes later by the other two. If the authorities had known where they jumped, it would have seemed like a randomly chosen spot. But downwind of it lay a small rented farmhouse. The men, all experienced in airborne operations, landed within a one-kilometer radius and soon converged on the place where, in an unattached garage, they would find a three-year-old Renault with four French passports in the glove compartment.

The runways in Frankfurt had been cleared, and the Delta Force unit on the ground waited for the three planes controlled by the terrorists. But instead of showing up simultaneously as Shannon Airport had been informed, Bosnia-Two landed alone at exactly 9:46 a.m. local time.

The tower had known not to expect communication from the aircraft as it came in, but after it had touched down and taxied to a stop, the pilots still remained in the cockpit. Finally two soldiers approached the nose of the plane, and through a mixture of shouting and sign language discovered that the aircraft had bombs on board.

Eventually the Germans sent a squad to disable the explosives, first on the two girls, then on the cockpit door. By the time this began, the second plane had landed, and the process was repeated.

Not long afterward, the 200 released "political prisoners," whose two aircraft had followed the Great Circle Route all the way from Atlanta and never come within a hundred miles of the Bosnian planes, landed. They pulled off to the side and waited for word from the tower to begin refueling for the second leg of their journey.

The authorities boarded the two Bosnian planes, and within thirty minutes they had turned the hostages over to waiting medics and begun debriefing the CIA pilots. The Delta Force commander, geared for a shootout, didn't know what to make of it when his men searched the plane and found neither terrorists nor gold. He sent word to the other contingent at Rhein-Main Air Base, already aboard a C-5 waiting to take off for Ar Ruṭbah, and told them to stand fast until they received orders to proceed.

Four hostages had been recovered, but what about the other thirty-one? The CIA flight engineers of both aircraft reported that there had been only two terrorists on each flight, the one in the cockpit and the one guarding them and the girls. What about the other twelve? Where was Drabeznic and Bosnia-One? And what about the $500 million in gold?

"At this point we owe Jason Blanchot a call," said the Vice President, "and I think you should be the one to make it, Mr. President."

It was a little after 5:00 a.m. in Washington, but no one had been sleeping when the message went out to assemble in the Cabinet Room. The President, red-eyed and looking a good ten years older than he had a few days before, wore a crazed expression. "Damn it, I need time to think!" he yelled. "Blanchot can wait. We've gotta develop a plan of some kind."

This time no one offered any suggestions, and in frustration the Commander-in-Chief suddenly wheeled on Gen. Helms and the acting Secretary of Defense. "I can't believe you people! First you fail to get the hostages out, now you lose a damn plane!"

Helms could have protested that he had nothing to do with the AWACS, but he kept silent. The acting Secretary, who would gladly have taken credit for any triumph by his subordinates, knew that their failure rested on him. "Sir," he said softly, "we did everything we could. The AWACS is among the most sophisticated—"

"I'm tired of hearing you say you did everything you could have done!" roared the President. "Then where's that friggin' Delta flight, huh? How exactly did they manage to make a couple hundred thousand pounds of steel disappear in thin air?"

"It wasn't magic," answered the acting Secretary patiently, "but something like it. By a little clever maneuvering, the northern plane managed to be outside the range of any of our AWACS for twenty minutes or so, and then . . . who knows? Maybe the jet with the gold was riding under it, and got away then. Whatever it was, it was damn clever, I'll have to say that."

"I'm glad you're so impressed," replied the President coldly. "Meanwhile we've just seen a guy who beats D.B. Cooper all to hell. Remember him? Supposedly jumped out of a plane with $200,000 about twenty-five years ago, and hasn't been heard from since. Cooper started the whole ball of wax rolling, with copycats everywhere, and now—*now!* This son of a bitch has outdone Cooper by a long shot. Can you imagine how many copycats there'll be now? Our borders aren't ever gonna be safe again."

Gen. Helms cleared his throat. "Sir, keep in mind the old saying, 'It ain't over till it's over.' We have every reason to believe that Mason is on the jet that got away, and is preparing to enact his plan—whatever exactly that is."

"Yeah," snorted the President. "A plan to make off with the money." He glanced at the Vice President, who had sat quietly through this interchange. "Like I said, Blanchot can wait. Right now, we've got to put all our energy into figuring out how we can get back thirty-one hostages and half a billion dollars in gold."

36

When the acting U.S. Secretary of Defense described his possible scenario of how Bosnia-One had gotten away, it had sounded implausible to his listeners in the Cabinet Room. But it was closer to the mark than anyone could have guessed.

As the two L-1011s with transponders had split, Bosnia-Two going south and Bosnia-Three going north, Bosnia-One (the former Delta Flight 20) had ridden below Bosnia-Three. The two planes flew at an extremely low altitude—just 1,000 feet over the ocean, where the clutter created by signals bouncing off the surface of the water made them much harder to track on radar. They had continued northward, out of range from the first AWACS, and in the twenty-one minutes before they entered the screen of the intercepting AWACS from Gander, Bosnia-One had split off onto a southerly vector while Bosnia-Three kept heading north toward the Great Circle Route. Flying low on its way south, it had stayed well off the course and the radar screens of the first AWACS following Bosnia-Two.

Just after they made their last mysterious turn, Dewberry had given Bass a set of coordinates to plug into their inertial navigation system, or INS, which put them east of the Bahamas. They passed over Great Inagua Island and flew down the Windward Passage between Cuba and Haiti, skirted around Jamaica from the north, and headed due west toward the marshy jungles northeast of Orange Walk, Belize.

At 4:28 a.m. Atlanta time, Watson—looking like he hadn't gotten any more sleep than his crewmates—was returned to the flight engineer's seat. He looked at his gauges, then at Dewberry. "What the hell?" His voice was thick from hours of silence on the long plane ride. "The fuel's down to—"

Dewberry held up a hand to silence him. "I reckon we burned up a little bit at that low altitude." Turning to Bass, he ordered, "Cap'n, you just get this thing landed, and when you do, you better damn sure make it so we can take off again. If you don't, you ain't never gonna see the outside of this cockpit."

He had just admitted what Mason had expected, that the flight wouldn't terminate in Belize.

"Alright, I'm gonna go buckle myself in," said Dewberry as he prepared to exit the cockpit door, "but once we've landed, don't any of you try to come out till we come for you."

As the door shut, Mason called over his shoulder, "How you doin', Rick?"

"Glad to have something to do after sitting all that time, but hell! Those boys sure did pull a fast one, didn't they?"

Bass told Mason to turn on the *Fasten Seat Belts* sign, then he made an announcement over the speaker system that they were in for a tight landing.

To the left of the aircraft lay the Caribbean Sea; to the right Mason saw the dark coastline of the Yucatán Peninsula. There, the coastal lowlands along Cozumel gave way to a thick swath of marshes that ran all the way from the tip of Mexico, through northern Belize, and into Guatemala. Just northwest of the Mexican island called Banco Chinchorro, Bass began turning landward, crossing a six-mile strip of Mexican property just above Ambergris Cay, Belize, and dropping altitude above the marshlands.

Below them they saw a narrow strip of concrete lined with acetylene torches running down the middle of the jungle. The field looked to be a mile long or more, plenty adequate for landing smaller aircraft but dangerously short for the overloaded L-1011.

Bass brought the plane in at the slowest speed possible without stalling, the flaps fully extended while the trees beneath them shook as though in a hurricane. At the moment the nose crossed the tree line and came over the landing strip, he yelled to Mason to drop the wheels, then he touched down hard, the aircraft bouncing and shaking like a car that has dropped to first gear at seventy miles an hour.

Immediately, Bass began standing on the brakes with all his strength, but the aircraft careened at a breakneck speed past the abandoned control tower and fueling station, the end of the runway coming up fast. He reversed the thrusters, and the jet shuddered as though it would explode. With the wheels burning rubber fast on the concrete and the end of the line zooming toward them, Bass pounded the brakes harder and harder. Everything in the plane that wasn't belted in or attached had fallen to the floor, and still the plane rumbled forward faster than a car on the interstate. Finally, Bass brought it to a hard stop with only 200 feet of runway between them and the trees ahead in the darkness.

As the aircraft lurched one last time and settled into place, Mason wiped the thick sweat off of his forehead and looked over at Bass, who smiled back a little weakly.

After the cockpit crew had shut off the engines, Dewberry returned and handcuffed them together before allowing them to stand up and stretch. As the three men stood in the doorway of the cockpit, one of the terrorists opened the left passenger door out into the thick night air. A truck with a makeshift wooden stairway backed up to the door.

The airstrip where they'd landed looked abandoned, except for two Piper-414 Twin aircraft, a towing vehicle, and a fuel truck parked on the edge. The surface of the runway was cracked, and would have had weeds growing through it if the concrete hadn't been poured many feet deep to accommodate the weight of planes taking off and landing. A chain-link fence around the little base had long since succumbed to the dense plant life around it, caving in under the weight of thick vines, and the two buildings to the side looked like something off the set of a B-movie. It was hard to imagine that this place had once been abuzz with activity, but it had been.

Officially deactivated, the former air base remained in the control of Belizean generals who supplemented their incomes by renting it out to the Cali Cartel for stops on the way to Miami. Though the DEA and U.S. military intelligence knew about it, they did nothing to render it unusable because Washington wanted to maintain good relations with the Belizean government. Certainly the U.S. officials, having completely lost track of Delta Flight 20, could never guess to what use the field was being put today. Nor did the Belizean generals, who thought they were renting it to smugglers at the fringes of the cartel; they had asked only about the price, and since the figure offered was much more than sufficient, they didn't require any further information.

Even in its best days, this hadn't been an impressive piece of real estate: just a crude runway 7,500 feet long cut through the jungles and swamps, and connected to civilization by a rough dirt road. With such a short field, landing would have been hard even under better weight conditions, but Captain Bass wondered how he would ever manage to take off again with such a short strip—especially with forty-odd tons of gold on board. The flight manual suggested 8,000 feet as a *minimum* length with full fuel capacity.

Mason, standing with Bass and Watson to his right, the three of them cuffed together, watched the faces of the hostages as the terrorists now paraded them one at a time down the aisle to the makeshift stairway. Their expressions still showed signs of fear, but clearly relief had sprung up within them too—maybe even hope.

He saw Michelle staring at him, to which he replied with an almost imperceptible nod of the head. The girls had been silent as they made their way past the flight crew, but as Michelle drew near, she spoke up. "Thank you for getting us down safely," she said, reaching for Bass's free right hand and shaking it with his two cuffed ones.

A terrorist stood glowering over her, but Michelle shook Watson's hand as well, an even more complicated maneuver because when the man's right hand came up, it brought Bass's left hand up with it. "And you too," she said. "I appreciate your help."

"No talking," the terrorist beside them ordered.

So Michelle said nothing when she shook the hand of the bald-headed co-pilot and slipped a piece of paper into his palm.

Mason felt it instantly and grabbed it with his thumb, keeping his other fingers extended.

"Move on," the guard said to Michelle, pushing her through the doorway to the outside.

The hostages assembled on the cracking concrete of the landing strip under a dim street lamp. They lined up as directed by the terrorists, in six rows of five girls apiece, with Michelle off to the side. Drabeznic had detailed only two of the terrorists to guard the hostages, while the vast bulk of the group, including the advance party, started preparing the L-1011 for another leg of its flight. Observing this, it was easy for Mason to guess that there had been a shift in priorities upon landing.

Drabeznic came out to the top of the stairs and addressed the group standing below him. "My friends," he began, "I regret to tell you that we have come to the end of our journey together."

As he spoke, a truck engine behind the small wooden landing tower started up, and a motor tanker pulled out from behind it in the direction of the plane. Meanwhile, members of the team that had come in on the L-1011 had opened up the cargo-bay doors, and a few of them jumped in and began moving boxes around.

"In a few minutes," he said, "we will remove the explosive devices and handcuffs from you, and you will be free to walk about. However,

I strongly advise you not to wander into the jungles on your own: you'll find nothing there but snakes and jaguars. On the other hand, if you remain on this strip—and we will reignite the acetylene torches upon our departure to ensure that you are more noticeable here, as well as to keep animal predators away—you will soon be discovered by the authorities. It is now 5:21 a.m. local time, meaning that the sun will rise in about an hour to an hour and a half. I have every reason to believe that before sundown, all of you will be on your way back to the United States, and from there to your homes.

"As for you members of the crew," he said over his shoulder, "we will be journeying together just a bit further. You, too, will get to see your families soon, though not quite as soon as these young ladies. In the meantime, I suggest that you comply with all our orders. That is all."

Half an hour later, the flight crew had been released from their handcuffs and returned to the cockpit. Outside, under the dim illumination of the street lamp, Mason could see the girls huddling together around Michelle, and he smiled to himself at how she'd instantly become their leader. By now the fuel truck had pulled away, and the terrorists had completed whatever it was they were doing with the cargo. It wasn't hard to guess what: up ahead he saw several of them struggling to heave sagging canvas bags into the much smaller cargo holds of the two Piper-414s.

The sight of Michelle speaking to the girls like a mother to a group of children reminded Mason of the note, which he hadn't had a chance to read because he'd had someone watching him from the moment he received it. But now, back in the cockpit with only Bass and Watson beside him, he was just getting ready to pull it out of his right jacket pocket when Dewberry burst in the door and said, "Alright, Cap'n, start your engines."

"Where to?" asked Mason, wheeling around in his seat with his right hand on his jacket pocket.

"Don't you worry about that." Dewberry glanced at Watson in the flight engineer's seat. "Don't get too comfortable—once we get airborne, I'm gonna take your place like before. In the meantime, y'all bring her up to 5,000 and head due west until we tell you otherwise. Now let's get going." As Dewberry stepped back out into first class,

Mason glanced past him and saw Drabeznic sitting with Tokai. Beyond them, tourist class appeared to be empty.

He suspected that Drabeznic might be keeping a few other terrorists hidden on board, but it definitely looked as though the bulk of them— even allowing for the handful of men who'd arrived here separately as the advance party—were in the two Pipers. Mason thought, *I hope those assholes have overloaded themselves with so much gold they can't even get off the ground.* But as he watched, the two planes took off and headed in a southerly direction, their lights soon gone from the dark jungle sky.

Watson checked the ramp weight card for the L-1011, which Dewberry had filled out a few minutes earlier. If the information on it was truthful, they had six hours of fuel, which when combined with the 85,000 pounds of gold cargo, put them at about 450,000 pounds—a lot of weight to heave off such a short runway.

Bass slammed his foot onto the brakes and began to rev the engines to three-quarters of maximum thrust. The plane lurched forward, trying to break loose from the tight grasp that held it. The captain applied more power until the brakes could no longer keep the aircraft in place, then he released his foot, slammed the throttle all the way forward, and bellowed, "Let's do it!"

The L-1011 lumbered down the runway, its three Rolls-Royce engines screeching as Bass attempted to utilize every ounce of energy in them. Trees whirred past, their fronds once more dancing wildly as the plane gained ground speed. As it had when they landed, the end of the runway loomed up fast, and at the last second Bass slammed back hard on the controls and yelled to Mason to pull up the gear. The wheels, which usually weren't returned to the fuselage until it reached an altitude of several hundred feet, were immediately closed up into their cavity to make a smoother surface and provide more lift.

"We're up!" Bass shouted, still pulling back as hard as he could. They had barely cleared the palm trees at the far end of the runway. In a few seconds, they were at 500 feet. "Let's head for 5,000 and put this on a course of two-seven-zero degrees, just like the asshole ordered."

"Where do you suppose we're going?" Watson yelled to Mason.

"Beats me, but my guess is that it would *not* be due west."

"The old reverse psychology?"

"Yeah, so the folks on the ground will point and say, 'They went that-a-way.' You wait—in five more minutes, we'll be changing courses again."

As the aircraft stabilized, Mason quickly fished from his pocket the note his second-in-command had handed him. Holding it in his lap, ready to shove it under his thigh if the cockpit door opened, he looked and at first saw nothing but a torn gray strip of paper. Puzzled, he ran his hand across it, and felt a slight impression. He looked down and, holding it at an angle to the light from the instrument panel, could barely make out the rude characters scratched there. Hurriedly he grabbed a pencil from a pouch on the side of his seat and rubbed it across the paper to reveal a four-word message: *ITS ONLY THE $.*

Mason guessed everything correctly except the amount of time it took for Drabeznic and Dewberry to return to the cockpit and order another change of direction: they waited eight minutes, not five. After sending Watson out, Drabeznic smashed the radio with the butt of his pistol. "Now there won't be any turning back," he said, dusting off his hands. "We'll maintain altitude, but change direction to due north and hold that for exactly five minutes; from there, Mr. Dewberry will direct you."

It was still pitch-black below them, but far to the east they could see the first patches of the sun's light turning the sky a reddish-purple as they swung around ninety degrees in the direction of Mexico's lush coastal lowlands. From a mile up, they could make out a few lights from Corozal to the east, and beyond it Chetumal on the Mexican side of the border, next to a small bay. After the five-minute mark had passed, Dewberry ordered them to drop to 3,000 feet on a heading of zero-nine-zero degrees, meaning that they would now turn—as Mason had guessed—in exactly the opposite direction from the one in which they'd taken off. Only now they were a good twenty-four miles northwest of where they'd started, well out of sight from the released hostages on the deserted airfield.

As always, Dewberry knew what he was doing, and he carefully watched the on-board Global Positioning System, or GPS. The Department of Defense operated twenty-four satellites in precisely controlled orbits two miles above the earth, which provided navigational data via the GPS to civilian aircraft. It took only three satellites in a triangular pattern to give the GPS operator his exact location within an error of only a few feet, information which the system relayed to him in seconds.

"Cap'n," he said after a few more minutes, "bring the aircraft up point-six-three degrees and continue on this course, maintaining altitude." By now they had crossed the coast and headed out over the Caribbean, with no land in front of them but Jamaica, 520 nautical miles away.

As Mason stared ahead toward the rising sun, the aircraft now racing toward it at 300 nautical miles per hour, he tried to figure out where they were really going. Montego Bay didn't seem a likely spot for terrorists to land a plane, and even if they did, what would prevent the authorities from seizing the aircraft? Drabeznic no longer had any hostages other than the pilots, and they were volunteers; without any bargaining chips, he'd end up in a firefight he couldn't win.

Maybe a true warrior for Islam, as he claimed to be, would have gone down willingly in a blaze of glory. But Mason had suspected Drabeznic's claims from the beginning, when he observed the calm and methodical way the leader of al-Ansar took over Fitten dorm and orchestrated the crisis up to the very end. When Gen. Helms informed him Thursday morning of the demands, including the gold, Mason's suspicions had only deepened; now Michelle's note confirmed everything he'd thought. It was all about money—and only money.

In the next forty-five minutes as they flew over the by now brightly lit Caribbean Sea, Mason forced his exhausted mind to process all the data he knew or at least suspected to be true. Drabeznic had planned everything carefully, never doing anything by accident, and he probably didn't care about any cause except his own enrichment. Therefore he would do everything he could to keep himself and the gold as close together as possible, and that required eliminating everyone who knew where he'd gone with it. *Everyone*, Mason thought. *That means Bass and Watson and me. And that means—*

He turned around in his seat and looked straight at Dewberry, who at that moment had his gaze fixed on Captain Bass. "In exactly five minutes," Dewberry was saying, "at a point approximately 18° 30' north and 82° 50' west, you will turn on a heading of one-three-five degrees." His eyes shifted toward Mason. "What the hell you lookin' at?"

"Just wanted to get one last look at the guy who pulled this whole thing off," said Mason with an admiring smile.

"Turn your ass around in that seat," Dewberry ordered.

"No, I'm serious." Mason kept up the smile, which he realized must have looked pretty foolish. "You were the guy I heard about on the news, weren't you? The one who posed as a Tech employee and set up the whole thing for those jokers in the back?" He was taking a chance, because he didn't know for sure how many of these facts had actually gotten out to the general public. But he had little to lose now, and on Dewberry's face he saw a faint smile of pleasure at this compliment to his performance.

And Mason was making a performance of his own: as he spoke, he fully became Robert L. Brown of Cairo, Georgia, a country boy who'd never had any experience with the terrorist underworld except through movies and TV. "I'll bet your boss back there is gonna pay you pretty good when this thing is over with. Lord knows he can give you top dollar, and still have plenty to keep for himself. What y'all got in them containers? Gold? I know something sure as hell is weighing this plane down."

"Let's just say that I've got a good compensation package," said Dewberry. "Now turn around."

Fifteen minutes later, at about 8:25 Atlanta time, they were on their way southeastward, with only two tiny dots directly between them and the South American continent some 700 nautical miles away. The two dots were called Bajo Nuevo, a tiny Colombian possession at the far northern periphery of half a dozen islands, reefs, and banks (perhaps twenty square miles of land) to which the Colombians had assigned the magnificent title "San Andrés and Providencia Intendancy." The Nicaraguans had another name for them—*Nicaragua*—and both nations claimed the area, all except for a minuscule island about forty miles southwest of Bajo Nuevo called Isla Gracias à Dios after a cape on the Nicaraguan mainland. Presumably neither Managua nor Bogotá wanted to add the island's residents, among the poorest in the Caribbean, to their responsibilities; but Bajo Nuevo, on the other hand, was uninhabited.

Again, Mason turned around. "Hey, listen—"

"I told you to face forward."

"Nah, come on, I'm a mystery buff. Just humor me. After a few hours, you guys'll be gone, and you'll never see us again, right?"

Bass kept his eyes forward, wondering what Mason was up to but knowing better than to get involved.

"What's your question?" asked Dewberry with a sigh.

"I was just wondering how you plan to collect all this money the man's gonna pay you."

Dewberry shook his head. "I don't know what you mean."

"Oh, come on!" said Mason with a friendly laugh. "Surely you're not just planning to land somewhere and walk off into the sunset with a couple tons of gold? It is gold, isn't it? Yep, I was right, I can see it on your face. So how're you gonna take the money and run?"

"You'll see," Dewberry replied with a mysterious tone that seemed to invite further questioning. Clearly he enjoyed having his ego stroked by this inquisitive "mystery buff."

"Let me guess. At some point we're gonna drop altitude, then someone in back will break open the cargo doors. I'll bet y'all did something back on the ground to make 'em easier to open, huh? Then they'll push those containers out with all that gold over some shallow spot—deep enough to hide it, but not so deep you can't go back and get it. Your boss back there probably's even got his own little handheld GPS, so he can plug in the numbers. Then later, you guys'll jump out, and after you've laid low for awhile, you'll come back with a scuba team and get the gold—am I right?"

"You're getting warm," said Dewberry. "I don't suppose it matters if you know, 'cause you can't do anything about it."

Mason appeared to think about this for a moment. "But there's one thing missing, far as I can see."

"The hell you say!" Dewberry snorted. "We've got this thing planned down to a gnat's ass. What am I doing talking to you about this anyway? I must be punch-drunk. Now turn your redneck ass around till I tell you otherwise."

37

Sure enough, Dewberry's curiosity overcame him a minute later. "Hey, Chrome-Dome," he said.

"Yes?" This time it was Mason's turn to smile mysteriously.

"Lemme see if I can straighten you out. What do you think is missing?"

"Oh, that's easy," Mason replied. *"You* are." He turned to face forward, but Dewberry reached up and grabbed his shoulder to make him look him in the eye.

"What the hell's that supposed to mean, *I'm* missing?"

"Hell," Mason answered lazily, "you think your boss—Drabeznic, that's his name, isn't it? You think old Drabeznic's gonna want any of us to know where he dumped the gold, or where he ended up his own self? Shit! Every friggin' law man in the world is gonna be looking for him and that gold too." He shrugged his shoulders. "I'd say everyone here except for him and his homeboys back there—and that means me and Charlie and Rick too—is pretty well doomed."

"Look, he promised he was gonna let you live—"

"I'm tellin' you," Mason shot back, "a man's promises ain't worth shit when this much is at stake. Look here, once them cargo doors come off, this plane won't be able to climb very high. And at this altitude, we're burnin' fuel worse than a '72 Cadillac, so there's no way the three of us can get this thing back to dry land once you fellas jump."

"Well, you're partially right," Dewberry admitted. "After we've ditched the gold somewhere, this aircraft will head on out over the Atlantic 700 miles or so, three miles deep in the water. There won't be a trace of it left."

Bass clenched his jaw at these words, but Mason stared at Dewberry without blinking. "And you?"

"It's all been arranged."

"Meaning you'll have someone to pick you up when you jump just before the plane goes down, right?" Mason nodded his head thoughtfully. "But what's to stop your buddies from jumping out when the gold goes? My guess is that it'll have to be fairly close to land so it won't be too deep for diving later on, and if they did jump, how would you know until it was too late? I mean, you're up here, they're back there. And if that's the case, then why let the plane fly on at all? Why wouldn't they just plant a bomb set to go off about thirty minutes or so after they jump? By the time you figure out you're on your own, they'll be long gone."

These were clearly the words of Thomas Mason, not Robert Brown, and he'd returned to his ordinary speaking voice in his excitement. But Dewberry wasn't listening: he had his eyes on a map of their route that Drabeznic had given him on the ground in Belize with a warning to keep it secret.

We're going to make the drop in the shallows around Bajo Nuevo, Dewberry could hear his boss saying, *then turn due east. We'll fly on to the 70th parallel, then jump, and a boat from Santo Domingo will be waiting for us. The aircraft,* Drabeznic had added with a sly smile, *will continue on with those three suckers on it, but at such a low altitude, it will never make it to the next piece of land*—Bird Island, a good 825 nautical miles away. It had seemed like a good plan to Dewberry, but even then he'd wondered why Drabeznic had ordered him to fly straight over the eastward island of Bajo Nuevo—why even pass over land, when the shallows ran a good twenty miles or more to the north? And when he'd asked Drabeznic to go ahead and issue him his parachute, Drabeznic had shaken his head. *No,* he'd said, *we'll keep it in the hold for you until you get ready to jump—do you want to tip off the flight crew to our plan?*

All of a sudden, the scenario described by the co-pilot was beginning to make sense, but Dewberry still resisted it. "Ah, this is bullshit," he said, shoving the map aside. "He needs me too much."

"Uh-uh." Mason shook his head. "He *needed* you, past tense. But now . . . ." He shrugged and smiled philosophically. "I'd like to say I'll see you in the next life, but I don't want to go where you're going."

"Watch it," said Dewberry. "I might be sending you there sooner than you think." Instinctively he reaching for the .45 stowed in his belt—but then he remembered he didn't have it anymore, because Drabeznic had borrowed it on the ground in Belize and never returned it.

Suddenly a squawk came over the hand-held radio. "How's it going up there, Dewberry?" asked Drabeznic's voice.

"Everything's fine," Dewberry replied. "We're set to hit the shallows at 0932 local time, and cross the northeast island at 0940."

"Excellent, excellent. In just a few hours, we'll be home free. Now, keep a close eye on those pilots, and don't leave the cockpit for any reason. It's very crucial that they not screw us up here at the last minute. Do you understand?"

"Got it."

After he clicked off his radio, Dewberry said nothing for a minute, then finally he looked at Mason, who was still gazing at him. "Let's just say you're right," he announced tentatively. "What the hell can I do?"

"I don't know, but you're gonna die just like us if you don't do something quick, whereas you're in a position to save your own life, plus Bass's and Watson's and mine."

Dewberry threw up his hands. "I can't turn sides now, man. If I go back to the States, they'll put me in prison for the rest of my life—maybe even death row."

"I'll bet if you helped us turn this around, there'd be some kind of plea bargain. I know you wouldn't get the death penalty."

Dewberry glanced at him suspiciously, for the first time noticing that the co-pilot didn't have the same drawl he'd maintained for most of the flight. "How do you *know* that?"

"It's not important how I know, but I do. Let's just say I'm in a position to make certain guarantees on behalf of the U.S. government."

"I knew you were planted!" Dewberry lied.

"Not quite," said Mason. "But we don't have time for explanations. Listen to me. If you help us unravel this whole thing, you're gonna get a lot lighter sentence than you would if the feds caught you. Hell, we might could guarantee you the witness protection program—you'd disappear from sight completely, new identity, new life."

Dewberry thought for a second. "Can you promise me that?"

"I can promise that," said Mason, not really knowing how to make his guarantee good once they got out of this jam. He pointed at Bass. "There's a witness right there, and I can tell you now, he's not got anything to do with the government."

"Well, shit," said Dewberry. "How the hell are we gonna get out of here? I'm not armed."

"I noticed." Mason got out of his seat, and glanced through the wide-angle viewer on the cockpit door. First class was empty—even Watson was gone—but the curtain had been drawn between it and tourist class. That meant that Drabeznic and his men had probably gone down to the cargo hold, and they might have Watson with them as security, so it wouldn't do to simply alter course or raise altitude. He had to get down below and stop Drabeznic himself.

"What're you doing?" Dewberry asked as Mason crouched down over the hatch into the forward avionics compartment and reached in.

"Hang on," Mason said as he struggled to feel for the device he'd stowed back at Hartsfield International in Atlanta. Withdrawing it, he said, "Looks like I'm the only one here who's got a weapon."

When Dewberry saw the Taser, he looked impressed, but said, "That won't do much against firearms."

"No," said Mason, "but it's all we've got. There doesn't seem to be anybody out there, so my guess is they're already down in the cargo hold."

"Hell, the door's locked from the outside," said Dewberry, who had de-energized the solenoid on the door that allowed pilots to lock it from the cockpit side. He touched the knob. "There, see what I mean?"

Mason turned the handle himself. "No, it isn't," he said, as the door opened against the little flip-up seat beside it. "See?"

And they both did see. Standing there filling the entire doorway stood the enormous figure of Tokai.

He must have been standing guard against the wall where they couldn't see him through the wide-angle viewer, and moved into position when he heard them turning the knob. In one hand he had a radio, in the other an M-11 submachine pistol pointed straight at them; for backup he had a .45—probably Dewberry's—stuck in his belt. He said some words into the radio, then Drabeznic's voice spoke back in English.

"Is there a problem, Dewberry?" Drabeznic demanded over the radio. "If so, Tokai will take care of it."

"I was just checking . . . ." said Dewberry, and Drabeznic said something to his man, who grabbed Dewberry before Mason could activate his Taser. With enormous strength, Tokai hurled his former comrade into the starboard lavatory, and the door swung shut behind him. After a few seconds of scuffling, Mason heard two quick bursts from the submachine pistol.

Then Tokai pushed the door back open, and the last thing he saw was the bald co-pilot pointing something at him. Instantly the two probes embedded themselves in his body. The voltage sent convulsions through his huge bulk, and his eyes rolled back in his head as he dropped his weapon and fell to the floor, writhing in pain and uncontrollable spasms but still conscious. Mason hit the charge again until the man's body jumped violently and he passed out.

"Damn, what'd you do?" asked Watson, who had raced into the first-class section after watching all this from behind the curtain. "Is he dead?" Suddenly a horrible stench filled the cabin. "He is dead, isn't he?"

Mason shook his head. "Nah, but he might need his diaper changed. I don't know how long he'll be out, so let's get him tied up."

Watson glanced around. "We don't have any rope . . . ." His eye fell on the compartment above one of the seats, and he popped it open to find three blankets in a neatly folded stack. He pulled one down. "Now, what can I use to shred these into strips?"

Mason, his hand still on the Taser, nodded toward a knife stuck in the left boot of the inert Tokai, and Watson pulled it out. As the flight engineer started cutting up the blankets, Mason called in through the cockpit door, "Everything okay in there, Charlie?"

"I'm alright," called the captain over his shoulder. "Where to now?"

"The mainland—Central America—if you can make it."

"Just barely. It's a good 300 miles, and we're burning fuel fast, but we've got a couple offshore islands in between here and there. None of them have anything remotely resembling an airstrip to land this—"

"Where's *there*?" Mason shouted back.

"The nearest airport is Puerto Cabezas, Nicaragua."

"Great—see if you can get them on the radio."

Bass turned around and pointed at the smashed instrument. "He took care of that 'way back there, remember?"

"Oh, yeah. Well . . . ."

"Alright," said Bass. "I'm gonna turn on a heading of two-five-two degrees and raise the altitude to just under 10,000 so we can conserve fuel. But I don't want to go any higher than that, because then we'll have to pressurize, and I don't think that's a good idea if there's gonna be fireworks on the aircraft."

Watson laid out the crude rope on the floor beside Tokai and knelt down over him, first pulling the .45 out of his belt and laying it aside, then struggling to roll the huge body onto the strips while keeping his hands well away from the seat of the prisoner's pants. Watson looked up at Mason, who was still holding the Taser, as he started wrapping the strips around the man's arms and chest. "You've got the easy job," Watson said, grimacing from the smell and the strain of lifting.

Just then Tokai's radio crackled with a voice—Drabeznic's. They had no idea what he was saying, but after fifteen seconds, he called again, and then once more. Mason and Watson exchanged glances.

Suddenly there was a loud, sharp jolt as though the plane had hit something in mid-flight, and a warning light flashed on the panel directly in front of the co-pilot's seat.

"What the hell was that?" Mason demanded.

"The mid cargo door's ajar," Bass called back.

"It's probably blown smack off at this speed," Watson observed as he tied the rope around Tokai's arms and moved to bind up his legs. "We're just lucky it didn't do any damage—that thing could smash against the starboard wing or hydraulic compartment, and we'd be in a world of hurt. Charlie, how's it look from up there?"

"I think we're okay."

"He would have had to be down in the cargo hold to take that door off," Watson said. "But how did he get down there?"

"Through the galley, maybe," Mason replied.

"But there's no way in there."

"I'm sure he made one if there isn't."

Drabeznic's voice returned to the radio, this time in English. "Captain!" he yelled. "I know you can hear me. Respond at once."

Bass looked around at Mason, who shook his head.

"Captain Bass!" Drabeznic yelled. "You would be well advised to answer. What have you done with Tokai?"

Again, Mason shook his head.

After a long pause, Drabeznic said, "If you do not respond in thirty seconds, I will be forced to detonate a bomb I have already put into place. By the time it goes off, my men and I will be long gone, but I'm afraid Delta did not include parachutes for its crew. Do you understand me, Captain? It does no good not to answer. I know you can hear."

Mason picked up the radio from beside Tokai as Watson fashioned a gag out of bundled-up cloth and tried to work the giant's mouth open.

"Drabeznic," he said in a calm voice, "I told you I'd get your ass."

The voice on the other end didn't answer for several seconds. "Who is this?" he asked finally.

"Sound familiar? We've been speaking for the last three days."

"Mason?"

"Like I said, one day you'll turn around and I'll be there, and even though you can't see me, you better just take my word for it. I'm here."

"How did you—?" Then he answered his own question: "Ah, yes, Mister Clean. I knew I recognized you! You just couldn't let it go, could you?"

"This is your wake-up call!" Mason shouted. "Now your ass is mine!"

The radio went silent.

"Hey Mason," said Watson. "I guess that's your real name, huh?" He gestured toward the bound and gagged body of Tokai. "What should we do with him?"

"Here." Mason gave Watson the Taser. "You watch him. If he starts moving around, give him another jolt."

"Why don't you just get rid of him?" Watson pointed at the weapons confiscated from the prisoner: the M-11, the .45, the knife.

"I'm not ready to play by their rules," Mason replied, picking up the .45 and handing it to Watson before taking the submachine pistol for himself. "Not just yet, anyway. Is there another way into the lower galley other than the elevators?"

"Not that I'm aware of, and I've been flying these planes ever since they came out. What do you plan on doing?"

Suddenly, Drabeznic was back on the radio. "Captain, this is your commander. Now listen closely to your instructions."

Mason answered for Bass. "We're not taking any more orders from you, Drabeznic. If you didn't notice, you left all your bargaining chips back on the airfield in Belize."

"I would think again, Mason. If by 'bargaining chips' you mean hostages, don't forget that I still have three: you and your two friends. Tell the pilot that if he tries to land this plane at any place and time other than what I want him to do, it will explode."

"With you on it?"

"Even if I am, it's better than prison. I have nothing to lose. Keep in mind, all it takes to blow this plane out of the air is a sufficient charge of explosives placed in the right position to take out all your hydraulics—like Lockerbie, remember?"

Mason said nothing.

"It wouldn't surprise me if you have a death wish," Drabeznic continued, "especially because you'll always be remembered as the man who let the freedom fighters of al-Ansar take over the Olympic Village. But what about your two friends? Are they so willing to die?"

Mason sighed, once again stymied by the man who had planned for every contingency. He walked over and handed the radio to Bass.

Drabeznic gave orders to turn around on a heading toward Bajo Nuevo, now twenty minutes behind them, and make no further deviations from the altitude of 9,400 feet he had established. In case the captain had thoughts of disobeying him, he warned that he had a Merlin GPS with parallel-channel receivers and a 3-D lock to give him their altitude as well as their exact position. Just as he was about to sign off, he ordered the captain to hand the radio to Mason.

"You know, Tom," he said, "I'm actually glad we're back together again for one last hurrah. Why don't you come down for a chat and we'll relive our experiences together?"

"Sounds great, Hakija," replied Mason. "Who's your welcoming party down there, El Homra?"

"Who says he's down here?"

Mason looked around. "He ain't up here. So that's his name, huh?"

Drabeznic laughed. "It hardly matters now. Tell me, how did you turn Dewberry against me?"

"By pointing out the facts. If you wanted to keep him on your side, you should have at least given him a parachute." By now Mason was standing beside the galley elevator near the center of the plane, inspecting it and trying to figure out how he could get down below without being killed.

"Yeah, yeah—what about Tokai?"

"He was shocked by my presence, so to speak. He might be dead."

Mason knew Tokai wasn't dead, and would need another shot of juice in a few minutes to keep him out. Maybe the bluff worked, because Drabeznic didn't say anything more.

Mason took control of the Tasers while Watson hurriedly drew him a schematic of the downstairs galley on the back of an air-sickness bag. Both lifts lowered into a small kitchen—an area easily covered by a single gunman. "So there's nothing other than the elevator?" Mason asked.

Watson shook his head.

"Okay." Mason thought for a second, then walked over to the lavatory door. He glanced at Watson, who'd probably never seen a freshly dead body up close, but Watson looked straight past him into the latrine, where Dewberry's blood-spattered carcass leaned against the wall. "Okay, he's gonna be hard to lift," Mason said as he took the dead man's radio and put it under his arm, "but I'm gonna take him with me into the elevator, and let him be my shield. Hey Charlie, as soon as I get on the lift, I want you to start shaking the plane from side to side, then take it into a short dive. Can you do that?"

"Sure," Bass called back warily. "But it has to be pretty damn short. Ninety-four hundred feet doesn't give us a lot of room to play with."

"Right. Take it down to maybe 2,000. If the asshole down there starts yelling at you on the radio, I want you to get aggressive with him—tell him it's something he caused by blowing the cargo door off. In the meantime, all that maneuvering should throw the goon standing guard in the kitchen off-balance, maybe enough to give me the edge I need."

"You're gonna have a helluva time getting out of that lift if Charlie goes into a dive," Watson observed. "Especially with 200 pounds of dead weight on your hands."

"It's the best I can do," said Mason, taking off his fake eyeglasses, along with his co-pilot's jacket and rolling up his sleeves. He made a face as he knelt down over the body of Dewberry and began lifting him from under the arms, the still-warm blood pressing against his shirt like sweat on a muggy summer day. "Damn, he's heavy!"

Watson let go of the Taser, shoving the .45 calibre into his belt and grabbing Dewberry's feet. "I'm going with you," he announced.

Mason shook his head as he strained to carry the weight down the first-class aisle. "I need you up here—besides, it's too dangerous down there. I don't know what I'm getting into, and I'm not gonna let—"

"Look, Mason," Watson insisted as they heaved the body toward the lift door. "Charlie can fly the plane all by himself, and the sooner we take care of those two assholes down below, the sooner we can get on back home." He nodded toward Tokai, bound and gagged and blissfully asleep in a pile of his own excrement. "He ain't goin' nowhere."

"Alright," said Mason, poking out his lower lip to blow on a ticklish trickle of sweat running down his temple. "Do you know how to use that .45?"

"Sure."

Fortunately, both elevators were at cabin level, so they didn't have to run the risk of alerting anyone below that the lift had been called back up to the cabin. Mason got into the one on the left side of the aircraft, and with Watson's help propped up Dewberry's body between himself and the door while Watson got into the other lift.

Bass began his buffeting maneuvers. The plane bounced wildly, and immediately Drabeznic's voice boomed over the radio. "What the hell's going on up there, Captain?"

"Why don't you tell me?" Bass yelled back. "You must have done something, 'cause I'm losing control."

"What are you talking about?"

"One of the control surfaces is out of commission. Did you screw up the tail section when you blew off the doors?"

"No. We allowed for that in our calculations."

"Looks like your calculations were off," said Bass as he continued jerking the plane back and forth.

Meanwhile Mason and Watson, on their slow descent into the bowels of the aircraft, felt the plane suddenly lurch forward as it began its 7,400-foot dive. Both men were thrust toward the ceilings of the two elevators.

As the aircraft leveled off, Mason flung his lift door open. Holding Dewberry's body in front of him, he looked around and saw a figure leaning against a wall to balance himself. Startled initially by the sight of Dewberry, the terrorist hesitated to shoot, but as he realized what was happening, he began to fire wildly.

Bullets ripped into the chest of Dewberry's body, and Mason dropped to the floor in the corner beside the lift door with the body in front of him. The shooter stood up to look at the body on the floor, giving Mason a view of his head. Mason unleashed the full force of the M-11 and watched the bullets rip through the terrorist's cheekbones and out the back of his head, spraying brains and blood all over the wall and the food carts beside him.

Mason cautiously pulled himself up and looked around. As he'd expected, Drabeznic was nowhere to be seen. He jumped up and removed the dead man's weapon, then to make sure he was really dead, felt of his carotid artery, all the time keeping his own weapon at the ready. Mason jumped when the other elevator door pushed open and Watson peeked out. Seeing Mason standing over the dead terrorist, Watson opened the door completely and stepped into the kitchen. His face was ashen.

"Is that Drabeznic?"

"No, but Drabeznic's around here somewhere. How do we get back to the cargo bay?"

"I'm telling you, there's no door back that way."

"Then what's that?" Mason said, pointing toward a hole in the wall directly in front of him, at the rear end of the galley. It looked as though someone had used some type of saw and cut through the aluminum bulkhead into the cargo area immediately behind it. Mason grinned at Watson and handed him El Homra's M-11. "You wait here and cover me. If you see anyone coming behind me"—he gestured toward the panel leading into the hydraulics compartment—"or if anyone comes through that opening up front besides me, shoot to kill."

Bass's voice came over the handheld radio. "Mason, are you okay down there?"

Shit, Mason thought. *I should have told him to maintain radio silence.* But it was too late.

"Nice trick," Drabeznic said over the radio. "You almost caught me off-guard. Captain, take us back to 9,400 feet and put this plane back on course if you ever want to see your family again. Once you get to Bajo Nuevo, I want you to circle the islands in a five-mile arc."

Realizing his mistake, Bass made no reply, but he did as he was told, and the two men in the galley could feel the plane regaining altitude.

Mason turned his radio down as low as he could and still hear it, then he cautiously walked over to the hydraulics compartment and raised the panel. With his machine pistol at the ready, he looked inside, but there was no one there. All the while he listened to Drabeznic giving course corrections to the captain, who'd used the buffeting maneuvers as an opportunity to change headings. He couldn't hear Drabeznic's voice except on the radio, so he knew he had to be somewhere further to the rear in the aircraft.

Finally he turned to Watson. "Cover me from here."

As the plane continued its slow ascent, it caused a slight downward incline toward the rear, and Mason held onto the wall as he walked along into the darkened area of the cargo hold. He could hear the wind blowing through the open hatch, and a little further on he could feel it across his face. A few feet further, and he saw a light coming through the gaping hole in the starboard side of the plane.

Ahead of him lay the fifteen cargo containers, lined up in one row of eight on the portside and another row of seven to starboard, with a small aisle between them. Suddenly, Mason had yet another idea, and he stepped back toward Watson. "Rick," he whispered, handing him his radio, "go back into the galley and start talking over this thing. Just say some kind of bullshit, it doesn't matter what. If Drabeznic has his radio on, I might be able to locate him."

Watson stepped back into the galley and began talking to Bass.

"Hey, Charlie, we've got this asshole in a squeeze play. In a minute, he's gonna be dog meat . . . ." And so on.

Meanwhile Mason crept cautiously into the cargo bay, the sound of the wind ripping through it getting louder and louder. The loose straps meant to hold the containers in place flapped in the heavy breeze.

Shit, I didn't count on all the noise down here, Mason thought. *I'll never hear the damn radio.*

But then he did. Further down on the left, twenty feet away, came Watson's voice saying, "Yeah, and they'll probably put him in the Atlanta federal pen. He'll be some prisoner's bitch."

Mason moved closer until he'd made it to the near side of the cargo container. Standing behind it, he judged the position of the radio and, holding his breath, jumped around the corner with his weapon at the ready.

There lay the radio on the floor, with Watson chattering rapidly about the prisoners who would likely gang-rape Drabeznic.

Oh, shit, Mason thought.

Then from the top of the container above him a voice said, "Checkmate."

38

Looking up, he saw Drabeznic pointing his M-11 straight at him. Mason dropped his own weapon. "Pick up the radio and call your friend," the man on top of the cargo container ordered. "Tell him you've got me, and to come on back."

"Call him yourself."

Drabeznic smiled. "Just thought I'd test you. Didn't think you would. Now, kick that weapon away from you and lie down with your hands behind your head."

Mason did as he was instructed. A second later, Drabeznic was standing over him, and he tossed Mason's weapon out the open bay door before firing a burst from his own submachine pistol up the corridor between the containers. "That will slow down your friend for awhile. Now get up."

As he did, Mason saw Drabeznic strapping on a parachute and locking it over his chest. "I'm afraid I'm going to have to be leaving you, Mr. Mason," he said before once again firing random shots down the corridor. Watson had just entered the cargo bay, and he jumped back behind the bulkhead.

"Come on," Drabeznic ordered Mason. He stuck the weapon into his prisoner's back, and together they walked toward the open cargo door.

A heavy canvas bag lay on the floor amongst several boxes that had been broken open. It was partially filled with coins, and now Drabeznic ordered Mason to finish loading it with as many as would fit.

Mason began working while Drabeznic peered back and forth between him and the corridor. Periodically, he fired bursts toward the front of the plane, just to keep the flight engineer in a cautious frame of mind. "Perhaps I should kill you before I go," he said. "After all, you're the man who loused up a perfectly good plan."

Mason ignored the threat, and as he worked he told Drabeznic what he'd figured out about that plan.

"Very good," said Drabeznic when he heard the scenario which

Mason had used to turn Dewberry against his leader. "You are quite the detective."

"I've also figured out that this doesn't have a thing to do with religion," Mason continued as he poured more coins into the bag. "All that stuff about Islam was just a ruse."

"Perhaps, perhaps. Keep working."

"So I don't guess you care about how this has affected the Bosnians? You've got your money, and they're left holding the bag as far as being blamed for this."

Drabeznic shrugged. "They should just be thankful for all the munitions I obtained for them—I'd say I'm a hero in their eyes."

"So are you really a Bosnian at all?"

"I'm a man without a country."

Mason was thinking of what the Russian diplomat had said to Drabeznic on Tuesday night, during one of his many attempts to coerce the Moscow government: *Your accent, it sounds familiar. Are you from the Caucasus?*

"Okay, if it's really important to you, I'm a Chechen," said Drabeznic, seeming to relent even though Mason hadn't said anything more. "There, are you satisfied? The Chechens, the 'niggers' as Russians call us, a nation of robbers and murderers. And I'm the worst of the lot. I had a pretty good living in the old days, when the central government contracted my services to various causes—"

"A mercenary, huh?"

"Call me what you will. I consider a mercenary a man who hires himself out to right-wing regimes, whereas I, because I worked exclusively for socialist nations, would be called an idealist."

"Yeah, you're pretty darn idealistic, I'd say."

"And much too smart for your CIA to catch up with, even though they've been looking for me under different names for years. But ever since the unfortunate demise of the socialist governments, I've been without a job and therefore have been forced to adopt the ways of capitalism myself. Hence this one last great coup, which I consider capitalism at its finest."

Mason looked up from his work. "Speaking of cynicism, don't you feel the slightest bit guilty about using the Olympics for your purposes? You know, the international festival of brotherhood and all that?"

"To hell with your brotherhood," said Drabeznic. "The Olympic Games were useful to me, no more, and for two reasons. Where else could I gain such a great world stage and bring pressure on the U.S.

government to meet our demands? Had we been only common criminals trying to abscond with a half a billion dollars, there would have been no hesitancy to take us out, but as Islamic fundamentalists in service to a higher cause, there had to be certain doubts." He laughed. "And as for my second reason, it is said that one of your great American bank robbers, when asked why he robbed banks, replied, 'That's where the money is.' So that's why I went after the International Olympic Committee—who else could turn over half a billion dollars to me?"

"Why stop at half?" Mason asked. "They've probably got much more."

"Perhaps someday I'll come back and get the rest," said Drabeznic philosophically, "but why be greedy? Half a billion, minus a little overhead, is enough for one man to live quite comfortably for a long time." Then his tone soured. "But thanks to you, I don't have half a billion. In that bag is probably only a little over a million. Still, it's more than I started with. Now finish packing up—I've got to get going."

As soon as Mason had finished, Drabeznic pointed to four life vests in the corner. He ordered him to tie the vests tightly to the bag, which by now weighed close to 200 pounds, then lie down with his hands clasped behind his head.

Lying on the floor face-down did not stop Mason from talking. "More than you started with?" he said. "Looks to me like you lost money—surely this whole operation cost more to fund than you've got in your little doggie bag there."

"You are partially correct," said Drabeznic as he attached a parachute to the bag. "The investment was $3.6 million, and I seriously doubt that I'm taking that much away. But I wasn't the one who invested, and I'm sure my backer is pleased with the return on his money. Look at the arms we have shipped to Bosnia, and the good men whose release we have secured—a lot of people are now in his debt without even knowing it. And I'm sure he took great pleasure in buggering you people for a few days."

Without moving, Mason turned his eyes toward Drabeznic, who was checking that the life preservers were properly tied on. "What investor?"

Drabeznic laughed. "I'll give you a hint: he hates your country even more than I do. Oh, I'm sorry, I don't suppose that narrows the field much. Uh, let's see . . . he's sitting on so much money that $3.6 million is what you Americans call chump change." As he talked, Drabeznic attached one end of a seventy-five-foot rope to the rip cord, the other end to his belt buckle. "Still don't know? Think south of the Mediterranean, north of the Sahara."

Drabeznic stopped to fire his M-11 up the corridor, and shots rattled off the wall. "I believe your friend is not much of a soldier, Mason. He should have been on top of us by now. Where do you suppose he is?"

"I don't know. Maybe he's right behind you."

"Never mind." Drabeznic took something from his shirt pocket and showed it to Mason. "Do you see this? It is an electronic transmitter with two buttons. The red button, which could cause an instant explosion of this aircraft, is covered up because it looks like I won't need to use it. The other button, however, gives the crew of this plane exactly seven minutes to live. So after I depart here at the appropriate time, which should be soon"—he looked down at his Merlin GPS—"I will push it. As I jump to safety, I'll think about you scrambling around, trying to find the bomb and disarm it. And even if you do, you'll discover that it's booby-trapped, so you might be better off just to jump out and hope for the best."

He looked out at the Caribbean shallows around Bajo Nuevo, almost 10,000 feet below him. "But please, Mason, don't try to play like in the Rambo movies and jump after me to grab my parachute in the middle of the air. I will have my weapon at the ready, and you would only be wasting your time."

"That's okay—I don't like heights anyway, Drabeznic."

"Hm. Perhaps I should have pushed you after all. But no matter. Okay, you bastard, help me push this out."

Mason stood on one side of the canvas bag, glancing sideways at Drabeznic and wishing he could take advantage of the moment to lunge at him. The two men edged the bag closer to the doorway. Mason could feel a rush of wind ripping across his face, and he wanted to reach out and grab Drabeznic so much he could almost taste it, but he knew the other man had all the advantage. The bag slid over the edge and began careening toward the blue-green water far below. As it did, Drabeznic pushed the green button on the transmitter.

"Good-bye, Mason," he said in that split-second. "Remember—seven minutes. And *Allah akbar!*" This last bit of cynical humor disappeared in the sound of the rushing wind as Drabeznic went flying out after the canvas bag.

Mason peered over the side and saw Drabeznic, already hundreds of feet away, facing toward him with the M-11. The man fired a burst in his direction, and the bullets whizzed harmlessly overhead, but they came close enough for Mason to jump back into the cargo bay.

No, he wasn't about to dive after him. He'd never even thought of doing that. Glancing at his watch, he calculated that ten seconds had passed since Drabeznic pushed the button. A second later, he looked back over the side and saw the parachute open on the bag of gold, soon followed by Drabeznic's chute.

Six minutes, forty-seven seconds to go . . . and counting. Hurriedly Mason picked up the radio Drabeznic had left, ordered Bass to turn the plane toward the nearest airport, and called to Watson. "Quick!" he yelled. "Come on up here now, and bring us a couple lights if you can find them—but hurry!"

Watson rushed into the cargo bay with two flashlights from the galley. "Where is he?" he asked.

"Gone," said Mason, pointing to the open door, "but he's left a bomb on board, and we've got a little over six minutes to find it and disarm it, or we're dog meat. Where's a good place to look?"

Watson pointed toward the hydraulic lines running forward along the top of the cargo compartment and the edge of the bulkhead. Quickly the men began working their way along them, searching with their flashlights for anything that looked unusual. Periodically, Mason glanced at his watch to keep track of the remaining time. With barely five minutes to go, Watson called out from the hydraulics compartment. "There's something here, Tom."

Mason ran through the galley to the compartment, where Watson stood pointing up to a small black box, strapped in to the bulkhead and tied in such a way that its blast would entirely sever all hydraulic lines. "That's it!" said Mason. "But keep looking."

He carefully inspected the explosive before touching it. The case opened, and gingerly he pried it apart to find a simple on-off switch and a red LED timer that said 0:48:03, counting down by the second. Something didn't seem right: this had to be the bomb Drabeznic had set previously, not the one engaged to go off in four minutes, forty seconds. Taking a deep breath, Mason reached up and flipped the switch off.

"Alright!" yelled Watson behind him.

"That's not it," Mason said. "You didn't find anything else?"

"Nothing."

"Damn." Mason looked around. They were now well below the four-minute mark. "There's got to be another bomb on board . . . ." He stopped. There was only one place in the cargo hold where they hadn't looked—or rather, fifteen of them. Suddenly he reached down and pulled out the pin holding the container nearest the door in place. "Charlie!" he yelled into Watson's radio. "Tilt this thing ten degrees to starboard and lift your nose."

"Whatever you say."

As the plane began to lift, the cargo container started sliding back on its tracks toward the bay door, teetering close to the edge.

"What the hell—?" asked Watson. "Have you gone nuts?" As the words left his mouth, the cargo container with some $30 million in gold seesawed back and forth, as though giving Mason one more second to change his mind. Then gravity pulled it out, and it went careening toward the blue waters below.

"That's where the explosives are!" Mason shouted. "Watson, undo every one of these bastards!" He yelled into his radio for Bass to level off so that they could safely remove the pins holding the containers.

Watson started pulling out the pins as told, but he didn't look convinced. "It's gonna be mighty damn costly if you're wrong," he said.

"I'm not wrong!" Mason shouted back. "He knew that the gold was the last thing we'd give up, so he put it there! If we dump it, at least the Marines or someone can go back and get it, but if we try to open one of these, it's gonna blow us and the gold and the plane from here to Jamaica!"

Soon all the remaining containers on the right side were loosened. "Alright," Mason said into the radio. "Do what you did a minute ago."

Every container weighed close to three tons, and the best Mason and Watson could do was let the force of gravity do all the work. Slowly the giant boxes moved toward the door, slamming into each other. Then first one went, then the next and next, and the two men didn't even have time to watch as one by one the containers—each holding more money than either of them would earn in five lifetimes—went hurtling toward the sea below.

"Level it off again, Bass," Mason shouted into the radio. "The ones on the starboard are all out."

As the plane stabilized, they loosened the containers on the port side. By now, they had less than two minutes left.

On orders from Mason, the plane again began the upward and rightward pull, pushing the weight to the rear and slamming the containers against one another as one by one they poured out the hole and down toward the Caribbean. Mason watched the sweep hand of his watch as it went below the fifteen-second mark. "Number thirteen is out!" he shouted to no one in particular. "Fourteen is free."

With eight seconds left, the fifteenth container slid out. "Gun this son of a bitch," he ordered Bass.

The plane lurched forward at full throttle, making a steep left bank which threw Mason and Watson to the floor.

Suddenly the L-1011 started to shake violently, and a second later they heard the sound of an enormous blast behind and below them. Outside the open cargo door, tilted up toward heaven, Mason saw a shower of tiny gold meteors going by. One of them fell into the open bay on its downward trajectory and landed three feet from his head. As it rolled toward him, he grabbed it: a Canadian Maple Leaf, gleaming in the bright sunlight that spilled into the darkened cargo hold.

He stared at it for a second, then passed it to Watson. "Here, Rick, have a memento!" he shouted. "No one will miss it."

Watson, his head still pressed against the portside wall as the plane levelled off, looked like he was going to be sick. "I wish I could say I wouldn't have missed *this* for the world," he replied in a weak voice, "but I think I would have."

"You did fine, my man. Maybe we'll recruit you for Defense when this is all over."

Watson shook his head, managing a smile. "Thanks, but I think I'll stick with Delta."

"Watson, Mason!" came Bass's voice over the radio. "Are you guys okay?"

Mason picked up the radio. "We're okay, Charlie," he said.

"Glad to hear it. We should make Puerto Cabezas in forty-five minutes, but without any radio, we'll just have to circle and try to get into the pattern."

Mason and Watson made their way back up to the cabin via the elevators, passing the bodies of Dewberry and El Homra. As they reached the top, the plane shuddered and began diving sharply to the left. Mason's first thought was that Drabeznic had tricked them, and put one more bomb on board.

He burst out of the elevator and began running toward the cockpit, with Watson following close behind, both of them struggling to maintain balance as the aircraft nosed downward. *Damn*, said Mason to himself as he saw the bundle of shredded blankets that had bound Tokai, *maybe I should have played by their rules after all.*

He must have regained consciousness and edged his way over to the knife Watson had taken from him. Then, taking advantage of the fact that Bass had his full attention on flying the plane, he had cut his bindings. Up ahead, the door flapped back and forth, and through it they could see the captain lying across his seat, the Taser wrapped around his neck in a makeshift garrote. The horizon through the window in front of him looked unnaturally high, meaning that they were pointed down toward the water.

Mason raced into the cockpit and pulled Bass's body out of the seat, knocking his foot off the rudder and his hand off the steering column. With the autopilot on, this quickly righted the aircraft, and he reached down to get his M-11, which he'd dropped.

In that instant, Tokai, who'd been hiding directly behind him inside the cockpit, raced forward and slashed at him with his knife, but Mason had ducked to pick up the submachine pistol. Caught off balance, Mason turned around to see the man grinning wildly and holding up the knife. Now Tokai ripped through the air, pushing Mason against the back of the captain's seat, and Mason grabbed the seat for support as he kicked at the man's chest. But Tokai was too strong for him: he staggered backward slightly, then came forward again with his knife.

Watson slammed in through the open cockpit and knocked the stout man to his side. In one swift motion, Tokai recovered and swung upward with the knife, slicing a big gash into Watson's right arm. Now the co-pilot's white shirt was red with blood, and he looked down in astonishment.

The diversion was all that Mason needed. He reached down, picked up his fallen M-11 pistol, and stuck it into Tokai's chest. The man looked at him for an instant, his eyes growing big, then Mason laid on the trigger and sent three bullets into his chest.

As Tokai slumped to the floor, Mason turned back to Watson, who'd fallen too, partly to get out of the way of the M-11 and partly from shock. "You've gotta fly this plane, Rick," he barked as he pulled him to his feet. "I'll take care of your arm."

"Shit, Tom, I'm bleeding bad."

"You're the only one who can land us." He helped Watson into the pilot's seat, with Bass's body lying to the side across the co-pilot's. "Where's the first aid kit?"

"In the first overhead compartment, portside. I think I'm gonna pass out."

"You can't."

Mason ran back to the first-class cabin, and in the insanity of the moment he wondered if he'd lost count of the terrorists, if perhaps there was one more on board. Within seconds, he had stepped back over Tokai's body and begun applying a tourniquet to Watson's left arm, where it appeared that an artery had been severed. Mason knew that he had to put on maximum pressure to stop the bleeding; he also knew he couldn't afford for Watson to pass out. With a radio, he might have a chance of landing the plane himself, but without it, there was no way anyone could talk him down.

Having attended to Watson, Mason felt Bass's carotid artery and realized he was dead. But he wasn't going to tell Watson unless he asked, and in the midst of all the shock and confusion, there was a chance he wouldn't have to—not just yet, anyway. During the next few minutes, he cleaned the bodies out of the cockpit, brought a bag of ice up from the galley, and put a dressing on Watson's arm. He gave him liquids and Advil, the strongest pharmaceutical on board, and prayed that his companion would make it.

"Okay," Mason said, checking the onboard GPS as soon as he saw the Nicaraguan coast up ahead. "We're gonna be approaching Puerto Cabezas in a few minutes—what's next?"

Watson tried to shrug, but winced from pain. "I don't have a chart for Puerto Cabezas, and I don't have any idea what the landing pattern is. We don't even have a radio, so we'll just have to buzz the field, circle around and look for other aircraft, then hold our breath and try to put it down. You'll have to control the engine speed for me."

"Gotcha—just tell me what to do."

Far below them, the startled tower commander at the Puerto Cabezas airport looked up to see a Delta L-1011 flying by, then circling and passing by again. Not knowing its identity, he yelled into his radio, "Unidentified Delta jet, unidentified Delta jet—come in. Come in. You need clearance to land. Repeat—"

But there was no response. The plane circled two times, and while it did, the personnel on the ground ordered two small aircraft awaiting takeoff to taxi back to the terminal. The tower sounded the siren, and the airfield's lone fire truck—a model almost twenty years old—lumbered out onto the edge of the tarmac.

Watson had begun to have trouble focusing as his consciousness ebbed in and out. Mason watched his face. "Stay with me," he begged. "Stay with me, man. We're almost there."

"It's okay, Tom," Watson said, gathering his strength. "I've got it."

He went out over the ocean again, and then began a long, slow descent to an airfield never built to accommodate a craft of the L-1011's size. The horizon in front of them bounced up and down, and Watson yelled, "Put the landing gear down. Do you see the switch?"

"Over here?"

"Yeah, that's it."

Mason pulled up on the switch, and the hydraulics-operated wheels dropped and locked into place. "Alright," Watson gasped. "Air speed should be 120 knots."

Mason eased off on the three slide controls regulating the amount of fuel to the three Rolls-Royce engines that drove the aircraft.

"Easy now," Watson called over the deafening roar of the rapidly decelerating jet. "Down to 110—flaps down, flaps down!"

Mason reached over and pulled the switch, popping out the flaps.

"Easy now, Tom! We're on final. When we cross the stripe there on the runway, I want you to drop it to 100 knots . . . . Alright, down to ninety. Okay. Touchdown."

The plane bounced in the air a good eight feet, then the gargantuan craft shuddered and bounced again.

"Reverse the engines, Tom! Reverse thrust! Help me put on the brakes—slam on the brakes!"

Both men pushed their feet down hard, and the plane screeched, slid, and skidded across the tarmac of Puerto Cabezas airport. "Cut them off," Watson gasped. "Cut off the engines." Mason put the engines in neutral and shut them down, sending the plane skidding forward and lurching to a stop just before the end of the runway.

"Great job, Rick," Mason said, looking over at his pilot. But Watson, his last reserves of energy drained, had passed out.

Mason ran to the door, opened it, and looked down at a cadre of local gendarmes and military, all of them pointing their automatic rifles at his head. Every one of them seemed to be screaming at him in Spanish, their words drowned out by the wail of the fire engine's siren.

EPILOGUE

In the early afternoon of the same day, Friday, August 2, a British Army contingent arrived at the abandoned airstrip in Belize. Making their approach over the marshes in their choppers, they could see dozens of girls in athletic suits frantically waving. But once they landed, they found a strangely reticent group. No one seemed to be heat-sick, yet a number of the hostages appeared to be in the early stages of shock that had finally taken hold once their captors left them there that morning.

Within two hours they were on a chartered plane from Belize City to Atlanta, accompanied by medical personnel who attended to the ones in shock. A crowd of thousands had gathered at Hartsfield for their arrival in Atlanta, carrying signs and banners and craning to look over the heads of the dignitaries and journalists out front.

Steve Kirk was at the front of the line as the former hostages arrived to a huge ovation. He and Michelle stared at one another for a moment, as though wondering whether they dared to make an emotional public display; then they rushed to embrace. Soon afterward, they retired to Kirk's apartment and pulled the blinds shut. No one saw them until late the next day, and the many people who called Kirk's phone got his voice mail.

The Air Force gave Charlie Bass—a distinguished pilot in Vietnam—full military honors at his funeral. Allan Boyd received a posthumous Medal of Honor, and he and the fifteen other SEALs who died in Atlanta were buried as heroes at Arlington National Cemetery in Washington.

Rick Watson, placed in the Puerto Cabezas hospital for treatment of his stab wounds, contracted a staph infection and hepatitis. The President ordered a medevac flight back to Atlanta—one of his few popular actions since the Olympic crisis began—and within six months the flight engineer had returned to work. Delta promoted him to full captain, with a substantial bonus, and in 1997 he received the Hero of the Year award from the City of Atlanta.

The Village siege and the long flight had only topped off two weeks of limited sleep for Tom Mason, and as soon as he got home, he took to his bed for a full twenty-four hours. Later, his wife Sandy told him that he must have had some terrible nightmares, because every few hours he'd sit up in bed and shout something like "Boyd, get the hell out of there!" or "Gonna get you—ends of the earth—don't ever forget this face . . . ."

During this time, she had to intercept dozens of phone calls from the Pentagon, and many more from reporters eager to talk to her husband. Two hours after he finally got out of bed, he was on an F-14 to Washington for his debriefing with Gen. Helms and the DCI.

He told them everything he knew about al-Ansar's operatives, its possible financial resources, and the man who'd commanded the whole operation. The CIA narrowed its files down to Chechens who'd served in clandestine roles with the old Moscow government, and they found a likely suspect who had served as an intelligence officer with the regime. This individual had disappeared in 1989, and was presumed dead, though no body had ever been found.

Mason spent one extremely uncomfortable hour with the President, who asked him over and over about the location of the gold and the reason why he'd dumped it. It turned out that the Navy, using sophisticated electronic sensors and mine-sweepers, had combed a 200-square-mile area surrounding the intersection of the 80th west and 15th north parallels. After going over every square foot of Bajo Nuevo, they had moved on to its inhabited neighbor Gracias à Dios, where they found a village of simple fishermen who wouldn't have known what to do with half a billion dollars if it had dropped out of the sky. In all, they recovered fewer than twenty bars of gold and several thousand coins whose value didn't begin to compensate for the cost of retrieving them.

The President kept assuring Mason he didn't consider him a suspect in the disappearance of the money, but a few hours after that conversation, Mason found himself in the middle of what the Pentagon called a "routine security clearance reevaluation." He submitted to three polygraphs, various psychological tests, and unending questions about everything that had ever happened to him since his parents brought him home from the hospital. But they found nothing on Thomas Mason, and the 100-page evaluation report concluded with the sentence: "Subject possesses a remarkably high degree of integrity and devotion to duty, which may be a sign of mild neurosis or merely an old-fashioned work ethic."

His hair soon grew back, and by early 1997—to the great joy of his wife and kids—Mason had retired from the Department of Defense. He quickly began making more money from paid speaking engagements than he had from his job, and he spent much of that year in front of his PC, pounding out his account of the events that had occurred during the four tumultuous days from July 30 to August 2, 1996. For help on the details he consulted his friend Greg Robbins, who had founded a private security firm. The book, *Black Cloud Over Atlanta*, stayed on *The New York Times* best-seller list for twenty-four weeks, and a movie of the same title soon followed. Mason found he liked the writing life, and turned his attention to fiction; over time he became one of the most respected espionage authors on either side of the Atlantic.

Michelle Hinton retired from her job as well, and married Steve Kirk. The two moved to Laguna Beach, California, and eventually had two daughters and a son. Steve became managing director for an international consulting firm specializing in the hotel industry, and Michelle, after an extensive tour of the talk-show circuit, gained renown as an intelligent fashion model. Once in awhile, she rounded out her work with small roles in motion pictures, and she and Steve were happy that their lives were never again as eventful as they had been during those four long days in July and August 1996.

Virtually every sovereign nation participated in the hunt for the remaining members of al-Ansar. Three days after the siege in Atlanta, French police stopped a Renault carrying four Eastern European-looking men over the border into Italy. The trunk was riding low, as though they had an enormous weight on board, and a search revealed six million French francs' worth of gold coins.

By international understanding, anyone who exchanged large quantities of gold coins for cash would be asked to submit to an I.D. check, and this resulted in the arrest of four more men in Peru, Fiji, and the Marquesas. Virtually every police precinct on six continents had copies of the Olympic badges used by the Bosnian handball team, and though some of the men had altered their appearance, one more was identified by a prostitute in Caracas and another by a nosy neighbor in Montevideo. The four men who had made up the advance party in

Belize, and one more of the terrorists who'd held Fitten dorm, managed to do themselves in by lavish spending.

The U.S. negotiated the extradition of all fifteen captured terrorists, and the FBI had to provide them with round-the-clock bodyguards because of the many death threats they received. Several of them tried to turn state's evidence by giving information as to the whereabouts of Drabeznic and one other member of their group who had managed to elude the authorities, but in reality they didn't have any useful leads to offer.

They all ended up in prison, where they joined some of the men whose temporary release their leader had secured. When the two aircraft containing the "political prisoners" from America had landed in Frankfurt on August 2, the Germans had detained them; as soon as they learned that all the hostages had been freed, they sent the prisoners on their way—back to the U.S. and the unfinished terms that awaited them.

Elizabeth Taggart, who recovered quickly from her gunshot wounds, swam at the World Aquatic Championships in September 1998. There she won gold medals in the 100-meter backstroke and the 50-meter freestyle, the latter a particular triumph because the Chinese and North Koreans had shut her out of the 50-free competition two years before. Yet the two Oriental teams still managed to grab all the limelight at the '98 Championships—only now it was for a different reason.

No fewer than twenty-four Chinese swimmers tested positive for steroids, and many more had masking agents in their urine. A new process, secretly developed over the past two years, helped doctors to find the entire North Korean team guilty of using the previously unde-tectable substance known as human growth hormone or hGH. FINA, the swimming federation, declared all North Korean medals at the '98 Championships void, and began to consider retroactively disqualifying all medals awarded to that country since 1992. Soon afterward, high officials in the Korean Workers Party denounced the members of their national Olympic committee as "bourgeois traitors" who had re-cruited foreign assistance to win medals for their own enrichment. They sentenced them to thirty years each in a work camp on the Chinese border.

The German skinhead accused of clubbing Hungarian decathlete Sándor Lukács stood trial in 1997. His defense implicated Hypershoe, the company that had invested $2 million in Lukács's competition, the Americans Sweeney and Rogers. Lukács's family then sued Hypershoe, and the company gave them a $1 million settlement. Therefore the sponsorship of the two Americans (Sweeney won the gold by a slight margin two days before the terrorist attack began) ended up costing the company far more than their original $2 million. But it paid for itself in name recognition.

In spite of protests from Civil Rights groups, Christiann Vervoerden became a U.S. citizen, and he did it without the help of his attorney, John Shapiro. By marrying JoEllen Cunningham, he instantly gained his citizenship, and one of his wife's first acts as his new manager was to fire Shapiro. Eleven fights over two years made him the world heavyweight champion for all three of the major boxing associations. Not since Rocky Marciano in the early '50s had a white fighter enjoyed such success—or such a blue-collar cult following—and five title retentions earned him over $200 million, which Mrs. Vervoerden invested with the characteristic cunning implicit in her maiden name.

But Christiann would live up to his own name. One night when he was driving drunk in the canyons above L.A. (he and JoEllen had moved to Beverly Hills), he flipped his Ferrari. When he came to in the hospital days later, he was shocked to meet the motorist who'd dragged his body from the burning car with the help of another, who had administered CPR to him: they were both black. The two men, one of them a Baptist minister and the other a deacon, prayed with Christiann at his bedside. He found Christ, renounced all his past ways, and became— except for his sometimes overly forceful proselytizing—an altogether agreeable human being.

But the new Christiann, his inner aggression gone, could no longer bear to beat other men to senseless pulps, and he retired from the ring. Within a few months, his former victim Tyrone Bennett had earned the heavyweight title, and his now bored wife divorced him in a settlement that left her $50 million richer. JoEllen celebrated the end of her short marriage with a spread in *Playboy* and an interview in which she said, "There's no limit to what an athlete can achieve if she goes at it with determination."

Three years after the Atlanta Games, an Israeli hit team led by Tom Mason's old friend Eli tracked down Ahmad Mahfouz. The leader and remaining member of the small action group that had attempted to blow up the Olympic Stadium was living in Beirut, helping to direct activities in Israel on behalf of several extremist Egyptian fundamentalist parties. When Eli's people located him, they sent a secret communiqué back to Tel Aviv: should they turn him over to the U.S. to stand trial for the bombings on I-85 south of Atlanta, in which case he would go through lengthy appeals and spend the remainder of his life in an American prison, or . . . ? Eli was advised to use his own discretion— a death sentence for Mahfouz.

But not even the Israelis could locate Drabeznic or the one other member of al-Ansar who still remained at large. The other man had taken only fifty pounds of gold, and with it he moved to a village in the mountains of Bolivia. This former terrorist arranged to receive the La Paz newspaper, already a month old by the time it got to him via pack mule, and over the ensuing months he read of his comrades' recapture. With each new report, his paranoia grew. He ended up burying his gold in a remote spot, and he lived out his days tilling a small potato farm, his life no better—in fact, much worse—than it had been before he signed on with Drabeznic.

Drabeznic himself vanished with his $1.2 million, and only two pieces of evidence indicated what he'd done after he jumped out of Delta Flight 20 over Bajo Nuevo. First there was an abandoned Piper aircraft found near Kingston with a dead charter pilot in the seat. Then, six weeks after the terrorist leader's disappearance, a body washed up on the beach at Pedro Cays off Jamaica, but even with his features half-erased from floating face-down in the water, the police knew it wasn't Drabeznic. The man was black, and fit the description of a boat pilot last seen leaving Santo Domingo harbor in his forty-foot craft early on the morning of August 2, 1996.

Hakija Drabeznic became a legend. Alleged sightings of him in the Serengeti, the Australian Outback, and the hinterlands of northern Canada became so frequent that *The National Enquirer* devoted a monthly column to them for several years. A medium in Johannesburg claimed to have contacted him via a seance and learned that he had died in a gunfight on the Falkland Islands, but a London tabloid that offered £500,000 for his body never gave away the prize. No one ever figured out his origins, and no one ever learned his destination.

The gold, like the man who'd stolen it, became a legend, and attracted professional treasure-hunters to the site where it had gone down in the central Caribbean. But they never found any of it, and many of them lost fortunes of their own in the search.

A few million dollars trickled back to the IOC from the capture of the various terrorists, who of course had managed to spend plenty of it, and in any case the mother lode—well over $475 million—remained unrecovered. The executive committee had an idea where it had ended up, and had sent a platoon of lawyers to get it, but with little success.

Then they turned to the U.S. government. Jason Blanchot swore that the White House had guaranteed the return of his money, but the President denied ever making such a promise. And even if he had "remembered" giving his word, it wouldn't have mattered because the Chief Executive lacked the authority to turn over federal funds to the IOC.

Therefore the IOC could not pay for the deficit resulting from the failure of the '96 Games. Facing lawsuits from sponsors, TV rights holders (led by Ira Greenberg of NBC, whose lawyers found a loophole in their indemnity agreement), and families of slain athletes, the IOC declared bankruptcy in 1997 and began to operate in receivership.

The bankruptcy allowed NBC to renegotiate the $1.25 billion they'd agreed to pay for Sydney and the 2002 Winter Games in Salt Lake City. Bidding on Sydney alone—they would have to "see how things went" before they reopened discussions on Salt Lake City—they offered $100 million, less than any U.S. network had paid since the 1984 Winter Olympics. And even that had to be contingent on successful completion of the Games; in the meantime, the funds would sit in escrow, meaning that they did the Sydney Organizing Committee no good.

With all the bad karma now associated with the Olympics, sponsorship sales dwindled, even when discounted from $40 million to $10 million, and the Australian government found itself with a projected debt close to one billion U.S. dollars. Then the finger-pointing began: the Sydney Organizing Committee blamed the American networks and sponsors, the sports federations blamed the Australians, and everyone blamed the IOC. Late in 1998, Sydney cancelled its plans for the 2000 Games.

It was the end of the Olympics, which Pierre de Coubertin had lovingly resurrected after fifteen centuries of dormancy. In their ancient form, they had lasted 1,170 years before politics and greed destroyed them. But in the modern world, things happened much more quickly: this time around, it took less than a tenth as long.

Soon afterward, Jason Blanchot's car went off a cliff in Monte Carlo. The police reported it as an accident, and if they believed that, they were the only ones. One newspaper hinted that big-money players had rubbed out the man who'd lost $500 million, though most observers assumed he took his own life.

These suspicions were more or less confirmed when his secretary found a note in the top drawer of his desk, dated a few days before the "accident":

> Who or what has destroyed my beloved Games, I ask, and the more I search my thoughts, the more I come back to one thing: *television*. Yes, the very same television that revived us in 1984 when we were close to death. It's not the first time that the medicine which saved the patient ultimately killed him.
>
> This drug elicits the most addictive emotion known to man: greed. Corporations under its influence willingly endanger the life of an athlete whose only crime is that he plans to compete with the gladiators they have sponsored. Nations who succumb to its charms turn their finest physical specimens into chemical Frankenstein monsters. Malcontents and psychopaths, hungry for the euphoria that comes from the camera's glow, will gladly hurl victims off buildings, or blow them up by the thousands.
>
> Do I claim to be innocent? I do not. We were all enticed by the mighty lure of the dollars and the spotlights. And yet what good have we done for ourselves or anyone else? None at all.
>
> And therefore, though I may consider it unfair that it is so, it has fallen to me to be the man who oversaw—and helped to create—The Last Olympics.

But what about the gold?

For years the name "Isla Gracias à Dios" had seemed ironic to anyone who knew the place. The fifty families who lived in thatched houses on the tiny island in the southwest Caribbean had earned a meager existence as fishermen for generations, and they didn't seem to have a lot to thank God for. Not until Friday, August 2, 1996.

That morning, as the fishermen prepared their nets for another uneventful twelve hours' work, they chatted and laughed amongst themselves, smoking cigarettes and telling stories. Suddenly a giant plane flew over, then they heard an enormous explosion. The men jumped to the ground in terror, and seconds later, it began to rain.

At least, they thought it was rain. They felt heavy droplets falling on them—so heavy they dropped to the ground and covered their heads with their hands. But then one of them noticed that the puddle gathering around him wasn't water. It was gold . . . gold coins.

Soon the entire population of the island had gathered at the dock to find treasure scattered in boats, on pilings, on rooftops. Much more gold had fallen offshore, and for days afterward, the islanders—expert divers almost from birth—sent out little expeditions. These parties came back again and again, each time carrying more wealth than the whole town could earn in a hundred lifetimes.

The village priest led the others in praising the Almighty for fulfilling the promise in their island's name. But he was not short on earthly wisdom either, and he knew that someone would soon come to recover their lost fortune. So he suggested that the villagers change the form of the gold by melting it down and recasting it in the shapes of the clay cooking pots they'd used for centuries. As an extra precaution, they hid this extremely valuable crockery in a deep cave at the center of the island.

Soon his insight became reality as legions of strangers began descending on the village, and groups of lawyers representing a strange, faraway entity called the International Olympic Committee demanded the return of their gold. The priest played dumb, and when the IOC went to Bogotá to obtain permission to search the island, they discovered that it was technically a sovereign state because neither Colombia nor Nicaragua had wanted to add this extremely poverty-stricken patch of ground to their nations. Both of them wanted it now, of course, but the wily priest was a step ahead of them, and had obtained some of the greatest legal minds in the world to assist his people in maintaining their independence—and their gold.

One of these lawyers took an interest in a bright young islander, and helped him gain admission to a great Ivy League business school in Philadelphia. With his education, the youth returned to lead his neighbors in the development of luxury resort hotels, a yacht club, a casino, and even a jet airport. Within a decade the sleepy town of Gracias à Dios had become the number-one tourist attraction in the Caribbean, with the highest per capita income in the New World.

Many years passed, and one day the son of the young man who'd gone to school in Pennsylvania had a great notion of his own: "We make so much money on this island," he told a group of other entrepreneurs in a speech at the local business club, "why don't we build a stadium and invite all the athletes of the world to participate in games here? After all, in my father's time God proved Himself most generous by raining treasures from heaven on us—why not share some of our wealth with the rest of the world? These could be the new modern Olympic Games!"

Everyone said it sounded like a wonderful idea.